THE MIDNIGHT BELL

The Northanger Abbey Horrid Novels

CLERMONT
Regina Maria Roche
Edited by Natalie Schroeder

CASTLE OF WOLFENBACH
Eliza Parsons
Edited by Diane Long Hoeveler

THE NECROMANCER; OR, THE TALE OF THE BLACK FOREST
"Peter Teuthold"
Edited by Jeffrey Cass

THE MIDNIGHT BELL
Francis Lathom
Introduction by David Punter

Forthcoming

THE MYSTERIOUS WARNING
Eliza Parsons
Edited by Karen Morton

HORRID MYSTERIES
Karl Grosse
Edited by Norbert Besch

THE ORPHAN OF THE RHINE
Eleanor Sleath
Edited by Angela Wright

Visit www.valancourtbooks.com to order or for more information.

Gothic Classics

THE

MIDNIGHT BELL,

A GERMAN STORY,

FOUNDED ON INCIDENTS IN REAL LIFE.

THREE VOLUMES IN ONE.

Francis Lathom

Introduction by David Punter

A round unvarnish'd tale.　Othello.

Kansas City:
VALANCOURT BOOKS
2007

The Midnight Bell by Francis Lathom
First published by H.D. Symonds in 1798
First Valancourt Books edition, August 2007

This edition © 2007 by Valancourt Books

Library of Congress Cataloging-in-Publication Data

Lathom, Francis, 1774-1832.
  The midnight bell : a German story founded on incidents in real
life, three volumes in one / Francis Lathom ; introduction by David
Punter. -- 1st Valancourt Books ed.
     p. cm. -- (Gothic Classics)
  Originally published: London : H.D. Symonds, 1798.
  ISBN 1-934555-12-6
  I. Title.
  PR4878.L175M54 2007
  823'.7--dc22
                                          2007024022

Published by Valancourt Books
Kansas City, Missouri
http://www.valancourtbooks.com

Composition by James D. Jenkins
Set in Dante MT

10 9 8 7 6 5 4 3 2 1

CONTENTS

INTRODUCTION

I<small>F</small> Francis Lathom is known at all, it will almost certainly be in the context of Jane Austen: this novel, *The Midnight Bell*, first published in 1798, forms part of the Gothic reading material on which *Northanger Abbey* is founded, and there is also on record a separate letter in which Austen, travelling with her parents in late 1798, informs us that her father is currently reading this salutary work.[1]

Lathom then may partly interest us because he is a Gothicist, even if perhaps of the second or third rank; but also because of what one might call his impossible biography. The so-called 'facts' of his life have been known for some time, although they have been passed down by a variety of less than reliable witnesses, from the Rev. A. J. Milne, minister of the parish of Fyvie, a village in the Northeast of Scotland, through to the egregious bibliophile and religious and political reactionary Montague Summers. As is the case, of course, with most 'lives', layers of rumour have accreted during the process of transmission. We need, however, for our purposes to offer some outline of that life, and in what follows we adopt some of the details of this conventionalised biography.

Francis Lathom was born in 1774 in Rotterdam. Moving back to Norwich, of which his father Henry was a native, he rapidly became a successful playwright. His first play was produced at the Theatre Royal, Norwich, when he was eighteen; and he went on to have a string of popular successes, while at the same writing and publishing a regular series of novels. The novels fell broadly speaking into two camps: the Gothic romances, of which *The Midnight Bell* is typical, and novels whose type is well summarised in the title of the first of them, *Men and Manners*—novels of upper-class social life, laced with variable amounts of wit and satire.

At some point while still a young man, Lathom left Norwich; the exact date is unknown, although it was probably in 1802 or 1803. He moved eventually to Scotland, and lived first at Inverurie and subsequently at Fyvie; in his last years he moved, with the family with whom he was lodging, to Monquhitter, very nearby, where he died in 1832. He was well-known in his lifetime as a minor author and dramatist, although his reputation died with him, and most of his works are now difficult to find.

And yet, having ascertained these 'facts', if facts they are, about the life of Francis Lathom we find ourselves up against a great many unanswered questions. Who, for example, was he? Sometime during the nineteenth century, the notion starts to crop up in the passing down of his life story through the *Dictionary of National Biography* and elsewhere that he was the illegitimate son of an English lord. As far as it has been possible to trace, no coherent proof has ever been put forward for this, and neither has any verifiable suggestion as to whom this errant, and presumably East Anglian, nobleman might have been. It certainly appears to be the case that his long sojourn in Scotland, a country with which, as far as has ever been ascertained, he had no prior connection, was continuously well-funded, to an extent not entirely to be accounted for by his literary career; but the sources of this money are unknown.

Why, to put another of the most obvious questions, did he ever leave Norwich? He was, by all accounts, well established; he was evidently well off, and even more evidently successful. If he had seen his career as lying in the theatre, then for Lathom to uproot to the Highlands of Scotland was the equivalent of sudden death.

Questions of this kind need answers, and if none are available, then they must be invented. The answer to the question that is most frequently found is that Lathom was homosexual. The story goes that he contracted a socially unfortunate liaison in Norwich, and had to leave town. As the years have gone by, so other related anecdotes have attached themselves to his life: we are, for example, assured by Devendra P. Varma in his introduction to the 1968 reprint of *The Midnight Bell* that while living in Inverurie, 'he became strongly attached to a farm labourer who enticed him away to Banff. Here Lathom was detained as a hostage until the labourer received a quarter's pay'.[2] Quite what the farm labourer was expecting to be paid *for* remains unclear in this startling little vignette of life in Banffshire in the early part of the nineteenth century.

However, one can see the way in which this solves the problem. Obviously, if things are getting tough for you in a large country town, the thing to do is to move to a succession of tiny villages in the heart of the Highlands, in the hope, presumably, that you may reside incognito. Lathom was, by all accounts, a sociable man, a gifted and unembarrassed *raconteur*, fond of extravagant dressing and even more fond of a drink. Quite apart from his English accent, he must have blended into the background very well.

But aside from this heavy irony, we need to consider, of course, this 'life', as it has built itself up over the centuries, as itself a construct, a narrative, in which the lines of connection from cause to explanation go through a series of undecidable inversions. For example, if a small village in Scotland suddenly finds itself playing host to an erudite and rather dandified former city dweller, then of course the imputation of homosexuality might well be brought forward as explanation, as might the legend of aristocratic birth. Whether it could ever have been seriously advanced without incurring a kind of opprobrium which does not seem to have been Lathom's lot seems, however, unlikely. Going a little further, we might say that we find in this life a curious entanglement of secrecy and display: a man who, apparently, was forthcoming to the point of tedium about himself night after night in the local hostelries of Fyvie but yet who, presumably, contrived to drop not a single reliable hint about his own family and ancestry; a man who relished the latest fashions and somehow always appeared to acquire the most recent metropolitan gossip, yet who chose, with every appearance of cheerfulness, to share these esoteric concerns with a bemused peasantry.

Secrecy and display: the very *fons et origo*, we might say, of Gothic fiction. How often in the Gothics do we come across figures with an uncanny resemblance to some aspects of Lathom's 'history': conspirators, for example, who on the one hand claim to be invisible, untraceable, yet who give themselves away at every moment by, for example, their surprisingly cultured voices, by the way each movement, each item of clothing, ineluctably brands them 'conspirator', by the way they announce their own role and destiny. Can we seriously suppose that any casual observer passing a Montoni or a Schedoni on some curving Alpine road would say to themselves, 'My word, that was an ordinary-looking kind of man'?

In what follows, it is necessary to pursue these themes of secrecy and display and some associated ones. One might, or need, to consider a variety of Lathom's novelistic and dramatic fictions from before 1800, but the necessary materials for an appreciation of his literary contribution can probably all be found in *The Midnight Bell*. Before embarking on this text in more detail, however, we need to keep in mind that Lathom, like many of the other Gothic writers, was not *only* a Gothicist; he clearly saw Gothic as one among a repertoire of popular styles, many of which interested him. To look for a deep attachment to Gothic on the part of its authors, to search for some direct inner psychological linkage, is not usually the best way forward; if the readers and critics of Gothic tended from time to time to see it as over-conventionalised and mechanical, then the same was certainly true of some of its authors, who tended to see a kind of perverse technical challenge in testing their ability to do something fresh, or at least readable, within Gothic's prison-like confines.

It is necessary now to give some account of *The Midnight Bell*, of which one contemporary reviewer wryly remarked that 'were the delineation of character an object of greater attention with him, he would avoid that intricacy of plot, that hurry and confusion of incident, which rather perplex than interest his readers'.[3] 'Intricacy of plot'; 'hurry and confusion of incident': in an attempt to go through this intricacy, I shall partly rely on Summers who, whatever his disastrous ideological agenda and his polemical proselytising for a variety of unworthy causes, nevertheless summarised more Gothic plots in his lifetime than I should ever care to do.[4]

We begin, then, with one Count Cohenburg, a Saxon nobleman, who has two sons. Alphonsus, the elder, is 26 when the novel opens, his younger brother Frederick 18. Alphonsus inherits the title and estate upon the death of his father, marries, and has a son, also helpfully named Alphonsus, who is the hero of the story. His father Alphonsus I, as it were, shares many excellent characteristics with his son, but is regrettably prey to the vice of suspicion. In particular, he is suspicious that his wife Anna and his brother Frederick have been entering into more than fraternal or sororal relations, and devises a scheme for finding out whether this is true.

The incidents that follow are not explained at the time. A report is received that Alphonsus senior has been assassinated; his wife Anna appears in Alphonsus junior's room, clasping a bloody dagger, and bids him flee for his life. He departs, whereupon the deserted castle acquires an unsavoury reputation, resting upon the false rumour that Anna has killed her son; in the castle, as the author tells us, 'a ghost begins to walk, and every night at twelve o'clock it tolls the great bell in the south tower, because that is the time she killed the young count'.

After various adventures the exiled Alphonsus, tortured by bewilderment, becomes sacristan at the convenient Convent of St. Helena. A priest there tells him the story of a young novice, Lauretta, with whom he, Alphonsus, promptly falls in love. The priest, perhaps rather surprisingly, marries them, and they go off to live idyllically in a small cottage near Innsbruck. Lauretta, however, attracts the attention of the licentious young aristocrat Theodore, who has her abducted by a couple of Teutonic villains called Ralberg and Kroonzer. By a singular coincidence, Ralberg turns out to be none other than Count Byroff, Lauretta's father, who has recently escaped from the Bastille, and thus the situation is saved.

Alphonsus now decides the time is ripe to investigate the mystery of the castle, and eventually, and not without many twists and turns, the secret is unveiled.

The reviewer quoted earlier on is, of course, right: the extreme complications of the plot allow almost no space for character development, and none of the figures in the text rise above stock characterisation. I have omitted some of the more tedious ones, such as a humorous French servant named Jacques who speaks an execrable Franglais but is, of course, loyal to the death to his master. Indeed, one could go further and say that any move towards verisimilitude is fractured from the outset, not so much by the plot itself or even by the burden of the many unexplained secrets the narrative has to carry from the beginning until nearly the end, but by the sheer time and space required in order for the characters to give their various explanations one to another. Character A is forever trying to explain to Character B his whereabouts for the last thirty pages, but being interrupted, either by a new plot development or by the arrival of some other lost soul with an equally engaging story to tell—sometimes, indeed, containing embedded within it other stories, and so on.

There is no need to deny the vigour with which all this is accomplished, or even the urgency of some of the narrative passages; but this alone, clearly, would be insufficient to claim much more of our interest. What else can we find in *The Midnight Bell*, and in what way, if at all, might we be able to frame some connection between Lathom and his own text; or, to put it in terms which might be preferred, between the narrative of the book and the narrative of the life—or to put it in still different terms, what would be the force of seeing these stories as mutual alibis, as fundamentally implicated in the web of signs that we might assign to the-author-as-Lathom? And where in all this might we continue the essentially Gothic, but also essentially critical, work of looking for secrets?[5]

We need, perhaps, first to think a little about the structure of secrets, and especially about the increasingly common critical assertion that all secrets are open secrets. What might we mean by this? Well, we might consider the structure of *The Midnight Bell*. Within it, we might initially try to distinguish between the content of the secret—in other words, what the secret might 'turn out to be'—and the structure of the secret—as that which remains to be revealed. But even as we try to effect this distinction, we find ourselves beached, as it were, as we were when we were children: beached in the sense that the holding of the secret always takes place, can only take place, under the sign of a curious duplicity. For there is, to put it simply, no point in holding, or being party to, a secret unless someone knows that we are, as it were, secret sharers, with all the ambiguity and complexity which Conrad's story of that name, for example, brought to the issue. What is the secret in *The Midnight Bell*? It is, in the most obvious sense, a question: a question about the significance of the tolling of the bell. What, we are enjoined from the beginning to ask, might this tolling signify? What, by a slight semantic shift, might this *telling* signify? We learn, as time goes on, that this tolling, this telling, this incomprehensible significance, comes to signify a truth; a truth, perhaps, about murder, about the killing of a spouse, about a series of incidents which have affected a birthright. If we turn this on its head, then we might suggest that it is our birthright to know secrets; just as it is our presumed right, as readers, to have secrets explained to us.

The midnight bell, we might then also suggest, is for us as readers also a midwife bell: it serves to bring about a birth, a birth of awareness. The secret is of our birth, is of our birthright; to reveal the secret prematurely would, of course, be to destroy narrative. We might think here of the crucial difference predicated by, for example, writing about trauma studies: a difference between the detective story, as an emblem, as the exemplary narrative, of modernism, and the ghost story, suggested to be the emblematic narrative of postmodernism.[6]

A crude formulation, no doubt; but what might it mean? The structure of the detective story is the structure of the relation, the display, of a supposedly pre-existent historical sequence; this might be seen as modernist insofar as it presumes a pre-existent story, a chronology which remains to be revealed, displayed, by the story of the text. The ghost story, on the other hand, never leaves us with this sense of a re-established certainty; on the contrary, it reminds us that the story can never be fully told, or re-told, in the present: what 'remains' in the present is only ever, indeed, a narrative of remains, a story of how the present is always haunted by an inexplicable past.

As we speak of these things, it is obviously doubtful that we are speaking of *The Midnight Bell* as an unusual narrative; on the contrary, we are speaking of the Gothic itself, the original Gothic, of that vast superimposition of the logic of the inexplicable upon the surpassed certainties of history. And we thus find ourselves also speaking of the specific cryptic complexity of the Gothic; the sense in the Gothic that the mystery to be unravelled will only ever inhabit the already impossible realm of the 'explained supernatural'; that the conflict between the 'naturalisation' of explanation will always turn out to conflict with the inexplicability, the undecidability, of the supernatural. In the world which *The Midnight Bell* inhabits, explanation takes place always under the sign of interruption: between the privacy of the secret and the public world of display, there will always be an interception, the impossibility of the completion of a circuit, all the phenomena will arise which Avital Ronell talks of—down the line—when she tries to speak of telephony, of the call that will never be properly answered, or even properly heard.[7] And the 'midnight bell' serves as an emblem for this; a bell, a tolling, a telling, whose meaning is always deferred, is never available on a simply public terrain.

But to speak of the midnight bell more specifically: it is clear in the text that it is the bell that tells us of the time of our birth, but also, and by an inseparable logic, tells us of the time of our death. Alphonsus yearns towards the bell—he needs to discover, to uncover, the secret of the bell because he needs to know the secret of his birth, of his particular trauma, a trauma in which he has known a mother but only to be cast out from the mother's presence, only to embark upon a life of ambiguous exile, from which he can only make every effort to return, effort that will enable him once more to enter the castle of his birth and to return to the possession of his realm, a realm from which his father has already been outlawed, but a return that can only be accomplished through the outlawry of his mother. What is the task thereby accomplished? It is the task of orphanage.[8]

From beginning to end, the story of Lathom is a story of the orphan. The story surprisingly erected around Lathom, the story held in the apparent mysteries of his birth and death—an unknown birth and parentage (so it is frequently assumed), and a burial under another name, in which his patronymic is suppressed (which is true—he is buried under the name of James Francis in Fyvie churchyard)—is a story of orphanage, a story about the uprooting, the cutting down of the family tree, and in *The Midnight Bell* this takes a peculiarly exorbitant form. Consider the very origin of the story, the first few sentences: we are here situated not in the simple world of father and son, mother and daughter, we are here in the realm of grandfathers, as we are throughout; there is a curious habit (and we all know how Gothic fiction might take place in the realm of curious habits, by which we now mean the realm of convents and monasteries) by which *The Midnight Bell* forever begins its stories, its attempts to account for origins, in the realm of the grandfather. What, after all, is Alphonsus senior to us, or we to him? In that parody of *Hamlet* we only reiterate the endless, and beginningless, set of allusions to *Hamlet* which structures the narrative (curiously, Lathom frequently misquotes the play).

Orphans; grandfathers; family trees; who is whose father? How can we know what a patrimony (the Castle Cohenburg) or a patronymic (Lathom's lost—last or first?—name) can possibly mean? What, again, is a secret? What secret did Lathom appear to bear when he was living as an exile, on foreign ground, a foreign body, an exile in a community which could only be a primal ground for the odd recipience of his words?

Let us think a little more about exile, and how exile might have to do with fantasies of the homosexual. It is becoming common-place, since the work particularly of Judith Butler, to think a little harder about the significance of heterosexuality; or, to put that in other words, to consider what the notion of the 'sexual natural' might mean, what other secret it might conceal. According to But-ler and others, the secret of the Oedipus complex is held elsewhere; not in the cross-over love of the boy-child for the mother, nor in the love of the daughter for her (so usually absent) father, but in the agonising renunciation of same-sex love, in the thwarted emu-lation of son for father, of daughter for mother.[9] Butler goes on to effect a curious connection, a connection which has now been drawn more closely together in a recent book by Guinn Batten, to which we shall return later, which brings together three cultural themes: orphanage, of which we have already spoken; the abstrac-tion of commodity and labour by capitalism, which, although we have not yet mentioned it, is no doubt an effect registered by the development of stories of the later eighteenth century; and, finally, melancholy.[10]

At which point something leaps out of *The Midnight Bell*, which is that it is a text repeatedly inhabited—infested, we could almost say—by melancholy. Space is too short to allow us to supply all the examples: they are many. At almost every available point we are reminded that the narrative is driven by melancholy; Alphonsus, for example, is at all points in danger of relapsing into melancholy; and mostly this danger is an effect of his unknowingness of the secret, whatever the secret might turn out to be.

But this melancholy spreads: Anna also is prey to melancholy; so is Lauretta; so too are the more austere, and even violent, mem-bers of the novel's feudal superstructure, Count Byroff for exam-ple, or even selected members of the banditti. Let us take it one stage further: let us suggest that the entire narrative thrust of *The Midnight Bell* can be considered as a sustained attempt to express and ward off melancholy. Obviously, it is indeed that for Anna: we might presume that the need to summon monks for prayer in the depth of the night could carry a further meaning; that the psychic collapse of 'the year's deep midnight' requires a corresponding solace. We have known now, of course, for many years that the fiction of the monk as 'father' has exercised a persuasive sway over the tropes of the Gothic; what better way to invoke, and indeed produce, a fiction of fatherhood in the context of an overriding orphanage than by summoning them? At precisely the right time of night, of course, to come to the bedside—which is also the coffinside, the repository, the crypt, the depth of paternity, which is also the holding (and therefore the withholding) of that same secret—in order curiously to 'reproduce' reproduction?

The reproduction of reproduction—on another scene. Melancholy, according to Julia Kristeva as well as the other sources on which we have been drawing, takes its form on the scene of an absence;[11] in economic terms, as the always doomed reproduction of a system of exchange which is no longer available, no longer meaningful. It thus takes its place as the reproduction of an absence, of a lack of sense; as the always deferred, the always unavailable solution to a problem which cannot be resolved. We might therefore be drawn to considering the relation, within the text of *The Midnight Bell*, between melancholy, the withholding of the secret, and homosexuality; but in doing so we might therefore always need to bear in mind in what the nature of the homosexuality of the text—the queerness, to use a more contemporary rhetoric—might consist.

In doing so, we are following in the long distant footsteps of Freud in, for example, *Mourning and Melancholia* and in *The Ego and the Id*. One might consider, for instance, his formulation to the effect that 'when it happens that a person has to give up a sexual object there quite often ensues an alteration of his ego which can only be described as the setting up of the object inside the ego, as it occurs in melancholia'.[12] Perhaps more pertinently, however, we are speaking also of the connection between melancholia and homosexuality established over a long series of more recent works by Butler.

For example:

If the assumption of femininity and the assumption of masculinity proceed through the accomplishment of an always tenuous

heterosexuality, we might understand the force of this accomplishment as mandating the abandonment of homosexual at-
tachments or, perhaps more trenchantly, *preempting* the possibility of homosexual attachment, a foreclosure of possibility which
produces a domain of homosexuality understood as unlivable
passion and ungrievable loss.[13]

Melancholia, melancholy, thus arises in this way:

> When certain kinds of losses are compelled by a set of culturally
> prevalent prohibitions, we might expect a culturally prevalent
> form of melancholia, one which signals the internalisation of
> the ungrieved and ungrievable homosexual cathexis. And where
> there is no public recognition or discourse through which such
> a loss might be named and mourned, then melancholia takes on
> cultural dimensions of contemporary consequence. . . . hetero-
> sexual identity is purchased through a melancholic incorpora-
> tion of the love that it disavows.[14]

Now, it needs to be said that this theory of the melancholic dis-
persal of a prior homosexual cathexis raises a number of problems,
not least in the sense that, while Butler claims to be on the cutting
edge of anti-essentialism, the uncomfortable fact remains that her
entire *oeuvre* to date appears to be devoted precisely to the setting
up of a master narrative, even if this master narrative can make
some claim to status as a counter-story of the psyche. But the more
urgent problem, it seems to me, comes when we try to look at this
kind of idea in terms of text, culture, the narratives of biography.
For there are several interesting possibilities. The most obvious, of
course, would be whether we can see in *The Midnight Bell*, and/or in
others of Lathom's writings, traces that would lead us in the direction of clues as to his actual sexual orientation: in other words, and
to put the question in more contemporary terms, is there a queer
writing?

One of Lathom's few commentators to date, Allen Whitlock
Grove, in a dissertation aptly titled 'Coming Out of the Castle',
concentrates on a particular scene of violent sexual remembrance
in *The Midnight Bell* as an instance of Lathom's potentially queer
concerns. Interestingly for us, Grove's locus for this is the Hermit's

Tale, one of the many 'dispersals' of melancholia in the book, couched as most of them are as confessional anecdote. This is interesting because we can see Lathom's life itself as a 'hermit's tale' of two kinds: the first being his ostensible sequestering in Scotland as, it seems, refuge from his own social crimes; the second being the curious disappearance of his biography into conjecture, rumour, hermitage indeed: a narrative embedded within a guessing game. That *The Midnight Bell*'s 'hermit's tale' should contain for Grove traces of Lathom's prior homosexual cathexis becomes therefore curiously resonant.

The hermit in question in the novel only becomes so once he is accused of murdering a young man, Dulac, with whom he has shared his bed. The connotations of this in a Gothic context might be enough to raise the issue of the homoerotic liaison, even without the additional rites of bloodshed, shame and melancholy with which Lathom dresses the aftermath. Symbolism aside, Grove believes the key to Lathom's agenda lies in the register employed to portray the interaction between the hermit and Dulac:

> Lathom describes the Hermit and his companion going to bed in a realistic, novelistic . . . loving language absent elsewhere in the novel. The minute details create a sense of domesticity and affection in contrast to the melodramatic and over-conventionalized relationships we find elsewhere in the novel. . . . The nosebleed and later the bloody sheets clearly indicate loss of virginity or sexual penetration, yet the compassionate and co-operative relationship of the two men suggests that any such action was entirely consensual.[15]

Grove further believes that the 'important presence' of this scene in the novel acts as a counterweight to the 'hollowness and superficiality' of its conventional ending. Perhaps, while the bloody sheets do speak of rape and death, and a secret interred therein, they also figure the birth, or rather re-birth, of the secret from the mother-place of the crime. In revisitation, Lathom/the hermit's 'secretions' are displayed.

However, just as the essentialist question about women's writing seems rightly to have dissolved recently under the pressure of our increased understanding of the mutual imbrication of discourses, so therefore presumably such a question as 'Is there a queer writing?' would also dissolve on closer inspection, leaving one free to think about the matter in other ways.[16] For example: might it even be that, within the texts themselves, *The Midnight Bell* for example, one might find alongside the focus on melancholy other traces, traces that might have been unconsciously perceived by readers at the time? Was Lathom regarded as queer not because of what he was but because of what he wrote? Such a case would be inordinately difficult to prove, and we are certainly not going to try to do so here; but we will point out a few features of the text that we might want to set alongside the theory of melancholia. The text moves, for example, from a homosexual structure, emblematically in the form of the two brothers and the present/absent father, through bloodshed to an eventual resolution through the aforementioned heterosexual marriage, reassigning the highly problematic, indeed murderous territory of the castle to a more domestic site. There is, we can say, nothing very remarkable in this; we are here merely within loosely comic conventions. What does, however, begin to appear more strange when we bring critical pressure to bear is a key part of the process by which Alphonsus becomes able to achieve this happy ending, namely the relationship between Count Byroff—Lauretta's father and thus, as it were, a potentially new father for Alphonsus—and the young Frenchman Jacques.

This begins when Byroff is imprisoned in the Bastile, and Jacques begins his fictional life as a young gaoler who feels an unaccountable sympathy for him:

> Some how, *monsieur*, I had taken a liking to you above any of the prisoners I attended; and all I kept wishing for, was some means of setting you at liberty, that we might run away together; I knew, if I could contrive it, you would not dislike it, and there was something in your countenance that told me you would be kind to me afterwards.

'You would not dislike it' and 'you would be kind to me afterwards'; odd terms, perhaps, in which Jacques expresses his view as to what the feelings might be towards him of one who had been saved from torture and a lingering death in the Bastille. But more than this goes on between them, and some of it is decidedly strange.

There is, for example, Jacques' plan for how to disguise themselves during the initial phase of their escape. Jacques' interesting scheme is to disguise himself as a black beggar, and to pass off Byroff, whom he attires in female garments, as his wife. 'Now, *monsieur*', says the ever-attentive Jacques, 'please to remember that, in carrying on my plan, you must, if you please, pretend to be my wife; your features are very delicate, and you may easily pass for a woman...' (133). But this is curious, and we might begin to suspect that something odd has happened to Byroff while in the Bastille, for when we first meet him this is not the impression we have at all of this 'handsome' man of whom his wife-to-be observes, 'I never knew a man better calculated to make a woman happy' (30)—furthermore, Byroff has spent many years disguised as Ralberg, a villain of 'scowling mien and haggard looks' (48), but then perhaps descriptive consistency is less at stake here than a logic of desire. Something there is here, certainly, about a certain alteration of form, transvestitism, shape-changing, something about a different form of relationship; but perhaps what is even more strange is Jacques' apparent conviction that a good way of going into disguise is to go around Europe as a black beggar with, of all things, a white wife—for that is what the text tells us.

Secrecy and display: perhaps after all one does seem to see some vestige of a pattern shimmering here, however illusory, however 'delicate'. The fantasy, for example, of some kind of reunification within a homosexual, fraternal whole. When the two of them arrive at an inn where they are to pass the night, Byroff says,

> I was rejoiced to perceive that our stratagem passed unsuspected; and when we retired to bed, which we did in the characters of husband and wife, the better to conceal our real ones, Jacques desired me to sit down, saying he must have a little chat with me before we went to bed ...

But also, perhaps, and inseparably from this cosy, domestic quasi-marital scene, there is something darker, something represented in the black man—Jacques adopts the inevitable name 'Caesar' and speaks only in a tongue which Lathom calls the 'vitiated' language of the Negro—something that might make us wonder in what sense exile can really be figured as an achievement, a stratagem, a question of secrecy and display, or whether on some other scene it plays itself out also as a shared abjection, as a violent ejection from even such curiously oblique safety as might be signified by a cell in the Bastille.

For there are stranger things to come which might have a bearing on this kind of interpretation. Towards the end of the book Jacques, perhaps inevitably on the terrain of such a dubious set of histories, tells Alphonsus a ghost story, which culminates when he sees the ghost itself in the form, he tells us, of 'a man in black, kneeling down, without a head; and when I called out for help, he got up and ran away as fast as ever he could, and when he had got a little way off, his back looked as white as snow' (167). The manifold peculiarities of this apparition are never explained. The phrase 'white as snow' is, perhaps, biblical, and if so the ambiguous allusion to the leper would confirm the trope of exile that seems now to run through the text. As for the headlessness, what do we have here? A black and white man, black and white now fused into one person, but at a cost, a cost of decapitation, castration, the emblem, perhaps, of a reassertion of a love that will join together the forbidden but at the same time will, in the same breath, lose all it holds most dear.

The question here might be about transgression: about how far it is possible to transgress and still remain within boundaries, within sight of the castle, no matter how dilapidated it may have become. Such questions, which might also be questions about exile and about self-exile, or to put it in the terms developed by Deleuze and Guattari, questions of deterritorialisation, reterritorialisation and the nomad, are certainly ones that exercise Count Byroff. For example, when he is first put in the Bastille, he finds that he can

> form no conjecture for the cause of my present containment, except that of the state of Venice having found a power of arresting my person for a crime committed within its dominions, even after I had quitted them; but this supposition appeared so repugnant to the idea that I had always been taught to entertain

that the authority of every state was bounded by the limits of its
territories, that I could not reconcile it to my mind ...

What a curious assumption, one might think; an assumption
which would be necessary, of course, if one were to suppose that
exile could save one's life, or if one found that one were figuring
the law as an all-embracing power from which escape would be
forever necessary, a force of prohibition which, in reality, knows
no bounds. Judith Butler again: 'The prohibition on homosexuality
preempts the process of grief and prompts a melancholic identifi-
cation which effectively turns homosexual desire back on itself'.[17]

Secrecy and escape, under this regime, would be both possible and not possible: would figure as an avoidance of law while at
the same time reinforcing an awareness that however bizarre the
disguise, however like the as yet unwritten plot of 'The Purloined
Letter' it might seem to try to hide precisely in the most unlikely
of scenarios, an event that of course had also not taken place yet in
Lathom's life if indeed it did at all, nonetheless discovery is inevitable, that not even meeting and enacting an exorbitant concept of
display on its own terms will be sufficient to prevent one's life, as it
were, from writing itself, from displaying within its own contours
the melancholia arising from a primal renunciation.

The question of how that renunciation and its consequences
are figured in the text would, through melancholia, be inevitably
bound up with death, and indeed there are many deaths in the
novel, treated with a kind of insouciance which seems undecidably
poised between a conventional psychic disavowal and the equal con-
ventionalities of the Gothic genre. There is, however, one epigraph,
the one to the novel's climactic chapter, that perhaps deserves a little more of our attention, from Nicholas Rowe:

There is but one, one only thing to think on,
My murder'd lord, and his dark gaping grave,
That waits unclos'd, impatient of my coming.

That waiting, of course, is again undecidably doubled: are we
speaking here of a waiting for the satisfaction of vengeance, or
of an always hovering but never consummated possibility of un-

ion? What, though, is important is the resonance of this obsessive
structure—'only one thing to think on'—with melancholia, which
relies upon the psychic institution, as Freud puts it, of a 'gathering-
place for the death instincts'.[18] For the entire trope of escape, as we
are beginning to see it figured in a complex weave of text and life,
is responsive, it would seem, to a further inweaving: to the question we may have to put about the possibility of escape from obsession, escape from the grave around which we hover, that grave
which, in *The Midnight Bell*, is always and everywhere the grave of
the father—as it is also a grave which is tended by 'fathers' of the
Church—but which can also be seen as the grave of a desire that
cannot emerge in the world, such a desire as that figured in the text
by Jacques, who can fulfil his wishes only in a comedic self-abase-
ment, in abjection, and simultaneously under the sign of another
race and another name.[19]

This no doubt bifurcated introduction is in need of two con-
clusions, one that will take us back to Francis Lathom himself, or
James Francis as he is called on his grave, in his grave, and another
that will allow us to speculate beyond his life and text. From a review of Lathom's *Men and Manners*, published the year after *The
Midnight Bell*, and concerning two young people called Alfred and
Rachel: Rachel refuses, we hear, to become Alfred's wife, and this,
the reviewer dryly remarks, 'proves fortunate, as they are discovered to be brother and sister'.[20] Yet the unveiling of such secrets, of
course, is commonplace, figuring as it does as a repetition of the
problematic condition of the orphan, or alternatively as the root of
narrative re-entry into heterosexual married life.

'The poet sings', says Goethe, 'to keep the monster at bay',
but a writer like Lathom might help to persuade us that we need
to concentrate on the ambivalence of this thought. The monster
must, of course, be kept at bay; for if it were allowed too close, then
there would be no secret any more, and no gap to fill with magic words. Or alternatively, if the monster were to be allowed too
close, then the carefully built barricades that are the patient work
of melancholy might break and we would be in a world without
boundaries, a world where there is no integrity of states, no border
enforced by the violent but necessary prohibitions of the law. Thus
far, I suggest, a first reading of Goethe. But it is also necessary for

the monster not to retreat too far; the poet's song, on this wider reading, would not be a lulling of the monster to sleep but a perennial enticement, a sirenian medley of attraction and repulsion, an enactment of an ineluctable fascination on a stage before the emergence of basic splitting in the sexed psyche.[25] There would be no escape from the object, no possibility of escape from the object, because, presumably, the monster 'out there' is a mere thing of fantasy, precisely a projection of the incorporated inner object, from which, as from the open grave in which it is partly buried, there is indeed no escape.[21]

Are these remarks actually about Francis Lathom? Perhaps they are not; perhaps they cannot be. Let us consider a further possibility: 'the book signifies, like the totem of the murdered father that Freud made the founder of human cultures, both death and hidden power'[22]. That sentence is from the book mentioned earlier, by Guinn Batten, called *The Orphaned Imagination: Melancholy and Commodity Culture in English Romanticism*, and essentially the thrust of her argument is to historicise the associations between melancholy and orphanage, exile and loss, books and death which we have been following. She is concerned, as she puts it, with

> the hole in language that Derrida calls 'dead time' and that Slavoj Žižek calls the *Reality* of language's own death that eludes the synchronic Law of the Father ... this void is a hidden, resonant 'place' between signifying word and signified thing, a place not unlike that which exists   between two words for whom rhyme serves both to evoke and to deny identity. That void is a blank monument to the fall into the (fatherless) Law that breaks apart son and parent, words and things, desire and its   fulfilment, labour and its products.[23]

It is necessary to say two things about this passage. First, Batten is asserting, following Kristeva, that there is an inseparable link between this gap, this hole, this void within language, and the experience of melancholia:

> Melancholia in modern cultures emerges explicitly at the troubled nexus of an increasingly interiorised and leisured self and a society that promotes the freedom of that self by colonising

(through ideology) the self's most private spaces of appetite and remorse.[24]

And thus the second point we might develop from Batten, and on which I shall conclude this introduction, is the question of history. The gap between 'labour and its products', she says; an 'increasingly interiorised and leisured self'. All of this is predicated on a continuing concept of alienation; in the background hovers the spectre of Marx, in particular of his early manuscripts, with their categorisation of the types of alienation attendant upon capitalism and wage labour.[25]

It is part of Batten's argument to assert that the late eighteenth-century poets were peculiarly aware of, at the same time as being crucially affected by, the spread of that alienation which both consigned them to recognise the inextricability of the connection between writing and earning, creation and consumption, and at the same time forced upon them a melancholia, a resistance to capitalist demands for productivity, which itself became the subject and insignia of their work.

The Midnight Bell shares a historical context with the early romantics, and it shares with them too an obsession with melancholia; but we are still left with many questions. Batten has in the end little helpful to say about the complexities of gendering, and although she uses some of Butler's arguments on melancholia as well as Kristeva's on depression and labour there would still be gaps in an argument that tried to fit all of these rhetorics seamlessly alongside each other.

Perhaps the fairest provisional judgement we can come to is this. Francis Lathom, in the eighteenth century, wrote a novel called *The Midnight Bell*, which increasingly as one looks at it seems to become a victim and exponent of *Nachträglichkeit*, of deferral of meaning, as though something had been deposited in the text that was destined to be acted out, performed later. Somewhere at the root of this twist, which is perhaps a twist common to all textuality or is perhaps more precisely situated in a time, in a place, under specific historical and geographical conditions, lies melancholy, and it is possible to read this melancholy in terms of separation, loss; at which point the whole structure becomes enmeshed in the complexities of gender differentiation. And this itself further enacts the text as commodity, as well as the 'life'; as also sites for our desire for value for money, for historical and fetishistic recuperation.

But then, of course, one might also say that in taking these kinds of approach to a text, what one is really doing is engaging in a kind of suspicion, and it is, as I said earlier, precisely suspicion and its unfathomable consequences that is the ostensible theme of *The Midnight Bell*. We can therefore safely, and without the least suspicion of a hidden under-text, leave the last words to Alphonsus, for they are the closing words of the novel:

> Learn, above all, my children ... to avoid suspicion; for as it is the source of crimes, it is also the worst of crimes, attaching itself with equal mischief to the guilty and the innocent; it is an endless pang to him who harbours it; for it dies only when he dies, and then too often leaves a curse on those that follow him; it is the influence of evil that breeds suspicion, the noble spirit of charity that subdues it!

DAVID PUNTER
Bristol

April 12, 2007

DAVID PUNTER is Professor of English at University of Bristol. He has published some 20 books of literary criticism as well as four volumes of poetry and hundreds of essays and articles on Gothic, romantic and contemporary literature, psychoanalysis and literary theory. His books on the Gothic include *The Literature of Terror* (1980), *Gothic Pathologies: The Text, the Body, and the Law* (1998), and *A Companion to the Gothic* (2000).

NOTES

1. See Jane Austen, *Northanger Abbey*, introd. Claudia L. Johnson (London: Campbell, 1992), p. 40; *Jane Austen's Letters*, ed. Deirdre Le Faye (new edn, Oxford and New York: Oxford University Press, 1995), p. 15.
2. Devendra P. Varma, 'Introduction', in Francis Lathom, *The Midnight Bell* (London: Folio Press, 1968), p. viii.
3. Anon., review of *The Midnight Bell*, *Monthly Magazine* (1798), V. 509.
4. See Montague Summers, *The Gothic Quest* (new edn, London: Fortune Press, 1968), pp. 311-13.
5. On the topic of the secret, see for example Frank Kermode, *The Genesis of Secrecy: On the Interpretation of Narrative* (Cambridge, MA: Harvard University Press, 1979), and Esther Rashkin, *Family Secrets and the Psychoanalysis of Narrative* (Princeton, NJ: Princeton University Press, 1992).
6. Cf. my 'Hungry Ghosts and Foreign Bodies', in *Gothic Modernisms*, eds Andrew Smith and Jeff Wallace (Basingstoke: Palgrave, 2001).
7. The reference is to Avital Ronell, *The Telephone Book: Technology, Schizophrenia, Electric Speech* (Lincoln: University of Nebraska, Press, 1989).
8. On orphanage, and on the law of the orphan, see also my *Gothic Pathologies: The Text, the Body and the Law* (London: Macmillan, 1998), especially pp. 200-21.
9. See Judith Butler, *Gender Trouble: Feminism and the Subversion of Identity* (New York and London: Routledge, 1990), pp. 79-141.
10. See Guinn Batten, *The Orphaned Imagination: Melancholy and Commodity Culture in English Romanticism* (Durham and London: Duke University Press, 1998).
11. See Julia Kristeva, *Black Sun: Depression and Melancholia*, trans. Leon S. Roudiez (New York: Columbia University Press, 1989); especially interesting are her comments on sadness and beauty at pp. 97-103.
12. Sigmund Freud, *The Ego and the Id*, in *The Standard Edition of the*

Complete Psychological Works of Sigmund Freud, eds James Strachey et al. (24 vols, London: Hogarth Press, 1953-74), XIX, 29.

13. Judith Butler, *The Psychic Life of Power: Theories in Subjection* (Stanford: Stanford University Press, 1997), p. 135.

14. This is particularly evident towards the end of *Gender Trouble*, where she speaks of 'a critical genealogy of the naturalisation of sex and of bodies in general' (p. 147).

15. Allen Whitlock Grove, *Coming out of the Castle: Renegotiating Gender and Sexuality in Eighteenth-Century Gothic Fiction* (unpublished dissertation, University of Pennsylvania, 1996), p. 41.

16. On this topic, see in particular Lee Edelman, *Homographesis: Essays in Gay Literary and Cultural Theory* (New York and London: Routledge, 1994).

17. Butler, *Psychic Life of Power*, p. 142.

18. Freud, *The Ego and the Id*, p., 54; see also Butler, *Psychic Life of Power*, p. 132.

19. The textuality of black abjection is too vast to name, but some of the clearest and starkest indictments can be sensed in a reading of W.E.B. DuBois, *The Souls of Black Folk*, eds Henry Louis Gates and Terri Hume Oliver (new edn, London: Norton, 1999).

20. Anon., review of Lathom, *Men and Manners*, *The British Critic* (1799), XIII. 666.

21. On incorporation, see Nicolas Abraham and Maria Torok, *The Wolf Man's Magic Word: A Cryptonymy*, trans. Nicholas Rand (Minneapolis: University of Minnesota Press, 1986), pp. 16-17; and 'Mourning *or* Melancholia: Introjection *versus* Incorporation', in *The Shell and the Kernel*, ed. Rand (Chicago and London: University of Chicago Press, 1994).

22. Batten, *Orphaned Imagination*, p. 185.

23. Batten, *Orphaned Imagination*, p. 53.

24. Batten, *Orphaned Imagination*, p. 73.

25. See Marx, *The Economic and Philosophical Manuscripts of 1844*, ed. Dirk J. Struik (New York: International Publishers, 1964), especially pp. 106-19; and Jacques Derrida, *Specters of Marx: The State of the Debt, the Work of Mourning, and the New International*, trans. Peggy Kamuf (New York and London: Routledge, 1994).

NOTE ON THE TEXT

For some reason, *The Midnight Bell* has fared better than some of the other "horrid" novels on Isabella Thorpe and Catherine Morland's reading list in *Northanger Abbey*. It was first published anonymously in three volumes by H. D. Symonds, London, in 1798. Ned Kelly quickly brought out a pirated edition in two volumes at Dublin the same year; Haly, Harris, and Connor of Cork issued the novel in three volumes, also in 1798. The novel's popularity extended far beyond the British Isles, however, with James Carey of Philadelphia publishing the book in three volumes in 1799; a French translation, under the title *Le cloche de minuit*, appeared in 1813. A second edition appeared in 1825, published by William Lane's successor at the Minerva Press, A. K. Newman.

The 20th century saw two editions of *The Midnight Bell*. The first, published as part of a hardcover collector's set of the *Northanger* novels, appeared in 1968 from London's Folio Press, with an introduction by Devendra P. Varma. Varma's introduction is chiefly interesting for his blatant plagiarism of Michael Sadleir and Montague Summers and for the unsupported claims he makes about Francis Lathom, some of which David Punter mentions in his introduction to the present edition. The other 20th century edition appeared in 1989, published by Skoob Books of London with an introduction by Lucien Jenkins.

The Valancourt Books edition follows nearly verbatim the text of the rare 1798 first edition. Unlike many early printed books, *The Midnight Bell* presents very few problems for the modern editor, as it largely conforms to modern standard English spelling, punctuation, and grammar. A handful of very minor errors have been silently corrected, nearly all involving extraneous or omitted quotation marks. Errors of grammar, spelling, and usage have been retained, as have Lathom's (or his printer's) mistakes in the occasional French words spoken by Jacques. Both the Folio and Skoob editions follow the trend in UK publishing to replace double quotation marks with single; we have not adopted this convention, choosing to retain the punctuation in the book as originally published.

JAMES D. JENKINS

The Midnight Bell

Volume I

THE MIDNIGHT BELL.

CHAPTER I.

I am not mad; this hair I tear is mine;
I am not mad; I would to heaven I were!
For then 'tis like I should forget myself.
Oh, if I could, what grief should I forget!
If I were mad, I should forget my son,
Or madly think a babe of clouts were he;
I am not mad; too well, too well I feel
The diff'rent plague of each calamity.

KING JOHN.

COUNT Cohenburg was descended from one of the noblest houses of Saxony; his castle, situated on a branch of the river Elbe, was one of the most magnificent in the German empire; his income was large, and his character celebrated, as one of the first men of his age.

At an early period of his life he espoused the second daughter of the marquis of Brandenburgh, and she blessed her husband with five sons; the eldest and the youngest of whom alone survived their mother.

At the time of count Cohenburg's death, which did not happen till he had some years buried his countess, Alphonsus, his eldest son, was in his twenty-sixth, and Frederic, his youngest, in his nineteenth year.

Alphonsus, now count Cohenburg, in his person was rather pleasing than handsome; his height about the middle stature, his mind well cultivated in every branch of learning, his temper mild and benevolent, but withall addicted to suspicion.

Frederic was a man formed to captivate; his features were regular, his countenance handsome and prepossessing, his figure tall and elegant; the advantages of education had been bestowed on him equally with his brother, but he had not so eagerly drank in instruction,—he was, however, an agreeable and even a fascinating companion,—he was passionate, but his anger was of a moment.

Arrived at his twenty-second year, Frederic became enamoured of a lady of Luxemburg; she was beautiful, but delicate in the extreme; she was an orphan, and possessed of a large fortune:—Frederic purchased a mansion in the vicinity of his brother's castle, and having espoused his beloved Sophia, every earthly happiness seemed to smile on him and his newly-married bride.

Within the year Frederic was blessed by the birth of a son.

Count Alphonsus was a beholder of his brother's happiness: he felt a wish for the same felicity Frederic enjoyed; he accordingly determined to marry, and selected from amongst the beauteous maids who adorned the German court, Anna, the only daughter of the duke of Coblentz. She was a woman in whom every engaging attraction was centred; her form was elegant, her manners affable and polite; there was something in her countenance that outshone regular beauty, and a vivacity in her conversation, that chained the senses of the enraptured listener.

Alphonsus was now as happy as his brother; and in the course of ten months his Anna brought him a son, on the same day on which Sophia gave birth to a second infant, which proved a female.

The name of his father was given to the infant son of count Alphonsus.

The following year Sophia brought her husband a third child, but the period of its entrance into the world was dated by the death of its mother.

The passions of Frederic were strong, and this proved a stroke which went nigh to unman his fortitude; the soothings of his brother however tended greatly to raise his depressed spirits.

Anna proved herself a not less affectionate sister to Frederic, than a mother to his children; she soothed them, consoled their father, performed for them every lenient action; and in short so forcible were her attentions, that she succeeded in lightening the burden of their sorrow.

Count Alphonsus loved his brother tenderly; he looked on his sorrows with a feeling eye; he would have alleviated them at the expence of half his worth; by any means, rather than by the assiduities of his Anna,—he conceived too highly of her to suppose her capable of bestowing on another the minutest particle of that love which she bore him;—he even repeated to himself that it was her love for him, which induced her thus to attend to his brother;—he knew the evil tendency of suspicion, and had always struggled to combat against it; but suspicion was a part of his nature, and would not always be subdued.

He watched his brother, and every turn of the countess's features when in Frederic's presence; he was convinced of his mistake; he was even on the point of apologising to his wife for the wrong he had done her in his thoughts; but he considered that he should, by so doing, only lay open to her an error in his heart, with which she was unacquainted; and therefore contented himself with the resolution of never again admitting a thought to her discredit.

Frederic's youngest child had survived its mother but a few hours, and, in the third year after her death, his eldest fell a victim to the grave: he recovered from this severe shock only to feel a greater,—his daughter died in his arms!—Misfortune seemed to have marked him out for her sport—he resolved to leave the scene of all his woes, and travel:—a hasty farewell was said by him to his brother and sister, and he departed.

In four years he returned; his manners were much altered; he was become dissatisfied, uneasy, absent; in short, no single trace of the former count Frederic was left.

Count Alphonsus was moved by his appearance, but his suspicious temper could not forbear revolving a subject which it had once disclaimed;—he determined however to bear his thoughts in silence,—he did so,—and in the course of eight months, Frederic again left Saxony.

The chief emotion which now swayed the breast of Alphonsus was pity; he fancied he perceived his brother's love for his wife, and his struggle to conceal it. The countess spoke frequently of the change in Frederic's temper,—her language served to convince Alphonsus that his brother was indifferent to her,—this was a point gained that gave him great satisfaction, yet he wished Frederic never to return.

Five years elapsed ere Frederic revisited Germany; he stayed but a short time in Saxony, and was then absent two more years; on his last return, his former disquietude of temper seemed converted into a settled melancholy; he retired to his mansion, and said he had formed a resolution to live a life of seclusion.

Alphonsus now imagined that he had found some means of gaining Anna's love, and that by pretending to keep himself retired in his own mansion, he thought to elude his brother's suspicion; he still, however, determined to keep a seal on his lips, but to open wide his eyes and ears.

The count's only son, Alphonsus, was now in his seventeenth year; his form was manly and well turned, his countenance rendered interesting and handsome by a pair of black eyes, and finely arched eyebrows, his cheeks were ruddy, his lips wore the smile of good-humour, and his short black hair hung curling round his neck; his intellects were strong, his genius discerning, and his mind well informed.

Nearly a year had elapsed since the arrival of Frederic in his native country, when an affair of consequence, relating to the will of his late father, called count Alphonsus to the metropolis of the German empire.

He visited his brother the day prior to his departure;—he bade a tender farewell to his wife and son—"My Anna is now in Frederic's power!" This idea a moment arrested his steps, as he was crossing the hall of the castle to the vehicle that awaited him:—"but is he not bound in honour to protect her?—he is!—and I will not suspect him."—He left the castle and proceeded on his journey, accompanied by an old and faithful servant.

Nearly two months had elapsed since the departure of count Alphonsus, ere the period for his return to the castle of Cohenburg was mentioned by him in his letters to his wife: he had written frequently to her, and every letter was replete with his anxiety again to behold her.

At length the time for his arrival was fixed; and the countess awaited it with every mark of ardent love; when, on the morning of the day which he had stated for his arrival, the servant who had accompanied him came to the castle alone; the anxious looks of the countess demanded a speedy explanation of his business,—"Was he the harbinger of the count?" she asked.

"Alas! no," he answered.

"Oh, he is dead! he is murdered!" she exclaimed, and sunk life-less on the ground.

Her fears were too well founded; the old servant brought the sorrowing information, that two ruffians, who had burst from a thicket about ten leagues distant from Cohenburg castle, had fallen upon him and stabbed him to the heart.

Tears came to the relief of Alphonsus; and the first words his sorrow permitted him to articulate, were an order to a domestic to convey the sad intelligence to his uncle, and request his immediate presence at the castle.

When recollection again returned to the unhappy Anna, she waved her hand in signal to the surrounding domestics to depart; and, upon being left alone with her son, thus addressed him:

"Alphonsus, thy uncle is the murderer of thy father.—Swear to me thou wilt revenge his death."

Alphonsus looked stedfastly on his mother in silent wonder.

Anna continued: "Thou marvellest at my words,—thou can'st not think the smooth-tongued Frederic so great a villain! but he is blacker than thy darkest thoughts can paint him!—Oh! I could tell thee"——she paused.

"Explain thyself, my dearest mother," cried Alphonsus.

"No! I cannot—I will not let thee think so basely of thy father's brother,—time may come, that thou"—she paused a moment,——"I cannot prove what I've alleged; therefore bury it in thy breast.—But swear to me, by heaven, whenever the murderer stands con-fessed, thou wilt revenge thy father's death."

"Oh, my mother! do you then think I would be careless in so great a point of duty?—No! let me but know him, and by all my hopes of heaven, my sword shall pierce his heart."

"Thou art my child indeed! good angels guard thee," cried the countess, and embraced him.—"Oh thou dost not know count Fre-deric; but time will teach thee him."

In due time count Frederic arrived; his countenance bore the marks of assumed grief;—Alphonsus could ill brook his presence;—he saw his mother's conjecture confirmed;—his tongue laboured to accuse the count of his villany;—his heart whispered him to await the proof of his guilt;—he bit his tongue in silence;—his sorrow burst into his eyes, and he rushed from the apartment inarticulately exclaiming, "Oh! my father!"

Towards the evening the count departed; the old servant who had brought the sorrowful intelligence was ordered instantly to return to the corpse, and get it conveyed to the castle with all convenient speed.

Count Frederic took upon himself to prepare for the obsequies of his brother.

After the departure of count Frederic, Alphonsus strongly solicited his mother to confide to him her cause for suspecting his uncle; "I must not—cannot,"—she replied: "time will develope and prove my words. Oh Alphonsus! remember what you have sworn."

"Sacredly I will maintain my vow."

On the next day, count Frederic again visited the castle of Cohenburg; Alphonsus shunned his presence, and retired on his arrival, to indulge his grief in solitude. After an interval of some time, thinking his uncle gone, he re-entered the apartment where he had left his mother: but what was his surprise, on his entrance, at seeing her kneeling before the count, and kissing his hand—she rose, and threw herself into a chair.—The count walked to the window:— "How does this conduct agree with the character my mother has given of the count," thought Alphonsus;—his mother perceived his eyes fixed on her; she wrung her hands, and lifted them in silent supplication to heaven.

In a short time Frederic departed.

"You have commanded me," said Alphonsus, after a pause, "not to ask an explanation of your suspicions"—he was proceeding, when the countess rose from her seat, and bursting into tears, left the apartment.

Alphonsus was stretched on the rack of doubt, suspicion, and perplexity; he traversed the apartment, he threw himself on the ground, he rose again, he walked about the room, he entered the garden; he walked, he sat: it was in vain; the mind cannot fly from itself.

The countess excused herself from appearing at supper;—Alphonsus knew not that the cloth was spread before him, though he leaned the arm on which he rested his head on the table.

At an early hour he retired to his chamber; it was in vain that he attempted to rest;—he read the letters he had received from his father during his absence; his tears ran swiftly down upon them;—he could read no more,—he threw himself upon his bed;—his lamp decayed in the socket, and the obscurity of the scene seemed in unison with his feelings.

The ghostly hour of midnight had just sounded, and all the castle of Cohenburg was wrapped in sleep, save the forlorn Alphonsus; the balm of wounded nature refused to heal his sorrows. Stretched on his restless bed, he lay ruminating on the occurrences of the preceding day, when a piercing shriek caught his ear, and roused him from his meditations,—it seemed to proceed from the chamber of his mother; he listened—it was not repeated—"Again her grief exceeds the bounds of reason!" he cried,—"Oh wretched woman! Kind heaven sooth her sorrows!" He sighed, dropped a tear, and sunk upon his pillow.

After a short interval, he fell into a restless slumber; he had not long enjoyed this first repose, since his father's death, when he was awakened by the opening of his chamber-door; the dawn of day was beginning to break, and served to show Alphonsus, that it was his mother who had entered his apartment;—her mien alarmed him,—her eyes were wildly fixed, her countenance betrayed the most visible signs of an agonized heart; she was wrapped in a loose garment, and her hair hung dishevelled on her shoulders.

"Alphonsus!" she exclaimed, "observe thy mother's words, nor ask their explanation:—instantly fly this castle, nor approach it more, as you value life!—as you value heaven!"

Alphonsus had lain down on the bed without undressing, and now starting from it,—"Why this sudden alarm?" he cried; "is it that you fear my uncle will perpetrate a second deed, horrid as the first?—fear not for me; I shall live to fulfil my oath."

She shrieked, then said, "You have undone yourself and me— your uncle is innocent—one only way can save us both—fly far from hence—fly from me—fly from your uncle—take that purse,— return not to the castle—saddle the fleetest courser in the stables, and depart while yet the earliness of the morn favours your escape unseen—embrace me—Oh! no! no! no!—it would—" a flood of tears prevented for a while her farther utterance; she then added, "Go! and may the blessings I can never hope from heaven fall on thee." She gave him the purse;—the palm of her hand was stained with blood! Alphonsus looked that he saw it; speech was refused him;—the countess met his eye; again she shrieked, "Oh, fly and save me!—I conjure you, fly!"—she cried; and, with a look that seemed to draw blood from her heart, she ran from Alphonsus's chamber, and locked herself within her own.

Thunderstruck by what he had heard and seen, Alphonsus debated some moments how to act; at last he cried,—"Has my unhappy mother lost her reason?—Oh, no! her manner is that of deep sorrow, not of frenzy; she undoubtedly has some strong cause for her commands; but then why conceal it from me?—My uncle, too, declared innocent!—what can she mean?—it is my duty to obey." He left his chamber; as he passed hers, she opened the door, and said,—"Speed thee, my beloved Alphonsus!"—He stopped, but she hastily closed it again. He descended into the hall, unbarred the heavy gates, and proceeded to the stables; having saddled his favourite horse, he mounted, and with a full and sorrowing heart left the castle of Cohenburg.

"Fly me,—fly this castle, as you value life,—as you value heaven." These words he repeated again and again,—he dwelt on them, till conjecture lost itself in a maze of thought;—he proceeded forwards about five leagues without slackening his pace, before he inquired of himself whither he was going,—and he then hesitated how to answer himself. In this dilemma, he perceived a distant village rising above some clustered trees on the brow of an easy hill: thither he directed his steed; the villagers were just risen to their labour as he reached it,—they looked at him with an eye of inquisitiveness:—he perceived that they knew him not, but that idle curiosity had attracted their attention; having refreshed his steed, he again set forward,—he wished, with all possible speed, to leave that part of the country where he was likely to be recognised; he felt that he had no cause for wishing to secrete himself, but he felt also, that he should experience an unconquerable embarrassment, should he encounter any friend, who might ask him whither he was journeying, or make inquiries relative to his family.

Towards noon he had proceeded many leagues into the heart of the country; his strength and spirits were equally exhausted; he dismounted from his horse; and having fastened him to the trunk of a tree, whose branches shaded him from the scorching rays of the mid-day sun, he threw himself down by his side.

Reflection, which clears not the point meditated on, wears away the time sorrowfully, but swiftly:—thus Alphonsus rose not from his bed of grass till the sun was far advanced towards the west; after riding three more weary leagues, a mean inn, where he meant to pass the night, received him; he drank a cup of wine, and was re-freshed,—it was the first nourishment, except some water which he had drunk at a brook from the hollow of his hand, that had that day passed his lips; he ate also, but sparingly, and that without relish. At an early hour he saw his steed safely bestowed, and betook himself to his chamber, though not to sleep.

CHAPTER II.

Canst thou not minister to a mind diseas'd,
Pluck from the memory a rooted sorrow,
Raze out the written troubles of the brain,
And, with some sweet oblivious antidote
Cleanse the stuff'd bosom of that perilous stuff,
That weighs upon the heart?

MACBETH.

THE night was spent by him, as the day had been passed, in vain lamentations and conjectures; towards morning he enjoyed a short slumber.

On waking, he turned his thoughts to find some means by which he might gain a reputable maintenance in life; the army appeared to him the most likely to afford him the asylum he wished, and he trusted to the change of dress and situation, for passing unnoticed in the world.

The German power was at that period engaged in a war against Poland, and he resolved to offer himself as a volunteer in one of the regiments which were then daily raising; for this purpose he determined immediately to proceed to Berlin; accordingly, having settled with the host of the miserable inn, he mounted his horse, and set forward.

His journey of the preceding day had been partly in an opposite angle to the high road leading to Berlin: he accordingly struck into a bye path, which was to conduct him to the high road.

With mournful thoughts he proceeded solitarily along, and gained the desired road about the middle of the day.

Two days served to complete his journey; on the evening of the second he entered the busy city of Berlin; he took up his abode for the night in a small inn, and on the following morning made inquiries for a purchaser for his steed; with this he had determined to part ere he entered into the service of his country, well aware that his pay would ill suffer him to support it.

He walked about the city, he admired the public edifices, he inquired who had been their founders and builders; and for the first two days, found a sufficient stock of amusement to divert his thoughts, in some measure, from the sad subject on which they were too forcibly bent; but as the novelty of the scene began to subside, reflection returned with redoubled perplexities and griefs;— sometimes he resolved to return to the castle:—"My uncle," he said, "my mother avows to be innocent,—why should I fear him?—but still, she conjures me not to see him:—some secret cause doubtless actuates her conduct,—why hide it from me?—Should she have leagued with him to murder my father!—have taken him to her bed, and driven me from the castle, that I might not be a witness of her shame!"—The thought went nigh to madden him. "She is not so base," he cried: "would she, had this been so, have supplicated the count on her knees?—it could not have been done to deceive me, for she expected not my entrance.—What cause could there have been for that mysterious conduct?—for her still more strange appearance on the morning she sent me from the castle?—for the blood that stained her hand?" Imagination could wander no farther:—"Some secret misery wrings her heart,—I cannot alleviate it, or she would call for my assistance,—and I will not aggravate her calamities by disobeying her commands." He prayed fervently for her happiness, and wafted up his prayers to heaven in a heart-felt sigh.

On the third day after his arrival in Berlin, his landlord found him a purchaser for his horse at a fair price; Alphonsus hesitated to strike the bargain; he had no friend left on earth; it had endeared his horse to him, and he felt a reluctance to part from the last remains of his late happy days. He debated in his mind:—what money he possessed would soon be gone, and then——! He cast a glance at the road before him, the path was gloomy—"He is yours," he cried; "take him, but use him kindly." He rushed into the house, refusing again to behold his favourite steed. The most needful article was then the last in his thoughts,—he recollected not the money, till the landlord awakened him from his reverie by pouring it from his hand upon the table.

His first step was now to offer himself for service; he received the bounty bestowed on a volunteer, and taking the military habit, found it made an alteration in his person which he little expected.

He felt an inexplicable unwillingness to lead to any discourse which might give him information of the general opinion of the world, if any tale relative to his family was current in it,—but of this he was ignorant; he resolved to drive the subject from his thoughts; it only became the more constant attendant on his solitary moments.

He had been about three months in the service of the empire, when the regiment in which he served, was ordered to march to a village about four leagues east of Berlin, till they should be called into action, for which they were commanded to hold themselves in readiness at a short notice.

In the course of another month they were called to the field; Alphonsus was strong, active, and possessed of much natural courage; he acquitted himself in the toils of war with the most becoming spirit and fortitude, insomuch that he gained the favour of his commanding officer, and was by him promoted in the regiment.

The name of the commander was Arieno; the Italian name struck Alphonsus; he was serving in the German army, beloved by his soldiers, had risen to his present rank by the favour of the emperor, fought with peculiar bravery in the German cause, and yet he was palpably an Italian.

Arieno became more and more attached to Alphonsus: he showed him his favour on every occasion. Alphonsus even began to be apprehensive that he was discovered:—but he was deceived.

When the army retired into winter quarters, Arieno invited Alphonsus to pass the winter with him; Alphonsus accepted the offer with gratitude, and retired with Arieno in the quality, as he supposed, of an attendant.

His imagination was pleasurably deceived; Arieno was himself the child of sorrow;—he had perceived by the dejected air, hesitating speech, and pensive mien of Alphonsus, that he was a prey to grief equally with himself: sympathy inclined him to regard the young count,—and the engaging mien of Alphonsus, though his brow was clouded with sorrow, had won Arieno's heart; and he resolved to make him his friend and companion.

The habitation of Arieno was a small retired mansion on the skirts of a village about three leagues east of Franckfort; an old woman, to whom the care of the house had been entrusted during the summer, was the only one of whom the family consisted in addition to the two friends.

Arieno was a man whose person, on first acquaintance, was little prepossessing; but as the virtues of his heart, which was the seat of every good quality, shone forth, he rapidly gained the love and esteem of those who had any knowledge of him: his conversation instructed whilst it pleased the hearer, and Alphonsus hung with delight on his accents, as he spoke of the vicissitudes of life, the fallacy of this world, and the stability of hopes placed in a future state.

Many days passed, ere Arieno touched on the string which tingled to the heart of Alphonsus; he then thus addressed him,—"I think my young friend, there is something in your manner, together with your knowledge of many abstruse subjects, that bespeaks your real rank in life to be far above that in which I first knew you."

Alphonsus was silent; but his reddening countenance betrayed to Arieno the truth of his observations, who thus went on:—"Some secret sorrow preys upon your heart; impart to me your cause of grief; I may have the ability to alleviate your sorrows; if not, I will sooth them."

Alphonsus was still silent.

"Do you not know me sufficiently," Arieno continued, "to be well assured, that the interest I take in your happiness, and not the gratification of an idle curiosity, renders me thus inquisitive?"

"Oh, my friend!" cried Alphonsus, taking Arieno's hand, "I owe you more than my gratitude can ever repay:—you are worthy to be trusted with my inmost concerns; but I would rather forego the comforts which I enjoy from your kindness and conversation, than impart to you the secrets of my heart;—indeed, indeed, they must lie buried in my breast."

"Far be it from me to distress you," returned Arieno; "fear not a repetition of these words from me."

A long silence ensued.

"You are an Italian," said Alphonsus, breaking silence.

"You are right," said Arieno; "and marvel, I doubt not, at my serving under the emperor of these dominions."

"I must confess, it has often excited my wonder."

"You shall conjecture no longer; my story is short, and I will tell it to you."

"I have no right to expect such a communication from you."

"I doubt not but you have good reasons for your secrecy; I wish my story to be known to the world."

Alphonsus bowed, and Arieno thus began.

"My father, count Arieno, was one of the richest noblemen in the state of Venice; his mansion, which was situated nearly a league distant from Venice, was magnificent in the extreme; his gardens were extensive and beautiful, and his gondolas rivalled in elegance any before seen. At an early age he espoused the daughter of a rich senator of Genoa, whom he had accidentally seen at the carnival: she was an only child; and at her father's death, which happened three months after her marriage with my father, she inherited his entire property.

"In the course of six years she brought my father four children, three sons and a daughter; my sister was the first born, I was the second son, my brother Stefano was the eldest. At an early age my youngest brother died; at the period from which I date my story, my brother Stefano was in his nineteenth and I in my eighteenth year. Stefano was in his temper haughty, proud, subtle, and very avaricious; his person was well calculated to hide the deformities of his mind; he was the darling of his mother, whom he much resembled in disposition; and she had entire dominion over her husband.

"In addition to this, when I tell you that from my childhood my brother showed his dislike of me by every means in his power, I have, I think, said enough to convince you, that my life was far from being enviable.

"Not far distant from the mansion of my father, resided a widow lady, Signora Bartini, with her two daughters; their fortunes were small, indeed barely sufficient to support them with any degree of credit; but they possessed a treasure, superior to riches, in their beauty and virtue; the eldest captivated a French chevalier; he married her, and she departed with him into France.

"The youngest, Camilla by name, had given me a wound which it was not in the power of art to heal. Convinced, however, that the inferiority of her condition in life to my own, would prove an unconquerable obstacle to my espousing her in the eyes of my family, I resolved to bury my passion in my own heart;—into my eyes it would, however, sometimes force its way, I even thought Camilla perceived it, and blushed congenial feelings. It was one evening, towards the end of summer, that, as I entered the small garden leading to the house of Signora Bartini (for I sometimes ventured to call, and enjoy the conversation of Camilla), my brother came from the house; as he passed me, he exclaimed, 'My visit is just ended in proper time, I perceive;' and passed on laughing.

"I had been so much accustomed to taunts of this kind from my brother, that I heeded but little what he said, and entered the house: I found Camilla weeping by the window, and her mother standing by her.

"Suspicion, of I know not what, immediately flashed upon my mind in the form of my brother; I tenderly inquired what had disturbed her; her mother gave some trivial and unsatisfactory reason for her tears, and immediately turned the conversation to another subject.

"I could not conceal the emotions of my heart, and in a short time took my leave.

"My father, mother, and brother, were just assembled at supper as I joined them.

"'I knew not whether we were to expect the pleasure of your company this evening,' said my mother.

"'Why, madam?'

"'Nay, perhaps you were not invited with Signora Bartini, and lovers must not be too forward.' She laughed loudly, and my brother did the same.

"I bit my lips with rage, then said, 'I could conceive no impropriety in visiting where my elder brother showed me the example.'

"They were at a loss for an answer, and again laughed.

"My father looked sternly at me, and said, 'You had best beware how you marry contrary to my inclinations;—remember that Camilla Bartini is the last woman I should choose for your wife.'

"I knew my combat was unequal, and remained silent.

"I now found myself more disagreeably situated than ever under my father's roof, and accordingly determined to travel; I asked his permission; he readily granted it, and likewise advanced me a handsome sum of money. His easy consent distressed me, though I wished to obtain it; affection seemed to have no part in so hasty a compliance.

"I went to Camilla's house: but what was my surprise to find that she had left it; she was gone on a visit to her sister in France.— There seemed something mysterious in her conduct; I could not summon resolution to ask signora Bartini to explain it to me. I took my leave of her; and the next morning I departed from my father's mansion.

"Ten months elapsed, and I heard not from any one of my father's family: I wrote to my mother, to inquire the cause of this long silence, instructing her to direct for me in Sicily. In about six weeks after, I received from her a few lines, informing me that my father had paid the debt of nature, and requesting my immediate presence.

"I lost no time in reaching Venice, and arrived at my late father's mansion, on the day of his funeral: the will was then opened; but conceive, if you can, my astonishment, when the following paragraph was read: 'To my second son Philip, in consequence of his disobedience to my commands, I bequeath only five hundred zechins, that he may know I have not forgotten him, but wilfully cut him off from all other share of my property.'

"It was a bolt of ice shot at my heart—it benumbed my vitals. Muttering curses on the villain who had belied me to my father, I left the mansion, darting a look at my brother, which I gloried in perceiving that he felt.

"I flew to the house of Signora Bartini: a female servant was standing by the door; she informed me that her mistress was gone to her daughter's in France.

" 'Where does she reside?'

" 'At Montpelier.'

" 'What is the Chevalier's name, who married her daughter?'

" 'The Chevalier D'Albert.'

"I will not trouble you with my reflections during the time that I was journeying to Montpelier: suffice it to say, that my suspicions were irrevocably fixed on my brother, as the villain who had taken from me the esteem of my father.

"Arrived at Montpelier, Madame D'Albert received me at the house of her husband.

" 'You will wonder to see me, Madam,' I exclaimed; 'but'——

"At this moment Signora Bartini entered the apartment: I saluted her; she made a sign to her daughter to leave us; I sat down by her; I hesitated how to address her.—What I had studied to say during my journey, had now fled from my thoughts, and I could only inquire for Camilla.

" 'Ah! Signor,' she cried, 'my child will soon, I hope, be well; the hand of death is heavy on her.'

"Till that moment, I knew not what misery was—my other sufferings had been light.

"I fell from the chair on which I was seated—a dead coldness seized me; and it was with difficulty that Signora Bartini restored me to life.

"When she perceived my senses were returned, she cried, 'Did you then really love my poor girl, Signor?'

" 'Love her! oh God, grant me words to prove how tenderly I loved her!'

" 'She loved you, but was taught to believe you wedded to another.'

"This was an additional wound to my already lacerated heart.

"She then proceeded to inform me, that, on the evening that I had met my brother coming from her house, and found her daughter weeping, he had been making the basest proposals to my Camilla, and that, fearing her refusal should incense his haughty spirit to any unwarrantable act of revenge, she had removed Camilla to her sister's in France: that Camilla, having heard that I had left Venice, had supposed that I had forgotten her, and given up herself to melancholy; and that, about two months before my arrival at Montpelier, she had received a letter, as from me, informing her that I was married. 'This,' said Signora Bartini, 'has driven her to despair; her faculties are impaired; and we hourly await her death, as the greatest blessing heaven can bestow on her.'

"The letter was shown me:—it was the hand-writing of my villanous brother.

"I informed her of the contents of my father's will, relating to me; I showed her how I conceived myself to have been doubly injured by my brother: she sympathised in my fate, and I in hers; our sorrow flowed from the same source.

"In the course of that day, my beloved Camilla breathed her last. How shall I relate my anguish on receiving the bitter intelligence? you, my friend, must conjecture what I have not words to describe.

"On the following morning, I was permitted to visit her corpse: oh, how altered was her once beautiful countenance! Oh, my God, what did I undergo during the moments I gazed upon her cold form! In an extasy of sorrow, I kissed her icy lips.—The scene was too much—it overpowered me;—I was dragged from her, I know not by what means, never again to behold the innocent and unhappy victim of falsehood, my loved Camilla!

"When her funeral obsequies were performed, I returned to Venice; a short time developed to me the perfidy of my brother; I learnt that he had gained the credit of my father to my marriage with Camilla, by showing him a forged certificate of our having been united in a parish church at Montpelier:—how did my heart pant for revenge!—cooler reflection taught me not to spill a brother's blood.—I disdained, however, to ask of him the small legacy portioned out to me by my father, and resolved for ever to leave the Venetian dominions; and having passed over into Germany, I offered myself a volunteer in the service of the emperor.—I have served under him about thirty-two years, and his goodness has raised me to the rank I now hold.—My brother possesses riches; but I enjoy a treasure whose blessings he will never know—an approving conscience."

Alphonsus thanked him for his recital, sympathised with him in his sufferings, and inquired if he had ever heard any tidings of his brother since the period of his leaving Venice.

"By accident I heard, about fourteen years ago, that he had married a woman of fortune immediately on his father's death; that my mother had not long survived her husband, and that his wife died in child-birth of her first infant, which was a female; I heard it by means of an officer who had visited Venice, and mentioned that the discourse of the city, whilst he was there, had turned solely upon the disappearance of the only daughter of one count Arieno. 'He is an avaricious fellow,' said he, 'and was bent on espousing his daughter to a noble as rich as himself, while the poor girl had fallen in love with a German count, whom she had seen at the carnival. Her father forced her to marry the noble; and a short time after she was missed, and no inquiries could discover whither she had fled.'—The name of her lover, I think the officer said, was count Cohenburg, a descendent of a noble family of Saxony:—thus providence punished his avarice by depriving him of his only child."

Alphonsus changed colour at the mention of his name; but Arieno perceived it not; and Alphonsus ventured to inquire, what was conjectured to have been the young lady's fate.

Arieno answered, that she was supposed to have fled with her lover, and eluded the diligence of her father's and husband's search.

Alphonsus's brain was now on the rack to decide on some part of his father's or uncle's conduct, that might tally with this account; his father had never been a sufficient time together absent from his castle to have formed any engagement of the kind; indeed, had opportunity been ever so favourable, he had always loved his mother too tenderly to wrong her in the regard she bore him;—his uncle, he recollected, had been much absent from Saxony about the time mentioned by Arieno; but he had several times at intervals returned to his mansion; and no one had accompanied him;—there were no others of their name in Germany;—he was convinced it was not his father—thus suspicion rested on his uncle;—his next thought was, whether what he had now heard could by any means be made to account for the death of his father, and the conduct of his moth-

er, or in any way be supposed to be connected with either.—Here
thought again lost itself in a maze of uncertain conjecture.

CHAPTER III.

Oh, day and night, but this is wond'rous strange!
HAMLET.

BEFORE the time of taking the field arrived, Arieno received information from the emperor, that his regiment was to be mounted for
the ensuing campaign. Alphonsus wished for his faithful steed: but
it was beyond his reach.

In the spring, Alphonsus and his Italian friend set out from the
hospitable mansion of the latter; Arieno thanked Alphonsus for the
pleasure his society had afforded him, and gave him a warm invitation to renew his visit the following winter.

About the middle of the summer, Arieno lost his life in an engagement on the borders of the empire; the receipt of this intelligence went nigh to cost Alphonsus his life. On the very same day,
a fall from his horse had fractured his sword-arm; and he heard not
of the tidings of his friend's death, till stretched himself on the bed
of sickness.

It was near the end of the campaign, ere Alphonsus recovered
from his wound; and in a very short time after the re-establishment
of his health, a decisive victory was obtained by the Germans over
the Poles. This put an end to a long and vigorously fought war:
most of the newly-raised regiments were disbanded, and every incapable soldier also received his discharge. The weakness which still
remained in Alphonsus's arm, made him unwilling to sue for his
continuance in the army; and he accordingly determined to seek
some other means of subsistence, attended with less danger to his
already fractured limb.

After much deliberation, he resolved to sue for employment in
the least laborious line, which the then lately-discovered silver mine
in Bohemia afforded. His regiment had been disbanded at Prague,
and thus he had not far to travel, for the purpose of putting his plan
into execution. He was readily hired by the contractor for working

the mine, and his labour fell short of what he had pictured to himself it would prove; he had felt much bodily weakness, proceeding from what he had suffered when he undertook the employment; and, conscious of his own inability, he had exaggerated in idea the labour of the task he had undertaken.

His fellow-labourers worked hard, and earned their pittance with the sweat of their brow; but it was the more sweetly relished by them at their moments of recreation.

They laughed, they sang, they told tales for each other's diversion; they related anecdotes that had fallen within their knowledge; and thus cheerfulness presided in the midst of labour.

They delighted much to hear Alphonsus recount the course of the battles in which he had fought: some amongst them had served, and to them his narrations were peculiarly interesting; and they ever and anon interrupted him to relate some similar circumstances which had occurred during the campaigns in which they had served.

Alphonsus had belonged to the mines nearly a year, when no new workmen having joined them, and their conversation thus beginning to grow insipid, and anecdotes, from often recounting, becoming stale, they resolved that at evening, when their tasks were ended, each miner should in his turn relate the events of his life.

Alphonsus was amongst the first to whom the lot fell to relate their adventures; he easily fabricated a short and simple tale, which served his purpose, and gained neither the approbation nor the contempt of his hearers: he joyed when the task was ended.

A few days after, the lot fell upon a youth, whose mirth had often drawn forth the loud laughs of his companions.—"Few words will tell my tale," he said, and thus began:

"My father and mother, good souls, rented a farm of count Cohenburg, in Lower Saxony, near the river Elbe."

Alphonsus was all attention.

"Oh, had he lived yet, I should not have been here! but I might have been much worse off: and so I thank the saints that I am here; and may I never fare worse, pray I.—Well, though my father did not come of a great family, a great family came of him; for, boys and girls, he had fifteen of us."—Here a loud laugh applauded the young miner's wit.—He continued—"Well, as I said before, my fa-

ther rented a farm of count Cohenburg; he was very good to the
poor, and promised my father he would do something for all his
children;—God rest his soul in heaven!—Let me see, I have now
worked in these mines two years and a half; it was about eight
months before that time, that the count went out to some foreign
part, for aught I know; or it might be only to see our emperor; I
can't tell, however, about some such thing"—

The suspense of Alphonsus for the conclusion of this tale, may
be easily conceived.

"So, on the day he was expected home, news was brought to
his castle by old Robert, who went with him, that his horse had
thrown him, and killed him, on his way home; and so Robert went
back with orders to have the count buried where he died.—Well,
now comes the most extraordinary part of my story; the good
dead count had a son about seventeen or eighteen years of age, a
fine comely handsome youth, not much unlike me,—only he never
worked in a mine."

Again the miners laughed, and Alphonsus heaved an inward
sigh.

"Well, two days after, he was missing, and so was the countess;
neither of them to be found, high nor low: now the folks say, the
good lady killed her son in a mad fit, for the loss of her husband;
and was so vexed at what she had done, when she came to herself, that she killed herself too—and directly after, a ghost began to
walk; and every night at twelve o'clock, it tolls the great bell in the
south turret, because that is the time she killed the young count."

"Well, and did you ever see it?" cried one of the miners.

"Oh no! no body has gone near the castle since; it belonged by
right to the count's brother; and he came to it; but he stayed only
a day or two; for he saw and heard such things, that he could not
bear his own life; and so he discharged all the servants, and locked
up the castle gates; and away he went, some folks say, out of the
country, and left the ghost to ring away by itself; and I fancy it is
pretty safe, for having all the supper the castle walls can give it to
itself, for no company will trouble it, I am sure.—Well, so, for want
of the count's help, my father went down in the world; and so we
most of us left him, to seek our own fortunes; and here am I, a jolly
miner:—and though ours is a low calling under ground, I fancy it

will bear looking into as well as many great men's upon the surface of the earth."

Here the youth ended his history;—a murmur of applause ran through the assembly, and they parted for the night.

Alphonsus slept not; he had now fresh food for unconfirmed conjecture.—A subject which he had not heard mentioned during two years' intercourse with the busy world, he had at length heard discussed in a mine; this led him to conjecture the story was not in current report.—"The castle deserted!—yet a bell tolled at midnight!"—In spirits he had no faith; and what could it avail any human being to live there, retired from the world? nor did he think it possible they could remain there undiscovered.—That his mother was dead, he did not in the least credit; the youth had said the same of him.—He ruminated again and again on what he had heard, but his meditations ended where they had begun.

Some time elapsed ere Alphonsus ventured to question the youth relative to what he had related of his family; and the only additional intelligence he could gain, was that some people suspected count Frederic to be the murderer of his brother, the countess and her son, for the sake of possessing the castle, which descended by the death of count Alphonsus to his son;—"But then, if this was the case," cried the youth, "what could make him run away, and leave the whole?"

"Conscience!" thought Alphonsus.—But his mother had declared his uncle innocent; and he was determined not to suspect him whom she had exculpated.

It was one day shortly after this time, that a gentleman travelling through Bohemia, came, attracted by curiosity, to visit the mine; Alphonsus and another miner were deputed to conduct him; the gentleman's servant accompanied him: in passing a deep cavity of the mine, over which a narrow plank was laid, the servant's eyes not being directed to the unsteady board over which he was passing, one of his feet slipped, and, unable to recover his balance, he sunk into the space below. The fall was, to any one, inevitable death:—he was dashed to pieces.

The gentleman, whose name was baron Kardsfelt, was much affected by the misfortune that had befallen his servant; he had lived with him many years, and had proved himself a faithful attendant.

The baron immediately returned to the surface of the earth, where the first objects that struck his sight, were his own and his servant's horses, fastened to a post at a short distance from the mouth of the mine: a difficulty immediately arose in his mind, how to get the animal he did not ride himself conveyed to the next town; he accordingly offered Alphonsus a liberal perquisite to ride it thither for him; Alphonsus willingly agreed to his proposal, and they mounted, and rode on.

Alphonsus had for some time considered his situation in the mine as a disagreeable one; he had entered into it from the same motive from which he had so long continued in it,—urgent necessity: he knew no other mode of procuring a subsistence, in which he could pass unknown; and yet he earnestly wished again to mix in the world, in the hope of gaining some light on the mystery which continually occupied his mind; accordingly he determined to offer himself to supply the place of the man whose death he had just witnessed.

The baron asked him many questions as to his abilities for filling the office he wished to undertake, and Alphonsus declared himself capable of every particular: what he had been accustomed formerly to have done for himself, he thought it no difficult matter to perform for another. There was something in his manner of application that interested the baron in his favour; he accepted the offer made to him by Alphonsus, and wrote a few lines to the superintendant of the mine, saying, that he should retain Alphonsus in his service.

The baron Kardsfelt was a man about thirty years of age, and unmarried; his manners were pleasant and his temper mild, unless he conceived himself to be ill-treated or affronted; and then his resentment knew no bounds.

He had at this time been on a visit to his sister, who was married and resided at Prague, and was returning to his own mansion at a short distance from Inspruck, when the accident took place which introduced Alphonsus to his knowledge.—Returned home, Alphonsus was made acquainted with the duties of his station, and executed them much to the satisfaction of his master, who behaved towards him with great kindness.

Alphonsus frequently visited Inspruck, and never missed an opportunity of starting some subject which he hoped might lead to the mention of his family, but he never heard the name. He was often a listener to the tales of spirits and witches, to which the common people in that part of the country give much credit; but the castle of Cohenburg was never spoken of; and he now began to distrust there being any foundation, except the imagination of some weak mind, for the tale the young miner had related.

The baron was fond of play, though he never staked large sums, and passed much of his time at the gaming-table. Having one day engaged a stranger in a game at draughts, his antagonist was accidentally called from the room in the midst of the game. The stranger had been much beaten by the baron: he was chafed by his losses, and, on his return to the room, asserted that the baron had re-drawn his last move. The baron's fiery temper was heated; he rose, drew his sword, and called on his antagonist to defend his assertion:—it proved to the baron a fatal summons, for he received his adversary's weapon in his side.

He was immediately conveyed home, fainting with loss of blood, and the wound pronounced to be mortal: speech was refused him; he beckoned Alphonsus to his bed-side, and gave him his purse; Alphonsus received it, kissed his hand, and retired weeping. The baron pulled the sleeve of his confessor who stood by him, and pointed to Alphonsus; the friar understood that he asked his protection for him, and answered by a significant inclination of the head: about an hour after the baron expired in great agonies.

Alphonsus gazed at him as he closed his eyes for ever.

It was a lesson to the gamester to play no more.

CHAPTER IV.

Ah me! for aught that ever I could read,
Could ever hear by tale or history,
The course of true love never did run smooth;
But either it was different in blood,
Or else misgrafted in respect of years;
Or else it stood upon the choice of friends;
Or if there were a sympathy in choice,
War, death, or sickness did lay siege to it,
Making it momentary as a sound,
Swift as a shadow, short as any dream:
Brief as the lightning in the collied night,
That in a spleen unfolds both heaven and earth;
And, ere a man hath pow'r to say—"Behold!"
The jaws of darkness do devour it up:
So quick, bright things come to confusion.
A MIDSUMMER NIGHT DREAM.

WHEN the friar had given the necessary orders, and made the proper arrangements for the funeral of the baron, he thus addressed Alphonsus,—"Young man, you seem greatly interested in the fate of the baron."

Alphonsus wept bitterly. Every added pang of sorrow deeply lacerates a grief-worn heart. "I have lost my only friend!" he cried.

"Do not despair," returned the friar: "the deceased baron has recommended you to my notice:—I will find some means of providing for your future life, be assured."

These words were balm to the wounded breast of Alphonsus.

"Farewell," continued the holy man: "place your confidence in the will of heaven to repair your loss, and be comforted; I will be here again to-morrow."—So saying he departed.

On the following day Alphonsus found himself more composed, and at the appointed hour father Matthias arrived.

"Good-morrow to thee, youth."

"The same to thee, good father."

"You have been much in my thoughts since we last parted. To every one the promise made to a dying man should be sacred,

particularly to those of our order. I promised the late baron that I
would see you provided for,—I have been revolving my mind the
means, and I think I have found them: I myself act as a confessor to
the convent of Saint Helena, about a league from hence; their sacristan has been dead about a fortnight, and they have not replaced
him:—should you like to become his successor?"

Alphonsus readily accepted the offer; and having heaved a farewell sigh over the body of his rash master, the friar undertook to
conduct him that evening to the convent, and at the appointed time
they set out together.

The convent of Saint Helena was a large and ancient edifice; its
ivy-grown towers indicated its antiquity, and the figures carved on
its walls bespoke the superstition they inclosed.

The friar opened a small door near the chapel, of which he
usually carried the key, and admitted Alphonsus into an inclosed
cloister, which led immediately to his apartments; thence a door
opened into the hall of the convent: it was spacious,—at the angles
were passages leading to the cells of the nuns; and in front, a wide
stair-case conducting to the upper range of cells. The apartment
in which the lady abbess usually sat, opened into the hall; the friar
entered it, and bade Alphonsus follow him: the abbess was alone;
father Matthias informed her who the youth was, and she received
him graciously. Some conversation then passed between her and
the friar in low voices, after which she spoke to Alphonsus, telling him, that, as he was unacquainted with the duties of his office, the porteress should accompany and instruct him in them for
the first three or four days and nights; she then, after some farther
conversation on the same subject, and exhorting him to be peculiarly diligent in his office, rang her bell; and the porteress attending
her summons, she was told that Alphonsus came to succeed the
late sacristan, was ordered to show him his apartment, and to give
him the necessary instructions. Alphonsus followed her out of the
room.

The porteress was about fifty years of age; she was deformed,
of a tart humour, and an incessant pratler. "Come, follow me," said
she, as soon as the door was closed: "I'll show you your room in a
minute; and a good comfortable one it is.—Oh! bow to the cross,
young man, bow to the cross." Alphonsus looked up, and perceived

one fastened over the arch under which they were passing; he obeyed Perilla's commands, and she continued, "Aye, you'll learn all our ways in time,—you'll have a fine, easy, happy life of it, I'll assure you:—let me see,—vespers are just over; at eight you must ring the bell, and prepare the chapel for prayers before going to bed; then again at twelve, for the midnight prayers; then at six, for matins; and at ten, for mass; and at four, for vespers; and that's all you have to do, except helping me to sweep the chapel, and keeping clean the ornaments; and all the rest of your time is your own."

They had by this time arrived at the apartment appropriated to the use of the sacristan. "There," cried she, throwing open the door, you'll live like a prince; father Matthias's rooms are on that side of you, and there is mine;"—pointing to the other side;—"and this," opening a door facing them, "is your way into the chapel; and you must take care that those tapers on the altar never go out; and when they are nearly done, come to me for some more; and now I think I have told you all, so you may come and sit with me till evening prayers if you like it." She proceeded, and he followed her into her apartment.

Perilla had yet a little taste for the world, though she had been thirty years removed from it, and now expected to hear much news of it, from her new acquaintance; but Alphonsus was the worst subject she could have met with for gratifying her wishes: she thought it might proceed from reserve and modesty, as being with a stranger, and immediately began to set him the example of communication, by relating to him various anecdotes of the nuns; at last, interrupting herself,—"There," said she, "the sand is just out, go, and ring the chapel bell.—Oh, here! but stay, stay, put on your surplice,—it is rather too tight about the neck, but we'll get you a new one;—come."

She proceeded into the chapel, and Alphonsus, according to her directions, tolled a certain number of strokes on the bell. "Now follow me," she again cried, and Alphonsus obeyed:—they crossed the chapel. "Here at this door the nuns come in; now you must take that bason of holy water, and hold it for them to dip their fingers into, to cross their foreheads, and keep them from the influence of the devil while they are at prayers. I'll light the candles at the altar for you, but you must do all yourself another time."

The nuns entered one by one, and throwing up their veils as they approached the hallowed ground, dipped each a finger in the vase which Alphonsus held. As soon as the nuns were all come in, the porteress beckoned Alphonsus to follow her once more; they passed behind the altar, and she instructed him, that he must now assist father Matthias in putting on his sacerdotal robes. Prayers were then chanted by the friar: the nuns joined him, and having sung an evening hymn, received his benediction, and retired to their cells.

Alphonsus then, according to the directions of the porteress, put out all candles, save the two never-to-be extinguished lights; and having locked the chapel doors, again accompanied Perilla to her apartment, where they supped. In a short time, "Come," said she, "father Matthias is in bed: you must go too." So saying, she gave him a lamp, and attended him to his chamber door, saying, "Good night, remember to wake at twelve."

Alphonsus slept not; he feared being found negligent in his office on the first trial, and only threw himself on the bed. Perilla's loud suspiration, however, soon convinced him that she had done otherwise; nevertheless at a few minutes before twelve she awoke, came to his chamber door, and warned him it was time to ring the bell.

The same ceremonies were repeated as before, and Alphonsus on their conclusion ventured to enter his bed; reflection, and the novelty of his situation, however, suffered him not to sleep soundly,—and when he heard Perilla again moving about, he arose and met her at the chamber door. Matins were chanted, and the nuns departed as before. "Now," said Perilla, "we must not go to bed any more; it is our duty to sweep the chapel." She then showed him what was required of him to perform, and afterwards set about her own employments.

Alphonsus was as much pleased with his situation as any line of life could, in his present state of mind, have rendered him; it afforded him shelter from a pitiless world, and he was satisfied. Custom quickly reconciled him to the hours of rising; and he even, in a short time, found little need to consult the hour-glass with which Perilla had provided him. The abbess was pleased with his conduct. Father Matthias paid him much attention; he discovered his mind to be informed above his rank in life: he hinted his suspicions to Alphonsus, who confessed their truth, but instantly declared the silence he wished to maintain. The holy father commiserated his lot; he supplied him with books to sooth his leisure hours, and, when his avocation permitted it, gave him his own society.

In the convent of Saint Helena were twenty-six nuns and ten novices; amongst the latter there was one named Lauretta, whose beautifully pensive countenance never failed to arrest the eyes of Alphonsus, as he held the vase of consecrated water. Had he known what love was, he would have felt that she had inspired him with the soft passion: her appearance gladdened his heart, and her departure from the chapel made him only wish for the hour of her return.

About six months after Alphonsus had become an inmate of the convent, as he was one day conversing familiarly with father Matthias, he ventured to inquire of him, who the young novice was that had so forcibly attracted his regard. "Ah! poor child!" said the holy man, "the lady abbess and myself are alone entrusted with the history of her birth; but as I think, from many instances of your conduct that have fallen under my eye, I may venture to trust you with her story, you shall hear it."

Alphonsus bowed acknowledgment for the compliment paid him by the holy man, who thus began:—

"It is now full seventeen years, since, one wet and stormy evening towards the end of December, a faint knock, twice repeated in a short space of time, called the porteress to the grate of the convent; a soft voice entreated shelter from the storm, and mentioned the name of our lady abbess: the porteress opened the gate; and a slender figure, a youth as she imagined, clad in the habit of a pilgrim, entered, leaning on a staff; the porteress closed the gate, and having conducted the supposed youth into the apartment of the abbess, the stranger had scarcely uttered, 'Oh! protect a suffering woman!' ere she sunk at the feet of the lady abbess.

"Exhausted by fatigue, and benumbed by the keenness of the element, the stranger was with difficulty recovered from the fainting fit into which she had fallen: after some time she drank a cup of balsamic cordial, administered to her by the abbess; and a flood of tears proceeding from the joy she felt, on the assurance given her of experiencing that asylum for which she supplicated, eased her full heart. After eating sparingly of the meal that had been set before her, she begged leave to retire to rest, unable to explain that night the mystery which accompanied her arrival in a male habit.

"On the following day she was much recovered from her fatigue, and her entreaties were earnestly made to the abbess not to deliver her up to any one who might demand her.

"The abbess promised her the full protection of the church and perceiving that she was still weak and ill, forbore to put to her any inquiries.

"In a few days she was much mended; but a deep melancholy, at times approaching to frenzy, clouded her mind; voluntarily, however, she communicated to the lady abbess and myself her afflictions; she afterwards (for she delighted to dwell on her sorrows) wrote down her little history, and presented me with it: there it is, I trust to your discretion not to reveal it out of the convent; peruse it whilst I go and pray by the sick sister, Velina."

Alphonsus promised strict secrecy, and receiving the manuscript from the hand of the friar, retired with it to his own apartment.

LAURETTA'S STORY.

"My name is Lauretta. I am the only daughter of count Arieno, resident near Venice; my mother died on the same day on which I was born; I had a fortune equal to my birth, and many were the suitors for my hand, more of whom I believe were swayed by interest than by any attachment to my person: at length, chance threw in my way count Frederic Cohenburg, a noble Saxon by birth, whom, were I to describe him to you as my burning fancy now paints him to my eyes, you would conceive to have surpassed his sex beyond the limits nature has prescribed; suffice it to say, I thought him all perfection.

"At first, I vainly imagined that the deference I paid him, proceeded only from my consciousness of his merit; and so far from being singular in my attentions to him, I should have been an exception to the females with whom I associated, not to have treated him as I did. But alas! I soon found that my regard proceeded from a softer motive, and I quickly perceived that I adored what others but approved.

"The infancy of love is too sweet to be easily shaken off:—at that delightful period, how little are we aware of the many anxious moments its maturity brings upon us!—fatal enchantment! how severe a scourge hast thou proved to me through life!

"A mutual affection glowed in our congenial breasts; I listened to his vows with rapture, and he heard my promises of constancy with equal delight.

"But an obstacle, to which the eyes of lovers are seldom open, had planted a hedge of thorns across the path which I vainly imagined was conducting me to the summit of earthly happiness.

"The only wealth which true love looks for, is an ardent return of affection: in that no one was more rich than my Frederic;—my father, who weighed merit only by wealth, had destined me for the wife of count Byroff, a nobleman of immense property, at that time on his travels; and he commanded me to check a passion grown too incorporate with my blood to hope a cure; nor did I endeavour to effect it; I would sooner have given up life, than to have lived and ceased to love my Frederic. His visits were now interdicted, on pain of my being immediately sent to a convent, if he was again seen with me.—How feelingly did I then taste that the bitters of love are more poignant than its sweets! Still had I not resolution to shake off my cause of sorrow.—If the idea for a moment entered my harassed brain, it was outweighed by the consideration that the uncertain wheel of fortune might one day turn in my favour, and give me to enjoy my Frederic's love without alloy.

"At length I contrived by stealth to meet him in the garden of my father's sister:—how did the sight of him rekindle the smothered flame!—I again vowed fidelity to him, and imprecated heavy curses on myself, if ever I swerved from the oath I had taken to be his only, and for ever.

"Not long after this, I was one day sitting alone in my chamber, ruminating on my hard fate, and bedewing with my tears a letter I had privately received from count Frederic, replete with vows, which, though often repeated, were still new and dear to me, when my father entered the apartment, and informed me that count By-

roff was returned to Venice.—How shall I describe to you the pangs
that at that moment rent my heart?—how relate to you the tide
of grief which burst its way through my swollen eyes?—But I will
leave it to be pictured in your susceptible breast.

"Had not the fulness of my heart sealed my lips, the too certain knowledge of my sentence having proceeded from a mouth
whence there was no appeal, would have prevented my giving utterance to ineffectual remonstrances.

"In the evening of that day, my destined spouse waited on my
father;—I was summoned to appear;—he rose and took my hand
as I entered the apartment; I cast my eyes upon the ground; I could
not bear to encounter those of a man whom I considered as the
bane of my future peace.—I must, however, in justice to him, say,
that, save only one, I never knew a man better calculated to make a
woman happy; his address was easy and elegant; his manners con-
ciliating; his person handsome, and his mind well stored with polite
and useful learning. He was a man that, had he been my brother, I
could have revered him; as it was, in spite of me, I respected him;
but with how widely different a passion did he wish to inspire me!
and in how mild, how gentle terms did he complain of that coldness with which I treated him! So far did his noble spirit win upon
me, that many times I formed the determination of disclosing to
him the fatal secret of my heart, and entreating his pity.—Oh, ye
powers! why did ye not whisper to my labouring breast the many
hours of anguish this confession would have spared me, and the
horrid deed that then had never been committed?

"At length the day I long had dreaded was fixed upon; and notice was given me the preceding evening, that I was, on the morning of the following day, to accompany count Byroff to the altar.—I
fell at my father's feet, and, clasping his knees, conjured him to have
pity on me; I endeavoured by the arguments of reason to convince
him of the impropriety and cruelty of his commands: I besought
him not to harden his heart against the entreaties of an only child;
I represented to him the remorse of conscience my future misery
would occasion him, when he considered that he alone had brought
it upon me. But his ear was deaf to every voice save that of interest,
and casting me from him, he exclaimed, 'Obey my commands, or
cease to be my daughter;' and, with a frown that pierced me to the

heart, left the apartment.—Exhausted with weeping, I sunk into a fainting fit, which lasted some time; as soon as my strength began to return, I took my woman, and, leaning on her arm, repaired to my aunt's, where I had before met Frederic; I informed her of all that had happened—she sympathised in my distress, but being entirely dependent on my father, durst not exert herself in my behalf; I entreated her to send in search of Frederic: she did so.—After two hours passed in tedious expectation, the messenger returned and informed us that he was not in Venice; he had been absent from it some days on urgent business, but was shortly expected to return.

"My aunt promised to send early in the morning, to inquire whether he was arrived, and if he was, to let me know immediately.

"I returned home like a malefactor, who, knowing his doom to be inevitable, makes no resistance when led to the stake.

"Entering my father's house, I passed quickly to my chamber, and throwing myself upon a couch, I again gave fresh vent to my tears.—My woman was afflicted at my distress; she had been my constant companion since the death of my mother; she loved, and endeavoured to comfort me: but alas! how vain were her counsels! she could only recommend resignation, where it was no virtue, and teach me to hope for that interposition of providence, which it refused to grant me.

"When I became somewhat composed, I began to reason with myself.—'Shall I,' said I, 'quit my father's house, and fly to Frederic?—surely he will receive me with joy, with rapture!'—I reflected a moment; I had been told that men were false, inconstant, and cruel; that those they professed to love in prosperity, were disregarded by them in adversity.—'Surely,' cried I, 'Frederic is not one of those!— oh no! what promises has he not made me!—what sacred oaths of fidelity has he not taken!—I will fly to him; he will meet me with transport.'—I sprang from the couch in extasy, and walked wildly about the chamber; when, oh cruel reflection! I at that instant remembered somewhere to have read, I know not where, that lovers' vows are made only to be broken.—'Oh heavens! should Frederic think thus,' I exclaimed; 'for who that has ever loved, but has sighed and sworn as he has done?—And shall I then throw myself upon him, to be accounted a burthen by him? perhaps upbraided for my love?—Oh credulity! bane of our sex! why have I so long been thy dupe?'—In a brain harassed as mine then was, any idea, however romantic, is easily admitted; and, half frantic, I loaded the faithful youth with every objurgation my rent heart suggested.

"I fear you will upbraid me with ingratitude, suspicion, and cowardice of nature; I confess to you, I seem to merit the reproach; but the torture of mind I then endured, may well apologise for my strange, and seemingly ungrateful, conduct.

"The thought of my lover's infidelity once admitted, I became more calm; I considered that if the vows of love were disregarded by those who were not compelled to break them, how innocent should I be, whom my relentless fates conspired to force unto it!—I even became in part reconciled to my approaching marriage.—You will marvel at my words:—but put yourself in my situation; conceive but for an instant the distracting thought of being abandoned, if not cursed, by a father; perhaps disregarded by the man to whom you should fly for protection; cast friendless upon an unpitying and prejudiced world: and the idea of giving your hand to a man whom you had already begun to esteem, will not appear in so dark colours as you may perhaps have drawn it.

"I did not retire to rest that night: early in the morning, my aunt sent to inform me that Frederic was not returned. 'It is well!' I cried; 'too sure he has forgotten me. Oh cruel, cruel Frederic! are these thy vows? is this thy boasted constancy?' All the pleasing scenes of future bliss I had once vainly flattered myself I should enjoy with my Frederic, now recurred to my imagination; and, in spite of my efforts to coerce them, a flood of tears again burst from me. I continued weeping till my father entered my chamber, and summoned me to attend count Byroff to the altar. 'To be for ever parted from my Frederic!' returned my heart. All my resolution again failed me, and I should have sunk senseless at my father's feet, had not the voice of count Byroff, inquiring for me in the tenderest accents, met my ear, and roused me from my lethargy of grief. He took my hand within his—it trembled excessively—he mistook the reluctance with which I suffered him to take it, for virgin bashfulness, and encouraged me with the most soothing expressions of affection.—We entered the chapel, and I returned from it a wife.

"My doom once fixed, my heart seemed lightened of a heavy

weight of anxiety, and I considered it as vain to afflict myself concerning a sentence which was now irrevocably fixed.

"The day was spent in festivity, and I constrained myself to appear cheerful; the awe in which I stood of my father caused me to wear a smile on my lips, whilst I could not forbear heaving a sigh unheard for Frederic.

"Innumerable were the gifts made me on that day by all my relations: count Byroff presented me with jewels to a vast amount, and many articles of dress not less costly in their kind: even my father's natural parsimony seemed relaxed; for he bestowed on me a valuable string of pearls, the only ornament I now possess, and which, notwithstanding his unrelenting cruelty, I still hold dear and sacred, in memory of him who gave it. Never did woman pass a less joyful bridal day than myself: when the bustle of festivity was subsided, and night again brought opportunity for reflection, I strongly felt that my love for Frederic had lost no ground in my heart.

"In the morning, my kind aunt visited me: I inquired eagerly after count Frederic;—he was not returned.

"In spite of my exertions to appear lively, I was depressed: count Byroff left no means untried to amuse, and render me cheerful. My father, who well knew the cause of my melancholy, let not the first opportunity slip of warning me to beware of raising his anger to a higher pitch than I already had done.

"About a month after my marriage, my most earnest wishes were crowned with success; my aunt informed me, that Frederic was returned, and half frantic at the intelligence she had given him. My father was luckily from home;—I immediately flew to my aunt's, where I once again beheld my only love. But oh! never was the parting of the most faithful lovers, doomed to weep away a sad and solitary life within monastic walls, more truly affecting than our meeting: my ardent lover gazed at me with a look of sorrow, that penetrated to my inmost soul; my heart shed tears of blood, and, in an agony of grief, I fainted in his arms. On recovering my senses, I entreated him to forgive the rash act into which I had been hurried by the threats of a cruel father, and the vain distrust of my own harassed mind: I besought him to pity me; nay, even more, to love me. Yes, I charged him to love me still, as I still loved him. Do not, I beseech you, misconstrue the meaning of these words, nor suppose me now a penitent for a crime which, the Supreme of all is witness, was far from my thoughts: my fates, cruel and relentless as they have been, were however satisfied with the resignation of my peace, and spared me the additional sacrifice of my virtue.

"Oh, Frederic! if some bright star thou reignest on high in yon exalted firmament, look down upon thy faithful Lauretta, faithful to thee, even in death, and witness for me the purity of a heart burnt up by love's devouring fire, yet never swerving from the rules of fairest virtue!

"I continued for some time constantly to meet Frederic at the house of my indulgent aunt, until some circumstances, however trivial in themselves, conspired to inform me that our meetings were discovered. I accordingly forebore to see him; and wrote to him, telling him my reason for absenting myself from my aunt's. A daily correspondence was now commenced between us, which, except that I saw not my Frederic, amounted to the same as if we had met; as, at our interviews, we had only uttered those lamentations, vows, and promises of fidelity, which were now conveyed in our letters. A faithful servant of my aunt's had the care of receiving and delivering them.

"About a fortnight after the commencement of our correspondence, I learned that my father and my husband were going a short journey, and would not return for two days. On the morning of the day on which my husband had told me they intended setting out, I dispatched a letter by our trusty messenger to Frederic, informing him of their intended absence, and that I would that evening meet him at my aunt's.

"In the afternoon my father and count Byroff bade me farewell, mounted their horses, and set out. In about two hours after their departure, I ventured to my aunt's; I informed her how things were circumstanced; she congratulated me on my pleasing prospect of seeing my Frederic, and then inquired for her servant, in order to learn whether he had found Frederic at home; but our messenger was not returned.

"Three hours were passed in anxious expectations and vain surmises: neither Frederic nor the servant appeared: the only conclusion I could draw, was, that Frederic was not in the city, and that our messenger was gone in search of him. But a short interval

convinced me of the horrible reverse. Oh! picture to yourself my
disappointment, my astonishment, my grief, when, hearing footsteps on the stairs, my aunt opened the door of the apartment, and
my father rushed in.—I uttered a violent shriek, and fainted at my
aunt's feet; when I recovered, I found myself on my own bed. 'Oh,
Frederic! art thou then lost for ever?' I exclaimed; for the first idea
which shot across my burning brain on my recovering my senses,
was, that the sword of count Byroff had pierced the heart of my
Frederic. How I got this intelligence, I am to this moment ignorant:
suffice it to say, it was but too true, and I infinitely miserable. My
husband was sitting by my bed-side; I upbraided him for his unjust
cruelty in the most extravagant terms, suggested by my excessive
grief: I laid before him all the history of my love for count Frederic;
I wept, I sighed, fainted, and upbraided him by turns.

"He informed me that my father had told him, that he suspected I entertained a connection with another man; which idea
he had at first endeavoured to confute; but my father persisting in
it, he had agreed to assist him in making an attempt at the discovery of the truth; that they had pretended to be going on a journey,
under the expectation of my then admitting Frederic into my father's house; but that, on the morning of that very day, my father
had seized our faithful messenger, and torn from him my letter to
Frederic, inviting him to meet me in the evening of that day at my
aunt's: that, having confined the servant, they had found means of
conveying my letter to him to whom it was addressed; and having
waylaid him in an obscure street through which they well knew he
must unavoidably pass in his way to my aunt's, count Byroff had
stabbed him. God alone knows what were my feelings during this
recital; and thanks be to him, that the fulness of my heart sealed my
lips, or I, in frantic rage, had cursed the author of my being.

"Count Byroff entreated me to be composed; he represented to
me, that my sorrow was now ineffectual, since the deed, which he
himself avowed to have been rash, was committed. He set before
me the resignation I owed to the will of a father, and endeavoured
to work upon me, by the shame I should incur in the opinion of
the world, if my conduct became publicly known. But I heeded not
what he said; I listened with disdain to words uttered by the murderer of my Frederic. At that moment, I should have scorned the

words of an angel, had they been incapable of recalling my Frederic to life.

"I absolutely refused all nourishment and repose: count Byroff became alarmed for my health; he continued with great earnestness to urge me to resignation; made me the most solemn protestations of his love; besought my forgiveness, and prayed me to tell him how he could sooth my anguish.

"I was silent, and count Byroff left my apartment: he had not been long gone, ere I commanded my faithful woman, who had been the companion of my sorrows, to go and inform my father and my husband, that I had fallen into a sound slumber; and warn them against entering my apartment, lest they should disturb me. Against her return, I had thrown on a long cloak and veil; and, having bribed her to keep my secret, I left the house unobserved. It was about nine o'clock in the evening when I set out: I moved towards the suburbs of the city as quickly as I was able: arrived there, I entered a narrow lane, in which I imagined I recollected the shop of a clothier. I walked down in search of it: to my great joy, I soon found it, and entering, I perceived there to be no one in the shop but an old woman. In imperfect language, intermixed with French, I told the woman I was journeying to Loretto, and wanted the habit of a male pilgrim. She immediately produced several: I purchased one, together with a staff and leathern bottle; and, having tied up my bundle, I left the shop, inwardly rejoicing that the old woman had been too busily occupied in praising the quality of her goods, particularly to notice me. I again set forward, and in a few minutes arrived in the great road leading from the city.

"Fortunately for me, the rising moon served to show me my way; and being arrived nearly half a league from the city, and perceiving no one near me, I ventured to exchange my garments for the pilgrim's habit; and having buried the clothes I had taken off under a sod, which I had with difficulty managed to cut up for the purpose of hiding them under it, I once more set forward, intending to journey to this convent, which I had heard my aunt mention, and where I had resolved, if you were so kind as to permit me, to pass the remainder of my days.

"Under favour of my habit, I travelled hither perfectly to my satisfaction, except the inconvenience I suffered from fatigue; but your benevolence and care soon brought me to the happy state in which I now find myself: and I trust I shall never prove ungrateful in my acknowledgments to you, and in prayers to the holy saint in whom you confide, to reward you for the humanity you have shown me."

Here was a part of the mystery, relative to the conduct of the uncle of Alphonsus, cleared up; count Frederic had loved and been beloved by the niece of his much revered friend Arieno; she thought him dead, and lived and died secluded from the world, mourning his loss. "Mistaken woman! oh that some angel," cried he, moved by the affecting narration of Lauretta's hapless lot, "had whispered to thee the falsity of that tale which drove thee forever from thy Frederic and the world!—Her loss was surely the cause of the grief which visibly preyed upon my uncle's heart!—Still this solves not the mystery in which I am concerned."—He sat a few minutes wrapped in melancholy thought; then returned to father Matthias's apartment.

"Well!" cried the holy man—"I perceive you feel what you have read;—you pity the unhappy sufferer?"

"Sincerely I do.—Her Frederic was five years since alive."

"Mysterious heaven!" exclaimed the old man: "explain to me, I beseech you, what you know concerning him."

"Indeed—I cannot now:—the time may come."—He paused.

The father looked disappointed; in a moment he regained his wonted serenity of countenance. "She died," cried he, "as she lived, lamenting the untimely fate of him she loved."

"How long have her cares been ended?"

"Grief wasted her frame to a skeleton, and she has sunk into the grave, now seven years."

"Were any inquiries ever made relative to her?"

"Never."

"But she mentions nothing of her child, nor have you spoken to me of her."

"When she delivered to us the manuscript I put into your hands, she knew not herself that she was about to become a mother.—With tears she some short time after declared her situation to the abbess; and called on heaven to witness that it was the pure offspring of her marriage with count Byroff.—Her sufferings moved the abbess, and she promised to connive at her situation, and protect her child. At the due period of time she gave birth to a female infant, which received its mother's name; this was to her great joy; for had its sex proved other, it must necessarily have been removed from her at an early age."

"And is the young Lauretta destined to a life of seclusion from the world?" asked Alphonsus.

"Her mother," answered the friar, "on her death-bed, ordained, that, should any part of her family by any means gain the knowledge of her having borne a child, and demand it of the abbess, it was to be delivered up to them; but in case of her remaining here unknown unto her eighteenth year, she was at that period to take the veil, as it was not likely that even she herself would then be remembered by them after so many years' absence; and on no account to inform her relations that a child of hers was in existence; dreading, as she said, that they should think it incumbent on them to take home the child, and either doubting the purity of its birth, or, in revenge for its mother's transgression, use it unkindly."

"Of what age is Lauretta?" asked Alphonsus.

"She has about four months attained her seventeenth year," returned the old man; "and I trust both her father, and count Arieno, are ignorant that such an angel is in existence.—She has been made acquainted with her own story by her mother: but the colours in which her parent painted to her her nearest relatives, leave her no wish to enter upon a world which she has never known, and of which she has heard so unprepossessing an account: she declares herself perfectly happy within these walls, and prepared to take the veil."

Alphonsus sighed; his eyes fell on the dropping sand, and it admonished him to ring the evening bell.

CHAPTER V.

————————————a matchless pair,
With equal virtue form'd, and equal grace;
The same, distinguish'd by the sex alone:
Hers, the mild lustre of the blooming morn,
And his, the radiance of the risen day.

THOMSON.

THE thoughts of Alphonsus were continually fixed on Lauretta; he every day felt a stronger prepossession in her favour; he began to conceive the nature of his regard for her, and wished to snatch her from the eternal gloom of a monastic life:—he longed to impart to her the sentiments with which she had inspired him: all intercourse with the females of the convent, save the lady abbess, and old Perilla, was denied him:—what means could he pursue to communicate to her his affection, or how did he know she would not disregard, nay perhaps despise him for the confession?

He resolved stedfastly to fix his eyes on hers as she entered the chapel: he was practically ignorant that love has a language of the eyes; but he conceived that the eyes might be made to express what passes in the heart.

He fixed on her countenance his black penetrating eyes: the blush of modesty o'ershadowed her cheeks; she cast her eyes on the ground, and proceeded swiftly along.

He was unacquainted with the sex, and knew not yet to distinguish between diffidence and displeasure.

He repeated his experiment frequently: sometimes it was returned in the same manner as on his first trial: mostly she raised not her eyes higher than the vase, and immediately dropped them again.

"No!"—cried he—"Lauretta feels no sentiment congenial with mine; she even meets my looks of love with indifference.—Unhappy Alphonsus!"

The next time she entered the chapel, he resolved not to raise his eyes to hers: a broken sigh burst from his heart. Lauretta sighed also. Alphonsus heard the sound,—it tingled on his heart.

He ventured once more to meet her blue eyes: he imagined a faint blush tinged her cheeks, and a soft smile stole over her countenance.

It was a confirmation of Alphonsus's most exalted hope. "She sees, and is not insensible to my fondest wishes!" he exclaimed. "Oh extasy incomparable!"

How light a breath turns the wavering balance of a lover's hopes and fears!

Fearless, he now met her eyes: her diffidence gradually wore off, and she encountered his fond glances with delight.

A method of conversing with her now entered his mind: he wrote to her the fondest declaration of his love, that the desire of its return could dictate:—he held his letter by the side of the vase; and as she extended her finger to touch the water, he slid the paper unobserved into her hand.

Three days elapsed ere he was released from the torture of suspense; on the third, at evening prayers, she put a note into his hand, containing these words,—"Oh, Alphonsus, what a conviction of the state of my own heart has the declaration of yours proved to me!—Oh, let it remain a secret to all besides ourselves!—Be cautious how you write to me again,—we shall be suspected!"

Alphonsus was truly happy for the first time; but extasy will cool, and bring time for reflection. It told him that he might never be more closely connected with Lauretta than at that moment.

About five months after this time, the lady abbess was seized with a violent illness. The friar, who was also the administerer of physic in the convent, was an unremitting attendant at her bed-side: in a few days she died, lamented by all the convent, and particularly by Lauretta, to whom she had been a second mother.

Her corpse was placed in its coffin, before the altar of the church; masses were performed three times each day for nine days successively, for the benefit of her soul; and three nuns and a novice alternately watched over her body for the same space of time.

Alphonsus thinking an opportunity might now be given him for presenting Lauretta with a letter, wrote one, informing her that he was the nephew of her deceased mother's beloved Frederic, and entreating her to agree to leave the convent with him on the first opportunity that should offer,—calling on heaven to witness the sanctity of his intentions.

On the evening of the fourth day, Lauretta was returning from her duty of watching the body, as Alphonsus was entering the chapel: she followed the nuns;—they had turned the angle of the chapel door, and Lauretta was in the door-way when Alphonsus met her. He cast a hasty look round,—saw no observing eye,—snatched her hand,—imprinted on it a fervent kiss, and put into it the letter.— The whole was the transaction of a moment.

The funeral obsequies of the abbess were performed at the stated time, with all the pomp of religion and superstition; requiems were chanted the whole night by the friar, and all the nuns and novices. It was morning ere they left the chapel; they were fatigued by their nocturnal worship; they rejoiced when it was ended, and retired hastily from the chapel. Lauretta contrived to be the last; she dropped a piece of paper; Alphonsus flew and hid it in his bosom.

"Explain to me, whither thou would'st fly."

He read it,—kissed it,—read it again, and tore it.

After much deliberation how to act, whether again to write to his beloved Lauretta, and inform her of the particulars of his unfortunate story, or only urge her to fly with him from the convent, he resolved to impart the whole of his history to father Matthias.

Accordingly he waited with impatience an hour when the old man was alone; and having entered his apartment, he hesitatingly informed him that he had a tale of confidence to impart to him,— which the holy man sacredly promised to bury in his own breast. Alphonsus then related to him every event that had occurred to him since his entrance into life. Having ended the narration,—"Now, good father," he cried, "canst thou solve the mystery that preys upon my breast?"

The holy man sat some minutes wrapt in thought; then, raising his eyes to Alphonsus, and marking his breast with the sign of the cross, he said, "Heaven forbid I should accuse any one unjustly! what I am about to say, is solely conjecture. Thy mother was frantic with grief, and had resolved on suicide."

Alphonsus shuddered at the idea: after a pause, he said, "But, father, her hand was bloody!"

The father paused an instant; then said, "She had grasped, in a moment of phrensy, the instrument she had destined for her destruction."

"Why did she send me from her?"

"Doubtless," returned the friar, "she forcibly felt the shame that would follow the act she was about to commit, and feared it would descend on her innocent son."

"Do you then impute to the same cause her accusation of my uncle, which she afterwards recalled?"

"I do."

"But, father, why has my uncle left the castle of Cohenburg?"

"His mind is open to sensibility; and the remembrance of those who had so lately inhabited it, rendered it unpleasant, and he doubtless retired to his own mansion."

"But why has he never inquired after me?"

"His inquiries may have escaped you."

"Your suppositions," cried Alphonsus, "are good: you consider circumstances; you know the nature of mankind: they may be just; but a heart, harassed as mine has been, pants for certainty."

"It will be difficult to attain it."

"Within these walls, I grant it."

"You do not wish to leave them?"

The hesitating silence of Alphonsus spoke for him in the affirmative.

"Your uncle, and the castle of Cohenburg," continued the friar, "are interdicted to you by your mother."

"But surely," interrupted Alphonsus, "it is not disobedience to act in opposition to the commands of a frantic parent?"

"You just now alleged, Alphonsus, and with reason, that my words could only proceed from conjecture."

Alphonsus felt the force of the friar's remark. The tears started in his eyes, and he exclaimed, "Oh! father! I cannot taste peace of mind till I gain some light on this mystery.—I am an unfit subject for the offices of religion,—my thoughts are too much centred in the world."

"How can you gain information but by visiting the castle?—and then how know you that your pains might not prove futile?"

"No! I would only mix with the world; the possibility of hear-

ing what I so earnestly desire would keep hope alive: here it lies
buried, and I have no pleasing thought to chear me."

"Whither would you go?"

"I have resolved to become a fisher on the banks of the Inn."

"The solitude in which you will there live, will soon cause you
to regret the happy station you wish to relinquish."

"I feel I was born for society; not to live with men alone, but to
enjoy the soothings of the softer sex."

"Beware of your choice."

"I would have you approve it."

"I am secluded from the world."

"But you intimately know her on whom I doat."

"Oh, shame! shame! Nurtured within our convent walls, art
thou the man to wish to break their sacred laws?"

"Lauretta Byroff is not bound by them."

"Have you ever conversed with her?"

"Never."

"How then can you tell her feelings are congenial with yours?"

"Be assured they are."

"I have promised her dying mother, that to no one, but her near
relations, I will deliver her."

"And should you then hesitate to deliver her to me?"

"You are not allied to her in blood."

"It is in your power to set all consanguinity a degree below
me."

"Explain thyself."

"Make me her nearest relative;—your promise is fulfilled, and I
am blessed."

Father Matthias paused awhile; he then said, "What would the
world say, should it ever be known that the descendents of your
two noble families were living in the obscure and humiliating situation you have mentioned?"

"Oh, father! what have those whom the world has so hardly
dealt with, to do with its censure?—I am well convinced that happiness is not confined to an elevated situation in life."

"Nor," returned the old man, "is it always to be found in an
humble state, answerable to the expectations of a warm lover." Fa-

ther Matthias again paused, then added, "Have you explained your
fortunes to Lauretta?"

"No."

"Declare them to her."

"But how, good father?—teach me the means."

"This night I will conduct her to my apartment, there thou shalt
meet her.—If she consents to share them (and I will pray that heav-
en guide her tongue for her true felicity), I will not be the means to
sunder those whom it has joined.—But mark me, if she refuses thy
suit, instantly she takes the veil.—I am hasty in this affair.—I feel an
interest in your fates; and what is done must be concluded ere the
arrival of our newly-chosen abbess."

Alphonsus kissed the friar's hand, and he made a sign to him to
leave him.

When evening prayers were ended, and Perilla was retired to
bed, father Matthias stole softly to the cell of Lauretta, and told her
to follow him to his apartment. She was reading; but having laid
down her book, and taken up her lamp, she drew down her veil and
followed him. He stopped at the door of Alphonsus's apartment,
and pointed to Lauretta to enter his; she did so, and in a few minutes Alphonsus was at her feet.

Joy and surprise made her hesitate to determine whether what
she saw was a vision, or him she really wished it to be.

The first moments, on the part of Alphonsus, were given up to
extasy; but he considered that the time allotted to him was short,
and that he had much to communicate; he accordingly began by
imparting to her the indulgence of the good confessor, proceeded
to the narration of his own life, and, lastly, recounted the plan he
had formed for their mutual happiness, if she deigned to share it
with him.

Her eyes spoke the consent that virgin bashfulness prevented her tongue from uttering;—she blushed:—he urged the friar's
words—the shortness of the time allowed her for the consideration—the possibility of their being separated for ever.—Her tender
heart melted at the idea;—her lips expressed the words her voice
scarcely sounded.—the enraptured Alphonsus sealed the sacred
bond with an extatic kiss.

Quickly after the friar entered, to warn them that the hour of twelve was near at hand; and he read in the eyes of Alphonsus the result of his conversation.

Lauretta returned to her cell, promising to visit the father on the following morning; and Alphonsus entered the chapel to prepare for midnight prayers.

Alphonsus and Lauretta passed the night in sleepless dreams of happiness to come.

At the appointed hour, Lauretta repaired to the apartment of father Matthias; he asked her confession—her heart was spotless, except a chaste and hidden love long entertained for Alphonsus, could be charged on the score of blame: he then represented to her the wayward fortunes that befall alike the good and evil in the world, upon which she was about to enter; he set before her the trials that all who live in it must sustain; he charged her well to consult her heart, that she might not, when too late, blame herself for an act which could not be recalled.

She did consult her heart, and found it firm.

The father had already conversed with Alphonsus to the same purpose; he was stedfastly fixed on again braving those vicissitudes of life to which he had already been exposed.

The old man now rose, and called Alphonsus into his apartment.

Alphonsus quivered with extasy.—Lauretta trembled, she knew not why.—She wept.

Father Matthias again exhorted them to reflection ere it was too late.

Their eyes met each other's; Lauretta's tears were dried, and Alphonsus ventured to answer for them both, "that they were resolved."

The indissoluble knot was tied.

"The grace of God shine upon you, my children!" cried the old man.—Alphonsus embraced his bride, while tears of joy sparkled in his eyes.

"To-morrow morning, with the dawn of day, you must leave these walls," said the holy man; "now retire to your respective apartments, and each collect together what little articles you may possess of value."

They followed his directions.

During the course of the day, the friar informed such of the nuns as were acquainted with Lauretta's story, that she had been summoned to leave the convent by her nearest relation; and they bade her tenderly farewell:—"She will depart early in the morning," said the old man; "and we shall, I fear, experience a double loss; for our young sacristan, wishing again to mix with the world, will leave us at the same period."

Perilla expressed much astonishment at his being dissatisfied with his present station,—told him, "he would find it difficult to meet with such another;" gave him "some lessons for his good," as she was pleased to term them, and comforted herself with the hope that his successor would prove more communicative, and thus a companion suited better to her garrulous taste.

On the following morning, after matins had been chanted, and the nuns had again returned to their private devotions in their respective cells, and Perilla was busied in sweeping the chapel, father Matthias went to the cell of Lauretta, and, having directed her to habit herself in the pilgrim's dress in which her mother had arrived at the convent, and which was now in Lauretta's possession, he led her down into the hall. Here she was met by the anxious Alphonsus;—"Accept that small purse of gold," said the good old man: "it may benefit you, my children; with me it lies useless."—They kissed his extended hand:—he gave them his last benediction, and unbarred the heavy gate.—Lauretta dropped a parting tear.—Alphonsus exclaimed, "Farewell, my kind friend!"—The old man raised his eyes and hands to heaven; then closed the gates on them for ever.

CHAPTER VI.

Which is the villain? Let me see his eyes;
That, when I note another man like him,
I may avoid him.
                                        MUCH ADO ABOUT NOTHING.

SUPPORTING herself on the arm of Alphonsus, an hour's journey brought Lauretta to Inspruck; where, wishing to avoid the questions of those who might perceive she was newly entered upon the world, she wisely concealed the surprise which was excited in her breast on beholding scenes to which she had hitherto been totally a stranger.

After a short repast, the travellers again set forward, and arrived about an hour after mid-day at the spot where Alphonsus had determined to fix his residence.—A small inn received them for the night, and in the morning Alphonsus repaired to the owner of the houses on the border of the river. Having bargained for the hire of one of the most commodious dwellings then vacant, and purchased the freedom of exercising his intended trade on the river, he next provided himself with the necessary implements for earning his subsistence; and in a few days entered upon the employment he had chosen for that purpose.

Fortune smiled on his endeavours; his Lauretta was the solace of his unemployed hours; and he enjoyed as great happiness as the mystery which had reduced him to his present humble situation could suffer a thinking mind to enjoy.—Retired from the world, not possessing either those riches or vanities which excite the envy of its inhabitants, Alphonsus and his Lauretta had hoped to live free from its cares and inquietudes; but they were quickly doomed to experience how short is the durability of human felicity, even in its humblest state.

The proprietor of the estate on which Alphonsus rented his humble habitation, was the baron Smaldart: he was a widower, whose wife had died in child-bed together with her infant. He was a man remarkable for his benevolence, hospitality, and mildness of temper.

His only sister had espoused the chevalier D'Aignon, a native of Burgundy, who, having been killed by a fall from his horse a short time after the death of the baroness Smaldart, madame D'Aignon had ever since resided with the baron.

Theodore, the son and only offspring of the deceased chevalier, now in his twentieth year, had for some time been receiving his education in France, and was expected shortly to return to his uncle's. His mother awaited his return with all the ardour of prejudiced fondness; but she was not permitted again to behold her son. She had for some time been slightly indisposed; and one morning,

about the time of Theodore's expected arrival in Germany, was
found lifeless in her bed.

This was a stroke which severely affected the baron: since the
loss of his wife, his sister had been his constant and much-beloved
companion: they had been strongly attached to each other; and he
had earnestly wished that she might survive him.

At the appointed time Theodore arrived at Smaldart castle: but
how great an alteration had taken place in him in the space of five
years! When a youth, his every wish had been anticipated by the
false indulgence of a kind uncle, and a doating mother; but still his
manners had been then unaffected, his deportment unassuming,
and his mind untainted with vicious habits. But now he was become haughty, impetuous, confident of his own opinion, and eager
to give it unasked. The pecuniary allowance made him by his mother had enabled him to pass the greater part of the time allowed for
his education, in a variety of dissipation: thus the acquisition of
knowledge had been utterly neglected by him: nor was he himself
conscious of his deficiency; having been hitherto connected with
a set of men too sensible of their own interest not to pay implicit
deference to his opinion on every occasion.

The baron had promised himself a pleasing companion in his
nephew: he had expected to reap edification and amusement from
the conversation of his well-informed mind; and hoped to find in
him a willing partaker of such diversions as the country afforded.

How mistaken were his expectations! Theodore's conversation consisted only in boasting of disgraceful exploits, in which he
was careful to hold himself up as the principal actor; and the only
amusement he found in the sports of the country, was to make
their pursuit a plea for injuring the lands of those who, from their
dependence on his uncle, he well knew would not venture to seek
redress. In short, had he aimed at making himself the object of
general contempt and hatred, he could not have pursued steps that
would more satisfactorily have gained him his wish.

He often averred that he despised the good opinion of inferi-
ors; and his actions plainly showed that he would submit to any
meanness to gain a smile of approbation from a superior in rank.

At the time of Theodore's arrival in Germany, Lauretta was in
an advanced state of pregnancy: but she appeared not the less fasci-

nating in his eyes; and, from the first moment of his beholding her, he marked her out for his lustful prey.

A mode of conduct but too common in life was now adopted by him: he used every means to show himself the friend of the husband, while he was labouring to become his blackest enemy. Often did he, by the most seductive flattery, make in imagination a step towards the heart of Lauretta; and as often did her awful virtue cause him to retrace his visionary path.

The perceptive mind of Alphonsus could not long remain ignorant of the hidden villany of the young chevalier; but, conscious of the strict chastity of his Lauretta, he determined to appear not to notice the actions of Theodore, whilst he in reality kept the strictest watch over them. His mind recoiled from being daily obliged to increase a debt of gratitude to a man who was studying to wound him in the tenderest part; but policy forbade him to refuse obligations he had once accepted, lest he should open to the chevalier the discovery he had made, and his measures become more determined.

At the expected period Lauretta gave birth to a female infant, whose being was but that of a few hours. Lauretta was much affected by the loss of her first-born: Alphonsus, though he rejoiced at the safety of his wife, dropped a tear in sympathy with her sorrow at the fate of his child.

Theodore appeared daily at the cottage of Alphonsus, making the most solicitous inquiries relative to the health of Lauretta, and offering to her, by means of her husband, the most liberal presents, which Alphonsus was slow to accept, and that sparingly:—of a refusal he saw the bad consequences.

In the summer, Alphonsus was frequently kept out nearly half the night by his occupation; but he dreaded not that his Lauretta would then suffer from the persecutions of Theodore, as he had never visited his cottage in an evening; and more particularly as he well knew the gates of the baron Smaldart's castle to be closed at an early hour.

The conduct of Theodore was, however, becoming daily more alarming to the timid Lauretta; and she obtained a promise from Alphonsus, that, if the chevalier persisted in it, he would appeal to the well-known humanity of the baron.

It was one night, not long after this time, that Lauretta, still weak from her late indisposition, having retired to rest before the return of her husband, was roused by the cries of a girl, whom Alphonsus had procured for her as a nurse and companion in his absence, calling out that the house was on fire; and the girl immediately ran out to procure assistance.—Lauretta, springing from the bed, threw on her clothes as quickly as her alarm would permit her, and was rushing towards the door of the apartment, when Theodore stood before her. She shrieked, and endeavoured to pass him: he seized her hand, and exclaiming "my lucky stars are at length predominant," dragged her into the outer apartment.

Lauretta again raised her feeble voice; but, alas! her cries, had they been heard, would have been thought to proceed from her alarm on hearing the cry of fire. "Oh God of mercy, assist me!" she cried. "Oh my Alphonsus, where art thou?" and, raising her eyes, which had hitherto been averted from the surly smiling Theodore, she perceived, standing near the door, two men, whose scowling mien and haggard looks terrified her more than the villain who held her; and she again uttered a faint cry.

Theodore cast at her a look of mingled triumph and contempt; and, waving his hand to the men, they approached Lauretta. She again struggled to release herself from Theodore; but the effort overpowered her, and she fainted in their arms.

CHAPTER VII.

Eye me, bless'd Providence, and square my trial
To my proportion'd strength.

MILTON.

LAURETTA, on recovering her senses, found herself in total darkness; and, by the motion which she felt, concluded she was in some vehicle, which was drawn swiftly along. It was some time ere she recollected the situation in which she had last seen the light, and she then exclaimed, "Gracious heaven, where am I?" No one answered. She extended her hand; it fell upon the hilt of a sword, and she immediately heard a rough voice, between sleeping and waking, mutter some words which she did not understand.

The image of the men who had so greatly alarmed her, recurred to her, and she shuddered.

The person who sat by her yawned, and turned himself towards her.

The night, although summer was far advanced, was damp: Lauretta was unaccustomed to the night air—she trembled with cold—and her teeth chattered violently.

Her companion again yawned; and then asking her, whether he should throw his woollen wrapper round her, relieved her from the apprehension under which she had at first laboured, that Theodore was the person who wore the sword she had accidentally touched.

That poignant anguish of mind which refuses to relieve the sufferer by an effusion of tears, is seldom more favourable to the utterance. Such was the grief of the unhappy Lauretta: her repeated attempts to articulate were ineffectual, and the pangs of her heart were redoubled by her involuntary silence. The tears, at length, as expressive of the painful efforts which produced them, stole singly down her cold cheeks, and with difficulty she again stammered out, "Where am I?"

"I must answer no questions," returned the man. His voice was hoarse, but by no means so blunt and harsh as Lauretta's fears had led her to expect.

"Whither am I going?" cried Lauretta.

This demand was thrice advanced, but no answer returned.

"Is the chevalier D'Aignon here?" she then asked.

"No," replied the man. "I believe I may venture to tell you, he is at the castle."

To no other question could she obtain the slightest answer: she knew not what to hope or what to fear; the gloominess of the night added greatly to the depression of her spirits, and the predominant idea within her breast was, that her companion was hired by Theodore to be her murderer, in revenge for his slighted love.

Her companion in a short time after addressed her; and, attributing her anxiety in a great measure to the chill, which, by the chattering of her teeth, he found still hung upon her, pressed her to taste some brandy out of a flask which had been almost unremit- tingly applied to his own lips.

Lauretta was insensible to his attentions. "Oh Alphonsus!" she cried, "shall I never again behold you?"—A flood of tears followed the exclamation, and her sorrow rose almost to phrenzy.

After three hours passed in a suspense more poignant than a certainty of suffering the most dreadful calamities that could have befallen her, the vehicle stopped.

Her companion immediately sprang up, and pushing past her, opened the door, and gave her into the arms of his comrade, by whose side stood another figure, holding a lantern.

The man who had received her into his arms, conveyed her into the kitchen of a miserable inn, of which it was difficult to say, whether poverty or dirt was the leading feature: he placed her in a chair, and then returning to the door, saluted the landlord with a volley of oaths, which conveyed the double meaning, that the horses were in want of provender, and his flask void of brandy.

He then approached the fire, and kicking away a dog which lay sleeping in the corner of the chimney, seated himself by Lauretta.

His companion now entered, and placing himself opposite the weeping fair, she imagined she perceived a faint gleam of pity shine in his eye. To avail herself of the moment in which she fancied she saw his heart open to the dictates of humanity, was her immediate resolution; and falling on her knees before him, she entreated him to have pity on her helpless situation, and restore her to her Al- phonsus. Ere he could answer, she heard his comrade start from his seat, and turning round her head, she observed that he had drawn his sword nearly out of the scabbard. All her fears now seemed veri- fied; she seized the hand of him before whom she was kneeling, uttered an hysteric shriek, and sunk senseless on the floor.

When she revived, she found herself still on the ground, with her head reclined on the knees of a woman, whose expanded fea- tures and brawny limbs seemed to deny her sex.

Whilst Lauretta had continued in a state of insensibility, the hostess had carefully chafed her temples with strong liquors, and now seeing life returned, pressed her to fortify her stomach with a dram of the same cordial, which she had before outwardly admin- istered.

She was now again placed in the chair which she had before oc-cupied, and casting her eyes round, she perceived that several other men had entered the kitchen: amongst them sat the ruffian who had lately given her so much cause for alarm; but she saw not him who had been her companion in the vehicle.

Her fainting fits, together with the extreme agitation of her spirits, had brought on a violent pain in her head; and unable any longer to support her drooping frame, she requested the hostess to conduct her to a bed; but with this petition, Kroonzer, the ruffian of whom Lauretta stood in so great dread, absolutely commanded her not to comply, saying, he must depart in a very short time. The hostess, though of so masculine a figure, seemed not devoid of the feelings of her sex, and now cast a look at Lauretta, which speak-ingly informed her, she wished to accord in her request, but durst not, from the awe in which she stood of Kroonzer.

After a short interval, Kroonzer ordered the host to bring out the horses and prepare for their departure: his commands were in-stantly obeyed.

Again lifted into the vehicle, how great were the apprehensions of Lauretta, on perceiving Kroonzer enter after her, together with another man, on whose countenance the light which proceeded from a lantern held by the host, falling, it appeared, if possible, more savage than that of the surly Kroonzer.

They again proceeded swiftly along, and for a length of time a strict silence was observed, not less by the men, than by Lauretta.

The faint taints of saffron hue which now began to streak the clearing sky, afforded extreme delight to the overburdened heart of Lauretta. She considered, that, had these men received orders to destroy her, they would in all probability have executed the deed, whilst the darkness of the night enabled them to evade the eye of man.

The first objects she descried by the rising light, were distant mountains, whose towering summits were rapidly gaining the gilded tinge of advancing day.—The tract of land over which they were journeying, was heathy and barren, save where, at intervals, some small clusters of unpropped vines grew spontaneously on the shelving hillocks.

Her fortitude in some measure returning with the much-wished-for light of day, she ventured to inquire, "whither she was going?"—"Not above a league farther now," cried Kroonzer, "whatever we may do at night."—And from this answer she hesitated not to conclude, that, wherever she was about to be conveyed, Theodore, apprehensive of a rescue, had cautioned her conductors against travelling in the day-time.

The road now turned into a valley: on the left lay high mountains which were speckled with cattle of various kinds; on the right, irregular lines of lofty chesnut and beech trees: it now wound round the mountain, and the sun burst full upon them between the boles of the trees. Never before had its chearing rays so greatly exhilarated the heart of her who now hailed its return from the bosom of the deep.

A few moments brought them to the extremity of the vale, and they entered upon a small but thickly planted forest; the ground was covered with furze, through which, as there was no distinct path, the vehicle found a difficulty in passing: at length turning an angle, Lauretta suddenly perceived a thatched cottage: here the vehicle stopped, and Ralberg, for such was the name of Kroonzer's comrade, having alighted, announced their arrival by a thundering knock with his fist at the door. It was opened by a man half dressed, whose appearance was that of a peasant, and Lauretta was conducted into an apartment which served for the double purpose of kitchen and chamber to the countryman and his wife, who, when they entered, was in the act of dressing behind a ragged curtain, which but ill concealed her from her newly arrived guests.

Lauretta, unable to stand, insensibly seated herself on a bench, which encircled half the fire-place,—unmindful of Kroonzer and his comrade, who had entered into close conversation with the countryman in low voices.

The good woman was no sooner habited, than advancing from behind her flimsy retreat, she began with an apology to Lauretta for not having been up ready to receive her, and ended by requesting her to accompany her to a better apartment. Lauretta, with tottering and uncertain steps, followed her hostess up a few stairs, scarcely superior either in breadth or safety to a ladder, and arrived in a small room, the furniture of which consisted of a mean bed, a disabled chair, and a large box, which served at once for a wardrobe, a seat, and a table.

Having closed the door, and pointed with half a courtesy to the only chair, Bartha again apologised for not having been risen to receive her; but alleged that she had arrived somewhat earlier than her husband had said he expected her.

"Were you then apprised of my coming?" asked Lauretta.

"Oh dear heart, yes," replied Bartha; "and so I got this chamber ready for you; for I said to Ugo,—lack-a-day, said I, she will be sorely tired with journeying all night, and glad to rest her wearied limbs, I warrant me."

"Oh!" cried Lauretta, clasping the hand of old Bartha, as she stood by her side,—"if you are acquainted with the purpose for which I am brought hither, for the love of God, I conjure you to inform me."

"The Holy Virgin wots, I know not," returned the woman.

"But, tell me, whither I am to be conveyed," continued Lauretta; "one of my guards insinuated that I am not to remain here longer than to-day."

"Ah! lack-a-day!" cried Bartha, "I know not indeed! Ugo says, women are tattlers, and should not be trusted with secrets. I pressed him hardly to tell me on what account you were coming hither; but he would not."

"Gave he no reason?"—inquired the disconsolate fair.

"No, by the saints, did he not. He only said, 'Bartha,'—said he, 'ask no questions; no harm is going to be done to any body; so make yourself easy.'"

"In what manner was he informed that I was going to be brought hither?" asked Lauretta.

"By my troth, I know not," answered Bartha. "He told me of it last night, when he came from work in that little forest you see there: he is a wood-cutter."

"Could you find any method of conveying a letter for me to my friends?"

"Not unknown to my husband, if it be far from hence."

"The estate of the baron Smaldart, on the borders of the river Inn, is the place I allude to."

"Lack-a-day, good soul, that is many leagues from hence; and I never go farther than the next village."

Lauretta hung down her head and wept, and Bartha left the apartment.

Unable to taste the refreshments with which Bartha in a short time returned, Lauretta threw herself upon the bed; and although she had never pressed bedding so hard and uncomfortable, the fatigue she had undergone soon closed her eyes, but not to peaceful slumbers: the scenes through which she had so lately passed, returned to her flurried imagination in more terrific colours than the reality had appeared to her,—now exaggerated by sleeping fancy.

CHAPTER VIII.

————Patience and sorrow strove
Which should express her goodliest.

LEAR.

THE day had been close and sultry; towards evening the sky began to lower, and the clouds seemed big with an approaching deluge of rain. Lauretta observed them with sensations of melancholy pleasure; the gloom in which all nature was clad seemed in unison with her feelings: she contemplated the scene before her, till, thought rising successively on thought, she became almost insensible to her own situation. Her reflections were at length interrupted by the entrance of Bartha, who brought her a cup of new milk, some fresh gathered fruit, and a slice of coarse bread, of which she entreated her to partake, as Kroonzer and Ralberg purposed proceeding on their journey in half an hour's time.

Lauretta, in order to please her kind hostess, rather than to satisfy the calls of nature, which were blunted by extreme grief, tasted the fruits, and sipped a small quantity of the milk, whilst Bartha again called forth every argument with which she was acquainted, to persuade Lauretta, that, as her husband had said she had nothing to fear, she was sure she had not. But this reasoning appeared to Lauretta, although she attempted not to confute it, too weak to afford her any solid consolation.

The voice of Kroonzer now called upon her to descend. The feeble resistance she could make, she well knew, would be of no avail; ready compliance might conciliate her guards; she therefore instantly obeyed the summons. Ralberg met her at the foot of the stairs, and taking her in his arms, placed her on a horse before his comrade, and then vaulted upon another himself, which the peasant held till he had mounted it.

A thick darkness blackened the horizon, and a dead silence prevailed, save when, at intervals, short gusts of wind announced a rising storm.

In a short time, vivid flashes of blue lightning momentarily illumined the atmosphere, and shot across the lofty mountains; the combating clouds rolled rapidly towards each other, and jarring, burst in tremendous claps, which, from their loudness, seemed immediately over the heads of Lauretta and her companions.

After an hour and a half, as nearly as Lauretta could guess, passed in journeying amidst this dreadful contention of the elements, and in almost incessant darkness, except when, at intervals, the darting flashes of lightning seemed to clothe the furze-grown earth in flakes of fire, the storm which, fortunately for the unhappy Lauretta, had been attended with but little rain, began gradually to subside, and a misty moon-light succeeded.

Their road, she now perceived, lay through a deep glen. "Oh, God!" she exclaimed, "should this be my destined grave!" and, chilled by the apprehensions her own imagination had raised, she insensibly hung down her head and closed her eyes.

A length of time elapsed ere she again ventured to look around her; and she then saw that they were entering upon a forest of lofty trees, thickly planted with underwood.

Ralberg and his companion had been in conversation together since the cessation of the storm; but she had not been able to gather any thing from their discourse that served either to diminish or increase her terrors.

Lauretta, becoming extremely fatigued and exhausted, again closed her eyes; and, notwithstanding the alarm under which she laboured, she struggled ineffectually against the attacks of sleep, which at length overpowered her fainting frame.

Suddenly starting from her involuntary slumber, she shivered violently, a dizziness seized her head; and although the night was become much clearer, she could not for some time distinguish any object.

A turret, which rose above a distant cluster of trees, now caught her gazing eye; and as she proceeded, she discovered that it formed part of a building towards which her guards were advancing.

Her eyes continued fixed on the object before them; and as she approached it, her alarm became extreme: her conductors spoke not, and she waited her doom in anxious silence.

The light of the moon, reflected on the building, showed her that one wing was entirely in ruins, and the whole edifice in a state of decay.

On being lifted from the horse, she was unable to stand; her knees knocked violently; and, almost insensible of her situation, she sunk upon the supporting arms of Kroonzer.

Ralberg having fastened the horses to a broken pillar of the colonnade, pushed back the heavy gate, which creaked loudly on its hinges; Kroonzer then entered the building with Lauretta in his arms, and as he placed her on a seat seemingly formed by a niche in the stone wall, he called to his companion, telling him instantly to strike a light, and chiding him for having waited his bidding. His words were re-echoed from every part of the building, and in sounds so dismally hollow, as caused Lauretta to shudder violently.

Ralberg made no answer, but began striking his flint:—for some moments Lauretta heard the uninterrupted jarring of the steel and flint; and, with a heart beating high with the anxious desire of seeing the joyful ray of light which was to release her from the horrid gloom in which she now trembled, she fixed her eyes upon the spot where the sound informed her Ralberg was stationed, when a flash of light drew them suddenly to the opposite side of the hall; it appeared to her to have proceeded from a lamp on the side on which she was sitting; she immediately turned round her head, and beheld a man who carried a lamp, with his back towards her, enter a door, which he immediately closed after him.

As the ruinous state of the building had not left Lauretta the least room to doubt that it was uninhabited, she immediately concluded the man she had seen to be Kroonzer, although she knew not whence he had procured the light, and again turned her eyes towards Ralberg; when, to her great astonishment, she saw them both approaching towards her with their lamp lighted. A shriek, which she endeavoured to suppress, burst involuntarily from her lips, and she immediately perceived the same door partly opened, and the arm and visage of a man, whose features she could not distinguish, appear within it. Theodore instantly recurred to her imagination; the recollection of him shot like a bolt of ice across her heart, and she sunk lifeless on the ground.

On the return of her senses, she was lying upon an uncanopied bed, and a dim lamp, which was burning in the apartment, showed her Ralberg standing by her side; she immediately cast her eyes round in search of Theodore;—the apartment was large, and the light thrown out by the lamp insufficient to convince her that he whom she dreaded was not within it;—raising herself upon the bed, she seized the hand of Ralberg, and, bursting into tears, conjured him "to save her,—to protect her from Theodore."—In as softened accents as his rough voice would permit him to articulate, he bade her be composed, and banish her apprehensions.—With a look of doubt, she again fixed on him her streaming eyes, and grasping more strictly the hand she had before held, she exclaimed, "May heaven reward you as you pity my misfortunes."

The sound of footsteps now called her attention to another part of the chamber. Kroonzer entered: he brought with him a cup of wine, some fruit, and bread; and, having taken the lamp from the ground, he placed them on a table near the bed; he then invited Lauretta to rise and taste them; she answered him only with her tears; he repeated his invitation; she endeavoured to speak, but her sobs prevented her utterance.—Springing from the bed, she threw herself at his feet, and clasped his knees; he pushed her from him, and beckoning to Ralberg to follow him, they left the apartment; and she heard the door locked and bolted after them.

The violent agitation of her spirits being somewhat abated, she took up the lamp, and walked round the apartment, in order to be certified whether any one was secreted within it.—Its form was circular; the roof high and vaulted; the walls of stone; the casements small, and many feet raised from the ground; and the entire appearance led her to conjecture, that she was now in that turret which had attracted her notice while journeying through the forest.

She then set down the lamp, and taking from her bosom a small ivory crucifix, which she placed on the table, she knelt, and, having fervently declared her gratitude for the sufferings of him in memory of whom she wore the sacred remembrancer now before her, she proceeded to implore of him fortitude, to enable her to bear up under the calamities which surrounded her, and his divine aid, against the evil designs of those whom she dreaded more than death; concluding by a declaration of her faith in his beneficence, and her unfeigned submission to his will.

Rising, and replacing in her bosom the crucifix, she felt a composure proceeding from her confidence in that power she had just addressed, which she little imagined she should have experienced; still, however, by no means sufficiently free from alarm to endeavour to compose herself to rest, she placed herself in a chair which stood near the bed, and, as from the stillness of the scene her terrors became gradually abated, she grew more collected, and better able to ruminate on the occurrences of the night.

The figure of the man whom she had seen was unremittingly before her eyes; and the feelings of her mind naturally assigning to him the person of Theodore, her fears began to return as strongly as ever; she sighed deeply, and the tears ran swiftly down her burning cheeks;—she rose, and walked slowly about the apartment, stopping at intervals and fixing her swoln eyes on the ground in mournful reflection on the past, and poignant anticipation of the future.

Faint and exhausted with fatigue of body, and anguish of mind, she again seated herself in the chair.—In a short time, the languor which hung upon her increased almost to inability, her eyes became dim, and big drops of perspiration started from her forehead;—shivering, she extended her trembling arm, and grasped the cup of wine; with difficulty she raised it to her head, and then, for some moments, her quivering lips refused admittance to the reviving cordial;—having twice swallowed a small draught of the liquor contained in the cup, the trembling which had seized her began to subside, the blood began again to circulate in her veins, and life seemed newly warmed within her heart; she again sipped a small quantity of the wine,—a glow succeeded the shivering fit, and a drowsiness, which she endeavoured in vain to shake off, stole gradually upon her, and lulled her into a profound sleep.

CHAPTER IX.

Tho' plung'd in ills, and exercis'd in care,
Yet never let the noble mind despair:
When prest by dangers, and beset with foes,
The gods their timely succour interpose;
And when our virtue sinks, o'erwhelmed with grief,
By unforeseen expedients bring relief.

PHILIPS.

LAURETTA, on waking, started from her chair, and cast her eyes wildly about, totally ignorant where she was; and, entirely forgetful of all that had passed the preceding evening. But busy recollection swiftly burst upon her with all its sorrows: she sighed, and raised her eyes to the high casements: the rays of the sun shone hot and full into her apartment; she conjectured it to be noon-day, and marvelled that she had slept so long and soundly; she moved towards the door; it was still fastened; and, from what she remembered of the disposition of the little furniture her prison contained, she saw not the smallest cause for suspecting that any one had visited it during the night. She examined the lamp; it was burnt out in the socket, and the cup of wine stood on the ground where she herself had placed it.

Towards evening, the creaking of the locks announced Kroonzer: he entered with a fresh supply of provisions; which, together with a flask of wine, and another of water, he placed upon the table; and, having trimmed the wick of the lamp, and replenished the wasted oil, he lighted it, and left the apartment, without uttering a single word.

The artificial light produced by the lamp tended swiftly to dispel the declining day; and, with the increasing gloom, the horrors of her situation were greatly accumulated in the imagination of the unhappy Lauretta.

Night had assumed her sablest form; when the fair prisoner, shivering from the inaction in which she had passed the solitary day, and still feeling a reluctancy to commit herself to the oblivion of sleep, began slowly to perambulate her chamber:—languid and feeble she stopped, and, reclining her arm against the flinty wall, her head sunk insensibly upon her hand, and she stood wrapped in painful thought. Suddenly, the trampling of horses struck her ear—she started, and listened—a shrill tucket was shortly after sounded, and she indistinctly heard the sound of voices. Burning with the chearing hope of rescue, her heart beat high within her breast, and her respiration became suspended. "The kind baron," she exclaimed, "has lent his aid to my Alphonsus, and they now come to my relief!"

An interval of dead silence ensued:—she moved towards the door, and, trembling with expectation, doubted whether or not she already heard footsteps. But sad conviction proved her agitated senses had deceived her.

Another interval longer than the first passed away, but no sound met her attentive ear. Delusive hope, however, raised in her harassed brain the flattering possibility, that her friends might be searching for her in some distant part of the building, and would still arrive at her prison.

A confusion of footsteps and voices seemingly approaching towards her apartment, now raised in her panting bosom a tumult of passions, amongst which fear was predominant. Till this instant, the pleasing expectation of enlargement, and restoration to her beloved Alphonsus, had solely occupied her imagination: now the hated Theodore recurred to her, and every footstep seemed to increase the dreadful probability, that she might the next moment be destined to fall a victim to his unruly passion, or breathe her last beneath his injurious arm.

The noise increased, and the persons seemed still to advance. "This way, this way," exclaimed an unknown voice; "follow me, this way." Lauretta breathed with extreme difficulty. A blow against the door thrilled her heart, and the same voice cried out, "The key is not here; ask it of Kroonzer."

Lauretta stood motionless: several voices now spoke at the same time, but so confusedly, that she could not distinguish a word they uttered. Suddenly, all the persons seemed to recede from her prison as swiftly as they had advanced towards it; and the sounds dying gradually away, an awful silence again prevailed.

Trembling lest they should return, Lauretta still continued near the door: she knew not how to account for what she had heard; and the more she ruminated, the more she was bewildered in her conjectures.

A length of time having elapsed, and not the minutest sound met her ear, her alarm began to subside; and the power of reflection returning, she felt in its fullest force the mortifying disappointment she had sustained: at that moment every future prospect of liberty seemed to have vanished in the present; she burst into a flood of tears, and, sinking upon the bed, gave way to the strongest parox-ysms of despair.

Oh hope! thou chearing shadow of each desired object! why does the blackening gloom of disappointment so often cloud the sunny path through which thou leadest us, glowing at every anx-ious step with warmer expectation? while fancy, strengthening with desire, *seems* the reality, and makes us in imagination blest; until the dream-dispelling dawn of reason opens our eyes, and shows us the wished-for goal, as distant still, as when we first began the imagi-nary course!

The mind, harassed beyond its bearing, seeks insensibly the balm designed by nature for its restoration. Thus the fair prisoner, on again opening her eyes to her solitary room, found she had tast-ed its efficacious sweets, although she had not courted its powers.

During the greatest part of the day, she continued upon the bed, lost in weeping and meditation. The approach of evening again introduced Kroonzer into her apartment: he had brought with him more fruit and another flask of water. He expressed great surprise at her not having tasted what he had set before her the former evening, and asked her to partake of what he had now brought. She paid little attention to his invitation; but besought him to explain to her the occurrences of the preceding night. He did not answer her; but, having prepared the lamp, he lighted it, and left the chamber; repeating the entreaty he had before urged, for her to eat some of the fruit and bread.

Not in compliance with the request of Kroonzer, but the calls of Nature, Lauretta eat of the fruit and bread, and drank a large cup of water: the wine she determined not to taste, concluding, from the effect it had produced on her the first night of her imprisonment, that its nature was somniferous; and, although she wished for an oblivion of her cares, she had not sufficient resolution to act herself towards the production of it; apprehensive of what might befall her in a state of insensibility.

Thus passed on six melancholy days, in a course of sad reflection, perplexed by a variety of conjectures, and cheared only by the idea that Alphonsus was ignorant of her sufferings.

No human being entered her prison save Kroonzer, who never failed at the accustomed hour; but observed an impenetrable silence to every interrogatory made him by Lauretta, relative to her situation.

No sounds similar to those she had heard on the second night of her imprisonment returned: she concluded herself a prisoner for life, and despair began to subside into calm melancholy.

Towards midnight of the seventh day, she was awakened from the soundest sleep she had for some time enjoyed, by a violent crash of thunder, which shook the turret: she sprang from the bed, and stood a moment in wild alarm, scarcely recollecting where she was, or knowing what she had heard; when a flash of lightning struck that side of the turret against which she was leaning; the wall instantaneously fell, and carried along with it the shrieking Lauretta.

END OF THE FIRST VOLUME.

The Midnight Bell

Volume II

THE MIDNIGHT BELL.

CHAPTER X.

Beneath a mountain's brow, the most remote
And inaccessible, by shepherds trod,
In a deep cave, dug by no mortal hand,
A hermit liv'd; a melancholy man.

HOME.

STUNNED by the fall, Lauretta lay a length of time amidst the ruins, insensible of her situation, till reason, beginning again to dawn, brought along with it a recollection of the accident that had befallen her. The tempest was abated, but it still rained violently: her head and right side were much bruised, and her left arm was burnt by the lightning: but, having fortunately dropped upon the wet earth, her body had sustained no other material injury. She lifted up her head, and cast her eyes around; but the twilight, obscured by the thick rain, was insufficient to show her any object but the ruined turret close by which she lay.

Resolved, however, if possible, to profit by an opportunity which seemed providentially given her for effecting her escape, she with difficulty raised herself upon her feet, and, although very weak, she determined to proceed from the castle as quickly as she was able, hoping perchance to arrive at some convent before she was missed—at least could be overtaken—by her guards, who had probably not heard the fall of the turret.

She had proceeded nearly a league without stopping, when the dawn of day, beginning to break, showed her that she was entering upon the precincts of a wood. The ground over which she had passed was heathy and uneven:—heated and panting for breath, she supported herself against the trunk of the first tree; her head ached violently; her arm and side were extremely painful, and her garments, drenched with the continued rain, clung round her, dripping with water. The inaction of a few moments produced a shivering chillness less tolerable than the fatigue of proceeding, and she again endeavoured to walk; but exhausted nature supported her trembling frame only a few paces, ere she sunk upon the rough ground: no prospect but that of a lingering death, or again falling into the hands of Kroonzer and his companion, now presented itself to her melancholy view: a flood of tears came to the relief of her full heart; she closed her eyes, and sobbed bitterly.

In this situation she had lain a considerable time, when she heard a voice articulate some words which she understood not. She raised her dim eyes, and beheld standing by her side a hermit of a benign aspect and venerable mien, on whose arm hung a flagon, and in whose hand was a staff, on which he supported his aged limbs.

"Praised be the saints!" cried he, as Lauretta opened her eyes, "I am deceived; I thought thee dead." Lauretta extended her feeble hand, which the hermit taking in his, knelt down by her side. "My strength is wasting fast," said Lauretta. After a short pause, she added, "Kind heaven hath sent thee to close my dying eyes."

"Rather do thou hope," returned the hermit, "it has sent me to succour thee from death: thy nature seems exhausted with fatigue; let me conduct thee to my cell hard by, and trust to providence and my endeavours to renovate thy strength."

"Alas, father!" replied Lauretta, "I fear I cannot reach it; I am too faint to walk."

"Let me entreat thee to essay it," cried the hermit.—The old man was feeble, and it required his utmost exertions to assist Lauretta in rising from the ground: he then put the staff into her right hand; and, encircling her waist with his arm, he held the other arm in his, and thus led her tottering steps through a winding path to his rude cell.

Having seated her on a bench covered with moss, the hermit laid a faggot and some dried leaves on the hearth; and, having kindled them, he warmed a small quantity of a restorative cordial he possessed, and gave it to Lauretta to drink. Somewhat revived by the medicine she had swallowed, the old man placed her before the fire, and, having given her a skin mantle, he left her to exchange her wet garments, whilst he went to fill his flagon at a neighbouring spring; which had been his errand abroad when he discovered Lauretta, but which he had left unaccomplished.

On his return, he found his fair guest in some measure refreshed, but still weak and ill. She complained much of the bruises on her head and side, and her arm also was extremely painful:—to this the hermit applied an assuasive balm; and, having given her a healing balsam with which to anoint her head and side, he conducted her into the inner division of his cell; and, having recommended to her to compose herself to sleep on his straw pallet, he left her to repose, whilst he broke his own fast in the outward division of his humble dwelling.

Soft sleep quickly visited the couch of Lauretta, and she embraced it as a friend whose caresses she was unwilling to forego; for she rose not till mid-day had been some hours gone by.

The kind hermit had baked for her some apples on his hearth; and of these, together with some brown bread, she made a sufficient repast, and drank plenteously of the water from the spring.

Lauretta's spirits returning with her strength, she voluntarily gratified the hermit's curiosity in regard to such particulars as led to account for the situation in which he had found her.

"A veil of mystery," cried the old man, as Lauretta ended her account, "has many years clouded that castle. The coward peasantry report it to be the residence of spirits: your words confirm me in the suspicion I have long entertained, that it is infested by a banditti. The castle formerly belonged to the family of Byroff, whose circumstances falling into decay, they have left this country; and their once stately mansion is now mouldering into a pile of ruins."

"Have they ever committed any depredations hereabout?" asked Lauretta.

"Never," answered the hermit. "If they are robbers, as I conjecture, caution would doubtless teach them not to assail the passenger near their haunt, lest it should be detected. But let us hope that the baron Smaldart, whom you represent as your friend, will find some measure for bringing them under the lash of justice."

"But how came Theodore connected with them?" said Lauretta.

"Time will develop that mystery," replied the venerable man:

and he added, "However artifice may for a while conceal his guilt, rest assured that providence in its own time will expose the machinations of the wicked, and turn their evil actions on themselves."

"The will of heaven be done," cried Lauretta. "But let me entreat your assistance in devising some method for my returning to my husband."

"We must be cautious in our steps," said the hermit, "lest they lead to the discovery of your retreat, and you again should fall into the power of your malicious enemies."

"By your counsel I will be guided," replied Lauretta.

"Thus then I advise," answered the solitary man. "I will provide thee with implements for writing unto whomsoever it shall best suit thy purpose; and on the morrow I will seek a trusty peasant, residing on the skirts of this forest, who shall convey what thou hast written to the baron Smaldart; and he may then concert some measure for thy safe return to thy husband."

Lauretta gladly adopted this proposal; and, having addressed a brief account of her sufferings and present concealment to her beloved Alphonsus, she inclosed it in a cover directed to the baron; she then drank a second cup of the cordial prepared for her by the hermit, and again retired to his pallet, which he kindly insisted on resigning for her accommodation, having prepared for himself a bed of dried moss and leaves in the outward part of his cell.

Early in the morning Lauretta arose, with a heart lighter than she had for some time felt it; and, having joined her kind host in his accustomed devotions, they sat down to an humble repast, and the hermit then sallied forth in search of the peasant who was to be Lauretta's messenger to the castle of Smaldart.

On his departure, Lauretta again habited herself in her own garments, which a constant fire had now rendered fit for wearing; and, not daring to venture without the cell, she sat ruminating on her happy and unexpected escape from her prison, and anticipating the pleasure of again beholding her Alphonsus.

The hermit, on returning, informed her that the peasant had willingly undertaken the journey; and that, in about five days, she might expect the arrival of her husband, or at least to receive some intelligence of him by the return of the messenger.

Lauretta expressed to him her gratitude for his kindness in the warmest terms; but he silenced her by observing that what he had done was but the debt of man to man, and that it were better not to know than not to perform it. She raised her hands to heaven, in thankfulness for the kind protector she had found; and at the same time dropped a tear for the sorrows of her Alphonsus.

In the course of that day, Lauretta ventured to inquire of her venerable host, what could have induced him, who, from his knowledge of the world, and the exalted sentiments of his heart, seemed to be so well calculated for the offices of society, to have secluded himself from all intercourse with men.

"Canst thou, daughter," he replied, "attend with patience to the tale of a careworn old man?"

Lauretta immediately expressed her anxious wish to be made acquainted with the history of her newly-gained friend.

The hermit heaved a sigh, and thus began.

CHAPTER XI.

When sorrows come, they come not single spies,
But in battalions.

HAMLET.

THE HERMIT'S TALE.

"IN me you behold the victim of a supposed crime; suffering where I had never erred, and denied the justification which, after years of misery, I was tantalised by having placed fruitlessly in my view.

"My father was a man of some small rank and eminence in the city of Berne, in Switzerland: he had been twice married; my sister was the fruit of his first marriage, myself of his second; and we were his only children.

"My sister was adorned with every beauty and grace that is captivating in a female form: a German count, to whom she by accident became known, grew enamoured of her, asked her hand of my father in marriage, and, as you may readily suppose, was not denied his request.

"About a year after the marriage of my sister, my father died:

my mother I never had known; I succeeded to the property of my father, and, in a letter of condolence written me on his death by count Harden (for such was the name of my brother-in-law), he earnestly entreated me to pass over into Germany, and visit my sister.

"The property which had devolved on me by my father's death, being sufficient to maintain me in a comfortable though not in an affluent style of life, I had not turned my thoughts to any vocation, and consequently had no bar to my accepting the kind invitation of the count.

"I accordingly wrote to him, with thanks for his kind remembrance of me, and informing him that I should with pleasure visit my sister at her new abode.

"A few days after, I set out on my intended journey, having resolved to travel on a favourite steed I possessed, for the benefit of the better enjoying the fineness of the country through which I should pass; and, strange as it may seem to you, this resolution was the foundation of a series of misery which has known no abatement.

"You will doubtless think my tale an improbable one;—oft do I myself look back on past occurrences, hardly able to convince myself they could ever be: but I have learnt, from sad experience, that the most trivial accidents may carry in their train a complicated and inexplicable string of misery.

"Let the words which I shall now relate, teach mankind not rashly to fix the stamp of guilt upon that brow on which unproved suspicion hangs, nor to shut the ear of compassion against the voice of him that is accused, because he may seem guilty.—Let my tale be known to all: to the wretched it will teach that he has a brother in affliction; and he on whom fortune has smiled, may gather from the misfortunes of another, a lesson of thankfulness and content.

"My first day's journey was prosperous; on the second, towards evening, when I was within two leagues of the village where I meant to pass the night, having carelessly let my bridle hang upon the horse's neck whilst I eagerly gazed at the delightful prospects which the country afforded, the animal having set his foot on a rolling stone, fell, and so severely wounded his knee, as to render it impossible for him to proceed.

"Perceiving at a short distance from me a neat mansion, I dismounted, and repaired towards it; the door was opened by a man who appeared to be between forty and fifty years of age; I told him the accident that had befallen me, and requested him to direct me to some person who might give assistance to my horse. He immediately called to him a lad of about fourteen years of age, who was working in a garden adjoining to the house, and ordered him to lead the horse to the stable. I was too much in need of assistance, to be very particular in my apologies, and thus willingly accepted his offer.

"It required much persuasion, and even force, to conduct the animal to the stable which had been so kindly offered for his reception.

"Having safely lodged him, my kind inviter himself administered to the wound, and then requested me to follow him into the house. A neatly dressed woman, who, he informed me, was his niece, rose at our entrance, and welcomed me, as did two beautiful little girls, her daughters.—My late accident served to commence our conversation; and the natural questions of whence I came, and whither I was journeying, with their subsequent answers, followed.

"The lad, whom I had left in the stable with my horse, presently entered, and, shaking his head, said, 'Ah, sir! this is a bad job; it will be some time, I doubt, before your beast will be able to set a foot to the ground.'

"I looked melancholy;—my host, whose name was Dulac, observed it, and thus addressed me:—'Nay, sir, don't let this account of your horse distress you; I hope the boy may be mistaken in his conjecture: at all events; if you can pass a few days with comfort to yourself in this humble dwelling, your company will be very acceptable to its inhabitants.'

"I bowed a look of thanks, for an offer by which I felt myself obliged, but hardly thought myself entitled to encroach upon the politeness of a stranger by accepting.

" 'Well, well,' continued Dulac, clearly perceiving, I believe, what passed within my breast, 'I must insist on your staying with us to-night; and to-morrow we will talk farther on the subject.—

Come, let us step into the stable, and see if our opinion coincides with Peter's.'

"I rose to follow him out, but he stepped back from the door, and, with an inclination of the head, waved his hand for me to precede him; I returned his salutation, and passed on as he directed me: he was then behind, and I heard his niece rise, and call him back. I entered the stable, and found, on examining the condition of my steed's wound, what Peter had said to be but too true. In a few minutes Dulac joined me; smiling, he said, 'My niece, sir, was fearful we should not be able to give you accommodation that you would like; for we have only one unoccupied bed, and my nephew Bertrand is gone to the next town, where he expects to meet his wife's sister and her husband, who are coming back with him to pass a few days here: but I told her not to be uneasy about that, for you were my guest, and if you would condescend to accept half of my pallet, you were heartily welcome to it.'

"I thought this a bad time to apologise for my intrusion; for if I did, it might seem as if I was dissatisfied with my accommodation; and I accordingly accepted his offer with as great warmth as he had made it.

"My frankness seemed to please him; and I could not fail being gratified with his kindness; as his words and actions plainly showed themselves to be such as proceeded from a warm and benevolent heart.

"In about an hour's time, Bertrand and his friends arrived; and Dulac presented me to his nephew, who welcomed me as cordially as his uncle had done. Shortly after, we sat down to supper: good humour presided, and I was happy to see that the party appeared by no means displeased with my society.

"At a late hour we parted; I believe, with mutual regret.

"From their conversation, I learnt that Dulac rented the farm on which he lived, and superintended the management of it himself; while Bertrand and his two sons performed the offices of tillage and husbandry.

"My first business in the morning was to visit my horse; and I was happy to find it in a much more salutary condition than my fears had led me to expect I should.

"Breakfast ended, Dulac invited me to walk with him; an invitation which the beauty of the surrounding country made me eager to accept. Through the most romantic scenery imagination can figure, my host, whose conversation was at once entertaining and instructive, led me to the margin of a small lake, on whose bosom the sun shining in its meridian of splendour, cast the most vivid gilding I had ever beheld; on the other side of the lake, a forest of various trees presented itself to our notice; on our right hand lay the ruins of an ancient monastery, with its decayed bridge, forming a hazardous pass over a bubbling rivulet; on the left, the open country afforded a prospect of many leagues in extent, speckled at intervals with clusters of trees; straggling cottages, easy hills, and browsing cattle; add to this, that the ground on which we rested was the extremity of a gentle declivity of greensward, on whose summit nodded tall and majestic pines, and that, as we reclined on the velvet turf, the falling of a neighbouring cascade met our ears; and you will not wonder that I was entranced by the scene.—At that moment I felt sensations of the most exquisite happiness; or, perhaps, I think them the greatest I ever experienced, because they were the last pleasing moments my heart ever knew.—With the setting of that sun, whose glories I then admired, set my felicity on earth.

"I left the spot of enchantment with regret; on our return home, I expressed in the warmest terms the delight I had experienced in the ravishing scenes I had just been beholding. Bertrand seemed to enjoy the praises I had bestowed on his situation; and promised he would in the evening accompany me to the same place, which he doubted not, he said, that I should view with increased pleasure, as the scene would be in some measure varied by the hour. I gladly accepted his offer, and about sun-set we reached the lake, a short time before the glories of nature in their full perfection had drawn forth my admiration.—A part seemed now to be vanishing, for the ingenious purpose of fixing the attention more strongly on that which was visible.—Bertrand threw himself on the grass; I stood by his side, gazing at the rising moon, who, courting splendour from the departing sun, faintly silvered those waves her rival orb had before deeply gilded, and listened with a melancholy pleasure to the falling of a neighbouring cascade, the view of which I had now so placed myself as to command, till the scene softened me into that extasy of sorrow, which must be exquisite if felt at all, and must be felt to be described.

"I had often indulged similar sensations on spots equally inviting, but they had never produced in me feelings so refined as I that evening felt:—how often have I since thought they were too surely the sorrowing omens of my future hapless lot!

"Bertrand made the signal for our departure, and I reluctantly complied with it.

"The exercise I had that day taken had somewhat fatigued me; Dulac observed it, and producing a skin of his old vintage, I drank with pleasure of the cup as it went round, and found myself refreshed and exhilarated.

"The evening passed off with the same harmony and satisfaction that the former one had done: at about the same time as the preceding night, we retired to rest, and sleep quickly overcame me.

"During the day, the heat of the weather had been unusually great; and the warmth of our chamber was oppressive, insomuch that, waking towards the dawn of the morning, I found it had caused me to bleed violently at the nose; I endeavoured in vain for some time to stop the flowing blood; and my restlessness awoke my companion, who, learning my situation, advised me to go and wash at the well, in a small yard adjoining to the garden: I immediately rose, and, having slipped on some of my clothes, was leaving the chamber, for the purpose of following his directions, when he called to me, asking me 'If I had ever opened the door which led out of the house into the garden?' I answered, 'that I did not recollect that I ever had.'—'Then,' said he, 'take this pocket-knife,' drawing one as he spoke from the pocket of his waistcoat which lay by his bed-side, 'and stick the blade under the latch with one hand, while you lift it up with the other, or you will find a difficulty in getting out.' I thanked him for his attention to me, and taking the knife from his extended hand, ran down stairs, and found it of much service to me in opening the door, the latch of which seemed to have been broken, and not yet mended; I then entered the yard, and, having drawn up a bucket of water, the cold soon produced the desired effect of stopping the blood; and having washed myself, I returned to the chamber. Dulac, who heard me come up, asked me, 'If I had shut the outward door?' I told him I had; and having got into bed, I turned on my side, and was quickly composed to sleep.

"On waking, I found Dulac was risen; I accordingly dressed myself, and went down, where I found the family assembling at breakfast. After the usual salutation of the morning, Bertrand inquired of me for his uncle: I told him, I had not seen him that morning; 'No more have I,' replied Bertrand; 'he has probably strolled down to the lake.'

" 'He will return, I dare say, before we have finished our meal,' added Martha; (for so was Bertrand's wife called) 'it is a very usual custom with him to walk early in a morning.'

"Bertrand's two daughters, the one about eleven, and the other about nine years of age, had finished each her cup of milk, before we had completed our meal, and immediately went up stairs, as Martha informed us, to attend to the duties of the house.

"Dulac did not return.—Bertrand began to wonder that he exceeded his accustomed time, and Peter went out to look for him,— as the family now conjectured he had mistaken the hour.

"In a few minutes the girls came running down stairs, with terror painted on their countenances, and the elder of them exclaimed,—'that her uncle's bed was all over blood!'

"Bertrand and his wife cast a look of surprise at each other—I blushed, and began immediately to apologise for what had happened; informing them also, that I had risen, by the advice of Dulac, and gone to the well, where washing had proved the remedy of my complaint.

" 'I saw a stain of blood upon the side of the well this morning,' said Bertrand, 'as also in the passage leading to the garden; but I had forgotten to inquire into the cause.'

" 'All my uncle's clothes are lying by the bed-side,' said one of the girls.

" 'How!' exclaimed Bertrand, and immediately ran up stairs.

"A general silence prevailed till Bertrand returned.

" 'What Nicola told us is too true!' said he. 'All his clothes, except his waistcoat, are in the chamber;—in that, he always wore his purse,' added he, at the same time darting at me a look of suspicion and scrutiny.

"Bertrand went on: 'He received thirty louis d'ors for his trees the day before yesterday: did he give them to you'—looking at Martha—'to lock away?'

" 'No,' answered Martha: 'he was counting them to me, when this stranger knocked at the door; and being interrupted, put them all into his pocket again.'

" 'This is a strange event!' said Bertrand, again looking at me.

"Astonishment prevented my utterance, and my silence, I believe, strengthened Bertrand in the suspicion of my guilt, which I afterwards found had immediately flashed on his mind.

"Bertrand, his brother-in-law, and the women, now began to converse together, in low voices, throwing, as I observed, at intervals, the most significant glances at me.—I felt confused beyond what I can express, and, had not a false shame prevented me, I should have fallen on my knees to pray for the return of Dulac, and to declare my innocence.

"In a short time, Bertrand's brother-in-law, Laval, left the house, and Bertrand, then turning to me, charged me with being one of a banditti, that had for some time, he said, infested that part of the country, and that having by some means gained intelligence that Dulac was to receive a large sum of money the day before, had planned the stratagem by which I had entered the house, for the purpose of plundering him of it. 'Not satisfied,' added he, 'with robbing him who kindly became your benefactor in an hour of pretended distress, you have endeavoured to shelter one crime by the commission of a blacker enormity: but tremble, young man; for offended justice is diligent in detecting the breakers of her law.'

"The terror I experienced at this open declaration of his sentiments, though I had before read them in his countenance, overpowered me so much, that it was with difficulty I kept myself from sinking on the floor; and my agitation, I am certain, confirmed Bertrand and his wife in thinking me guilty.

"The door was now locked upon me, to prevent my leaving the house, and I was given to understand that Laval was gone to the neighbouring town to fetch the officers of justice.

"In a short time, however, I gained courage from reflecting on my innocence, and I besought Bertrand to hear my vindication; he did not seem to attend to me, nor I believed listened, whilst I laid

down at length all the particulars I recollected relative to the preceding night.

"Every sound that met my ear,—every footstep that I heard
fall,—made my heart flutter with the hope and expectation of seeing Dulac enter; and oh! how forcibly did every new disappointment add to the load of anxiety that weighed down my heart!

"Presently after, Peter returned from his search of Dulac. 'He
had,' he said, 'looked for him in vain.' Bertrand seemed to receive
the intelligence he expected.—Martha began in a low voice to communicate to her son what had passed in his absence; and I could not
help bursting into tears, as my thoughts continued to dwell on my
unhappy situation.

"In about two hours after, the officers of justice arrived, and,
on the accusation of Bertrand, Laval, and their wives, bound me
their prisoner.—Bertrand then requested that I might be searched:
when,—with what words or feelings shall I relate it?—one of them
drew from my pocket—open, and bloody—the knife which Dulac
had lent me for the purpose of opening the door. In my agitation
the circumstance had entirely fled from my mind. Thus I had not
related that part of the night's occurrences to Bertrand: no one
would now hear me explain it; and it was decided by all, that it had
been the instrument of Dulac's death.

"Deaf to my remonstrances, they led me to the next town, and
I was thrown into prison, there to lie, till the period at which I was
destined to take my trial, should arrive.

"I apprised my brother-in-law of what had happened: he immediately set out for my prison, and having learnt my unhappy
story from my own mouth, he, without delay, began to exert such
interest as he could command in my favour, against the day of my
trial.

"Dulac returned not:—every possible inquiry was made after him by my advocates, but they all proved in vain; and the fatal
day arrived, without any one circumstance having occurred which
tended in the slightest degree to convince the world of my innocence. The well, it is true, had been searched, and no body found in
it; but still that was not reckoned a circumstance sufficiently strong
to operate against that of a bloody knife having been found upon
my person.

"My trial was short, and I heard myself condemned to die: that sentence was the death-blow to my sister; for, as I have since heard, she never recovered from the shock given her on receiving the tidings of my condemnation. I was taken back to prison, and a confessor was ordered to attend me: my situation moved him; he began, I believe, from my unshaken firmness at the approach of death, to think me innocent, and promised to use his influence in my behalf. His entreaties, joined to what degree of weight my brother count Harden possessed in the city, obtained for me life, on the terms of becoming a galley-slave for the remainder of my days.

"Death would surely on such a condition have been preferable, had I not hoped that something unforeseen might still occur to prove me guiltless, and restore me to my country.

"I pass over the agonising separation from my beloved sister, and my tedious journey, to the moment when I was chained to the oar.

"Ten years' service in the island of Corsica, for to that king had I been sold, inured me to the hardships I experienced, but did not abate the anxiety of my mind. Oh! what a sensation is that of an innocent heart, struggling amidst the most complicated and severe trials, without the means of proving how distant it is from meriting the load it labours under!

"At the end of this period a war broke out between the power to whom I was subject, and the emperor of Morocco. In the course of a year the emperor obtained a great victory over the Corsicans, and I, amongst other prisoners, became the property of the grand vizier: here it became my office to cultivate the gardens belonging to the vizier's palace: my labour was less, but I was still a slave; and the task-master was more severe than he to whom I had before been subservient.

"Thus did I pass on twelve more years, void of comfort either for my mind or my body, when, by an exchange of slaves, with the cause of which I was unacquainted, I was sent to work in a garden belonging to the palace of the emperor.

"On the third day after my removal to my new situation, I observed an old man in a slave's habit, whose countenance I thought was familiar to me. He observed me not at first, but as I passed nearer him, the better to examine his features, he no sooner cast his eyes on me, than he pronounced my name; and his voice instantly convinced me, that it was no other than Dulac who stood before me!

"After our mutual expressions of surprise were ended, I began to inform him of all that had befallen me since our separation,—and with eagerness I then inquired of him, by what means it had been effected.

" 'Oh!' said he, 'what hardships have I not suffered since we parted!—what misery have I not undergone!—But I will not murmur; for the decree of heaven is just, and unchangeable till its due time ordains a revocation of it.

" 'Not long after you had returned to bed, on the morning on which I last beheld you, I imagined I heard some one enter the house, by the door from the garden; I immediately drew on my waistcoat and slippers, and running down stairs, I beheld in the kitchen, attempting to open the door which led to my private closet, wherein I kept such bonds, papers, and money, as I possessed, two of my nearest neighbours, whom I had long known to be of suspicious characters, from their being connected with a set of smugglers, who resided on the coast of France.

" 'Their astonishment at seeing me you may well conceive; they immediately seized and gagged me, and having some moments concerted how they should dispose of me, to prevent my appearing in evidence against them, which by signs I endeavoured to convince them I would not do, if they would depart, and suffer me to remain unmolested, they resolved on carrying me to what they called their cave.

" 'Without the house there were two other men, their accomplices, whose countenances I knew not, waiting to assist them in carrying off such booty as they might chance to obtain; they were not a little disappointed at seeing me only brought out to them: but, as I afterwards found that they made a point of securing all who might be liable to act towards their discovery, they dragged me on between two of them, muttering curses on me for having interrupted their plunder, and sourly smiling as they vowed vengeance against me.

" 'The cave they had mentioned, was dug out of the earth, some three leagues distant from the spot where I resided, and served for the purpose of concealing their contraband goods. Thither they conducted me; and having searched my pockets, in which was unfortunately a sum of money I had two days before received for some elms, they set by me a pot of water, and some dry crusts of bread, and left me.

" 'My prison was shut from the faintest glimmering of light; the air admitted into it was so confined that I found a difficulty in breathing, and its scent was most nauseous; to which, add the agonies my mind was undergoing from the knowledge of my being in the power of these wretches, and torn from those I alone regarded, together with my anxiety for their concern at my unexpected and extraordinary disappearance, and you will easily picture to yourself the agonising feelings of my heart.

" 'In the dusk of the evening two other men entered the cave, and having gagged me, led me forth; after some hours' walking, we came up with a body of men, who I soon found were colleagues of those who now conducted me: along with them were fifteen other prisoners, bound and gagged in like manner as myself, and who had been taken in similar caves by these inhuman robbers.

" 'After some additional hours' travelling, we arrived at another cave, much resembling that in which I had been confined during the former night; and here the other prisoners, together with myself, were led down, and deposited in an inner division: the outer one, we found, was inhabited by the smugglers themselves.

" 'Many were the conjectures we formed with regard to our situation; and though it was impossible we should assign any degree of certainty to any one of them, we could not still forbear drawing them.

" 'The next night we were again led forth as before, and after several hours' travelling each night, for six successive nights, and being lodged by day in caverns similar to those I have already mentioned, we found ourselves on the sea coast: we were immediately put on board a vessel lying a short distance out at sea; and we soon understood that its master bargained with these smugglers for slaves, which he sold in Morocco, chiefly to the emperor.

" 'There is but one sure friend in misfortune,—resignation to the divine power, and confidence in its will to convert all we suffer here to our glory in a state hereafter: I armed my heart with this chearing thought; and my communication of my feelings had, I believe, much weight on the minds of my fellow-sufferers.

" 'After a passage of fatigue and hardship, we arrived where you now find me; here have I dwelt a slave ever since;—and if providence has decreed me here to end my unfortunate days, I bend to its almighty will.'

"With what sorrow did I behold him who had been my kind protector, in the unhappy situation I now saw him, and reduced to it, as I could not help thinking, partly by my means; as, had I not on that fatal night arisen from my bed and broken his repose, he in all probability would never have heard the entrance of those ruffians to whom he had now fallen a prey.

"I imparted to him my thoughts, and the anxiety they occasioned me; but he kindly chid me for forming my judgment from events, and declared that my lot, from the probability of its enduring so many years longer than the natural course of nature threatened him with a painful existence, was his greatest cause of disquietude.

"From the first moment of my finding Dulac, every nerve of thought was unremittingly on the stretch to devise some plan of effecting our escape, fondly anticipating the triumph I should enjoy, were I ever allowed to be the means of restoring him to his country and relatives.

"Whilst my mind was thus employed in forming various stratagems, all of which, however, appeared ineffectual, an occurrence, as unforeseen as unexpected, and which then appeared to me the happiest of my existence, took place: this was no other than intelligence being brought to Morocco, that a French nobleman, lately dead, had left by will, as an expiation of some crime he had committed, a sufficient sum of money for the liberation of fifty European slaves who had been the longest in captivity. And it is, I think, needless for me to relate to you the joy experienced by Dulac and myself, on being informed that we were of the happy number.

"Our slaves' habits were exchanged for European garments; and in a few days we embarked on board a French vessel, which was to transport us to the coast of Languedoc, whence we were each to be conveyed to our respective country.

"Our voyage for the first six days was prosperous: on the seventh, towards sunset, the wind, which had blown freshly through the day, became extremely violent; the angry clouds rolled over each other, producing tremendous claps of thunder, and the flashes of lightning, reflected on the expanse of water, appeared alarmingly vivid. The ship was tossed in an uncertain course by the foaming billows, which at intervals washed over the deck, and then again yielded to the dividing bow of the ship. A general consternation seised every one on board; and, with a silence that increased the awfulness of the scene, each seemed to await the next moment as his last. At length, driven upon the side of a rock obscured by the rolling waves, the vessel split into two equal parts, and an universal cry seemed to announce instantaneous destruction.

"The boat was lashed to that partition of the ship on which Dulac and myself were standing: a sailor instantly ran to it; and, having launched it into the deep, sprang into it. I hesitated not an instant to follow him; and, having gained the boat, I received Dulac from the side of the ship, in my extended arms. Immediately the foaming billows dashed us to a considerable distance from the ship; and in a few moments after we saw her swallowed up in a whirlpool.

"We beheld the sight with horror, and knew not, as yet, whether to be thankful that we had not shared the fate of the unhappy sufferers. In the space of an hour the wind began to abate, but the billows still rolled mountain-high; and it was with extreme difficulty that we could by any means balance our little bark. For some hours we contrived to effect it; till our limbs becoming benumbed by the wet and cold we were enduring, a wave dashed over us, and overset our boat. I could swim; and immediately raising myself in the water, I caught the boat, and exerting strength which was called forth by the urgency of the moment, I managed again to place myself in it. I immediately looked round for Dulac: he had vanished from my sight. An arm was now raised from the water; I seised it, and lifted from the deep the sailor who had been the means of effecting my escape from the ship:—Dulac was gone for ever.

"This was the completion of my misery; but as the preservation of life, when threatened with danger, is always the predominant idea in the breast of man, however his mind may be clouded with sorrow, I did not at that moment feel in its full force the loss I had sustained.

"Towards the break of morning, a small vessel, bound to Villa-Nuova in Spain, perceived our situation; and having sent out to us its boat, we were taken on board, and such accommodation as the vessel would afford kindly bestowed on us: and not till then, when the recollection of the horrors I had lately been exposed to began to subside, did I feel how much more miserable and destitute a being, than I had even before been, the loss of Dulac had rendered me.

"The sailor who had been my companion in the boat, a very short time after our entering the vessel, fell a victim to what he had undergone. Oh! why was I, with so great cause to loathe the world, spared from sharing his fate?

"On the following day the Spanish vessel gained her destined port, and I landed on a country where I was an entire stranger, and possessed neither of the means of purchasing my subsistence, nor of earning it, as I understood not the language of the kingdom.

"Fortunately for me, the captain of the vessel was conversant with the French language; and, being a man of generous disposition, he at my request furnished me with the habit of a seaman; and having given me a piece of gold, I set forward, thinking, in my present disguise, I might reach count Harden's mansion in the vicinity of Ulm, unknown.

"Seven weeks served to complete my journey: when, conceive my disappointment!—on reaching the spot where I had hoped to meet the warm embraces of an affectionate sister, I learned that she had but two months survived my exile; and that count Harden had also some years paid the debt of nature.

"I inquired whether my sister had left any offspring. I was informed, that she had never borne but one child, a daughter, and that she was also dead.

"I believe I had already been wounded so deeply by affliction, that an added pang was imperceptible to my grief-worn heart. I can no other way account for the firm composure with which I heard this defeat of my last and only hope.

"In my way to Ulm I had passed this cell; I had found it was deserted; its late possessor having been some years dead. I had no interest in the world, but rather a wish to secrete myself from it, lest I should be recognized by any of Dulac's relatives; and I possessed nothing in the world, for my property had been confiscated on my receiving sentence of banishment. I accordingly determined to make it my dwelling: and having found that I had sufficient money left, from what I had collected on my journey from the charitable, under the disguise of a shipwrecked sailor, to purchase me a woollen robe, a scrip, staff, and flagon, I immediately repaired hither, and have resided here ever since, indebted for my subsistence to the peasantry round about, in addition to the fruits and berries I collect in the surrounding wood.

"I have now dwelt here fifteen years; and, save the little intercourse I hold with the peasantry, you are the first whose conversation has cheared my solitary dwelling.—I am now fourscore and two years old: may you attain my years, without the sorrows that have numbered mine! and may you await the hour of your death, my now only consolation, with a heart like mine, full of forgiveness towards those who may have injured you."

Here the hermit concluded; and Lauretta, wiping away the tear from her eye, which had been drawn forth by the sufferings of her benefactor, thanked him for the confidence he had reposed in her, and of her own accord promised to be the faithful guardian of his sad tale.

To dwell on the sorrows of others, when the mind is agitated by misfortune, tends only to depress the already sinking spirits. Thus Lauretta now felt a gloom cloud her mind, which she found herself unable to shake off; and her attempts to appear chearful only added to the depression which in reality weighed down her spirits, while the tears stole insensibly from her downcast eyes.

The old man perceived the melancholy which had seised upon his fair guest, and began to converse on various topics, which he hoped might engage her attention from the gloomy subjects on which he well saw they were dwelling: but finding his endeavours to be in vain, he again heated for her a cup of his balsamic cordial; and having bathed with a mollifying ointment her head and arm, which were now in a healing condition, he prevailed on her, as night was rapidly shutting in, to seek relief for her agitated mind in the composure of sleep.

On the following morning, Lauretta arose at the moment the old man returned from fetching his accustomed measure of water; and he joyed to find that the refreshment of sleep had dispelled the gloom of sorrow which had on the preceding evening clouded her brow.

The hermit had also been to a neighbouring cottage, where he was constantly supplied with bread, and had brought from thence a bunch of fresh-gathered grapes, as a present to Lauretta.

During the course of the day, Lauretta expressed to her host her astonishment at Theodore's never having visited her during her late confinement; as, had he conveyed her thither from the love he bore her person, it was natural to suppose he would have immediately followed her, and by force have rendered her subservient to his base desires. The hermit bade her be contented with the knowledge of having escaped the evil she had dreaded, nor sink her spirits with dwelling on a gloomy retrospect, now a smiling prospect of hope was placed in her view.

"But should it vanish," cried Lauretta, "should the wicked Theodore have by any means cut me off from again beholding my Alphonsus"——she paused, and the tears started in her eyes.

"Why thus unnecessarily afflict thee, by visionary phantoms of distress?" exclaimed the solitary man. "From the evils experienced in this life of probation no one is exempt: it is a chequered scene, wherein the most submissive to their fate endure the less affliction here, and ensure to themselves the greater reward hereafter: whereas, to anticipate misfortune, is to double our earthly calamities, while we endanger our future felicity, in drawing upon us the displeasure of him who alone can bestow it, by our want of confidence in his will and ability to protect us."

Lauretta felt the force of his words; but she felt also, that it was easier for a man, dead to every connection with the world, to give philosophic counsel, than for her to cease to be anxious for the fate of him whom alone she loved.

Towards evening, a sprightly fire cheared the hermit's cell, and various discourse wasted the hours pleasantly, till the hermit gave the signal of retiring for the night; and Lauretta having joined him in fervent prayer, they each betook themselves to their respective pallet.

About midnight Lauretta awoke, and Alphonsus immediately becoming the subject of her thoughts, she lay ruminating on what might have befallen him since their separation, when a faint sigh caught her ear; somewhat startled, she raised herself upon her couch and listened; but instantly recollecting the near situation of her host, she smiled at her vain apprehensions, and turning on her pallet, fell insensibly into a second sleep.

On waking in the morning, she called to the hermit, inquiring the hour; and receiving no answer to her demand, she concluded him gone to the spring; she accordingly rose, and entered the outward division of the hermitage, when, what was her astonishment on beholding her venerable benefactor stretched lifeless on his mossy couch!

She uttered a loud shriek, and sunk upon the ground; but there was no one near to hear, or to raise her: at length, with tottering steps she ventured to approach the clay-cold corpse,—she gazed upon it awhile in silent anguish; then, bursting into a flood of tears, she exclaimed—"Hard, when I had found a friend to soothe the loss of those from whom the base designs of villany have for a while exiled me, that the hand of death should, at that needy moment, have wrested him from me!—Oh! that I had flown to him when I first heard that passing sigh! his last breath, doubtless, then hung lingering on his lips, and my timely aid might have recalled it!—Oh! preserver of my life, pardon my unwilling neglect of thine: and if, after death, exalted saints (for, surely, such thou art) have influence here on earth, unseen by man, Oh! cast a thought on the unhappy wretch thou didst not here disdain to succour."

Weeping, she cast herself upon the bench which had not long before supported the old man and herself in chearful conversation over the crackling embers;—a dead silence now reigned, broken only by her sighs.—Three tedious days and equal nights were before her, to be passed in solitude, irksome in itself, and which she yet feared to see interrupted by any unwelcome visitant, before the time would elapse, at the expiration of which the hermit had taught her to expect the return of her messenger.

Day was nearly closed ere she awoke from the lethargy of grief and reflection into which she had fallen; and having then eaten a small quantity of bread, and drank a cup of water, she cast a look of sorrow at her deceased friend; and having prayed fervently, she cast herself upon her pallet, relying for protection on that being who, in the trials to which he subjects us in this transient state, consults

only our welfare, by fixing our thoughts more forcibly on the blissful scenes of an endless futurity.

CHAPTER XII.

Oh, my wrongs,
My wrongs! they now come rushing o'er my head.—
Again, again, they wake me into madness.

HARTSON.

WE now return to Alphonsus, whom we left on that fatal night
on which Lauretta was conveyed from him by the villany of
Theodore.

The night was far advanced, when Alphonsus returned from
the water; and, on approaching his little habitation, his surprise
was instantly excited by seeing the door open, and no light burning
within against his return;—he entered,—all was silent.—He called
on Lauretta, and on the girl who attended her; no answer was given
him:—he sought her in every part;—again he called on her, it was
in vain.—Frantic with surprise and fear, he ran to the habitation
nearest to his own: he awoke its inhabitants, and, scarcely knowing
what he said, or able to explain his own ideas, he asked for Lauretta; she was not there.—He then flew to the next cottage, and so
on to every one in succession:—Lauretta was not to be found, or
any information to be gained respecting her.—He again returned
to his own dwelling; again he searched it, and again he called on his
beloved Lauretta; but Lauretta answered him not.—"She is gone!
lost for ever!" he exclaimed—"Theodore, the cursed Theodore, has
torn her from me; he triumphs over me, and tortures her!"—In the
wildest agitation he threw himself on the ground; then starting
from the momentary trance into which he had fallen, and with his
net still on his arm, as he had brought it from his boat, he rather
flew than ran towards Smaldart castle.

The baron was just risen as Alphonsus reached the castle:—Alphonsus perceived him in the garden, and flying to him, apologised
for his abrupt intrusion, and then requested the baron to inform
him whether Theodore was absent from the castle.

The baron answered, that he had not seen him since the preceding evening; and immediately asked his reason for the inquiry; and Alphonsus, in as collected a manner as the agitation of his spirits would allow him to speak, related to the baron all that had passed since Theodore's arrival in Germany.

The baron was too well acquainted with the disposition of Theodore, to doubt either what Alphonsus had said of him, or his being the means of Lauretta's being torn from her husband, and immediately dispatched a servant to the chamber of Theodore, to ascertain whether he was in the castle.

The servant quickly returned, with information that Theodore was still in bed.

"I did not suppose he had left the castle," said the baron; "I am well acquainted with his extraordinary temper, and see the motives of his entire conduct;—not love, but pride, first edged him on to supplant you in the affections of an amiable and lovely woman; the triumph he there sought to gain was defeated by your Lauretta's virtue; revenge is now the only passion left open to him, and he seeks its gratification in separating the persons of those whose affections he could not divide:—but rely on my friendship and services; he has doubtless entrusted your wife to the care of some bribed peasant in the neighbourhood till he can find an apt moment for carrying her beyond your reach:—saddle the fleetest horses in my stable, take two of my domestics to accompany you, and visit every habitation in the circle of my estate, commanding them in my name not to retain her.—I will in the mean time be answerable that Theodore shall not pursue her."

With terms of unfeigned gratitude to the baron, Alphonsus ran to the stables, and having announced what the baron had authorised him to perform, in a few minutes' time departed from the castle, together with the two domestics appointed to accompany him.

Theodore, if he had slept at all (and sleep is rarely the portion of even the most secure villany), had been awakened by the entrance of the servant into his chamber, and had immediately risen, and descended into the hall; he was inquiring of every domestic the cause of his uncle's having asked for him at so early an hour, when the baron entered from the garden; and perceiving Theodore, who was listening with the utmost counterfeited composure to the story of Lauretta's disappearance, as relating by one of the servants to his fellows, he beckoned him to follow him into an apartment.

Theodore obeying his uncle's call, entered the room, and threw himself into a chair; the baron closed the door, and thus addressed him: "Theodore, the unlimited indulgence of a too fond uncle has been your ruin,—boyish errors, left unchastised, have ripened with your years into crimes; those crimes, either from their having been confined within the limits of too lenient laws, or from the inability of those you have wronged, to punish, have escaped with impunity; on this presumption your haughty spirit, triumphing in its imaginary security, seeks revenge for every thwarted inclination; but know, that the forbearance of an uncle may be too far imposed upon, and the laws of your country too highly insulted. I greatly fear you have been tempting the former, and abusing the latter."

Theodore rose in great agitation, and was beginning to speak.—

"Be calm, and hear me," continued the baron; "your passion of revenge has been excited against two amiable persons, sufficiently unhappy in their knowledge of you without the addition of your cruelty: but it was not enough for you that they were not miserable;—this was only to be done by tearing them asunder, and you have effected it: but they shall meet again to your confusion."

Choaking with rage at this open declaration of the sentiments of the baron, when he had buoyed himself up with the idea of having so dexterously conducted the villanous act, as to have removed all fear of the slightest suspicion falling upon him, Theodore exclaimed, "Me! accuse me of having carried off the wife of Alphonsus the fisherman! You pay an exalted compliment to my taste, and to my knowledge of my rank in life."—Then, with a satirical smile, he added, "But I beg the female's pardon, 'tis unfair to decide on the merits of her I never saw."

"Never saw!" returned the baron, fixing his eyes stedfastly on his nephew.

Theodore met the baron's eyes;—he read in them his knowledge of the falsehood he had uttered; and a frown of passion succeeding the sneer of contumely which had before sat upon his countenance, he cried, "No, I swear by heaven, that"——

"Hold," interrupted the baron, "violate not heaven by an oath, which, ten times repeated, would not convince me. I cannot suppose that the man whom I suspect to be the perpetrator of a crime, heinous as that of which I now accuse you, will hesitate the commission of a second, whereby he hopes to clear away the imputation of the first."

Perceiving the baron to be firm in the point he was urging, and thinking a patient show of innocence to be most likely to win on the baron in his favour, he said, "If you are determined to think so hardly of me, sir, I must trust alone to the conviction time will give you of my innocence, for my return to your good opinion; in the interval I have, however, my own heart to refer to for consolation."

What villain is not skilled in fair words?—The baron was too well acquainted with the human heart, to ask the confession of Theodore. He knew that guilt is stubborn, and that the urgency of entreaty tends only to harden, not relax, its obstinacy.

He accordingly thus addressed him. "Theodore, you *may* be innocent with regard to what has occurred; it would greatly delight me to find you so, but I much fear you are not. If you are guilty, the restraint I am about to impose on you, will be only what you merit: if otherwise, the elucidation of this mystery will be to your honour. I am resolute in my determination, that the two apartments at the end of the northern gallery shall be your prison, till Lauretta is restored to her husband. Should it be possible that she has fled from Alphonsus on any other account, or with any other person, you have no business to interfere in what concerns them only: if you have conveyed her hence, it is my duty to prevent your pursuing her, and I will take care to put an effectual bar to your further annoying her peace."

Theodore raised his hands and eyes with a look of astonishment and sorrow, then walked slowly to the window with his handkerchief to his face.

The apartments to which the baron had alluded, were immediately prepared; and Theodore, in sullen silence, entered them; and the lock was turned upon him by the baron's own hand.

The key of the apartments wherein the chevalier was confined, was given, by the baron, to a trusty servant; with orders to visit him frequently, and to supply him with every necessary of life, and any article of amusement he required; but on no account to suffer him to pass the limits of his prison.

Late in the evening, Alphonsus returned much fatigued, and his spirits greatly depressed by the want of success that had attended his numerous inquiries.

Exhausted as he was, he immediately sought the baron, and requested permission of him to exchange his steed, and again set out in search of his beloved Lauretta. The baron informed him of what had passed between him and Theodore since his departure; and besought him, for his health's sake, to await the morning, before he again set out. But no consideration of what he might himself undergo, could restrain Alphonsus from the pursuit of one whose safety was so essential to his happiness; and, having scarcely permitted himself to partake of a hasty repast, he mounted a fresh horse that had been prepared for him, and set out in a different direction from the castle to that he had before taken.

In the course of the following day, the baron visited Theodore. Confinement, to which he was unaccustomed, had already gone far towards curbing his crabbed disposition; and, on seeing his uncle, he burst into a peevish exclamation, which sued for liberty; and during which it was with difficulty that he restrained his tears. The baron having looked round the apartments in order to satisfy himself that they were secure in every part, and the accommodation of his nephew good, left him without speaking a single word.

Midnight brought back Alphonsus to Smaldart castle: the fatigue of body and mind he had undergone, had so far exhausted nature, as to require the most assiduous attention being paid to him; and being lifted off his horse, he was immediately, by the baron's order, conveyed to a bed in the castle.

"She is gone for ever, for ever!" he exclaimed, as the baron approached the side of the bed on which he lay: he endeavoured to say more, but weakness overpowered him.

The baron used every argument he could devise to chear him, but he was too miserable to be soothed by any consolation, save the presence of his Lauretta.

Early in the morning the baron sent out four horsemen, commanding them to take a more extended circuit than Alphonsus had done, and to omit no possible means that might lead to the discovery of the object they were going in pursuit of.

A fever in the blood had seised upon Alphonsus, and towards evening the wildest delirium possessed him: at intervals, with returning reason, he asked for tidings of Lauretta; then again raving, in thought, beheld her standing by him; and again, reason returned to prove the pleasing vision a fallacy.

Thus passed on eight days of the most unhappy nature to all parties: to Theodore the most irksome imagination can conceive; the success of his base plan alone affording him a slender satisfaction, which was nearly outweighed by the idea that suspicion fell too heavily upon him to be easily shaken off. A thousand plans had he formed for escaping from his confinement, and as many obstacles arose to render them impracticable: worn out by curbing his violent temper or venting it on empty air, he at length submitted to entreat, where before he had scarcely deigned to command; and in the humblest language, interlarded with the most liberal promises which the hope of obtaining his wish could instigate, he besought the domestic whom the baron had appointed to serve and watch over him, to favour his escape.

The servant, on whom the baron's injunctions had been too forcibly laid, to hesitate a single moment in the discharge of the trust reposed in him, ventured to remonstrate with the chevalier on the impropriety of the request he so strongly urged, and the inadequacy of any reward to the loss of the baron Smaldart's favour.

The baron, who had not visited his nephew since the second day of his inhabiting those apartments, now entered, and thus put a stop to a further conversation. Theodore, on beholding his uncle, burst into a flood of tears, and calling on heaven to witness his innocence, besought a remission of his confinement.

"I had weighed well my reasons for the punishment I have doomed you to," cried the baron, "ere I enforced it; and those tears, the effect of disappointed villany, shall not impel me to relax its severity. Is every thing here to your satisfaction? I wish you to undergo no farther inconvenience than what you may suffer in being prevented from leaving these walls."

To one subject alone could Theodore attend; he reiterated his declarations of innocence, and in louder accents implored for his accustomed liberty.

The baron had too tenderly loved Theodore, to be entirely un-moved by his protestations and entreaties, and accordingly left the apartment, lest they should exact from him an indulgence he might afterwards repent.

Towards evening of the eighth day Alphonsus' fever began to abate, and the frantic sorrow which had before possessed him be-gan to subside into a silent melancholy.

On the following day the messengers returned; they informed the baron, that they had met with an old woman, who had told them, that a female, answering to the description of Lauretta, and who had talked much of Smaldart castle, had been brought in a vehicle by two men to her cottage, early in the morning of the very day on which Lauretta had been missed, and had remained there during the whole of that day; the woman, they said, had pointed out to them the road along which the men and the female had journeyed, and they had followed the track many leagues, but all their endeavours to discover the object of their search had proved equally fruitless.

Farther conviction of Theodore's guilt beamed upon the baron in this account delivered by the old woman; but conjecture only tended the more to perplex him, and he determined to see her him-self, and gain from her such intelligence as she was able to give him: he accordingly commanded two of the horsemen to refresh themselves, and be prepared to set out again with him in an hour's time.

The conduct of Theodore was now exhibiting in striking col-ours, that villany will submit to the most humiliating meanness, in the hope of gaining its desired ends. Whenever the domestic visited him, he raved, fawned, and prayed by turns, for the grant of his supplication, till the domestic, sensible how wrongly he should be acting were he to acquiesce, and wishing Theodore not to flatter a hope which he did not mean to realize, gave him a gentle refusal.

Contradiction from a servant Theodore had never yet experi-enced, and even in his present humiliating state he could not brook it; he therefore seised the domestic by the throat, and throwing him upon the ground, gave a loose to his rage. Stunned by the blow, the man lay in a state of insensibility: Theodore perceived his situation, and determining to avail himself of it, hastily searched his pockets, and having found the key of the outward apartment, he unlocked the door, and sallied cautiously forth, again closing it as he went out.

An hour after mid-day the baron arrived at the cottage; and its hostess, who was no other than Bartha, gave him the same information she had delivered to the horsemen; adding, that the young woman had much wished to write a letter to be conveyed to Smaldart castle, but that she had not been able to furnish her with the requisites; and that her husband had meant to visit the castle on the following day with the message she had then desired her to get conveyed thither, being the first day he could spare from his laborious avocation. The message was only, that she had been conveyed to the cottage by two ruffians, whom she knew to be the instruments of Theodore, and an entreaty that the baron would assist her husband in finding some means to accomplish her rescue.

The wood-cutter, Bartha's husband, then told the baron, that on the afternoon prior to Lauretta's being brought to his cottage, two men had accosted him whilst at his daily labour in the neighbouring wood, and inquired whether he lived near that spot; whether he would give them the use of his dwelling on the following day; and whether money could bribe him to secrecy. "I am very poor," continued the woodman, "and extending my hand to receive a couple of pieces of gold which one of them held in his, I told them I would do any thing but murder to serve them. 'We require nothing but secrecy,' he returned:—'we shall bring a young woman, for whom you must provide a bed, early in the morning, to your cottage, and stay with you all day.' I agreed to this, and having walked with them a few steps to show them where my cot stood, they wished me good night, and left me."

"Proceed," said the baron.

"Well, sure enough, early in the morning they brought a young woman, and my wife took her up stairs, and then one of the men went away with the vehicle in which they had brought her, and came back with only the horses; and at night one of them took the young woman on a horse before him, and they gave me another piece of gold, and away they went, and we have neither seen them, nor heard of them since."

"Would you had informed me of this sooner!" exclaimed the baron. "But complaints are useless where there is no remedy for the evil." So saying, he presented Bartha with a piece of money, and returned to his castle.

Hoping that this incontrovertible proof of Theodore's guilt might be efficacious in drawing from him a confession of the truth, the baron proceeded towards his apartments, where, to his astonishment, he saw extended on the floor, the servant, just recovering from the blow he had sustained, and unable to give any account of Theodore. As his escape had not been long effected, he could not consequently have proceeded far distant from the castle; accordingly every domestic and even the baron himself, ran out in search of him.

Theodore had, during this interval, concealed himself in his bed-chamber, and now seeing from its window the servants and his uncle issue from the portal, he ventured to descend into the hall of the castle, where having met with no interruption to his progress, he ran hastily out of the postern gate, and having reached the stable, he saddled and mounted his steed: all danger now vanished before him, for he knew his pursuers to be on foot, and he was well acquainted with the fleetness of the horse on which he rode; accordingly he clapped spurs to his beast, and galloped dauntlessly forward.

Thus providence in its all-wise direction allots a certain portion of triumph to the machinations of the wicked, which ultimately shall edge them on to become the instruments of their own conviction and punishment.

Shortly after the baron returned to the castle, and four of his vassals were immediately commanded to mount their horses, and set off, in hope of overtaking Theodore. His horse was now missed, and this information caused the baron the more earnestly to urge their speed.

As the slight information which the baron had received relative to Lauretta, tended only to prove that she was in the power of Theodore's agents—a circumstance which the chevalier's recent escape had rendered the more distressing—he forbore to inform

Alphonsus either of what he had heard, or of what had that day occurred at Smaldart castle.

Early on the next morning the baron entered the apartment of Alphonsus, and on meeting his eyes, which the opening of the door had drawn towards the baron, he exclaimed, "Joy! joy, Alphonsus! Lauretta is found! Lauretta is in safety!"

The intelligence was too smiling for Alphonsus instantly to believe that his senses had been true to him; he feared to ask a repetition of the baron's words, lest the pleasing idea should vanish in his reiterated voice. He seised the baron's hand, and pressing it in his own, the tears gushed from his eyes.

The baron now put into his hand the letter of Lauretta's own writing, which he had a few minutes before received from the peasant commissioned by the hermit, who had that morning reached the castle.

Although the fever under which Alphonsus laboured had been much abated by the skill of an able physician whom the baron had procured to attend him, yet while the cause, namely, the violent agitation of his spirits, continued, it was not possible that the effect could have been removed; and he was reduced to so weak a state by what he had undergone during the last ten days, not less in body than in mind, that, on receiving tidings at once so joyful, and yet, from the desponding state of his mind, so little expected, it was with great difficulty for some time that life could be retained within him.

At length an hysteric fit of laughter, accompanied by many tears, relieved his overburthened heart, and he pressed alternately to his lips and to his bosom the paper which contained the account of his Lauretta's safety.

When Alphonsus was sufficiently recovered from the phrenzy of joy that had possessed him, to attend to the words of the baron, that kind friend informed him, that he would take upon himself the office of being Lauretta's guardian and conductor to the castle.

Alphonsus sprang from the bed in which he had before been scarcely able to raise himself; and, declaring himself to be now recovered, entreated to accompany the baron: but to this the physician gave a stern denial, declaring that it was absolutely necessary to his health and safety, that he should not yet leave his bed, or have his composure broken by any avoidable means.

Sufficiently secure of the safety of his Lauretta under the protection of the kind baron, Alphonsus reluctantly yielded to the remonstrances of the physician; and the baron departed, accompanied by two of his servants, and the peasant who was to conduct him to the hermit's cell.

The baron had not proceeded far on his journey to the hermitage, ere he was met by his returning vassals, whose pursuit of Theodore had proved ineffectual: and, as he now knew Lauretta to be removed from the reach of the chevalier, he commanded them to discontinue their search.

On the third day after the baron's departure, Alphonsus was so much recovered as to be permitted to leave his chamber:—his fever had quitted him;—his strength was returning, and his spirits were highly elated, as he dwelt on the mortification which Theodore, whom he vainly imagined still to be the sullen inhabitant of the prison his uncle had decreed him, would in his turn experience, on his seeing Lauretta safely restored to the arms of her husband. Theodore's escape the baron had judged it most advisable to conceal from Alphonsus, as the knowledge of it could only increase his fears for Lauretta's sufferings.

On the evening of the fourth day, the baron was expected to return; and Alphonsus awaited on the tiptoe of expectation the hour that should bring him to his castle. Midnight sounded, and the baron did not arrive: Alphonsus endeavoured to console himself with the possibility of the baron's journey having deceived him in the length of a few hours, and sat listening with anxiety for sounds which he might construe into the approach of the expected carriage. Morning dawned, and disappointment still prevailed: day passed on in a state of inexplicable inquietude; and night closed in with increased apprehensions to the trembling Alphonsus.

About the first hour of the morning, as Alphonsus was traversing his chamber, with a mind swelled with the most hideous phantoms of the fate that might have befallen her in whom his every wish and thought were centred, the distant approach of a carriage fell on his ear. He seised his lamp, and the increasing sound of joy accompanied him as he descended into the hall of the castle. Unacquainted with the exact method of opening the door, and his hand being infirm from agitation, it was some time ere he could effect it; and he drew it back on its hinges, at the very moment the carriage stopped.

Alphonsus issued out with the lamp in his hand; and, having scarcely permitted himself to salute the baron as he left the carriage, he sprang forward to meet Lauretta. Vain thought! Lauretta was not within it.

Grief and astonishment petrified Alphonsus.

The baron took his hand in his, and led him into the hall of the castle.

"Tell me the worst at once," cried Alphonsus. When, at length, after many ineffectual efforts, articulation was again granted him, "Tell me she is dead; the sound will be my summons to her grave."

"Afflict thee not so deeply: she is not dead, though gone from us."

"Gone! how? whither? by what means?" exclaimed Alphonsus, his eyes rolling wildly in their sockets. "Has the vile hermit betrayed her to . . . . . .?"

"Sully not unjustly his venerable name," interrupted the baron. "He has, I fear, suffered much in her cause: when I reached his humble cell, the first object that presented itself to my sight was his lifeless form, stretched on the earth."

"And Lauretta!" cried Alphonsus, waiting to have the sentence filled up by the baron.

"Has baffled my most diligent search of her," added the baron.

"Mysterious heaven!" returned the youth; "who could have learned her retreat?—who have carried her from thence?—Is not the chevalier at this very moment in the castle?"

"Is Theodore then returned?" asked the baron eagerly.

Alphonsus started, and fixed a look of inquiry, surprise, and suspicion, on the baron, that at once convinced him how unguardedly he had spoken, and how fully explicative of Theodore's escape, which he had hitherto so carefully concealed from Alphonsus, the few words he had just uttered had proved. He endeavoured to retract what he had said; but Alphonsus flew to substantial proof; and the deserted apartments, which had been the chevalier's prison, were but a too certain conviction of all his fears.

Ye who have felt, can alone conceive and participate in the poignant feelings of Alphonsus, on this heart-rending discovery:— by turns silent agony and frantic grief possessed him. The plan which one moment suggested, the next taught him to reject; and, from a chaos of ideas, his perturbed mind could fix on no one to adopt in the present moment of despair and madness.

Descending into the hall, he for a short space of time traversed it with hasty and uncertain steps. Suddenly stopping, he exclaimed, "It may not yet be too late to save her! Just heaven, nerve my arm, and guide my steps to the object of my search!" and fled from the hall with hasty steps.

The baron, alarmed by the wild mien of Alphonsus on his dis-covering the absence of Theodore from Smaldart castle, had as-cended to the apartment of the physician, to inform him what had occurred, and summon him to the aid of his patient, at the same moment that Alphonsus had run to investigate the late prison of the chevalier. And, having first sought him in the northern gallery, then in the apartment which had been assigned to him in the castle, and lastly in the great hall, he saw not for some minutes the open gate which bespoke his having left the castle. Immediately on per-ceiving it, he ran out in search of him: but it was too late: he had mounted a horse, which he had taken from the stable, and departed unseen by any one.

CHAPTER XIII.

On her white breast a sparkling cross she wore,
Which Jews might kiss, and infidels adore.
POPE.

DURING the two first days after the death of the hermit, Lauretta's solitude remained unbroken; and the expectation of being quickly restored to the protection of Alphonsus, tended alone to solace her in the gloomy scene she was constrained to contemplate.

On the evening of the day prior to that on which she had been taught to await the return of the peasant, she had about an hour retired to her straw pallet, when whispering voices met her ear: her heart beat high, her breath became suspended, and she listened awhile in that state of silent anxiety which fears to move, lest it lose the sound it wishes to catch. In a few moments she plainly heard footsteps in the outer division of the cave, and immediately after a voice said, "Give me the light." The light was produced, and the first object which it showed to the expecting eyes of Lauretta was the visage of Theodore.

Lauretta shrieked; and immediately the man who had held the lantern, having given it into the hand of Theodore, advanced, and taking her arm in his, led her from the cave. Theodore secreted the light under his garment, and closely followed them.

The moment Lauretta had so much dreaded was now arrived: agony inexplicable filled her heart, and choked her utterance. Her guide continued to walk quickly forward, and she of necessity suited her steps to his:—neither Theodore nor his companion spoke;—and, when the power of speech returned to Lauretta, she well knew how callous the flinty heart of the chevalier would be to any entreaty she could offer up to him; and she judged also, how deaf to the cries of misery must he be, who would hire himself to be Theodore's agent, whether he was acquainted with his base designs, or had blindly sold himself to execute his will.

A few faintly shining stars served to light them on their way; and Lauretta shortly perceived that they had entered the forest through which she had passed on the morning on which she had so miraculously escaped from her confinement in the castle. They still continued to proceed; and, as they advanced, Lauretta began to discern the fatal building rising above a gentle acclivity, which they were ascending.

Presently a tucket, much resembling that Lauretta had heard on the second night of her imprisonment in the castle, sounded at a distance: her heart thrilled at the recollection of the delusive hopes that sound had once raised in her panting breast, and she started as the sound met her ear. Her guard, who probably, from the sudden motion of her body, conjectured she was endeavouring to disengage herself from him, drew her arm more strictly within his, and at the same instant turning round his head to Theodore, said, "There they are."—"Then let us stop a few minutes," returned Theodore. "Oh no!" replied the man; "they will be housed long ere we reach the cavern: besides, were they not, they would not see us." "'Tis well," answered Theodore; "proceed then."

"The cavern!" echoed Lauretta's heart; and busy thought, ever ready to torment the breast it inhabits, pointed out that cavern as her destined grave.

The tears burst from her eyes:—the horrible idea of never again beholding her Alphonsus, at that moment so forcibly impressed on her mind, was too heart-rending a sensation for the tide of grief with which it swelled her aking breast to be suppressed; and she was on the point of falling on her knees, and endeavouring to move the mercy of her guard, when a voice, at some distance from her, exclaimed, "Lauretta Byroff!"

"Oh God!" cried Lauretta, "what is it I hear?"

They were still amongst the trees. Theodore called to the man who conducted Lauretta to stop: he obeyed the summons, and they looked round on all sides: no one was to be seen, and all was still.

"This is astonishing," said Theodore. "These words were addressed to you," turning to Lauretta: "explain them, I charge you."

"I am unable," answered Lauretta.

"Is it not your name?" rejoined Theodore, hastily.

"You know Lauretta is my name."

"You equivocate. I ask, whether Byroff is also your name?"

"No," said Lauretta.

"What is it, then?" asked Theodore. "Beware not to deceive me."

"It is Byroff," replied Lauretta: a moment's thought had reminded her not to utter a name her husband had so cautiously laboured to conceal: and she was too innocent in deceit to substitute a feigned one.

"Your own words have proved upon you one falsehood," cried Theodore. "How am I conscious you have not uttered another? Therefore, unravel the mystery of that voice, or this moment is your last."

"By heaven, I cannot!" answered Lauretta.

"Then I will," exclaimed Theodore, drawing from its scabbard his sword, on which he had laid his hand when he first demanded

Lauretta's confession; and, commanding her guard not to leave her, he rushed amongst the trees from whence the voice had proceeded.

Lauretta and her guide followed him with their eyes in silent wonder for some moments, when a sudden blow from an unseen hand levelled her companion with the earth, and, from the firmness with which he had held her arm, he in his fall drew her upon him. Astonishment closed her lips; and in an instant, a man muffled up in a cloak lifted her from the ground, and whispering in her ear "Be silent," he took her arm under his, and led her swiftly along: they continued for some time to approach towards the decayed castle. This was a matter of surprise to Lauretta, for as she could not doubt his being one interested in her safety, it was natural for her to suppose that he would have led her as far distant as possible from the spot that contained Theodore's companions in iniquity. She was now, however, in the power of this stranger; and she was well aware that if he was her enemy, her questions could render her little service; if a friend, that an inquiry would be breaking an injunction on which, perhaps, her safety materially depended.—She suppressed her curiosity: the little portion of thought she could spare from her present mysterious situation, convinced her that the voice of him who now conducted her was familiar to her ear; but she could not recollect where she had heard it.

Being approached within about a furlong of the castle, her guide turned into a narrow glen which lay on their left; they had not proceeded many paces, when he stopped, and disengaging himself from Lauretta, he stooped down, and having drawn aside a bunch of furze and brambles which lay against the side of the glen, he took from an inner pocket of his coat a lantern, which, holding downwards, showed to Lauretta the mouth of a stony rock, which seemed hardly large enough to admit a person on their hands and knees.

Her guide knelt down, and creeping forward, in a low voice called to Lauretta to follow him;—she hesitated a moment:—"This was doubtless the cavern Theodore and the ruffian, who had brought her from the hermit's cave, had alluded to."—She shuddered.—"I conjure you, follow me," said her guide:—his accents seemed mild and persuasive:—Lauretta crossed herself, and followed him.

After having proceeded a few feet, they arrived in an apartment which, by what Lauretta could distinguish of it by the partial and gloomy light thrown out by the lantern of her guide, appeared to her a large vault; they crossed it, and entered a long and narrow passage cut out of the rock;—their footsteps echoed as they traversed it; and Lauretta could not forbear frequently turning her head to assure herself they were not pursued.

Having attained the extremity of the passage, they entered another vaulted chamber, larger than the first.—Her guide opened a door on one side, which presented to their view a flight of stone steps; her guide began to descend them;—Lauretta paused.— "Quick, quick, I entreat you," said he, taking her hand: again the recollection of his voice struck her, and she suffered herself to be led by him down into a passage much resembling that through which they had passed above; on the right hand was a small door, which the guide opened, and presented to her view a small room, in which were a seat, a table, a bed, and a lamp: they entered, and the guide throwing off a long robe and cowl which he had hitherto kept closely round him, discovered to Lauretta the person of Ralberg.

Lauretta was petrified with astonishment;—she knew not what to hope, or what to fear.

"Be not alarmed," he said, "at beholding him you once thought your enemy; he was never willingly so; and be assured that he will now protect you at the hazard of his life: but your safety and my own both depend on my instantly leaving you:—fear not to be interrupted here, and rely on seeing me again very soon."

He lighted the lamp, and was departing.

"Oh! do not leave me," exclaimed Lauretta, catching hold of his garment.

"For heaven's sake, do not detain me to your own destruction.— If you should chance to hear footsteps, extinguish the lamp.—Angels guard you!" So saying, he hastily closed the door, and Lauretta heard him lock it and depart.

For some moments Lauretta remained motionless on the spot where Ralberg had left her.—When before in his power, she had felt no sensation but fear: now, his words had given her room to hope the greatest kindness from him; and yet the air of mystery that had accompanied them, outweighed every consolation they might otherwise have brought her.

Why had this man, who had so lately been an assistant in her misery, so suddenly changed his principles? A man who, when she had before beheld him, had worn on his brow the sullen frown of discontent; yet, she recollected, she had then remarked that the roughness of his voice had appeared assumed, and his whole manner that of restraint.—"May not fond hope again deceive me in this imagination?" she cried; "and yet the softness of voice with which he now addressed me has proved me right in one conjecture; his mien also is varied, the frown on his brow is dispersed, pity and anxiety are mingled in his eye, and a smile of satisfaction sits on his lips.—My name, too! by what means can he have learnt that?"— This was a mystery, to the unravelling of which she had no clue.

Her eyes had hitherto been fixed in deep thought on the ground: she now raised them;—the first object which attracted them was the lamp, and she beheld lying by it on the table—a dagger!

Her blood chilled;—she perfectly recollected that that instrument was not on the table when she entered the apartment; thus no doubt could remain to her of Ralberg having placed it there.—He had declared he would guard her life at the hazard of his own; that very declaration seemed to prove that he knew her life would be attempted: then why had he brought her to a spot over which such imminent danger was impending?—And if he had really meant to protect her, why had he left an instrument of death in her view?— No idea occupied her mind, but that Theodore meant to visit her where she now was, and that the alternative of suicide or dishonour would alone be left to her.—But then, if Ralberg still acted in the interest of the chevalier, how could she account for the occurrences that had so lately taken place on the skirts of the forest?—Perhaps Theodore had doubted the faith of the man whom he had brought with him to the hermit's cell, and had taken those means of freeing himself from him under the cloak of mystery: and this seemed the only conjecture that could in the slightest degree account for her being brought by a man who pretended to be her friend, to the very spot to which her professed enemy had declared his intention of carrying her.

For several hours no sound interrupted the stillness of the scene, and Lauretta with a trembling heart awaited her doom in anxious silence; at length she heard a footstep quickly approaching.—She immediately recollected Ralberg's injunction to blow out the light, but she wanted courage to comply with it: it struck her that her murderer, unable to view her dying agonies, might wish to perpetrate the deed of death in darkness.

The key was now placed in the lock: Lauretta started from the bed on which she had been sitting; the door opened, and Ralberg entered.—Having placed on the table a small basket he had brought with him, he closed the door, and taking Lauretta's hand, thus addressed her:—"Did I understand you rightly this evening in the wood? did you confess yourself to be Lauretta Byroff, when I unseen addressed you by those words?"

"I did," answered Lauretta.

Ralberg now drew from his pocket the ivory crucifix which Lauretta had been accustomed to wear suspended from her neck by the string of pearls, which were presented by her grandfather to her mother on the day of her marriage with count Byroff. "This then is doubtless yours?" said Ralberg, as he produced it.

"It is," replied Lauretta eagerly; "I well remember that I left it in the turret of the castle, and often since have mourned its loss."

"'Tis then dear to you?" said Ralberg.

"As the dying gift of a lost mother can be!"—Recollection became painful as she uttered these words: she wept;—Ralberg sighed, and for an instant placed his hand before his eyes.

"Where did your mother die?" he asked.

"At the convent of St. Helena."

Again he seized the hand of Lauretta, and, with an energy that seemed to wring his heart, he exclaimed:—"Who was your father?"

"Count Byroff," she answered.

The tears started in Ralberg's eyes. "Deceive me not in this point," he cried, "I conjure you;—I charge you!"

There was something in his manner that awed Lauretta. "On

my faith I do not," returned Lauretta. "My mother's dying breath declared him such."

"My child! my child!" uttered Ralberg, in a voice scarcely audible, and fell upon Lauretta's neck.—"I am thy unhappy father! I am he that was count Byroff."

What a blissful sound was this to the grief-worn Lauretta: she had found a friend that would protect her; and, in that friend, a father. She met his embrace with the warmest fervor, and he for some moments held her clasped in silence to his bosom. At length, "that cross," said he, restoring it to Lauretta, "was my first gift to your mother. Oh! tell me! tell me! all that has befallen her.—But no—I must not risk the hearing now; it will too long detain me; I must instantly leave you, or perhaps never see you more."

"Alas!" cried Lauretta, "have I only found a father to be again bereft of him?"

"Oh my child!" said count Byroff, "I blush to confess to you the situation in which you meet that father. Misfortunes had driven me to despair, and that despair tempted me to——hark! surely I am not discovered?" He paused,—then continued, "No, all is still."

"To what?" asked Lauretta.

"To connect myself with a set of wretches, whose existence disgraces humanity.—Hark! is not that the trampling of horses?" he cried.—"I must fly, or I may lose thee for ever!—Farewell; it will be some time ere thou wilt see me again."—He went hastily out, locked the door upon Lauretta as he had before done, and the sound of his footsteps in a few moments dying away, an awful silence prevailed.

It was some time ere Lauretta could convince herself that the transaction of the last minutes was more than a dream, and, when conviction did beam upon her, she wept tears of joy.

When reflection again returned, she began to meditate on the last words her father had uttered, and endeavoured to solve the mystery of his present situation: it baffled her attempts, and his declaration that it would be some time ere she again saw him, raised not less her wonder than her sorrow. "I am in safety," she cried, "but my Alphonsus is ignorant that I am so, and what pangs will not he experience on arriving at the hermit's cave, and finding me gone:—the situation, too, of my deceased benefactor will lead him to credit, that violence has been used against us both.—Oh! why did I not entreat my father to find some means of quieting the apprehensions of my Alphonsus?—When he returns, it may be too late for him to meet the object of my anxiety!"

She slept not that night: a variety of sensations ruffled her mind, and drove off the attacks of sleep: in the morning she examined the basket count Byroff had, on the preceding night, left on the table: it contained provisions which seemed calculated to last her for two or three days; a bottle of wine, another of water, and some oil in a flask to replenish her lamp.

Day passed on, and the solitude of her prison remained uninterrupted:—night arrived, and she still enjoyed little refreshment from sleep; her thoughts were occupied by the disappointed expectations of Alphonsus on not finding her in the hermit's cave. She rose from her bed, and endeavoured to compose her mind by prayer; but the crucifix which she placed before her, only afforded a fresh subject for thought, by recalling to her mind all the mystery dependent on the discovery and conduct of her newly-found parent.

The following day passed on, and count Byroff visited not his daughter. Lauretta's apprehensions were now raised for his safety; she began to fear that the discovery of his last visit to her, which he had seemed so much to dread, had taken place; and the only ray of comfort which shone upon her harassed mind in this fresh cause of alarm, was, that, had this been the case, they who had made the discovery of his visit, would, in all probability, ere this, have made it their business to discover its cause.

Her spirits had become much fatigued by continual watchings, apprehensions, and anxieties; and a few hours before midnight, a sound sleep closed her eyes for a short time; but, on waking, what was her grief to find, that, having too long neglected to feed and trim her lamp, it had burned out. The utter darkness in which she now found herself, appalled her senses; and again throwing herself on the bed, the tears flowed quickly down her burning cheeks.

Fearing, she knew not why, to quit her present situation in the darkness which now surrounded her, she remained upon the bed, till she conjectured it to be nearly midnight. The echoed responses of her own sighs were the only sounds she had heard, till a footstep approaching cautiously towards the door of her apartment, reillumined a spark of hope and pleasure in her breast: she raised herself on the bed, and a few moments presented to her view count Byroff, habited in the garment of a friar.

Lauretta sprang forward to meet him; he embraced her, and without noticing the darkness in which he found her, and which he might perhaps imagine she had effected in compliance with his instructions, he immediately assisted her to muffle herself in his robe, which he had on the first night left in that apartment, and then told her to follow him with all possible celerity.

The count had reached the door of the apartment, when, stepping back, he took the dagger from the table, and sticking it in his under girdle, again commanded Lauretta to follow him closely, and proceeded swiftly along.

Lauretta followed her father's steps in silence; and by the light of a lamp which he held, she perceived that he was re-conducting her by the path which had led her to the dreary apartment she had just quitted. She remarked that his hand trembled, and on his countenance was depicted the wildest anxiety.

Being arrived in the glen, count Byroff threw down the lamp to extinguish it; and having closed up the mouth of the cavern, he loosened a horse which had been fastened to a stump of a tree near unto it, and having led the animal to the level ground, he mounted it, and taking up Lauretta before him, he clapped spurs to the beast, and they galloped swiftly forwards.

They proceeded nearly a league in silence, except when it was broken by the count addressing himself to his horse to increase his speed: at length Lauretta ventured to inquire, in a low accent, "Whither they were going?" "You must presently direct our road," returned the count;—"but be silent now, I conjure you; some one may be concealed amidst these trees." Lauretta obeyed her father's injunctions; but as suggestion but too often breeds suspicion, she could not forbear turning her eyes by turns on all sides, and watching every shadow as she passed it, fearing it should wear the form of man, and often conjecturing she beheld what she feared.

It was one of those nights when the waning moon sinks to the horizon full and crimson, and casts a tinge of fire upon the objects over which perspective seems to show it impended; and as the travellers turned a sharp angle of a narrow wood through which they had been passing, it suddenly burst upon their view. The scene was mournfully romantic, and Lauretta suffered it to occupy her thoughts;—at intervals a clump of trees intercepted it from her sight, and she then sought its partial light darting momentarily from amidst the breaks of the interwoven branches;—again it darted in full splendour upon her sight, and again an intercepting hillock, whose gilded crown reminded her where it was obscured, shut it from her eyes;—presently its reflected beams played on a crooked lake, along whose bank they were passing, and then again, attracted to the silken leaves of the elm, seemed for a time to clothe its branches with purest snow:—at length its nightly reign being ended, it imperceptibly sunk under the horizon, gradually stealing from the surrounding objects the gilded hue which it had lately sent to beautify them.

After travelling three hours and a half, the count and Lauretta arrived at a mean cottage. In a few minutes its door was opened in compliance with the request of the count; and its inhabitants, a middle-aged man, and a lad his son, shepherds by trade, readily granted admission to the count and his daughter.

The count quickly extorted from them a promise that they would not on any condition suffer any person to enter the cottage whilst he remained in it, or confess that any stranger was concealed within it, should inquiry be made of them. To this petition they agreed not less readily from the temptation of the large reward by which he offered to bribe their secrecy, than from their fear of his resentment falling on them or their flocks, should they betray him; for his habit had immediately led them to believe that he was a brother of some religious order, a circumstance which the count plainly perceived, and in which, from his acquaintance with the natural superstition of the lower ranks of people in that part of the country, he placed his chief dependence for ensuring such secrecy as he should require during the intervals in which he judged it expedient to interrupt his journey.

Having seen his horse safely bestowed, the count questioned Lauretta, whether she wished to compose herself to sleep; but she declared that her mind was too strongly agitated to suffer her to seek repose for her body: the count then hinted to her a wish that she would unfold to him the history of her life; she inwardly lamented that he had not first offered to communicate his own; but considering that his curiosity must be as strongly awakened as hers, in compliance with the obedience due to her father, she immediately acquiesced in his wish; and having retired with him to the only apartment of which the cottage consisted, in addition to that occupied by the shepherd and his son, she informed him of every particular that had occurred to her from the first moment of her entrance into the world, to that on which he had rescued her in the wood from Theodore and his accomplice.

CHAPTER XIV.

This is the state of man; to-day he puts forth
The tender leaves of hope, to-morrow blossoms,
And bears his blushing honours thick upon him:
The third day comes a frost, a killing frost,
And when he thinks, good easy man, full surely
His greatness is a ripening, nips his root,
And then he falls, as I do.

KING HENRY VIII.

IN relating the occurrences of her own life, Lauretta omitted not to lay before the count such particulars as he was unacquainted with in that of her deceased mother; and the stress which she laid on the declaration of her mother's innocence, with regard to the suspicions which had been raised against her, on account of her continued acquaintance with count Frederic Cohenburg, her first and only love, seemed much to affect him.

"Oh!" exclaimed count Byroff, "had she but explained to me the state of her heart, we might now have both been happy, and I free from guilt."

A short silence ensued: the count then said, "Now, my child, attend to the tale of thy father's fortunes, and learn from thence that the commission of one rash act imperceptibly leads on the human heart to crimes once most distant from its imagination.

"My father and his sister were the only children of my grandfather, count Byroff, a German nobleman, who resided on a small estate about twenty leagues distant from Vienna; for as fortune is not always the sure companion of rank, his narrow circumstances had obliged him to retire from the splendour of the court.

"My aunt had the good fortune to captivate an Italian marchese of immense property; and having received her hand in marriage, he carried her with him into Italy.

"My father married a woman of rank, whose circumstances were but too much in the situation of his own; he did not many years survive his union with the woman of his heart, and dying, left my mother and myself, his only child, to the protection of my grandfather.

"Many unforeseen and cruel misfortunes had occurred to lessen the small property the old count possessed; and by his death, which happened just as I had attained my eighteenth year, I found the fortune which had devolved on me slender indeed. My mother and myself, however, resolved to live retired from the world, and by frugality to increase that little stock which my rank in life forbade me to attempt any other means of increasing.

"How weak are the prejudices by which we suffer ourselves to be ruled!

"A short time after the death of my grandfather a letter arrived in Germany from my aunt, informing us that her husband was lately dead, that the greater part of his property had devolved on her by his will, and inviting my mother and myself to pass over into Italy, and reside with her.

"Being a paternal estate on which we had resided, it would have been deemed a disgrace to a nobleman to sell it; we accordingly left Germany without assigning any reason for our departure.

"My aunt, the marchesa del Parmo, who resided in an elegant mansion in one of the most eligible spots in Venice, received us with the warmest cordiality, and exercised towards us the most friendly attentions; but my mother lived only a short time to be sensible of the marchesa's kindness. On her death my aunt seemed to double her assiduities to me; she told me, that she had resolved never to marry again, and should, with the exception of a few legacies, leave me heir to her entire property; I expressed my gratitude to her in terms suited to the extensive promise she had made me: she then told me, that she had provided for me a tutor, with whom she wished me to travel for a couple of years, before I formed any plan of settling in the world. She at this time was well acquainted with my attachment to your mother, which had begun a very short time after my arrival in Italy; and she as well as myself imagined that my attentions were far from being unfavourably received by her.

"The youthful mind pants for novelty; and the offer made me by my aunt was too fascinating not to induce me for a short period to forego the society of my Lauretta, flattering myself that from the improvement of travel I should return more worthy of her; for the marchesa having spoken in my favour to count Arieno, he had immediately assented to my proposal of espousing his daughter.

"When I had been absent from Italy about eighteen months I received a letter from the marchesa's steward, informing me that she had died suddenly, and had left me her sole heir.

"I immediately returned to Venice to take possession of my newly-acquired fortune, and had arrived there only a few hours when count Arieno paid me a joint visit of condolence on the loss of my aunt, and congratulation on my acquisition of fortune. Before his departure he reminded me of the verbal contract subsisting between us relative to his daughter, and at the same time entreated me, if I observed a dejectedness in her manner, not to notice it, as I should only renew an acute sorrow which had been preying on her spirits since the sudden death of an intimate friend, and which was now gradually wearing off.

"I readily acquiesced in a proposition which I imagined would conduce to the tranquillity of her I loved; and on visiting my Lauretta I was sensibly touched by the frown of grief which I observed settled on her languid countenance; I endeavoured to sooth her sorrow without reverting to its cause. I could not forbear noticing the striking change in one so tenderly beloved; she wept, and doubtless misconstrued the meaning of my words, as I did the cause of her sorrow.

"Whenever I visited her, I remarked that her father always remained in the apartment with us. I now see the cause of a conduct which then much surprised me; he knew the awe in which his daughter stood of him, and by his presence resolved to prevent an explanation on her side from taking place.

"Curses on the sordidness of a father, who dooms his child to misery, that he may swell his own proud coffers!

"I now never saw count Arieno, that he did not advance arguments to induce me to hasten my marriage, which, from my regard to the recent death of my aunt the marchesa, I had thought it consistent with propriety some time to defer. In a short time, however, his reasonings, from their co-incidence with my real feelings, prevailed over my scruples, and I was united to your mother.

"After the solemnization of our marriage, count Arieno insisted that we should pass at least a couple of months at his mansion; his reason, I then thought, was his averseness to part from his daughter: I now perceive that he wished to keep her under his own eye, in order that he might be the better able to inspect her conduct, which he was well aware his cruelty had given him reason to suspect, and which he hesitated immediately to communicate to me.

"I used every means in my power to restore to your mother that chearfulness which had once been her never-failing companion; but a settled melancholy, which I found it impossible for me to dissipate, had taken possession of her mind.

"Six weeks after our marriage, I again mentioned to count Arieno, as I had before frequently done, my uneasiness at the unhappy state of my wife; and he then confessed to me, that he had but too much reason to believe I had an unworthy but favoured rival in the heart of his daughter.

"This was a blow which struck at once at the root of my happiness and pride: the whole mystery of count Arieno's interested conduct was in one moment exposed to my view, and I looked with contempt on the wretch who had made a traffic of his child.

"He now declared to me all the particulars of your mother's affection for count Frederic Cohenburg; was lavish in his praises on himself, both for the parental authority he had exerted over his daughter, and for that management which had made me his son-in-law.—He was the wretch who could pride himself on having, by one stroke of keen deceit, stamped the misery of an only child, and inveigled me into a state of eternal suspicion and unhappiness.

"I upbraided him with his base conduct;—he listened to me whilst I spoke, and smiled, as one secure in the completion of his own wish, and regardless of the fate of others: when I stopped speaking,

" 'What prevents you to rid yourself of this rival?' he cried.

" 'Whither can I fly from him?' I returned—'No where, but where he can follow.'

" 'End him!'—exclaimed Arieno.

"I had never yet drawn my sword against a fellow-creature, and I shuddered at the idea.

"Arieno perceived it; and, pretending to finish a sentence which he had left uncompleted, he said,—'or suffer patiently that infamy which the world will attach to a man who tamely bears dishonour in the tenderest point.'

"His imputation on my honour pierced my heart.

" 'Give me proof of your suspicions,' I returned, 'and I will instantly challenge him.'

" 'You shall have proof, rest assured,' he answered, and with these words he left the room.

"To what a state of misery had this intelligence reduced me!— to learn that I was an object of abhorrence to the woman in whom I had placed my hopes of future happiness, and the victim of the joint pride and avarice of her father.

"Still, however, I resolved to bear my feelings in silence till the promised proof was produced to me: at one time doubting the truth of count Arieno's assertion, and at another, fearing I saw it fully confirmed; and alike despising the vile author of my doubts, whichever opinion swayed my mind.

"About a fortnight after my last conversation with count Arieno on the subject of my anxiety, he one day entered the apartment where I was sitting, with an open letter in his hand; he seated himself, and thus addressed me:—'I yesterday morning gave out that you and myself should this evening set out on a short excursion into the country, from which we should not return in two or three days; the object of my having said this you will clearly perceive, when I tell you, that it has answered my expectation in producing this epistle, which I have contrived to intercept.'

"He gave the letter into my hand; and, to my extreme mortification, I read in it an invitation to count Cohenburg from your mother, written by her own hand, to meet her that evening at her aunt's.

"Count Arieno, when I had concluded reading the letter, which I several times perused ere I could convince myself that my senses were not deceived in what I had read, proceeded to inform me in what manner he had gained it from the servant entrusted by my wife, and what means he had taken to prevent his return to his employer.

"I listened to him without attempting to speak, for my feelings were unutterable; and I was on the point of tearing the fatal letter to atoms, when he hastily sprang from his seat, and snatching it out of my hand,—'Hold!' he exclaimed, 'on this depends our hopes of vengeance.' He again seated himself at the table; and having sealed the note as it had before been, he summoned into the apartment a trusty servant, to whom he confided to carry the epistle to him to whom it was directed.

"Still absorbed in thought, my silence had been broken only by heavy sighs, till, on the servant's quitting the room, the count asked, 'Whether I had perceived what he had done?'

"I told him that I had; and inquired what purpose he meant to answer by it.

" 'Count Cohenburg,' he replied, 'will doubtless attend to the invitation given him for this evening; he must necessarily pass through a dark lane in his way to my sister's, which is the place of appointment with your wife; it must therefore be our business to provide those who will there way-lay him: such may easily be found, and such as may be relied on.—We ourselves must leave the city at the hour I had mentioned we should set out; thus suspicion will be hoodwinked, and your rival fall an easy prey into the snare you will have spread for him.'

"I heard him pronounce these words with very different emotions from what I probably should have done had I been an Italian:—when he stopped speaking, I exclaimed, 'If he deserves death, why should I fear to be myself his punisher? If there be a palliation for shedding human blood, 'tis surely in behalf of him whose injuries loudly call for revenge: why then should I tempt another man to become criminal,—and, by paying the price of blood, add to the guilt that would still be mine, by having instigated him to become the instrument of an act whereof I should in reality be the agent?'

"It was some time before I could work upon Arieno, living in a country where the performance of murder is alike venal with other acts of hire, to listen to the arguments I advanced in favour of my being myself the redresser of my wrongs, and before I could prevail on him to promise to accompany me in the evening to the dark lane through which he had informed me count Cohenburg must inevitably pass in his way to the house of appointment with your mother: at length he promised to point it out to me, and we parted till the hour arrived at which Arieno had given out the preceding day that we should set out on our journey; we then mounted our horses, and rode to a small house about a quarter of a league out of the city, the habitation of a man who had formerly lived in the service of the count, and where we had pre-determined to leave our horses, and in the dusk of the evening return to the city on foot.

"We arrived in the dark lane nearly half an hour before the time mentioned in your mother's letter.—I drew my sword, and we placed ourselves under the shade of a low portico.—In a short time we heard footsteps.—A person muffled up in a cloak advanced rapidly towards us; count Arieno whispered to me, "'Tis he, 'tis the count himself.'—I immediately sprang forward to meet him, and in the name of a villain I called upon him to defend himself against the vengeance of an injured husband!—He made a blow at my sword with a stout cane which he held in his hand, and attempted to rush past me; but I quickly stepped back a few paces, and received his body on the point of my sword: he instantly fell, with a deep groan; and distant voices at the same moment assailing the ears of count Arieno and myself, we fled with all possible speed, I to the count's mansion, and he to the house of his sister, where he expected to find your mother, and from thence to re-conduct her to his own.

"What misery did I that night experience, on entering the apartment to which your mother had been conveyed on her return to her father's house! how did the cries and upbraidings of her agonised heart wound mine, although I conceived myself to have been so deeply injured by her!—She confessed to me all her love for count Frederic, but called on heaven to witness how free she was from the imputation of guilt laid upon her by me and her father.—I hardly dared credit what she affirmed; and yet so forcibly did the recollection of the ardent passion I once bore her plead for her in my heart, that I endeavoured, by every attention and every promise of future regard, to lull her into the oblivion of him she had lost, by fixing her mind on the assiduities of him she retained, fully resolving in my own mind, if she but ceased to upbraid me with the loss of count Frederic, again to take her to my bosom, and use every means of proving to her her loss replaced in an equally tender and affectionate lover.

"She that night altogether refused to listen to me; and I left her chamber with a heart as deeply lacerated as her own.

"Towards evening on the following day, I had again been endeavouring by repeated attentions to win on the heart I had embittered with sorrow, when I was summoned from my painful yet willing task, by count Arieno calling to me hastily to descend to him.

"I immediately went to him, and he in a few words informed me, that count Frederic had escaped; and that the person whom I had killed on the preceding evening proved to be the son of one of the first senators: that five thousand zechins were offered in reward to any one who might apprehend the murderer; and the punishment of exile and confiscation of property denounced by the state of Venice against those who might be acquainted with the perpetrator of the murder, and delay to deliver him into the hands of justice.

"What were my feelings on being informed that I was the murderer of an innocent man! I cannot describe, or you conceive; pain, poverty, sickness, loss of friends, or any other misery in its most aggravated state, and even all these combined, can give no faint idea of the pangs he feels, who has shed blood, which even the effusion of his own cannot re-animate.

" 'Now,' said count Arieno, 'what would that friend merit, who would undertake to rescue you from the danger hovering round you?'

"If I were apprehended, death, I well knew, would be my doom; and death I at that moment could have received with extasy from any hand but that of the executioner: from dying on a public scaffold my heart, humbled as I felt myself, recoiled, and I eagerly answered, 'Every thing.'

" 'Then,' said he, 'I will be that friend.—Now attend to the means: should you be apprehended for this crime, you are well assured your entire property becomes confiscate to the state.'

"I replied, that I was fully convinced it did.

" 'Your safety,' he continued, 'depends on your immediately flying from this country; in such case, it is impossible you can collect the value of your possessions in so short a time as it is necessary for you to depart, in order to carry them with you; what you leave behind you in your own name, will be immediately confiscated; thus make over to me your personals, by far the greater division of your property; leave your estate open to confiscation, as some small atonement for your offence; make your escape instantly, while it yet remains in your power to effect it; and depend on my remitting to you what you shall make over to me, as soon as you shall have reached a place of safety.'

"There was a kindness in this offer of count Arieno to assist me in my distress, that made me overlook his past conduct; and with thanks I acquiesced in his proposition, and quickly proceeded to put it in execution.

"I had scarcely put my hand and seal to the deed which transferred to count Arieno my personal property, dispersed through many parts of Italy, when information was brought us by the physician who had attended your mother, that she had fled from her father's house. The count seemed to receive the tidings with indifference; and I was too much occupied by my own safety to give any farther thought to what I had heard, than that she had learned count Cohenburg's existence, and found means of escaping to him.

"A few hours afterwards I set out from the Venetian dominions, and in little more than a week I arrived in Paris, the place where I had determined to seek shelter from the laws of Venice, as I little doubted, from the number of spies I well knew to be employed by that state, I should soon be discovered to be the perpetrator of the deed on which I shuddered to reflect.

"On the day after my arrival, I wrote to count Arieno to inform him of the place of my retreat; I thought it unnecessary to add that an immediate remittance would be welcome to me, as he well knew that I had taken with me only what cash I happened to have in my possession at the time of my departure, and a few trinkets of small value.

"In about three weeks I received from him a letter, the purport of which, to my great consternation, and, I blush to add, astonishment, knowing what I already did of his infamous character, was nearly in the following words:—That the state had gained information of my being the assassin of the senator's son, and had accordingly confiscated such of my property as was publicly known to be mine; that he lamented this discovery having so early taken place, as it would inevitably prevent his being to me the friend he had pledged himself to be; for that, as a Venetian senator, he should incur the fear of death, by being known to assist any man now lying under the penalty of its laws; and could accordingly only send me his thanks for having, by the deed that had passed between us on the evening of my leaving Venice, given him the power of profiting by a sum of money which could never again on any terms be mine, and which would otherwise have fallen to the use of the state.

" 'Upright senator!' I exclaimed, on perusing this infernal epistle; 'cautious in observing the outward forms of that state that he hesitates not privately to plunder!'—Oh! my child, how many villains wear the mask of worth like him, and, with the garb of office, cover a heart which knows no interest but its own; and contemplates no crime, of which an accumulation of its private wealth and pride will not seem to authorise the performance!"

The count paused a moment, then continued—"The keen sense of my own feelings, on a revisal of the villany that had been practised against me, may perhaps have tempted me to draw too harsh a stricture on mankind in general: but surely I cannot be wrong in asserting, that he who will act villanously in the transactions of private life, cannot lay aside his nature when he acts for the public.

"To what a situation was I now reduced! my whole property consisting of only fifteen zechins, and two rings of small value, without the possible means of recovering what had so basely been wrested from me, or of seeking redress from him who had so deeply injured me, without exposing myself to the greatest of dangers;—in a city where I was an entire stranger; without a friend to whom I could apply for assistance; without an acquaintance to whose conversation I could fly for a transitory relief of my painful feelings, and without a chearful thought that would afford me a momentary consolation within my own breast!

"My first step, however, was to avoid detection; as I knew not what power the state of Venice might have of demanding my person, should my retreat be discovered; and sometimes feared that Arieno, to insure to himself the possession of my property, might give information to the state whither I was fled, and have me apprehended, that, by my death, all doubts of my ever regaining what was lawfully mine, might be done away; but then again I considered, that he would be well aware, that, in case of such an accusation from him, revenge would prompt me to declare the state, rather than him, the possessor of that property I was myself doomed to forego; and this quieted my fears of any farther molestation from him: but, at all events, judging it to my advantage to obscure myself as much as possible, I changed my habit to that of the country I was now in, and called myself Montville, resolving still to remain in Paris, as the place where I was most likely to escape observation, well knowing that I should be most free from observation in the midst of a crowd.

"I had taken a lodging in an obscure part of the city; and my only amusement was the frequenting of a tavern in the neighbourhood, much resorted to by young men, who, though perhaps not in the most exalted stations of life, were however men of fashion and fortune.

"Every evening they met, in a greater or smaller number, at this house, and draughts were their entertainment: as a stranger, I had been generally noticed by them, and solicited to play; I knew myself to be an adept in the game, and thus readily accepted their invitation. The sums they staked were not large, or I could not have hazarded an engagement. I found some my equals in play; and when I engaged with these, good and bad fortune were alternately mine; but as my play was far superior to the generality of those who engaged with me, and as my circumstances, as I was sometimes tempted to think, induced me to place more attention on my game than my adversary usually gave to his, I was commonly, at the hour of retiring, the winner of a trifling sum; a circumstance which in my situation I considered of the most consolatory and promising nature: my precarious situation had taught me, hard as the reverse

was, to be an œconomist; and in the course of six months I had collected nearly fifty louis-d'ors, and I now began to turn my thoughts
to a subject to which they had before been directed; namely, whether I should pursue any means of discovering the retreat of your
mother, and of revenging myself on the destroyer of my peace.

"After many debates with my own heart, I drew this conclusion:—'Will the death of count Cohenburg restore my peace?—
No!—Will it not add guilt to hands already too deeply imbrued in
blood?—It will!—Can I hope that my wife will be to me what she
ought to be?—No!—Why then seek after her who shuns me, and
add another sting to an already wounded conscience, by the murder of one whose death cannot restore my lost tranquillity?'

"Having resolved that it behoved me to forget an object lately
so dear to me, my mind became more calm; for, when an opinion is
once firmly adopted, every subsequent thought seems to strength-
en the justness of that opinion.

"When my thoughts at times did turn back to your mother,
amidst the censures my injuries raised against her in my heart, I
still felt a portion of pity for one who had been driven to despair
by the cruelty of an unfeeling parent.—For that parent, when my
mind reverted to him, and too often, alas! it did, I felt the abhorrence I should have done against a dæmon.—'Is it possible,' I would
cry, 'the earth can contain a monster capable of his accumulated
crimes?—the sacrificer of an only child to his avarice!—the lurer of
a youth into a marriage into which he had deceived his senses!—the
instigator of that youth, when become his daughter's husband, to
murder him who ought to have possessed her hand!—the ravisher
of that youth's property, by the abuse of that faith which can alone
bind man to man; and by the same act, the plunderer of that state,
whose rights he had pledged his most solemn vow and life to defend!'"

CHAPTER XV.

What equal torment to the griefe of minde,
    And pyning anguish hid in gentle heart,
That inly feeds itself with thoughts unkinde,
    And nourisheth her own consuming smart?
                                        SPENCER.

COUNT BYROFF was now interrupted by the entrance of the old shepherd, whose son having just returned from milking, the good man
had brought the travellers a bowl of warm milk. The count commended his attention, and Lauretta drying those tears which had
been drawn into her eyes by her sympathy in the misfortunes of
him who had given her being, drank of the milk, and found herself
much refreshed by it; the count did the same; and the peasant retiring well pleased at the satisfaction expressed by his guests in their
acknowledgments of his kindness, count Byroff thus went on.

"I had resided nearly two years in Paris, when, returning one
day from walking in the suburbs of the city, two men, whom I had
for some time perceived to be observing me, followed me into the
house where I lodged, and introduced themselves into my apartment. On their entrance I raised a look at them which as plainly
inquired their business with me, as if I had demanded it in open
words. 'You must go with us, Monsieur, if you please:' said one
of them.—'Whither?' I instantly asked.—The man who had before
spoken replied to my question, by drawing from his pocket a paper
sealed at one corner, which he held out to my view with one hand,
whilst he pointed to it with the other. On seeing the paper, it immediately flashed upon my mind that these men were emissaries
sent in pursuit of me from the state of Venice; but guess my astonishment when I learnt that the fatal paper was a *lettre de cachet* to
convey me to the Bastile.

"The two men hurried me into a carriage, the blinds of which
were drawn up: we rolled rapidly through the streets, and in a short
time I felt myself passing over the draw-bridge which leads to the
mansion of wanton tyranny and despair.

"When the carriage stopped, I was taken from it by two men whose countenances I had not before beheld, and conducted through a paved court bounded by a lofty wall, into the first hall of that building, the bare glimpse of whose stubborn walls had so lately frozen my blood. Alas! how far was I then from conjecturing I was myself about to pine in solitude within them.

"Through two other halls and many intricate passages, my guards conducted me, till, arrived at an iron door which was nearly at the end of a long gallery terminated by a narrow window, through which the iron bars, fastened across it, suffered but a small portion of light to enter, they stopped; and the door being unlocked by a person who had met us in the second hall, and from thence preceded us, and whom I afterwards found to be the governor, I was commanded to enter, and the door was locked upon me; a small square room presented itself to my sight; a broken table, a stool, a mattrass, and a quilt, were its only furniture: the walls, which had been of plaster, were mouldering away in many parts, and in others being covered with a green scurf, confirmed me in the dampness of the place, which the chill that had seized me on entering it, had first caused me to remark.

"The stillness of the scene now gave me room for reflection on my situation; I could form no conjecture for the cause of my present confinement, except that of the state of Venice having found a power of arresting my person for a crime committed within its dominions, even after I had quitted them; but this supposition appeared so repugnant to the idea that I had always been taught to entertain that the authority of every state was bounded by the limits of its territories, that I could not reconcile it to my mind, though still I could discern not even the shadow of any other cause for my present confinement.

"I well knew on how slight and even falsely grounded suspicions of acting against the government, many unhappy men had been condemned to waste away a life of solitude and misery within the dreary and unrelenting walls within which I was now a prisoner; but I was so conscious that the little interest I had felt in the public affairs of a kingdom where I was an entire stranger, had led me still less ever to join in a conversation of which they had been the topic, that I felt too secure in my innocence on that point, to give it a second thought connected with my present confinement.

"For some hours I wandered about my prison in that state of suspense which is perhaps the most acute suffering the mind can undergo; towards evening a small portion of bread and water was brought me by a man who appeared to be an inferior jailor, and who immediately left my apartment on having placed my scanty pittance on the table.

"As night shut in, the horrors of my situation seemed to accumulate: there was only one window in my prison, and it was strongly grated with iron bars; I placed the stool under it, and having got upon it, I perceived that the window looked into a court, similar to the one through which I had passed when conducting to my prison.

"Night passed in intervals of sleeping and waking, and morning brought back my jailor with another scanty portion of the same fare that had been brought me by him the preceding evening.

"Thus passed on three days without any interruption of my sorrows or solitude, save the morning and evening visits of my jailor: for the first two days I had put to him many question relative to my situation; but as his sole answer had been a shake of the head, sometimes accompanied by a sour smile, I desisted from my inquiries.

"On the fourth morning the governor, accompanied by two guards, entered my prison. 'You must take the air to-day,' he said, 'or your health will be injured by your confinement.' The guards took me between them, and followed him out of the apartment into the gallery; he descended the first flight of steps, crossed a short passage, and then ascending a few stone stairs, at the top of which was an iron door, he opened it, and I was led by my guards upon a platform of about twelve feet square, but so closely surrounded by other parts of the building, that no object except the sky was discernible from it.

"The guards stationed themselves one on each side of the door; the governor had gained the middle of the platform: I went up to him, and besought him to inform me of the reasons of my confinement; he refused to answer me, and immediately left the platform. The guards were left with me, and I tried to draw them into conversation, but my efforts were ineffectual. In about half an hour the governor again appeared on the platform, and I was immediately reconducted to my prison in the same manner as I had been led from it.

"Every fourth day I was led out to take the air and exercise allotted to me; and with this sole interruption of my solitude, crept on seven weary months.

"One morning about this time my prison-door was opened, and the governor and two of his guards entered, not a little to my surprise, as I had visited the platform the day before; the guards took me between them, and following the governor as on other occasions, conducted me into a large hall, where sat at the upper end of the table a man, who, I was given to understand, was the lieutenant de police, and below him sat two other persons. I was placed at the lower end of the table; an oath that I should deliver only the truth was administered to me by the secretary; and the lieutenant then said to me, 'You call yourself, Montville?'

" 'I do.'

" 'Is it your real name?'

"I hesitated to answer; and he continued, 'Remember you are on oath. Is it your real name? I ask.'

" 'It is not.'

" 'What is your real name?'

" 'I have particular reasons for wishing to conceal it.'

" 'Note that accurately,' said the lieutenant, addressing himself to the secretary; and then said to me, 'Are you a Frenchman?'

" 'No.'

" 'You are an Italian?'

" 'No.'

" 'Do not attempt to deceive me, or it will be the worse for you. You say you are not an Italian?'

" 'I am not.'

" 'But you came from Italy to Paris?'

" 'I did.'

" 'How long have you been in France?'

" 'Twenty-two months, exclusive of the seven I have passed here.'

" 'What brought you to Paris?'

" 'My motive I must decline revealing.'

" 'You know it then to be a criminal one?'

" 'Why should you draw that inference?'

" 'You are to answer, not to question, young man,' said the lieutenant surlily. He whispered to the man who sat by him: they turned over the leaves of a book which lay before them, pointed to different parts of various pages,—again they whispered, and the lieutenant then asked me, 'By what means I was supported?'

" 'Does any one accuse me of gaining my means unjustly?' I said.

" 'I shall not a third time warn you that you are here to answer, and not to question,' said the lieutenant. 'How are you support-ed?'

" 'I brought money with me from Italy.'

"After many other questions of a similar nature, and which in the aggregate seemed to me to amount to little, though on some of them the lieutenant had laid great stress, I was remanded to my prison, equally ignorant of the charge on which I was arraigned as when I first entered it.

"About two months after I was again summoned to appear in the hall as before; the oath was administered as on the preceding occasion, and the lieutenant began by asking me many questions even more trivial than the former ones had been: at length, starting from the train of questions in which he was advancing, he said, 'On your former examination, you confessed yourself, I think, an Ital-ian.'

" 'I did not.'

" 'You avowed yourself then to be employed by that state?'

" 'I did not.'

" 'You alleged that you were lately come from Italy.'

" 'I did.'

" 'And that your motive for coming hither was a criminal one.'

" 'You drew that inference, but I did not subscribe to it.'

" 'Why did you not confute it by a declaration of the truth?'

" 'May I, before I answer this demand, make one myself?'

" 'You cannot oblige us to answer it, though we can force you to reply to ours.'

" 'Admirable administration of justice!' hung on my tongue:

but I stifled my emotion, and said, 'Am I permitted to ask one question?'

" 'Name it.'

" 'On what charge am I here a prisoner?'

"The lieutenant de police, and the man on his right hand, whispered together some minutes, and the lieutenant then said, 'You stand here arraigned of being employed by a foreign power as a spy upon this government.'

" 'By all my hopes of heaven the accusation is falsely founded,' I cried.

" 'Where are your proofs?'

" 'You shall have them.'

"The lieutenant smiled contemptuously.

"The innocence of my heart, however, in regard to the accusation now supporting against me, made me view his supercilious countenance with indifference; and knowing myself now not to be retained at the instigation of the state of Venice, I comparatively felt no fear in confessing a crime committed against it, when I hoped by so doing to free myself from my present alarming situation; and I immediately related such parts of my story as tended to show my motive for having taken up my abode in Paris.

"When I had concluded my story—'We will inquire into the truth of this,' said the lieutenant; and, making a signal to the guards, I was taken back to my prison.

"For some time I felt myself comparatively happy, as I did not doubt that enlargement must be the result of the promised inquiry; but as the mind, in reflecting on any agitated subject, leans alternately to the side of hope and fear, I began to apprehend, that the state of Venice, should it, by means of the lieutenant's inquiries concerning me, learn my present situation, might find means, as I was in prison, of having me retained there for the crime I had really committed, though I might be absolved of that under which I was now lying falsely accused.

"Eight months elapsed in an alternate succession of fear and expectation, before I was again summoned to appear in the hall; and the result of what then passed was, that no satisfactory corroborations of the story I had related having been procured by those employed for that purpose by the lieutenant, the tale I had told was

deemed either to have been framed by myself for my own preservation, or an invention delivered to me by the state of Venice when
commissioned by it into France, and which I had been commanded
to recount in case of my being apprehended, as an excuse for my
ambiguous conduct; and that the space of two days only would be
allowed me to consider whether I preferred, by confessing my real
character, to throw myself on the mercy of my judges, or, by persisting in my deceit, to provoke them to draw from me the truth
by torture.

"In answer to this decree, I could only repeat, in the most solemn terms, my innocence of the fact of which they accused me.

"They undoubtedly heard my declarations without interruption, but I could clearly perceive that their opinions were decided,
and that either they were not, or would not be, moved by my vows
and asseverations.

"On entering my prison I threw myself on my mattrass, and
amidst the sorrows that seemed to await me, the only idea which
induced me to look forward with a degree of calmness and resignation to the fate with which I was threatened, was, that the unjust
punishment I was about to suffer, might be accepted by him who
alone could read my heart, in expiation of the innocent blood I had
shed.

"At length, the day big to me with terror and agony arrived; at
an early hour I was once more led into the hall, and the lieutenant
again inquired, 'Whether my stubbornness had relaxed, and I was
willing to confess my crime?'

"I reiterated my vows and asseverations of innocence; but they
and my prayers for mercy were heard with equal indifference, and
I was dragged into that earthly hell, where demons, in the shape of
men, riot in acts of wanton cruelty.

"Innumerable instruments of torture, of which I knew not the
use, but feared too soon to learn it of each I beheld, were suspended against the walls, and scattered on the floor. At one end was
an immense fire, which, notwithstanding its size, two men, whose
savage countenances were by no means the least terrific features of
this soul-harrowing scene, were feeding with every provocative of
fierceness.

"Again it was recommended to me to confess ere it was too

late, and again I could only repeat, however incredulous were my hearers, that I had nothing to confess.

"I was then placed in a chair, and a circle of about three inches in diameter on the top of my head shaved bare of its hair.

"The soles of my feet and my breast were afterwards bared, and being fastened in the chair, it was drawn near to the fire, to the fierceness of which the naked parts of my body were exposed, whilst large drops of the coldest water were made to fall singly on the crown of my head.

"In a few minutes the pangs produced by the contrast of feelings I was undergoing, became so intense that I shrieked violently. The lieutenant approached me, and asked, 'if I was willing to end my punishment by confession?'

"Had I at the moment been able to have conceived any other means of freeing myself from the sufferings I was enduring, I should without hesitation have adopted it; but I was well aware, that if, to liberate myself at the present moment, I uttered a false confession, I could not afterwards retract it, and that I should in the end probably only suffer the more severely for having allowed their false accusation to be a just one; I therefore only continued to declare my innocence, and in the most moving terms to supplicate for mercy.

"In a quarter of an hour's time the torture inflicted on me became agonising, past all endurance, and I besought my tormentors to give me death: my hands and feet were bound; I had bit my tongue, till the blood streamed from my mouth upon my breast; and my eyes, which the pain I was undergoing had widely extended, from being exposed to the fierceness of the fire, were far from forming the least part of my sufferings.

"Every moment was now so forcibly diminishing the powers of nature, that the physician, who had been brought to announce to my tormentors when I had undergone what my frame could endure, commanded me to be gradually removed from the fire, and the water to cease dropping. I had been drawn back only a few feet, when, exhausted by the agony I had endured, the little strength I had remaining fled from me, and I fainted whilst yet bound in the chair of torture."

CHAPTER XVI.

Each substance of a grief hath twenty shadows,
Which show like grief itself but are not so;
For sorrow's eye, glazed with blinding tears,
Divides one thing entire to many objects;
Like perspectives, which, rightly gaz'd upon,
Shew nothing but confusion; ey'd awry,
Distinguish form.

KING RICHARD II.

"ON recovering, I found myself lying on my mattrass: a blanket had been added to my quilt; and the physician, on my again opening my eyes, administered to me a cup of wine, the first variation of my daily food of bread and water that had passed my lips since my entrance into the Bastile.

"For several days the physician continued to visit me; and having youth and strength on my side, in a month's time I began to recover the use of my bodily and mental faculties, both of which had been much injured by what I had undergone. The greatest cause of remembrance that remained to me of what was past, was the weakness of my eyes when they met the light.

"Near six months passed ere I was again led out to the platform for air, and I even then found my limbs very inadequate to the task of supporting me more than a few minutes at a time.

"Day rolled on after day, and month after month, but still I received no information whether what I had undergone was deemed a sufficient confirmation of my innocence, or not; and as I was still retained a prisoner, I kept looking forward with increasing apprehension to a trial more severe than the one I had already passed through.

"I must here mention a circumstance which, however trivial it may appear to you, dwells on my mind, and seems to claim my attention.

"Nearly a year had elapsed since my undergoing the torture, when one morning a small part of the window having been left open to air my prison, a red-breast flew into the apartment, and perching on the table, began to peck the bread which had just been brought me as half my day's provision. I approached a few steps towards it, that I might the better observe it; for in my present situation, any object which engaged my attention, afforded me a moment of unexpected happiness. I perceived that it saw me, and I stopped; lest I should drive it away; but the food seemed to be a greater attraction than my presence was a cause of fear, and, to my satisfaction, it went on pecking the bread.

"Its plumage was rough, and raised against the cold, and it bore every mark of having suffered from the inclemency of the season, which was that of a severe frost; a deep snow had some time covered the ground, and the eagerness with which it preyed on its newly-found prize, showed that the weather had proved to it, whose feeble claws were unable to turn up the depth of snow, a season of famine.

"I pitied it for what it had suffered, and participated in its present apparently great satisfaction;—'Yet, poor foolish wanderer!' I cried, 'thy native timidity, when the call of nature is satisfied, will again drive thee to the piercing cold and hunger from which thou hast now found protection!—Thou art not wise enough to insure it to thyself, and mayest perhaps perish for want of that which thou shouldst never lack by living here, could I but teach thee to know my good will towards thee!'—In the energy of what I felt, I drew nearer to the table; and the bird, having either finished its meal, or being terrified by my approach, flew two or three times round the room, in search of the spot by which it had entered, and having found it, vanished in a moment from my sight.

"'Thou art gone!' I exclaimed, 'never to return hither!'—There was a charm in the last words I had uttered, that seemed to render even the biting air and keen famine to which the little animal would be exposed, an enviable situation when compared with my own.— 'Many are the hardships thou wilt endure,' I cried; 'but thou hast a balm for all thy sufferings,—thou enjoyest liberty,—the choicest gift and richest blessing heaven pours on its created beings; deprived of it, all other ills in life are light.—Knowing what I have learnt from experience of the bitterness of its loss, I would not be the wretch to inflict it, e'en on the little bird I have just beheld, no! though my own enlargement were the price of its captivity!'

"On the following morning, to my great delight and surprise, the little bird again flew into my prison; I threw it some crumbs; it picked them, hopped about the floor, flew upon the table, fluttered about the room, and again left me.

"Every morning I was now visited by the red-breast; I had nothing else to occupy my attention; and I found a great source of amusement in waiting the arrival of my feathered visitor: I never failed to feed him plenteously, and used every endeavour to divest him of his natural timidity, and dispose him to receive my caresses; and I even flattered myself that he began to view me without fear, as he sometimes remained several hours in my prison; but, alas! when spring began to exhale her inviting sweets, my little companion, wearing too much the complexion of the world he inhabited, forgot his fosterer in the hour of adversity, nor returned to sooth his solitary moments. Spring, summer, and autumn passed, and I began to think that some accident had befallen him, or that he had entirely forgotten the spot where he had been so hospitably received, and gave him up as lost.—On the part of my persecutors also, a strict silence as to my doom had been observed towards me, and I began to fear I was a prisoner for life.

"Winter was now again advancing, when, as I was one morning reclining on my hard bed in mournful meditation, a fluttering in the room called my eyes to the part where I had heard it, and I beheld on the table my long-lamented bird!

"I felt the glow of unexpected pleasure mount into my cheeks; and I immediately rose and crumbled for him a piece of bread: he chirped in thankfulness for my gift, and I even imagined he seemed as pleased as myself at the renewal of our acquaintance.

"During the winter he continued to visit me, as he had done the former one; and having made for him a perch, which I contrived, by means of a crooked nail, to form out of a long splinter which I had shaved from my table, and which I fastened up in one corner of my prison, by supporting it in a small niche I made in either wall, he often remained with me during the night, as well as the day, and sometimes for four or five days successively; and the pleasure which, shut out as I was from all intercourse with my own species, I enjoyed in the unrestrained visits of this little bird, was undescribably great.

"With the spring he again deserted me, and with the winter he again returned to my prison; and thus, till the seventh year after his first visiting me, did he continue to be my companion during the winter season.

"It was one day, about the middle of the seventh winter, that he happened to stand sleeping on his perch, with his head folded in the feathers of his wing, when the jailor entering with my breakfast, and observing him, darted across the prison, and, ere I could stop his cruel arm, seized my unconscious favourite, and wrung his neck.

"Need I blush to own that the tears burst into my eyes?

"I would have remonstrated with the unfeeling wretch on his barbarity, had I not immediately considered that what I could now say would be of no avail, but to gain me the derision of him who had deprived me of my only source of solace and amusement; and I contented myself with requesting him to give me the dead body.

"Without answering me, he aimed to throw it out of the window; but, missing his cast, it fell back into the room; I sprang forward to seize it, but he had snatched it up, and his second aim being more successful, it was gone for ever ere I reached the spot; I followed it with my eyes, and when it disappeared, I still stood gazing on the window.

"The ruthless jailor left the prison in the silence in which he had entered it.

"I immediately placed the stool under the window, and sprang upon it, hoping I might find the body rested on the outward frame of the window: but the hope was vain.

"I descended from the stool, and standing with my arms folded in the middle of my prison, reflection again led me to draw a comparison between the present situation of myself and that of my lamented bird; and the only inference I could draw, from a long train of thought, I expressed in a short exclamation, which I insensibly uttered aloud,—'Thou, little bird, art still the happier.'

CHAPTER XVII.

Seldom, when
The steeled jailor is the friend of men.
MEASURE FOR MEASURE.

"ANOTHER year passed in solitude like the former ones; and the space of time I had now been imprisoned, in all ten years since my first being brought to the Bastile, began to reconcile me from habit, to that state which seemed to be marked out as the condition of my remaining life.

"No change had taken place in the treatment shown me, but that milk and thin wine were sometimes brought me instead of water with my bread, and that I was not now so frequently led out for air upon the platform as I had formerly been; being now seldom conducted thither above once in eight or nine days.

"About this time a man whom I had never before seen, brought me my morning and evening portion of provision, instead of the jailor who had been accustomed to attend me; he appeared to be about twenty-five years of age, tall, and strongly built, but of a benign aspect, that seemed ill to suit the office in which he served.

"As he visited me for several successive days, and the mildness of his countenance encouraged me to address him, I inquired whether he who had formerly attended me was dead.

" 'Oh no!' he answered, and immediately left me, as fearing to say more; whilst his features plainly showed that it was not from want of inclination on his part, that our conversation had been so short.

"I often endeavoured to tempt him into farther conference, but he could never be prevailed by me to utter more than one sentence at a visit. One day, however, when I asked if he knew whether I was a prisoner for life, he cast his eye to the door, as if to be assured no one was watching him, and then putting his face close to mine, he said hastily, and in a low voice, 'Pray don't question me again, but rely on my being your friend,' and again departed as precipitately as he had done on former occasions.

"The first ray of hope, in the course of ten tedious and painful years, now burst upon my afflicted heart, and every nerve was strained to form a conjecture how this youth could be interested in my welfare.

"Five months passed, and this youth still visited me; nor did I once behold him who had before attended me; but still I perceived, from the conduct of my newly-declared friend, that no fit opportunity for conference was given us, for he always hastened from my prison as quickly as possible, seldom however forgetting to cast at me a look of sympathy, which served to keep alive the feeble spark of hope he had lighted in my breast.

"One evening about this time, when he brought in my supper, he said, in the same mysterious way he had always spoken to me in, but apparently with greater signs of fear than he had ever before shown of being overheard, 'Don't go to sleep to-night.' I obeyed his injunctions, and awaited with the greatest impatience the hour that should disclose to me his meaning.

"The clock had just struck two, when a person in an under voice at the grating of my window, which I immediately knew to be that of my new friend, said '*Monsieur, monsieur!*'

"I felt for my stool, and placing it under the window, mounted upon it, and our faces then nearly meeting, he said, 'If I should contrive your escape from this place, and this kingdom, will you let me be your servant?'

" 'Say rather my friend,' I replied.

" 'Only say you won't let me starve, *monsieur.*'

" 'No, by heaven!' I returned, forgetful how destitute I myself was of the means of subsistence.

" 'Enough said,' he resumed; 'then don't refuse to drink any thing that is offered you; and leave the rest to me.'

" 'Drink!' I repeated, but the young man was gone.

"I remained some minutes at the window, but he did not return, neither did I hear the faintest sound. I then left my station, and throwing myself on my mattress, I began to ruminate on the words which I had just had addressed to me; and the only idea I could suffer myself to connect with the last sentence the young man had uttered, was that I was intended to be poisoned.

"At an early hour in the morning, I heard my prison door unlocked, and a friar entered; he commanded me to kneel by him; and having prayed that I might bear with fortitude the sentence he was about to announce to me, he told me that I was condemned to die on that day.

"A few hours before, I should have thought death the greatest happiness that could have befallen me; but now, with the faint hope of enlargement which my new friend had given me, prepared as I was to receive this sentence, and even tempted to believe that by his means I should escape it, I felt an undescribable shock on its being first announced to me.

"I am inclined to think that the emotions which this intelligence produced in me, were to me of essential service, for I am well convinced, that the sudden change my countenance underwent was so great, as to have baffled the suspicion of the priest, had he entertained any, of what had passed between me and the young jailor.

"He asked my confession. A seclusion of nearly eleven years from the world could have added no sin of magnitude to my account of former misdeeds, and of them I had made a confession on the very morning on which I had first been brought to the Bastile; thus this task was quickly ended. He then again ordered me to kneel, and having prayed by me full two hours, he gave me his blessing, and departed.

"In a few minutes the governor, attended by two guards, and the young man in whom my last and only hope rested, entered.

"Obeying the governor's orders, the young man poured from a phial which he had brought in his hand, a thick black liquor into a small bason, which the governor then took, and holding it out to me, commanded me to drink it, the two guards meanwhile levelling their bayonets at my breast, as a tacit threat in case of my refusing the draught.

"I crossed myself, and drank; the bason fell from my hand, and I raised my eyes in search of my friend: he had left the prison; the governor made a signal to the guards; they went out; he followed them; and I heard him turn the lock upon me.

"What a moment of horror was this! Uncertain whether or not I had swallowed the draught of death: if I had, how near the brink of eternity was I now standing!—if I had not, how dreadful a fate might await both me and the young man, should his stratagem fail!

"Within the course of an hour a faint sickness seized me. I lay down upon my mattress, and pulled the blanket over me; an icy coldness ran through my veins, and big drops of perspiration started on my forehead: in a short time a heaviness, which I could not struggle against, weighed down my eye-lids, and in less than two hours after my swallowing the draught, I sunk into what I then thought the sleep of death!"

Thus far had count Byroff proceeded in his narrative when the shepherd entering the room, informed him, that two men, who had seen his horse in the stable, had declared they knew it, and insisted on coming into the cottage in search of him, and that his son was then endeavouring to prevent their entrance.

The count raised his eyes in silence to Lauretta; they betrayed the wildest agitation and fear; Lauretta rose from her seat, and threw herself upon her father's neck, and at the same instant the voices of Theodore and Kroonzer were heard by them in the adjoining apartment.

Count Byroff started up, and snatching his dagger from his side, prepared himself to meet their entrance into the chamber.

The chevalier was the first that appeared; the count made a dart at him, which he resisting, threw the count upon the floor, and treading on him with his left foot, drew his sword, while he muttered curses on him for a villain and a traitor.

Lauretta, instigated by the scene before her, caught his arm, and falling on her knees by the side of her father's body, she exclaimed, "Here, in this bosom sheath thy sword; but spare, oh spare my father!"

Count Byroff's prayers and struggles confirmed Theodore that Lauretta had truly named him her parent; and a momentary surprise suspended his power of action. This count Byroff perceived, and availing himself of the astonishment of his antagonist, by an instantaneous effort raised himself again on his feet, and dropping his dagger, made himself master of the sword Theodore had just drawn. Kroonzer immediately drew his weapon, and springing forward, presented himself to oppose the count in defence of the chevalier, whilst Lauretta, regardless of herself, her thoughts centred only in her father's safety, and almost made frantic by the danger in which she now beheld him, ran without the cottage, piercing the air with her cries and calls for assistance.

Theodore was in an instant at her heels; and then first recollecting her own danger, on beholding herself so closely pursued by him she most dreaded, she flew to the young cottager who was standing without the cottage door, and clasping his hand, she cried out, "Oh! save me from him, I conjure you!"

The lad, who was still standing with the oaken staff in his hand, with which he had endeavoured to repulse the entrance of the chevalier and his accomplice, and still panting from the unequal combat he had sustained, moved either by the impulse of humanity, or fired by the beauty of his interesting suppliant, flew upon Theodore with the desperation a wolf flies to the combat when attacked by a lion, and conscious that he must either conquer or die.

For some moments the struggle was maintained with equal valour and dexterity; but at length the superior strength of the chevalier prevailing over that of his antagonist, Lauretta beheld her champion levelled with the ground; again she shrieked, and again she attempted to fly, but her trembling limbs could no longer support her, and she sunk on the earth in a swoon.

END OF THE SECOND VOLUME.

The Midnight Bell

Volume III

THE MIDNIGHT BELL.

CHAPTER XVIII.

My soul's delight, my utmost joy, my husband!
I feel once more his panting bosom beat;
Once more I hold him in my eager arms,
Behold his face, and lose my soul in rapture.
   Essex. Transporting bliss! my richest, dearest treasure!
My mourning turtle, my long absent peace,
Oh come yet nearer, nearer to my heart!
My raptured soul springs forward to receive thee;
Thou heav'n on earth, thou balm of all my woe.
The Earl of Essex.

A FERVENT kiss, imprinted on her cold lips, recalled Lauretta into existence, and she opened her eyes in the wildest apprehension: but oh! what a glow of mingled extasy and delight warmed her frozen blood, when she perceived that it was Alphonsus, her beloved Alphonsus, who had bestowed the kiss that had awakened her from her trance.

In an unbounded transport of joy she embraced him as he stood by her side; then springing from the bed on which she had been laid, she flew to meet the embrace of her father, and then again sunk on the neck of her Alphonsus.

When their mutual effusions of joy gave room for an explanation on the part of count Byroff, Lauretta learnt from the lips of her father, whom it had been her first care to teach Alphonsus to know as such, that she was still in the shepherd's cottage, that Kroonzer had been put to flight by the united efforts of her father and the peasant, and that the chevalier had been killed by a blow from the hand of her husband, with the oaken staff which he had first obtained from the young peasant when he overcame him, and which Alphonsus had wrested from him.

Alphonsus then briefly informed Lauretta of the manner in which he had early that morning left Smaldart castle, and by the most fortunate chance had arrived to her rescue at the moment she was on the point of falling a prey to the villany of Theodore.

Lauretta shuddered at the idea of the danger she had so unexpectedly escaped, and again clasped to her breast the author of her preservation: he returned her embrace with all the fervor of that warm affection he bore her, and then turning to count Byroff, he said, "Advise me, I beseech you, what course to follow, whither to bend my steps."

"What opposes your now returning to your humble dwelling immediately?" asked the count.

"To meet the baron Smaldart?" rejoined Alphonsus.

"The law is on your side:" resumed count Byroff.

"I should feel less reluctance to behold him if it were against me;" replied Alphonsus. "I cannot bear to meet the man I have so deeply wounded, when I know him void of the means of redress.— He has ever considered Theodore with the partiality of a father, and consequently must have viewed the enormity of his crimes with a softening eye; can he then do otherwise than detest the man who has deprived him of the darling of his heart?—I am convinced I have not acted wrongly: thus I cannot submit to sue for his forgiveness; and the compassion I feel for the grief I shall have excited in the breast of one who has behaved towards me with the kindness I have experienced from the baron Smaldart, commands me not to return to a spot where my presence might seem a triumph over the sorrow I had occasioned: no! I will seek some distant asylum, where, living forgotten, I shall not renew his misery."

"From a selfish motive," said count Byroff, "I warmly subscribe to your idea of leaving this part of the empire; for, having been seen by Kroonzer, it is absolutely necessary for the preservation of my life, that I should fly immediately from hence; thus, should you resolve to return to your late dwelling, I must forego the society of my child: should you remove to some distant spot, I may still be your companion."

The happiness of his Lauretta was at all times the first consideration of Alphonsus; and as he now read speakingly in her blue eyes, her dislike to her separation from her father, he instantly declared that he was resolved on not returning to the vicinity of Smaldart castle, and prepared to travel in any direction the count should dictate as most likely to ensure his safety.

Mutual satisfaction beamed in the eyes of the count and Lauretta, at this declaration of Alphonsus; and the count pressed that they might set out immediately.

In a few minutes the horses were prepared by the peasant, whom count Byroff having liberally rewarded for his exertions, and, at the instigation of Alphonsus, commanded him to send a messenger to Smaldart castle, with a full and exact account of the transactions of the morning, they departed, bending their course, in compliance with the directions of the count, towards the north.

Having stopped during the day no longer than was absolutely necessary for the refreshment of themselves and their horses, they arrived towards night at a little inn, where count Byroff said he trusted himself to be in safety.

Immediately on their being left alone in an apartment of the inn, Lauretta asked of her father the conclusion of his history; eager to learn the mystery of the situation in which she had at first seen him, and the cause of the danger he had so strongly expressed of being overtaken during the course of their day's journey.

"My child," answered count Byroff, "I confess that your curiosity has been strongly excited, but weightier considerations must supersede its gratification; we must look forward to the necessities of the future, ere we allow ourselves leisure to indulge in the remembrance of the past." Then addressing himself to Alphonsus, "Have you formed any plan of future life?" he asked.

Alphonsus answered, not.

After a pause, count Byroff continued, "You have appeared thoughtful during our journey: I conjectured you might have been deliberating on some measures which you were undecided whether or not to adopt."

"You conjectured rightly," replied Alphonsus, "in thinking my mind thus employed."

"What were your thoughts?"

"I fear you will not approve them; however, be assured I will do nothing without the concurrence of yourself and my Lauretta."

Count Byroff besought him to proceed.

"My Lauretta," he continued, "has doubtless related to you the ambiguous and sorrowful event which marks my early life?"

"She has."

"I cannot die happy, unless I solve the mystery by which I am driven a wanderer upon the world; its recollection clouds every moment of my existence, and renders me, in the summer of life, a gloomy and thoughtful companion to her, who, knowing the cause of my melancholy, bears, with an angel-like patience, the sour effects it will at times, in spite of my endeavours to coerce them, produce in me. Were it not better at once to end these agonising doubts, to visit the neighbourhood of Cohenburg castle, and, by discovering if possible the truth, learn at once my future doom?"

"It is a point," returned count Byroff, "whereon I cannot pretend to advise you; your sole guide must be the impulse of your own heart."

"But," said Lauretta, "whence is the intelligence you wish to procure to be gained?—The country round Cohenburg is doubtless unacquainted with the truth, or the young miner, the son of one of your father's vassals, must have known it:—your uncle, he informed you, was gone, no one knew whither, and your mother dead!"

"He said the same of me," returned Alphonsus; "thus his information in this point sways me not.—But he pronounced the castle to be deserted; this was a matter in which he could not be deceived; thus if I visit it secretly, I can offend no one by so doing; and I will guard against wounding my conscience by the relation of any discovery I may there make, should its secrecy seem to be required of me by the injunctions laid on me by my mother: and Oh! I have for some time laboured with an undescribable prepossession that I shall gain knowledge of moment, if I do visit it."

"You are then resolved?" said count Byroff.

"I have nothing wanting to complete my resolution, since you and my Lauretta do not seem to oppose it, but the means of accomplishing my journey."

"I have that in my possession," replied the count, "which, with frugality, will yet support us many weeks."

"Then to-morrow, with the dawn, I will once more turn my steps towards my native soil," said Alphonsus.

The remainder of the evening was spent by them in concerting the route they should travel; and having planned it to their mutual satisfaction, they at an early hour retired to rest.

Reflection on what might be the event of a long-wished, and at length projected, undertaking, suffered Alphonsus to sleep but little, and he rose with the dawn to awake his fellow-traveller: the count instantly obeyed his summons, and at sun-rise they set forward on their journey.

As they proceeded, count Byroff lightened the way by again commencing the narrative of his life, in complaisance to the curiosity of Alphonsus; and being arrived at the period to which he had deduced his story, when in the shepherd's cottage he had related it to Lauretta, he thus went on.

"When I had recovered from the influence of the draught I had taken, which had been only a sleeping potion of a very strong nature, the first object on which I opened my eyes, was a black man sitting by my side, in a dry ditch, under the shade of a hedge; the time was twilight in the evening, and being too dusk for me accurately to discern his features, I perceived not, until he spoke, that my companion was the young jailor, with a new countenance: and when I did know him, I was some moments at a loss whether to express my astonishment first, at his change of colour, or my own extraordinary appearance, for I found myself habited in the garments of a French woman of mean rank.

" 'Ah, *monsieur!*' cried he immediately on beholding me open my eyes, 'how glad am I to see you awake again, and out of that vile prison!—Don't you know me, *monsieur?*' continued he, observing that my eyes were fixed on him in doubt.

" 'I think I do now,' I returned, after having been convinced by his voice who he was: 'but I hardly know myself.'

" 'I thought how it would be when you awoke,' replied he; 'I contrived these disguises that we might pass unnoticed as beggars;—but here, *Monsieur*, take a sup of wine, and eat a bit of bread,' said he, pulling a flask and a crust from his pocket, 'and refresh yourself; for you must be faint with so long fasting.'

"I readily accepted his offer; and while the flask was at my mouth, he exclaimed, '*Dieu merci*, that we are out of that horrid place!'

" 'Why, you were not a prisoner?' I said.

" 'Oh no, *monsieur*; but I felt so much for the poor creatures that were, that I could not bear to see them suffer any longer.—But, however, we are out now, and I hope for ever:—woe be to us if we get in again!'

" 'But how did we get out, my good fellow?—How did you contrive our escape?' I asked.

" 'I'll tell you another time, *monsieur*: we must not talk about it any more now, for fear we should be overheard:—*Jacques Perlet* will tell you all about it another time.—Oh, but, *monsieur*, you must not call me Jacques now, but some other name, such as blacks go by:—what shall it be, *monsieur*?'

" 'Shall it be Cæsar?' I replied.

" 'Aye, *monsieur*,' said he, 'as well as any.—Now, *monsieur*, please to remember that, for carrying on my plan, you must, if you please, pretend to be my wife; your features are very delicate, and you may easily pass for a woman; and leave the rest to Jac—Cæsar I mean, *monsieur*."

"I readily agreed to any plan of security in my present situation; and Jacques then told me we must now walk forwards to a small *auberge*, which he said he knew stood rather sequestered from the road, and where we were to pass the night.

"In our way, I asked him how far we were from Paris.

" 'Oh, nine or ten *lieues*, *monsieur*,' answered he.

" 'By what means did we perform the journey?'

" 'It is so dark, *monsieur*,' said he, 'that I can't see whether any body is near us or not;—I durst not tell you any thing till by and by."

"I checked my curiosity, conscious how judiciously my guide was acting; and we arrived within sight of the little inn in silence.

"According to the directions of Jacques, I asked in French for a mean supper and bed, while my companion only occasionally spoke in the vitiated manner in which negroes usually pronounce a language which they have no opportunity of learning but by the ear.

"I was rejoiced to perceive that our stratagem passed unsuspected; and when we retired to bed, which we did in the characters of husband and wife, the better to conceal our real ones, Jacques desired me to sit down, saying he must have a little chat with me before we went to bed, for his tongue was burning to tell me how nicely he had managed our escape.

"I was, as you may suppose, anxious to learn how my salvation from death had been effected during the time of my insensibility; and placing myself on the foot of the bed, I desired him to begin; he seated himself on the ground by my side, and leaning his arm upon the bed, spoke thus:

" 'In the first place, *monsieur*, I must tell you a little about who I am, that you may the better understand my reasons for what I have done.—My father, *monsieur*, was a very honest *savetier* in the *fauxbourg St. Antoine*, and at one time earned a very comfortable living; but misfortunes will happen to the best of people, and one mishap or another had obliged him to borrow small sums of money from several of his neighbours, chiefly to defray the expenses of my mother's illness and funeral, all which he would honestly have repaid, I am sure, if he had lived; but he died, poor man, soon after, and left me without a friend in the world, except my uncle Perlet, the old jailor at the Bastile, and a brother we had none of us heard of for many years.

" 'Well, I had been brought up to my father's trade; and if he had not left me heir to his debts as well as to his business, (which God forbid I should blame him for; for how could he have helped it, if even he had known he had been going to die?) I might have gained myself a pretty livelihood: but his creditors threatened to arrest me for the money, and so my uncle Perlet, too avaricious to pay it for me, and too proud to see his nephew confined in a jail, though he lived in a prison himself, took me to serve under him in the Bastile.

" 'I did not like going there at all; but what could I do, *monsieur*? I thought it was better than starving; but by the time I had been there a couple of months, which was about the time I first came to bring you your portion of bread and water, I would almost sooner have died than have staid much longer where I was; for the frightful things I saw, and the groans, and moans, and shrieks I heard in that dismal place, would freeze your blood, and make your hair stand on end, *monsieur*, if I was to tell you them all.'

"I sighed in the affirmative to Jacques' exclamation; and he continued: 'Ah, *monsieur*, you have had your share of their devil's works, I dare say?'

" 'It is past now, so let us drive away its remembrance,' I replied.

" 'I wish I could, *monsieur*: but I shall dream of it many a night to come, I dare say.—My uncle,' continued he, 'had a room where he and I used to sit by ourselves in an evening: and as my head was continually running upon the poor unhappy wretches I attended in the day-time, I could not forbear questioning him about them; and many a time, when I heard the story of a poor helpless creature condemned to die by the rack, or poison, I could not help thinking of the fate of his persecutors at a future day, that all of us must see.

" 'Sometimes I used to remonstrate with my uncle on the cruelty with which he often assisted in using the unhappy prisoners; but his answer always was, 'Jacques, I am a true lover of my king, and I'll never treat those kindly, depend upon it, that it is his pleasure to have otherwise dealt by.'—'But may not obedience,' I would answer, 'be carried so far as to make conscience troublesome?'

" 'Impossible, child,' he once answered me, when I had thus spoken to him; 'the king is the representative of God on earth, chosen by himself; thus we can never be doing wrong, while we implicitly obey his commands.'—'Then,' returned I, 'how careful ought the king to be, for his own sake, that his conduct is kind, merciful, and forgiving, since, as you say, the consciences of all his subjects, if they have done amiss in compliance with his commands, are cleared from guilt; of course the weight of all their bad actions must lie upon his conscience instead of theirs, and he be punished accordingly hereafter.'

" 'You are a foolish boy,' cried he, 'and don't understand these matters.'

" 'I made him no answer; for truly, *monsieur*, I did not wish to know more than I already did of a conduct that seemed to me void of reason and humanity; I had only a mind to ask him whether he prayed to the king instead of *le bon Dieu*; but I durst not, for fear he should think I was laughing at him, and use me as hardly as he had done others for less offences.'

"I could not help smiling at Jacques's philosophy; he laughed too, and thus went on—

" 'Well, *monsieur*, every day I began to long more and more to quit my situation: but it was a thing I almost despaired to be able to do; for I was well aware that my uncle would never give his consent to my leaving the Bastile for any other employment, for fear I should tell tales out of prison; so I knew the only method must be to run away to a distance from Paris; but then I had not much money, and I did not much like to make such an attempt without a companion.

" 'Some how, *monsieur*, I had taken a liking to you above any of the prisoners I attended; and all I kept wishing for, was some means of setting you at liberty, that we might run away together; I knew, if I could contrive it, you could not dislike it, and there was something in your countenance that told me you would be kind to me afterwards.

" 'Oh, *monsieur!* how often have I wished to sit and talk half an hour or an hour with you, and tell you how much I pitied you, and how I wished to serve you; but I durst not, for all the walls in that Bastile have eyes and ears, I believe; for nothing can be said or done but what is known by my uncle and the governor.—I often inquired of my uncle something about you, and I learnt, a little at a time, that you were, as most of the other prisoners are, a gentleman; and that you were only retained in prison because they were afraid to let you out, for fear you should expose the secrets of their tyranny.

" 'And is it owing to the king that the poor gentleman suffers all this for nothing?' said I.

" 'Partly,' my uncle answered, 'and partly to those who first represented him to *sa majesté*, as obnoxious to the state.'

" 'Then the king has some good friends, who lighten the burthen of his conscience by taking a little of it upon their own,' said I.

" 'My uncle answered me with a look which determined me never to hazard a joke again, on what he deemed so sacred a subject.

" 'About five weeks ago, my uncle told me, as he had given up the care of half his prisoners to me, I must fill every part of the office myself, and accordingly on the next morning must carry a dose of poison into the apartment of a *marquis*, who was condemned to die: I was afraid of disobeying my uncle; and I knew besides that if I did not do it, somebody else would, so that my refusal would be of no service to the poor wretch; and thus, at the time appointed, I attended the governor to the cell, just as I came with him into yours, *monsieur*, on the morning when he thought he was giving you your last dose: but I was too sly for him,—eh, *monsieur?*

" 'When the poor gentleman had swallowed the draught, and the governor had left the apartment, my uncle locked the door upon the dying man, saying, 'nobody must go in any more till he was dead.'

" 'What! must we leave him all alone at this terrible moment?' asked I.

" 'Why, does he want any body to help him to die?'" returned my uncle.

" '*Ah, pauvre diable!* I wish it was over with him,' said I.

" 'It won't be long, I'll answer for it,' he replied, and then commanded me to leave the door by which I was standing, and could not help trying to listen what was passing within.

" 'In the evening, when all the prison doors were double locked for the night, he called me to follow him up stairs, and we went together into the poor *marquis's* apartment. Oh dear, *monsieur*, I shall never forget it. There lay the poor gentleman dead and cold, and all his features so dreadfully distorted, and his eyes and mouth wide open, that I should have run out of the room with fright if my uncle had not held me by the collar.

" 'Now,' said my uncle, 'we must carry the corpse into the *cimetière*, and bury it.'

" 'I was forced to obey, and we carried down the body to the spot he had named, where stood a coffin ready to receive it.

" 'I suppose you think,' said he, 'I am going to bury this man? No! no! I know a better trick than that; I'll never bury a corpse whilst I can get well paid for letting it remain above ground.' He then told me, that a surgeon in *La rue de Saint Etienne le grand* always bought the bodies of him to dissect; and that as he had the privilege of passing the draw-bridge when he pleased, he had always carried them to him by night; 'but,' said he, 'I'll contrive for you to carry this one, and I'll bury the coffin in the mean time.'

" 'Well, *monsieur*, the body was put into a sack; I pretended it was so heavy I could not carry it; my uncle knew better, and I was forced to set off according to his directions: he went with me to the draw-bridge, and having whispered the guards, they let me pass.

" 'Do you know, *monsieur*, I'd wager my life, the governor and he went shares in selling the dead men; for nobody, I had often heard my uncle say, could go over the draw-bridge without the governor's knowing it, and giving leave.

" 'Notwithstanding the weight of my burthen, I ran all the way; for not being accustomed to be so near dead people, I thought every moment I could feel him stirring and groaning.

" 'When I had got quit of my load, I began to consider whether I should go back or not; I felt in my pocket to see how much money I was worth in case I took the chance of running away, when, *pardi, monsieur!* if I had not left my purse at home. I did not know what to do now; for having nothing to support myself with, I thought I could not go far without money, so might be heard of by my uncle, taken back to the Bastile, and perhaps roasted alive for what I had done, by the great fire in that room where all the irons are hanging about: I trembled at the very thought of it, and so ran back as fast as my legs could carry me.

" 'When I returned back to my uncle, he gave me an *écu de six francs* out of his profits, as a reward for what I had done, saying, he would double it the next job, for he was determined I should not want for encouragement, and I should soon have another, for *monsieur Montville* had not much longer to live.

" 'I was not a little surprised and disturbed at hearing this, *monsieur*, as you may suppose; and I was sure that if any thing could be done, it must be done directly. Well, I kept thinking, and thinking, and no way could I contrive to get you out; at last a plan came into my head, and I resolved I would try it whether it succeeded or not. I complained to my uncle that I had got a very bad tooth-ache, and told him that I had frequently been subject to it, and that my father had been used to give me some laudanum to cure it, and begged that he would too.

" 'He gave me a small phial about half full, warning me to be very careful how I used it; I immediately ran with it to my own chamber, and having poured it into the phial that had held the poison given to the poor dead *marquis*, and which I had washed out for that purpose, I let fall the empty phial: it broke with the fall, just as I wished; I ran down to my uncle with the broken pieces in my hand, and telling him my misfortune, begged him to give me some more.

" 'The old fox was taken in for once, *monsieur*, and he brought me about as much as before.

" 'I suppose,' said I, as I took it from him, 'if I was to drink all this stuff, it would kill me?'

" 'Twice as much would,' he replied: 'that would make you sleep for about two days.'

" 'I found by this that my first quantity would have been enough for what I wanted with it, but however I thought it was no bad thing to have two doses by me, in case any accident happened to one of them; and so I put them both carefully by, and by the next night my tooth-ache was gone.

" 'Well, *monsieur*, at last the day was fixed for you to die upon: I found means of coming to your window, as you must recollect, the night before; and when I told you not to refuse to drink any thing that was offered you, I said it because I was afraid you might by some means spill the potion that would be given to you, thinking it to be poison, as you could not know I had contrived to give you laudanum in its stead, and then might be obliged to take the poison indeed, as a second dose would have been brought you, that I should have had no opportunity of changing.

" 'When I left the outside of your prison window, I went and got one of my phials half full of laudanum. Now the poison phials are always full; so I knew my false one must be so too, or it would discover the trick. I durst not put in any more laudanum for fear I should kill you, and if I filled it up with water, it would look so much paler than the poison; so at last, what do you think I did, *monsieur*?—why, I filled it up with treacle and water, and it looked quite black, just like what it should have been.

" 'When morning came, I was called to attend the governor: my uncle gave me the phial of poison; and I, to deceive him, said in a low voice, 'to-night I shall earn *deux écus*.' He nodded significantly, and I followed the governor and his guards. At the turn from the last flight of stairs into the gallery, I stopped an instant, and snatching my phial from my bosom, and slipping the other into its place, I made a noise with my feet as if saving myself from falling; and then running a step or two after the governor, and rubbing my knee as if I had bruised it, 'better so than a broken leg,' I cried: the governor turned round and looked at me; still rubbing my knee, I drew up a face which made him smile at my supposed accident, and he walked on without suspicion.'"

The travellers at this moment arrived within sight of a small house, and Alphonsus interrupted the count's narrative, by proposing, that, if it proved a house of public accommodation, they should make it their abode for the night, as the twilight was already beginning to fall. To this proposal count Byroff agreed; and the habitation proving to be such as they wished it, they here put an end to their day's journey.

CHAPTER XIX.

Wish'd morning's come! And now upon the plains
And distant mountains, where men feed their flocks,
The happy shepherds leave their homely huts,
And with their lusty pipes proclaim the new-born day.
The chearful birds too, on the tops of trees,
Assemble all in choirs, and with their notes
Salute and welcome up the rising sun.
There's no condition sure so curs'd as mine!
                                        OTWAY.

REFRESHED by the salutary balm of sleep, our travellers awoke to one of the most glorious mornings that ever burst from the heavens; the sun was beginning his progress towards his meridian of splendor, without a single cloud to obscure his expanding rays; the pearly drops of dew were still hanging on the dripping leaves, and studding the blades of grass; every bush resounding with the grateful notes of its feathered inhabitants, hailing the return of morn; and every flower exhaling sweets in gratitude to the rising presence of their fostering orb.

Again blessed with her Alphonsus, Lauretta's feelings harmonised in the universal gladness of nature: Alphonsus strove to be

chearful, but his efforts were ineffectual; Lauretta observed his
dejectedness, and without remarking upon it, endeavoured to divert it. She was sometimes successful: again Alphonsus sunk into
thought; she varied her attentions; he returned a smile of gratitude
for her endeavours to please, and she was happy.

Having made a delicious repast of new milk and fruits, they
again proceeded on their journey, and after a short conversation on
various topics, count Byroff thus pursued his narrative—

" 'Well, *monsieur*,' continued Jacques Perlet, 'all day long I was
wishing, I hardly knew why, to come and take a peep at you; however I should not have been allowed if I had asked it, and at all
events I thought it was much more prudent not. At night my uncle
called me to go up with him about the same time he had done before, and, oh dear, how frightened I was all the way up stairs!—for
it had just come into my head you might not be asleep yet; and
then, when I found you was asleep, I was as much afraid my uncle's
rough handling, or some unlucky blow in lifting you, might awake
you.

" 'However, *Dieu merci*, we got you down stairs, and into the *cimetière* quite safe: I trembled a little when my uncle said he thought
you was very warm; but I soon recovered again when he added,
that he thought nothing of that, for that he had carried away many
a one before they were half cold.

" 'In a few minutes I got you put into the sack, taking care to lay
you with your head towards the mouth, and away I went, leaving
my uncle to bury the coffin, and wait my return.

" 'Instead of going to the surgeon's, I made the best of my way
for *la porte de Saint Jean*; and being got out of the city, I looked for
the first hedge I could find, and setting down my load on the side
farthest from the road, I pulled you out of the sack, terrified to
death for fear I should have smothered you; and pleased enough I
was, when I put my hand to your side, and felt your heart heave. I
directly set about putting on you this gown and petticoat, and hat,
and apron, and cloak, that I had taken from the old woman in the
Bastile that is kept to make my uncle's and the governor's beds. I
did not rob her of them, *monsieur*, for I put a *demi-louis* into her box
when I took them out; and the manner I contrived to bring them
away with me, was by buttoning them in between my coat and

waistcoat, and telling my uncle it was a lump of cloth I had put there to keep the weight of my load from hurting my shoulder.

" 'When I had dressed you, I set about disguising myself, and having turned all my clothes inside outwards, I dyed my hands and face with some stuff I had brought in my pocket for that purpose; I then threw the clothes I had taken off you, together with the sack, over the opposite hedge, into a deep ditch, and then sat me down by your side, anxiously waiting till some cart might come past that would carry us a little farther from our old abode.

" 'About day-break I heard the wheels of some carriage coming from the city; I peeped over the hedge, and saw a waggon full of luggage, in the front of which sat one man, on a bench large enough to hold three or four; I called to him, asking, 'Whither he was going?'—'To Desmartin,' he answered. Then, pretending that I was hardly able to express myself in French, I told him that I had a sick wife almost at the point of death lying behind the hedge, and that I would give him a trifle to carry us some way on our journey, which lay his road; after a short dispute about what I was to pay him, he consented to carry us, and I lifted you into the waggon and placed you upon the seat, carefully holding you, lest you should fall out.

" 'We stopped several times during the day; some pitied my poor wife, some laughed at me for a black *fourbe*, and some were charitable enough to give me a *petit sous*, and bid me take care of *la pauvre ame*; and I directly bought the wine and bread in their presence, which I gave you under the hedge, for which they all called me a *bon garçon*, and one old woman doubled her charity.

" 'I had not taken you out of the waggon all day, for fear, if I did, the people should crowd round you out of curiosity, and discover the imposition: evening was coming on, and you did not wake; we were within a *lieue* of Desmartin, and I did not know what to do; at last I remembered this little *cabaret*, which stands a few hundred paces from the high road, for I had once in my life travelled as far as Desmartin; and telling the waggoner I meant to pass the night there, as inns in towns were too expensive for me, I desired, when we came in sight of it, to get out. He accordingly stopped, and having taken you out, and paid him his promised fare, we wished one another *bon soir*, and on he drove.

" 'Well, *monsieur*, I knew it could not be long before you woke; so I determined not to go to the *cabaret* till you did; so I entered the first field with you in my arms, and having spied the dry ditch where we were when you awoke, I laid you down in it, and seating myself by you, chuckled not a little to myself at the success of my plan,—and when you awoke I was just thinking how you and I should both laugh if we could see ourselves in a *miroir.*'

"When Jacques had ended his account, having thanked him in the warmest terms for the interest he had so kindly taken in my welfare, and commended the adroitness with which he had effected our escape, I told him that it behoved us immediately to conclude on some plan for leaving the kingdom with all possible expedition; for if my being alive was not discovered, he would doubtless be sent in search of by his uncle, and that if one was taken, the other would in course share his fate, and then both, beyond a doubt, fall sacrifices to the butchers in the Bastile.

" 'Why, *monsieur,*' replied he, 'let us set forward as fast as we can to your home, wherever it is.'

"How astonished was the poor fellow to hear I had neither home nor means of subsistence! He had expected to find me a man of rank and fortune either in Italy or Germany, he knew not which, and who would liberally repay him for his services. He, however, bore his disappointment with the most honourable fortitude, and he drew tears into my eyes by exclaiming, after a short pause of reflection—"Well, *monsieur*, if you had been *un homme de bien*, I am sure you would have taken care of *pauvre Jacques*; as you are not, Jacques will take care of you as well as he is able: as long as that money lasts, half of it is yours;" and so saying, he pulled from his pocket his whole worldly treasure, and threw it upon the bed.

"After much deliberation, we resolved to travel into Germany in our present disguises, for what purpose neither of us knew, except that we must leave France, and that all places were equally indifferent; for to take possession again of the mansion and estate I had once quitted, I knew to be an impossibility for me at the present moment to attempt, incumbered as it was with debts and mortgages.

"Next morning at a very early hour we set forward on our journey, and to our great satisfaction arrived in about ten days' time in

Germany, without having suffered more on our journey than what was occasioned by fatigue, and our own fears. During the whole expedition, Jacques' conversation was confined to two subjects—his apprehension of being pursued and overtaken, and his wish of being acquainted in what part of the empire was his brother, who had left Paris about four years ago with a man whom nobody knew, and with whom he had only said, he was going into Germany. 'He was an idle fellow,' continued Jacques, 'and, I dare say, took to some lazy kind of life; and *pardi*, so was his former one, for he could not have a much easier business than *valet de chambre* to a *marquis*: it suited him, for he got fine clothes, and strutted about like a *singe poudré*: I might have had his place when he went away, but I preferred homeliness and hard work to such frippery; and you see how I am rewarded for my honesty; but hard fare here, better hereafter, says *l'évangile*; so I am never cast down, *monsieur*, happen what will.'

"There was something consolatory to me in the reasoning of my humble companion, and I determined to put myself under the guidance of one so cheerful amidst misfortunes, and confident in providence under its painful inflictions, and accordingly told him I was resolved to be entirely directed by him in what course to follow for gaining our future subsistence.

"After some deliberation, Jacques proposed that we should endeavour to push our way to the capital of the empire, where he said he should stand a chance of being better paid for exercising his trade, as the value of his work would there be better estimated, being, as he assured me, an excellent workman.

"On the first day of our arrival in Germany, Jacques took advantage of a pool of water somewhat sequestered from the road, again to change the complexion of his face and hands, but it was some days ere he could accomplish a perfect triumph of the ivory over the ebony; however, having turned his clothes into their proper situation, his appearance became decent; and at the next town, having purchased for me a wrapping coat and a hat, I changed the outward form of my sex behind the first hedge we came to on our again proceeding on our journey.

"The cash Jacques now had left, consisted, in all, of a *louis d'or* and *deux écus*; accordingly, in order to housewife the money we possessed, it not appearing to us so easy a matter to acquire more when it was spent, we resolved to buy a loaf and some cheese, of which we ate, when hungry, under a tree; and, as the season was the middle of summer, we determined to sleep under hedges or in any out-houses we might meet with, thus to avoid the unnecessary expense of entering inns on the road.

"Necessity reconciles measures, which, to those who have never been reduced to adopt them, appear insurmountable; thus we experienced nothing more than accidental inconvenience from pursuing our plan. In the enjoyment of liberty I ever forgot care; and Jacques never failed to declare once every day, that he had rather sleep in a ditch with mud for a feather-bed, than on down in the Bastile.

"Journeying on one night by moonlight, the decayed castle wherein you, Lauretta, was an unfortunate prisoner, attracted our notice: its ruined condition seemed to bespeak it uninhabited; the gate stood open; we entered the hall, and without much farther observation, we determined to make it our abode for the night.

"We lay down together in a corner of the hall, where we had scarcely composed ourselves to sleep, when the sounding of a shrill tucket aroused our attention.—We listened without speaking:—In a couple of minutes a man entered the hall from a distant part of the building, and proceeding to the gate, called out, 'All's safe,' immediately we heard the trampling of horses approaching close to the gate; a number of men, who were talking confusedly, dismounted from them and entered the hall; and the first sentence I distinctly heard, and which opened to me at once the nature of this strange adventure, was, 'curse the barrenness of the road! one can find nobody to plunder,' uttered by one of the men as he vaulted from his horse.

"Presently another man entered the hall from the interior part of the building, carrying a lamp: in an instant Jacques sprung from my side, and running to the man, threw his arms around his neck, exclaiming, '*Ah mon frère, je vous retrouve! Ah mon cher frère! mon cher frère!*'

"In his eagerness to embrace his brother, Jacques had knocked the lamp out of his hand, which being extinguished by the fall, the party was left in darkness to exercise their imaginations on what they had heard; and, from what motive I cannot pretend to say, whether from surprise or any supernatural fear, a general silence prevailed till another light was brought into the hall; on the appearance of which, Jacques, regardless of surrounding objects, came running back to me, all the way introducing me to his brother as his 'très bon ami.'

"The banditti, for such, you will have perceived, were the inhabitants of this decayed mansion, immediately came round me; I rose and began to apologise for our intrusion into their dwelling, by stating to them the truth of our circumstances, which Jacques summed up by telling them we were almost pennyless, having just escaped from the Bastile.

"Avowed enemies to tyranny, and plainly perceiving there was no deceit in the relationship of the brothers, the banditti invited us to enter that part of the building which they inhabited, and partake of their supper before we retired to rest, when we should be accommodated with a bed.

"I thanked them for their kindness in the warmest terms, and they conducted us into a hall where a repast had been prepared against their return. I ate in complaisance to my entertainers,—and Jacques, because variety, to which he was unaccustomed, whetted his appetite.

"After supper I was requested to relate my adventures, Jacques having awakened their curiosity by repeatedly referring to our late escape; and though I should have preferred retiring to sleep, I felt myself bound to comply with their request.

"When I had concluded my story, the leader rose, and taking my hand,—'We are your brothers in affliction,' he said; 'most of us whom you here behold, have been driven from the haunts of men, by the cruelty of man; but there is not one of us whose heart has been steeled by his misfortunes into inhumanity: never has the traveller whom we have plundered borne the marks of our violence,—never have we left the poor man destitute,—the rich and profligate alone have been our prey,—the unfortunate at all times our care;—you are unfortunate, and we are willing to receive you as a brother; will you then become one of us, and live free from the despotism of tyrants, and the malice of an envious world, enjoying perfect liberty, subject only to laws of our own, and those useless where honour presides?'

" 'Well said, noble captain!' cried Jacques, starting up: 'honour amongst thieves is an old proverb of my father's: I'll make one of you with all my heart.'

"During the time I had been reciting my adventures, Jacques had been drinking pretty freely of the palatable wine the table afforded; and having taken somewhat too potent a dose, it was rather the spirit of the wine than that of his own courage which spoke for him in the last sentence. The captain perceived his situation, and commanded his brother to conduct him to bed; but he promised faithfully not to drink another drop, or speak another word, if he might but be permitted to sit up as long as his *cher maître.*

"During this little altercation between the captain and Jacques, I had a moment of leisure to reflect on the words which had been addressed to me: I thought they appeared rather an apology for a mode of life which the speaker himself knew to be culpable, but was from necessity constrained to follow, than an eulogium which might tempt me to embrace it: I accordingly requested that I might deliberate on his proposal till the morning; a request readily granted me: Jacques and I then retired for the night,—Jacques assuring the captain he had resolved to serve under him.

"A few moments served to change the powers of the deceitful liquor which had produced Jacques's valour; for he was no sooner in bed than his boasted prowess was forgotten in a profound sleep, and I thus left to my own reflections.

"During the greatest part of the night I remained awake, undecided what plan to follow. My mind revolted from becoming a determined robber; but I felt a still greater antipathy to again mixing in the ensnaring scenes of that world from which I had already experienced so much perfidy and sorrow; and I at length resolved to accept the asylum which had been offered me.

"In the morning when Jacques awoke, all the occurrences of the preceding night had entirely fled from his memory, and he awoke me in a great fright, inquiring whether we had got into the Bastile again. Just as I had sufficiently roused myself to begin to rally his recollection, his brother entered to call us to breakfast, and his presence saved me the trouble of farther explanation, as, on sight of him, Jacques immediately recollected where he was.

"On seeing the captain, I immediately declared to him my resolution; and was welcomed by him into my new situation, as also separately by every voice of the community.

"The captain then turned to Jacques, and reminded him of his promise.

"Jacques stared vacantly, and inquired 'what it was?'

" 'To become one of the fraternity over which I have the honour to preside,' returned the leader.

" 'Did I promise that?'

" 'You did.'

" 'Well then, I'll keep my word; and if you will but feed me and clothe me, I'll be *savetier* to you all for nothing: and what more can you desire of me, if you will but consider that a cobler ought to stick to his last?'

"His brother joined me in interceding for the grant of his petition; and his native mirth, rather than any other qualification, obtained for him the majority of votes in his favour.

CHAPTER XX.

———————Yes, yes—'tis she!
This little cross—I know it by sure marks!
AARON HILL.

ON the preceding night, the faces of such of the banditti as had been out prowling, had been disguised with some colouring, which was always their custom when going on any expedition; and being now cleared from it, Jacques recognised, in the person of Kroonzer, the man with whom his brother had left France, of which occurrence this was the brief account: Kroonzer was the son of a German man and French woman; his residence had been chiefly in France, and his trade, from his infancy, none of the most creditable; his parents having been people, who, by assuming various disguises and characters in various places, had made these their means of imposing on the credulous, and defrauding the ignorant; thus gaining a fortuitous subsistence, whilst they cautiously kept within the pale of the law, and yet were in reality little better than common thieves.

"This mode of life had initiated Kroonzer into all the intrigues of Paris; and from his first herding with the banditti, to whose knowledge he had been led by accident, he had become extremely useful to them, by going annually into France, and finding means of disposing to advantage of such rings, watches, and other trinkets of value, as had fallen into their hands, and, before their knowledge of Kroonzer, had proved of little worth to them, as no one amongst them had ventured to hazard the experiment of changing them into money.

"It was in one of these expeditions that Kroonzer became acquainted with Jacques's brother; and having found him to be a man whom he believed would be a valuable acquisition to their society, he had enticed him into Germany under false promises, nor made the real truth known to him till he introduced him to his comrades; a measure which he had however been strictly forbidden by the captain ever again to repeat. Guillaume Perlet was, as it fortunately happened for the security of the banditti, an acceptable subject; for, preferring any kind of idleness to work, his new mode of life was pleasing to him the first moment of his being made acquainted with it.

"The captain treated me with great kindness and attention, and indeed my health required it, for the sudden change from eleven years of inactivity, to the great fatigue I had the last twenty days been undergoing, had reduced me to a state of excessive weakness.

"For the first year, I was not required to do any thing more in the various business of our household, of which every one in his turn took a part, than what I chose for my own amusement; nor during the whole of the time I lived amongst the banditti, in all nearly eight years, was any thing more asked of me than to take my turn in the evening and nightly watches.

"The evening watch was to answer the tucket sounded by the banditti, on their return from an excursion, that, in case of the officers of justice having entered their haunt during their absence, they might thus be apprised of it, ere they entered the castle, and, by flying, prevent their being taken with their spoils upon them, which would prove sure evidences of their guilt.

"Of the night watch this was the import; that those who did not go out in the quest of plunder watched for two hours alternately in the hall of the castle, that the fraternity might not be surprised in their sleep.

"During the first six years of my residence amongst the banditti, no circumstance worth relating occurred; and as I was not constrained to act the part of a plunderer, considering myself comparatively free from guilt, I felt myself tolerably happy: at the expiration of that period the captain died.

"A ballot immediately took place for appointing him a successor, and the majority of suffrages fell upon Kroonzer.

"About three months after his becoming leader of the fraternity, was the time at which he had always been accustomed to visit France; and as no one was deemed so fit for the business of that expedition as himself; he again undertook to perform it, notwithstanding his rise to his present situation; and accordingly, having appointed a deputy to guide the helm until his return, he departed as usual.

"The time of his absence was marked with an event of some moment: this was the death of Guillaume Perlet; and for some weeks it required all my most eloquent persuasions and remonstrances to keep Jacques from exceeding the bounds of reasonable sorrow on the loss of his brother; and he declared, that the thought of leaving me alone in my present situation, was his only inducement to struggle against death.

"At the stated time Kroonzer returned, and with him came the chevalier D'Aignon.

"Kroonzer had one fault,—it was that inordinate thirst of money which often leads its possessor to gratify in a heedless moment his ruling passion, and to repent at leisure that he did not subdue it. Conscious that he had acted wrongly, and yet too honourable to attempt a deceit which might endanger the security of those to whom the strongest ties of fellowship connected him,—when Theodore had retired for the night (for no one has a right to question the captain, and thus we knew not yet on what motive Theodore was brought amongst us), he candidly confessed the inconsiderate measure of which he had been guilty, and asked our advice how to act.

"He informed us, that during his visits to Paris, he had been much in the habit of frequenting gaming-tables, at many of which he had for the last three years frequently seen the chevalier, and had at times, he said, won of him sums of money to no small amount.—'He always paid his money without concern, and was so eager to enter into any measure for squandering it,' continued Kroonzer, 'that I soon found him to be a fit subject to exercise my talents upon. No very favourable opportunity offered to forward my plans on him, till a few days ago, happening to meet him at a tavern where he was engaged at dice with a young nobleman, and a dispute arising between them, and swords being called in to adjust their quarrel, the young man fell by the hand of the chevalier: his rage was now lost in fear for his own safety, and he exclaimed madly, that he was lost, ruined, and a dead man. I was the only one in the room with them; and approaching him, I told him if he would sign a draft for five hundred louis-d'ors, which I drew from my pocket, I would insure his safety: he immediately acquiesced, and I gloried in my success, till the reflection of a few moments told me how wrongly I had been acting, since I had no other means of securing him but by bringing him hither; and I could not steel my heart into being the villain to desert him, now he had paid me so liberally for his protection; I accordingly effected his escape, and I have secured my reward: but how shall we secure our own safety?'

"At length it was agreed that Theodore should take an oath, by which he imprecated vengeance on himself if ever he betrayed us, or our haunt; and that we each separately, in his presence, should bind ourselves by a solemn vow, to seek his life, if ever he was known, by the slightest insinuation, to disregard the oath by which he was restricted.

"He willingly agreed to this proposal, probably foreseeing that a refusal would have caused him to have been retained a prisoner amongst us for life; a plan which was first suggested by one of the banditti; but which Kroonzer feared to adopt, knowing that if by any means the haunt should be detected by the officers of justice, the finding a man of rank imprisoned in it, would be an unsurmountable evidence against them on their trial.

"A short time after, on the promise of three hundred louis-d'ors from the chevalier, in addition to the sum Kroonzer had already received, he again set out for Paris, in order to gain intelligence of Theodore's antagonist; and on his return, brought information that the wound had not proved mortal, and that the young nobleman was in a fair way of recovery.

"Theodore immediately left us, and we heard no more of him till three days before your being brought to the decayed castle. It was one night about this time, that the man who held the night watch gave the alarm, having seen, as he said, a man on horseback riding amongst the ruins: the banditti, to whom every unknown person wore the dread appearance of a spy, or officer of justice, immediately prepared themselves for defence; but a few minutes eased their doubts, by their hearing the voice of the chevalier in the hall of the castle.

"Kroonzer then first lamented that he had not interdicted to him their haunt; but still a prey to interest, he again consented to serve him, and Theodore departed before day-break.

"On his departure, Kroonzer informed us that Theodore had bought him, by one thousand louis-d'ors, to secrete in the castle his sister, who, he said, had formed an engagement with a man much her inferior in life, and which he meant to prevent from taking place, by immuring her in a convent, when he had found one suited to his wishes; but should in the mean time leave her with us, judging it expedient immediately to carry her away from her paramour.

"Kroonzer had promised to fetch this supposed sister, whom he had been told to treat with the greatest kindness, and requested me to be his companion in the expedition.

"The story told by Theodore had appeared to me plausible, and his conduct by no means improper: I accordingly consented, and another of the banditti was chosen to attend us; and at the appointed time, having disguised ourselves, we set out on our journey in an old carriage which had been left in the castle before any of the banditti had known it, and in which we carried provision to supply us on our journey.

"We stopped only twice for a short space of time; the first inn Kroonzer did not like, being in too public a situation: accordingly we proceeded to the cottage where you remained an entire day, and bargained with its owner for our admittance on our return, for he had already been cautioned by Theodore against travelling in the day:—as to the second inn, as he proposed staying at it only a short time on his return, and that in the dead of the night, he paid little attention to its situation.

"We proceeded to the spot where Kroonzer had agreed to meet the chevalier; a tap at the window was the signal to the little girl who attended you to give the alarm of fire, and then open the door to the chevalier under the pretence of running out to call for assistance; we entered, and when you fainted in our arms, we immediately carried you to the vehicle by which our companion was waiting for us at a short distance from your cottage; he entered it with you, and Kroonzer and myself mounted the horses and drove on. Your dress, and the cottage in which we found you, so ill suited to the character of the chevalier's sister, first raised suspicions in us of the truth of what Theodore had told us; but he laughed at our scruples, and explained them away, though I must confess not very satisfactorily either to Kroonzer or myself.

"At the little inn where we first stopped, a plausible story, told by Kroonzer, lulled the curiosity awakened in the host and his guests by our appearance; and at the retired cottage of old Bartha we did not think it necessary to render any account of our actions."

Lauretta could not here forbear interrupting her father to inquire, why Kroonzer, since he had no design upon her life, had drawn his sword, on her supplicating the pity of him who had been her companion in the carriage?

Count Byroff informed her, that it had been drawn by him as a tacit threat to his companion, to prevent his informing her of her destination, which had been particularly forbidden by the chevalier, and which he had not yet had an opportunity of imparting to his comrade.

"After we left this inn," continued the count, "we became your companions; and our comrade, the driver, having fastened our third horse to the back of the vehicle, and being arrived at Bartha's cottage, we sent our companion forward upon it to the castle to prepare for your reception, which had been forgotten by Kroonzer in the hurry of his setting out.

"The vehicle so long disused had been so shattered by the journey, the greatest part of which lay, as you must have remarked, over uneven ground, that we thought it unsafe to proceed farther in it; and accordingly, whilst you were in the cottage, we carried it into the middle of a neighbouring wood, where we left it, and returned with the horses to the cottage:—our journey from thence to the castle I need not repeat."

"It was doubtless, then," said Lauretta, "one of the banditti whom I saw enter a door in the hall of the castle, and whose appearance so much alarmed me, from my conjecturing him to have been Theodore?"

"It was," replied the count; "he knew not that we were returned, and having unguardedly entered the hall, made a precipitate retreat on seeing us; for we had determined, if possible, not to let you suppose the castle inhabited, that in case of your escaping from us, or hereafter, by any means, mixing again with the world, you might have no clue for suspecting those on whom your anger would have fallen to be concealed in a nest of deserted ruins."

"Who were those persons that approached my prison door on the second night of my confinement?" asked Lauretta.

"Some of the banditti," answered count Byroff, "who having been out for nearly three days on an expedition of plunder, knew not where you were lodged, and were proceeding to hide what they had acquired in a secret closet in the apartment where you were confined, but were immediately recalled by Kroonzer."

Thus was the perplexing mystery of Theodore's villany, and Lauretta's fears, explained away. Lauretta heard it all with wonder and secret satisfaction at the evils she had escaped. Count Byroff paused in silence, while his daughter offered up a short but heart-dictated thanksgiving to the power who had given her fortitude to bear up under her sufferings, and rewarded her confidence in him by his benign interposition: he then proceeded to inform her, how he had discovered her to be his child.

"You must recollect, that on your recovering from the swoon into which you fell in the hall of the castle, and finding yourself on the bed in the prison, you supplicated my protection: it was at that moment that your voice and features struck me, as bearing a strong resemblance to those of your deceased mother, when, on the last night I ever beheld her, she upbraided me with being the supposed murderer of count Frederic Cohenburg; but not knowing that she had ever borne a child, I could only wonder at so strong a resemblance between two persons whom I could not for an instant suppose to be connected by the most distant ties of blood, and I endeavoured to forget it.

"Kroonzer took upon himself the office of attending you; I wished it had been assigned to me; but as I could give no reason that would have appeared satisfactory to the banditti for asking to share it with him, I forebore to express my thoughts.

"On the morning of your escape from the castle, through the chasm in the wall of your prison made by the lightning, I was the first who discovered that you were gone."

Lauretta here interrupted her father, to remark to Alphonsus her providential escape with life in falling from so great a height; but count Byroff, smiling at the miraculous deliverance which she imagined she had experienced, explained to her, "that at that end of the castle which was inhabited by the banditti, stood seven towers, which rose gradually above each other, and that she had been confined in the lowest of these, the floor of which was not above three feet raised from the ground.

"None of the banditti in the retired parts of the building heard the falling of the wall: the one who had the watch in the hall of the castle heard the rumbling of falling stones, but it was so customary a sound amongst those decayed walls, which continually were crumbling on every slight shock of the weather, that he did not attend to it.

"Morning was far advanced, when passing by the turret in a short ramble I was taking for the benefit of the air, I perceived what had occurred; and entering to look whether you were still there, though I was well convinced I could not expect to find you, the cross which is now on your neck, and which from the figures carved upon it, I instantly recollected to be that I had given your mother, caught my eye, and so forcibly did this circumstance strengthen my belief, that I had not been deceived in imagining that I had discovered in you a likeness to my lost Lauretta, that I no longer hesitated to pronounce you her daughter, and count Frederic Cohenburg your father.

"Convinced as I now was that you was the offspring of my lost wife, and conscious that she could not have been a sufficient time from me to have borne a son of Theodore's age, even if his name, and Kroonzer's knowledge of his family, had not baffled the suppo-

sition, I immediately again began to doubt the veracity of the tale
Theodore had related concerning you, but resolved to conceal my
thoughts till Theodore's future conduct should elucidate the truth
of this mystery; I accordingly concealed the cross in my bosom,
and proceeded to inform Kroonzer of your escape.

"Kroonzer heard my intelligence with sorrow, and alarm for the
community, upon whom his temerity in introducing Theodore to a
knowledge of their haunt, might bring the worst of consequences,
provided you were not regained, and Theodore took measures of
vengeance against Kroonzer for his negligence, as he might deem
it, in suffering you to escape.

"Horsemen were immediately sent out in pursuit of you, but
no success attended their endeavours: the following evening Theodore arrived; disappointment rendered him almost frantic, and he
himself went in search of you, still solemnly vowing you were his
sister.

"Thus passed on several days, the banditti continually going
out by turns in pursuit of you, and again returning unsuccessful
to receive fresh orders from Kroonzer or Theodore, one of whom
remained constantly at the castle.

"At length one of the banditti, who had been out disguised,
brought intelligence, that a peasant whom he had questioned, had
told him, that on the very day you had escaped from the castle he
had seen the old hermit, who lived on the skirts of the forest, leading a female to his cell.

"Theodore had before this commanded the most secure place
about the castle to be prepared for your reception, in case you
should be retaken by him; and Kroonzer had prepared what was by
the banditti called the cavern, and to which there was a communication from an apartment in the castle; accordingly having learned
that it was in readiness to receive you, he took one of the banditti,
and as all the horses were out with others of the fraternity on an
expedition of plunder, set out on foot towards the hermitage.

"I resolved at once, if practicable, to ease my doubts, by informing myself whether you had any knowledge of my deceased wife;
I accordingly followed them, and having stationed myself amidst
some trees, close by which I knew they must pass in their return
to the castle, provided they found you in the hermitage, I resolved

at all risques to pronounce the name of my wife, supposing that if you had any knowledge of her, you must of course be acquainted with her name, and would on thus unexpectedly hearing it, utter some exclamation, from which I might gather what I so earnestly wished to learn; determining, if you were the child of my Lauretta, to befriend you for the sake of the love I had once borne her.

"Your answer thrilled my heart; it recalled to me more forcibly than before the recollection of her I had lost. Whilst Theodore was questioning you, I gained a stand opposite to the spot whence I had spoken to you, and when he rushed to the place from which the sound of my voice had proceeded, I rescued you from his accomplice, and then conducted you to the cavern, which, as having been the place mentioned by Theodore himself, I thought least likely for him to suppose to be your present place of concealment, as he would imagine you taken from him almost by supernatural means.

"Without any suspicion of my having been absent, I arrived at the castle some time before Theodore, who had been delayed by the assistance he had been obliged to give to his companion before he could restore him to his senses: I grieved that I had so hardly used one who had never injured, or even offended me; but it was my only method of rescuing you, undiscovered; and the anxiety of the moment would, I fear, had necessity required it, have tempted me to have done more; I thank heaven that it did not.

"The dagger which you doubtless beheld on the table, I left you as a safeguard against the violence of Theodore, should he by any means have discovered your retreat, and have assailed your person.

"I had the watch that night; trembling I flew to you, and I returned hardly able to contain my joy, that I had preserved, unhoped for, unexpected, my own daughter!

"Again Theodore and the banditti scoured the country in search of you, and horrid was the vengeance Theodore denounced against your protectors.

"I ventured no more to visit you till I again held the watch, against which night I had prepared for our escape, which the eye of providence, regardful of suffering innocence, prospered with its blessing.

"I durst not impart to the banditti the discovery I had made, lest

they should refuse their consent to my leaving them; and the alarm
I yesterday testified during our day's journey, proceeded from my
fear of their overtaking me, and separating me for ever from you; as
Kroonzer yesterday morning, when he departed after the death of
Theodore, refusing to hear me, bade me beware the vengeance due
to a traitor. But," continued the count, "we will seek some retired
spot where the secrecy to which my own safety at present enjoins
me, will, I trust, be my safeguard against the threatened danger."

Here ended the eventful history of count Byroff, who, with the
tear of parental affection starting in his eye, declared his sufferings
overpaid by their having led him at last to find an angel he knew not
to have been created; to whom he was bound by the most tender
ties of nature, and in whose smiles and endearments he might forget to reflect on past calamities.

CHAPTER XXI.

———————Let me be your servant:
*   *   *   *   *   *   *   *   *
———————I will follow thee,
To the last gasp, with truth and loyalty.
AS YOU LIKE IT.

DURING the day our travellers continued to advance on their journey, and when towards evening they again stopped for the night,
Alphonsus confessed himself so ill, as to be immediately obliged to
retire to bed.

The exertions of body together with the coldness of the air
on the night of his leaving Smaldart castle, in conjunction with the
precipitate and violent changes from grief to joy which his mind
had been lately undergoing, added to his endeavours for the last day
and night of concealing that he was otherwise than well, in order
to expedite their journey, and the safety of his Lauretta's father, had
reduced him to a state of great danger; his fever was returning with
increased violence, and with less strength on his part to combat
against its attacks.

Such medical assistance as the village afforded, count Byroff made it his immediate business to procure: Lauretta and her father watched over him during the night, and the morning brought with it increased symptoms of danger.

Till the fifth day the violence of his fever had abated only for short intervals, and the physician had given but slender hopes of his recovery: he now pronounced his patient free from danger, at the same time warning the count and Lauretta, against any indulgence which might endanger a relapse.

Lauretta had hitherto been the constant nurse of her husband, insomuch that count Byroff, moved by her entreaties to suffer her to remain with him she most loved, had, with no little alarm for her own safety, now seen her pass five nights without sleep, and an equal number of days without having retired above two hours together from her husband's chamber, which she had always passed rather in prayers for his amendment, than in attempts to enjoy that repose of which she stood so much in need for the preservation of her own health. On the pleasing change however in the fate of Alphonsus, he had rather commanded than prevailed with her to retire regularly for the night, having promised to be himself the nurse of Alphonsus during her slumbers; and if any material change took place in him, to bring her immediate intelligence of it.

Lauretta had not been long retired, when Alphonsus requiring some drink which was preparing by the hostess, the count went down to fetch it: as he was descending the stairs, he heard a confused noise of talking and laughing, which ceasing at momentary intervals, rendered audible the voice of a person whose lamentations seemed to produce the laughter of the hearers, and the words, *"que le diable m'emporte*, if I would not give all I am worth to be dead,"* followed by an ill restrained cry of the speaker, and a laugh, exaggerated beyond their feelings, on the part of the audience, brought him to the door of the kitchen. His attention, excited by what he had heard, was converted into no less astonishment, when, on his entering, a man, whose features the dim lamp hanging over the chimney had not at first suffered him to see distinctly, rising from his seat, and dropping from his hand a pot of wine, which he was just lifting to his mouth, ran up to him, and falling on his knees before him, clasped his arms round him, and exclaimed, *"Oh, vous voila! vous voila!"* he recognised the person of Jacques Perlet.—"He

is crazy, he is mad," called out two or three of the by-standers, and
again a loud laugh burst from every mouth.

Joy for some moments suspended the utterance of Jacques, and
surprise that of the count; which silence the host misconstruing
on the part of the count, advanced to rid him of his troublesome
detainer, and for that purpose, seized with both his hands Jacques's
left arm; this rough handling first recalled Jacques to his recollection, and immediately springing on his feet, he levelled a blow at
the host for attempting to tear him from the count, which, had not
the count arrested his arm, and thus prevented its full execution,
might have proved of fatal consequences to the unwarranted inter-
ferer.

Those who laugh irrationally at trifles, laugh equally whoever
is the cause; thus the whole merriment of the kitchen was now
turned against the precipitately retreating landlord; but as ridicule
has often produced valour in a breast which nature never implanted
in it, the landlord, with a countenance which seemed in return for
this raillery to wish every one present in his situation, with exactly
his feelings (by no means a slender punishment), was advancing to
the combat, when the count stepping between the combatants, explained in as few words as he could convey his meaning in, that the
offender was a person in whom he felt interest, and that he wished
the dispute to cease.

A smaller plea would have quieted the fury of the host; and
all Jacques wished for, was a moment for testifying the joy and triumph he felt at again finding the count, which he did by a loud
huzza, and exclaiming "that the count was the only good man ever
created, except his own father, who was dead."

The confusion of fists being ended, the confusion of tongues
ensued; Jacques stood on one side of the count, exclaiming inco-
herently, "Ah, *monsieur*, how could you run away and not take me
with you? I am sure I would have been faithful to you: you know I
would.—I would not have staid there without you for all the world;
it was worse than the *maudite Bastile*:—well, *Dieu merci*, I have found
you now, and if ever I leave you again, I wish my uncle and Kroonzer
may both catch me the next minute."—On the other side stood the
host, who, regardless of Jacques's ejaculation, contended to relate,
that Jacques had arrived there on foot about two hours before, that

he had inquired for a person, by whom the host now found him to have meant the count, whose dress he could not describe, and with whom he had sometimes said he expected to find a lady; sometimes a lady and a young man, and sometimes that he was alone; in short, that he had talked so inconsistently, and so much in French, that they had not understood above half what he said, only that he had often mentioned the Bastile; that they at last conjectured him to be mad, and when the count entered, he confessed they had been amusing themselves at his expense, till he had wept for vexation; added to this, the hostess, whose voice was none of the softest, was continually interlarding her husband's story with her own emendations and additions, and no one else in the kitchen desisted from giving their own opinion, whether it was attended to or not.

The count seized the first moment of silence, which many attempts to articulate at length gained him from that part of his audience by which he wished to be heard, to announce to the host and hostess that Jacques was a person for whom he entertained a warm friendship, and to desire that he might be accommodated to his ease, making himself answerable for the charge: he then turned to Jacques, and having easily convinced him that he was under the necessity of leaving him to watch over a sick friend, and with a caution to be careful what he said, and promising to see him early in the morning, he returned to the chamber of Alphonsus with the drink he had left it to procure.

Count Byroff was far from being displeased at so unexpectedly again meeting with Jacques Perlet; he knew him to be faithfully attached to him, and promised himself that he would be a useful companion on their intended journey; that Jacques had contrived to escape from the banditti, after having effected it from the Bastile, could not much excite his wonder; but what chance had fortunately conducted him to the spot where he now was, his curiosity was raised to learn.

At an early hour Lauretta returned to the chamber of her husband; she found him fallen into a soft slumber: the count stole silently out of the room, and left his daughter to the willing task of watching over her Alphonsus.

Early as the hour was, Jacques was risen, and the count descending, found him waiting his arrival, seated on a bench without the door of the little inn, where he was practising his trade on his own shoes, which were a good deal the worse for the journey they had performed.

On seeing the count, he sprang from his seat, and shaking him by the hand with both his, reiterated his joy at their fortunate meeting: the count in return acknowledged the pleasure it gave him, and having told Jacques to resume his seat, and placed himself by his side, he began to inquire what accident had brought him to that spot.

"No accident at all, *monsieur*," replied Jacques, "but chance; as soon as I had got away from the old castle full of robbers, I resolved to walk all over the empire, and ask every body I met after you, till I found you; and you see, *monsieur*, what good fortune I have had, *graces à Dieu*; and I hope you won't send me away from you now, *monsieur*."

The count immediately eased his doubts on this head, and then proceeded to inform him of the occasion of his having left the banditti, and also gave him the outlines of such occurrences as had befallen him since their last meeting.

"Well, *monsieur*, and how do you think I got away from them?" cried Jacques, in return to the count's narrative.

"I know you have a ready invention," returned count Byroff, "but cannot possibly presume to guess in what manner you exercised it in effecting your escape."

"Then I'll tell you, *monsieur*:—when Kroonzer came back at night, and told us of Theodore's death, and that the lady was your daughter, some said one thing of you, and some another; however they all agreed that it was natural enough for you to go with your child, and that they believed you were too much a man of honour to betray them, after they had been so kind to you; so they resolved not to seek after you, or to hurt you, if you again fell into their hands. Well, *monsieur*, when I heard you were gone, I had a strange inclination to be gone too; but I durst not ask, for I thought perhaps they might not put so much trust in me as a man of honour, as they did in you, and would keep such a tight watch over me, that I might never get away from them at all; so I only pretended to cry, and be very unhappy, because I might never see you again; and I declared, that if you did not come back next day, I would kill myself: they only laughed at me, but, however, I knew what I was doing, and did not mind them a straw; next day I was quite melancholy, and at night they asked me, whether I would keep my word; I did not answer them, but went and threw myself on my bed, drest as I was: when they were all asleep, I got up, and running past the man who had the watch in the hall, I made for the muddy pond on the west side of the castle, and having thrown in a great stone, a hat, and handkerchief, I climbed up, like a cat, into the top of the old willow that stands on its margin; presently several of the banditti came and dragged for me in the pond; the hat which they saw left them no room to doubt that I had thrown myself in, and not finding my body after some time searching, they concluded me sunk into the mud and smothered, and away they went neither pleased nor sorry at what had happened: when they were gone I came down from the tree, and ever since, *monsieur*, I have been wandering about, I hardly know where."

The physician arriving to attend his patient put an end to their conversation, as count Byroff rose to accompany him to the chamber of Alphonsus.

In the course of the day Jacques was introduced to the knowledge of Alphonsus and Lauretta, the former of whom received him as graciously as his situation would permit; the latter, in a transport of gratitude, as the sole means of her having ever known a father.

Alphonsus continued rapidly to regain his health and strength, and at the expiration of ten other days the physician pronounced him able to recommence his journey; our travellers accordingly, with the addition of Jacques to their former party, again set forward on their route, and no occurrence worthy of notice happened till their arrival at a solitary inn, which was situated in the road between Cohenburg castle, and the mansion of count Frederic, and about a league distant from each.

CHAPTER XXII.

How many things are there that the fancy makes
terrible by night, which the day turns into ridicule!
                                        SENECA'S MORALS.

FORTUNATELY for Alphonsus, who wished not to be known, the little inn had changed its inhabitants since he had last visited it; thus
no suspicion of their being any other than common travellers was
entertained by the landlord when they entered his dwelling.

Shortly after their arrival Alphonsus took occasion to lead to
the subject on which his thoughts were unremittingly bent.

"That's a fine castle that stands about a league from hence,"
said he, addressing his host.

"Yes, sir," was the answer.

"Who inhabits it?"

"Nobody."

"To whom does it belong?"

"To the Cohenburg family."

"And why do they not reside in it?"

"Ah, sir! they are all dead but one poor gentleman, the brother
of him that used to live there, and he can no where find rest for his
guilty mind: folks say he is gone into a monastery to repent of his
sins, and make his peace with heaven."

"Of what crime is he accused?"

"Why, sir, I have not lived here long, but as I have heard people
say, count Frederic, the youngest brother, he that I now speak of,
and who used to live in a handsome mansion about a league from
hence to the left, and which is now inhabited by one count Radvelt,
was so jealous of his brother's castle and riches, that he had him
murdered by assassins in the Wolf's Wood, in his return home to
his castle, from Vienna; and then killed his brother's wife and son
with his own hand. The matter was pretty well hushed up at first;
it was given out that the countess had died of grief for the loss of
her husband, and that her son had killed himself in a fit of madness:
nobody much believed it, but as nobody had any proofs to the con-

trary, nothing durst be said; but the villain soon betrayed himself, for he staid at the castle but two or three days, and then went no one knows whither."

"And did he leave nobody in the castle?"

"No, sir, nobody; people do tell strange stories that it is haunted, and that he was frightened away by the ghost of the murdered count; and some say, that a bell is tolled by it every night at midnight."

"I have a strange curiosity to visit this castle."

"You had better not, sir."

"Why so, friend?"

"Why, sir, people think that the reason of the ghost's ringing the bell is, that it is shut up by priestcraft within the walls of the castle, and prevented from coming out; and that it tolls the bell to call somebody in, that it may reveal the murder of its body to them, and frighten them into promising to revenge its death. Nobody goes near the castle on that account."

Alphonsus pretended to smile at the tale related by his host, but it had an effect on his feelings which he could ill conceal: all his efforts to coerce the wish of immediately gratifying his curiosity he found to be in vain, and he declared to the count and Lauretta, that he felt an impulse he could not resist, to certify himself that night as to the tolling of the bell: in vain did they remonstrate, and endeavour to prevail with him not to leave the inn until the morning; but there was a resolute and anxious wildness in his countenance to follow the impulse he had described, which seemed to bid defiance to every objection.

The tears however of Lauretta, whose alarm was raised, she could hardly express on what account, to a pitch of agony, at the idea of Alphonsus that night approaching the castle, brought him to consent to defer his visit to the following day, on condition that if he could gain no light on the mystery which occupied his mind by traversing the castle, and examining his father's cabinet, she would not object to their there taking up their abode, which he declared would be an alleviation of his sorrows and perplexities.

After a sleepless night, Alphonsus rose to an uneasy morn; every the most minute circumstance attendant on the mystery wherein his happiness was involved, had been turned over in his thoughts during the night; and as heretofore, instead of deriving any clue of elucidation from reflection, the mystery had only thickened upon increased conjecture.

Again he felt scruples arising in his mind against opposing the injunction laid on him by his mother: again his doubts were lulled by the secrecy he had vowed to maintain, relative to any discovery he might make in the castle, which, notwithstanding the strong impulse he felt to visit it, reason seemed to contradict he should do; and then again he felt a momentary fear, for which he shuddered to account, that a snare might be spread for taking his life if he returned to the castle.

Judging it however most consistent with the faith he owed himself to go alone to the castle, he avowed his intention to his Lauretta, and resigning her after a fond embrace to the care of her father till his return, he departed, followed by the eyes of Lauretta till the intervening branches of the trees shut him from her sight.

Alphonsus rode swiftly forward, lost in a maze of fluctuating thought; at length taking a turn of the well-known road, Cohenburg castle burst full upon his sight; he beheld it with mingled sensations of melancholy pleasure, and awful apprehension. Crossing the moat, he proceeded to the stable from whence he had taken his steed on the morning on which he had last departed from the castle: fond remembrance was hasty to contrast the present gloom of desertion with former scenes of happier aspect;—recollection became too painful to be constrained, and burst its way from his eyes in burning drops of sorrow.

Having left his steed in the stable, he proceeded to the castle-gate; it was locked, and bade defiance to his repeated efforts to open it: he next attempted the postern-gate, it in like manner resisted his endeavours. He ran round the castle, gazing upon it in every part, and trying to recollect some window by which he might effect his entrance; he would not trust to recollection for believing them all too high, and too strongly barricaded to favour his attempts, but examined every one separately in the circuit of the castle.

Tortured by having his attempts thus baffled, he threw himself upon the ground in despair; in a few minutes, however, recollecting that inactivity could add little to forward his wishes, he rose from his situation, resolving to return to the inn, and ask advice of count Byroff how to proceed in his present dilemma. Once again he exerted his utmost endeavours to open the two gates, but they proved equally vain with his former efforts; he mounted his steed and returned to the inn.

Alphonsus immediately related his adventure, and opened a consultation with the count, on what steps were the best to be taken by him.

"Much deliberation," the count said, "seemed to be required on a subject of so delicate a nature: the gates of the castle being locked might be construed into an indication either of its being inhabited, or not being inhabited. If it was inhabited, the prevalent idea of its being deserted plainly proved it was the shelter of some person who wished to live in obscurity, and would, from this motive, perhaps, revenge the entrance of any one who dared to trespass on his retirement."

"How can he wish to live unknown?" cried Alphonsus, "who every night publicly announces his dwelling by tolling the castle bell?"

"Have you any proof of this?" said the count.

"The young miner, and now again our landlord, both assert that it is so."

"But they never heard it; nor likely any one who trembles while he relates it, has any authority for it but the dream of some old woman, who having talked all day of the occurrences at the castle, had seen them in her sleep in aggravated colours."

"I will certify myself in this point," returned Alphonsus, "before I proceed to any measures for entering the castle; I will watch the tolling of the bell this night."

After promising Lauretta that he would use no means for entering the castle that night, she consented that he should watch on the outside, in order to learn the truth of the story which had been related of the midnight bell, provided her father accompanied him; but as Alphonsus declared that he could not leave her at the inn with satisfaction to himself, unless the count remained with her, it was at length agreed that Jacques Perlet should be the companion of Alphonsus on his nightly expedition.

As Alphonsus was well aware that his going out in the night could not fail being known by the host, and excite his curiosity, he determined to inform him, that he meant to go and listen for the tolling of the singular bell he had mentioned to be sounded every night at the castle; the host, unsuspicious that Alphonsus meant more than his words conveyed, endeavoured to dissuade him from his purpose by all the arguments of blind superstition, and vulgar fear; and finding him resolute in his purpose, besought him to wear a little cross on his expedition, which, he said, "had belonged to his deceased wife, and which having been kissed by the pope, would secure him from the influence of the devil, and his fiends."

To avoid the imputation of obstinacy and irreligion, Alphonsus accepted the offer of the sacred cross, and placed it within his waist-coat.

At a little after ten Alphonsus and Jacques set out for the castle on foot.

Where flesh and blood were to be contended with by day-light, Jacques was no coward, but a breath of wind, or a shadow in a dark night, were great settlers of his valour. Count Byroff knowing his disposition, had not made him acquainted with any of the particulars which constituted Alphonsus' curiosity in regard to the bell which was sounded at the old castle; and as he fortunately had not heard of any dreadful appearance which had been seen in the vicinity of this building, he endeavoured all the way to keep up his courage by repeating to himself, "that the sound of a bell in the night could be no more than the sound of a bell in the day."

Alphonsus, wrapt in reflection, was not much disposed to converse, and they had proceeded nearly a third of the way without speaking, when Jacques suddenly exclaimed, "Do you hear it, *monsieur?*"

"What?" asked Alphonsus.

"The bell, *monsieur?*"

"We are yet too distant from the castle to catch the sound," returned Alphonsus.

"So I thought, *monsieur:*—that was the reason I asked."

Had Jacques spoken the truth, he would have confessed that he found it very melancholy to proceed so far in silence, and that he despaired of drawing Alphonsus into conversation by any other subject, than the one on which his thoughts were then bent; his stratagem, however, answered but little to his wishes, for Alphonsus again sunk into silent reflection.

"The moon will be up presently, *monsieur*, it begins to grow a little light already."

Alphonsus raised his eyes for a moment to the atmosphere, and again dropped them to their former situation.

"I wonder how many stars there are, *monsieur*:—did you ever count them?"

"No."

"Nor I, *monsieur*;—I wonder whether any body ever did?"

No answer was returned.

"I dare say there are more than a thousand in all; I am sure I can see five hundred to-night, and there are often as many more on a clear night; a'n't there, *monsieur?*"

"Of what?"

"Stars, *monsieur*."

Jacques now anxiously waited for a rejoinder, but his hopes were deceived. Alphonsus had spoken to the few words he had accidentally heard, without entering into the subject to which they belonged.

Now the silence had been once broken, its recommencement appeared more unpleasant to Jacques, than whilst it had remained totally uninterrupted; his tongue ached to relieve his eyes and ears, which were unremittingly looking out for shapeless monsters, and listening for uncouth sounds; singing and whistling by night he had heard ridiculed as betraying fear; and he could for some time think on no other expedient to divert the way; at last a lucky thought entered his head: "I think I'll try and count the stars myself, *monsieur*," he said, and immediately began counting, *une, deux, trois*, &c. passing them, as he pronounced the number, on his fingers: he chuckled at this happy expedient; it exercised both his eyes and tongue, and amused his hearing; thus passed on another third of the way; Jacques never the nearer in his knowledge of the numeration of the heavenly bodies, but quite as near in reality as he wished to be. At last wearied by his employment, and not at all satisfied with hearing only his own voice, he desisted from his calculation, and lowered his eyes to the spot where he supposed to find Alphonsus walking by his side; but he was not there; for a few moments he stood motionless, then looking round on all sides, as far as the slender light of the faintly shining stars would permit him to carry his sight, and not beholding his companion, he ran straight forward in the path along which he supposed Alphonsus to have proceeded, as fast as he could move his legs, and attended by all the noise his overstrained voice could make.

Alphonsus, inattentive to every object but what was passing in his own mind, had insensibly passed his companion, whose pace had been retarded by his pretended studies, and had gained some ground upon him ere Jacques perceived his advance; now, however, roused from his reflections by Jacques' exclamations, he stopped for him, and they were quickly again united, to the no small satisfaction of one party; when an explanation of their parting took place on both sides, and Jacques determining not to let the conversation he had now raised, flag, asked Alphonsus "how many ghosts he had ever seen?"

"Not one," replied Alphonsus.

"Then you have seen one less than me, *monsieur*; and that's what always makes me afraid of being alone in the dark."

"Now I, on the contrary, should have supposed the dark to have been very agreeable to one of your credulous disposition."

"Why so, *monsieur?*"

"Because I should conceive that in it you could see neither objects to please nor alarm you."

"Oh dear, *monsieur*, how you talk! why ghosts always light themselves."

Alphonsus had not spirits either to rally Jacques on his false ideas, or to endeavour to correct them by the arguments of reason, and he remained silent.

Jacques had now a clue for conversation, and he chattered on about spirits, ghosts, and witches, to his own joint amusement and terror, till a few minutes brought them within sight of Cohenburg castle, and all his faculties were then absorbed in the use of his eyes.

They advanced within a few yards of the building to a small elevation of the turf, where Alphonsus proposed they should sit down, and wait the expected sound of the bell. The moon was breaking from under a retiring cloud, and, shedding her partial influence on the building, while its shadow fell upon the place which Alphonsus had chosen for his watching post, gave a pleasing yet melancholy aspect to the scene. It produced sensations in the mind of Jacques which he felt at a loss to explain, and after repeated hesitations how to express himself, he exclaimed, "Well, if ever I am to see another ghost, I am sure this is just the place I should expect to meet it in!"

"Folly!" cried Alphonsus: "how should you expect to see what never existed?"

"*Mon Dieu, monsieur*, how you talk! why all the priests in the world should not make me believe, I did not see one that time I was going to mention to you."

"Well, well, then you did," said Alphonsus, softened by the scene into reflections too dear to be easily shaken off, and wishing to prevent their farther interruption by coalescing in opinion with his companion.

"I thought you would believe me at last, *monsieur*," said Jacques, who flattered himself he had made a convert of Alphonsus: "I'll tell you the whole story,—may I, *monsieur?*"

"Oh yes," replied Alphonsus, thoroughly determined not to attend to it, and hoping, by this indulgence of his friend's garrulity, to free himself from the trouble of replying to his questions.

Having cast his eyes around, as a kind of security preparative to his dismal story, and moved a few inches nearer to Alphonsus, Jacques, thus began: "When I was about fifteen years old, *monsieur*, my father lived in a little village about a *lieue* from Desmartin, on the road to Paris; ours was a lonely little cottage, for it stood quite at the end of the village, and above a hundred paces distant from the next house; my grandmother was alive then, poor old soul, and she was as much afraid of a ghost as me; so one winter's evening, just before we went to bed, there comes a rap, or indeed it was more like a scratch at the door. 'Come in,' says my father; nobody answered, nor the door did not open; so my father bid me open it, and I did, but nobody was there to be seen; so as I thought it might be somebody that had a mind to frighten us, and had hid themselves behind the wood-stack at the corner of the house, I ran to look, for it was moon-light; and there I saw a man in black, kneeling down, without a head; and when I called out for help, he got up and ran away as fast as ever he could, and when he had got a little way off, his back looked as white as snow.

"Well, *monsieur*, frightened enough I was, as you may suppose, and so was my father, for he saw it too: and a little while after my grandmother died. 'Now the murder's out,' says my father: 'that was a warning of *la bonne's* death: we shall see no more ghosts now.' 'I hope not, I am sure,' said I; but he was wrong: for about a month after, one night when the wind was high, there was such a noise in the kitchen after we were gone to bed, that it waked us all, and in a minute or two the door between my father's chamber and mine burst open, as if *le diable lui même* had kicked it; then again we heard the noise in the kitchen, and in a few minutes came such a crash, as if the very roof had split over our heads; I covered myself with the bed cloaths; father said he would go down and see what it was, when, just as he was getting out of bed, there was such a rustling on the stairs; and then it seemed to come into the chamber under the door, and all on a sudden a long, deep, hoarse, frightful . . . ." At this instant the bell in the south turret of the castle tolled several strokes, which sounded on the air hollow and dismal; Alphonsus started from his seat, and Jacques remained sitting on the turf in a state of fear scarcely a degree removed from petrifaction.

CHAPTER XXIII.

O, matter and impertinency mixt!
Reason in madness!

                              LEAR.

COUNT BYROFF and Lauretta, eager to learn the result of Alphonsus's watching, had determined not to retire to rest till his return, which they imagined could not be later than an hour after midnight: however, he arrived not with the expected hour, and to add to their consternation, two o'clock brought back Jacques alone, with a countenance distorted by fear and anxiety.

Running up to count Byroff, he exclaimed, "Oh, *monsieur, monsieur!* the devils have got him; they have shut him up in that cursed old castle; I'd wager my life he never gets out again: *pour l'amour de Dieu*, let us raise the village here hard by, and pull down the walls."

Count Byroff could not be a moment at a loss to understand to whom he referred; but Lauretta, who had fainted, demanded his care prior to his asking an explanation of Jacques's words.

The landlord brought a glass of water to Lauretta.—"I told the young gentleman how it would be," he said, "if he would but have taken an old man's advice, and not have gone, he had been safe; I said there was no good in the spirits ringing that bell."

"I have seen three of them," returned Jacques, "as tall again as you or me, and all over as black as a crow, face, hands, and all."

"The virgin bless us all!" said the landlord, crossing himself, and raising his eyes to heaven.

In a few minutes Lauretta revived,—she flew to Jacques,—"Where is my Alphonsus?—is he in the castle?—answer me."

"Yes, locked in," replied Jacques; "but don't be afraid, *madame*: I dare say the ghosts don't mean to hurt him, for they are all gone away, and left him."

"Explain your words: what do you mean to convey by this inconsistent jargon?—Speak plainly, tell us every thing as it happened," said count Byroff.

"Why, *monsieur*, when the bell tolled—"

"Oh, then you have heard it;—aye, I knew I was right," interrupted the landlord.

"Oh yes, heard it, *mon Dieu*, I shall never forget it. When the bell tolled, *monsieur* Alphonsus said, he was sure then there must be somebody within the castle; and so he ran away to watch whether he could see a light in any part of the other side of the castle, and ordered me to keep my eye fixed on that opposite to which I was sitting. I sat still more than half an hour, and he did not come back: sometimes I ventured to look, and sometimes I did not: at last I saw him coming towards me; pleased enough was I, and I ran to meet him; he had seen nothing, no more had I. He said it was very odd, and he would only just try whether the gates were locked yet or not, and come back alone in the morning; and I told him I thought it would be much the best way. The great gate was locked: but when we came to a little gate at one end of the castle, it was partly open. He seemed very much surprised; and without saying any thing more to me, than bidding me wait for him where I was, and on no account to follow him, he ran in."

"In the dark?" said Lauretta.

"Yes, *madame.*"

"He cannot be in any danger on that account," said count Byroff: "he doubtless knows every footstep about the castle."

"Angels guard him!" exclaimed Lauretta; the tears rolled swiftly down her cheeks.

"Go on," said the count to Jacques.

"Well, *monsieur*, I waited and waited, and he did not come back: I was frightened to stay very near the castle, so I went and sat myself down at a little distance opposite to the little gate, when presently out came the three black things I told you of, and——"

"What things?" eagerly asked Lauretta, who had not heard Jacques mention them before.

"Why, *madame*, ghosts I am sure they were, for they stalked past where I was sitting, without speaking, and I could not hear them set a foot; and the last of them locked the gate as he came out, for I heard the key turn in the lock."

"Did you try whether it was locked?" asked the count.

"No, *monsieur*, I durst not go near it, for fear they should appear again, and take me to task for meddling; so when I had waited a good while longer, and *monsieur* Alphonsus did not come, I ran home to tell you what had happened; and a fine solitary walk I have had of it, *monsieur*; *graces à Dieu*, that I got here at all;—only feel how warm I am with running," continued he, turning to the host.

Count Byroff and Lauretta fixed their eyes on each other in silence, but both their countenances expressively asked the important question of what steps could be taken for the best.

They could ask no foreign assistance without betraying the secret which Alphonsus so strongly wished to remain unknown, and the mystery attendant on which he might at the very moment be solving.

The determination of one moment, the reflection of the next rejected. Lauretta was suffering on the rack of apprehension, and count Byroff was tortured by the agony he perceived his child enduring.

In little more than an hour, a loud knock at the door called out the landlord; Alphonsus rushed in, and threw himself upon a seat, regardless of surrounding objects.

Neither the congratulations of Jacques on his safe return, nor the caresses of his Lauretta, could for some moments obtain even a look in return: a frantic wildness was depicted on his countenance, and his stretched eyes were fixed on vacancy.

Count Byroff requested the landlord and Jacques to retire, they reluctantly complied with his petition.

"Oh, Alphonsus!" said Lauretta, throwing herself on his neck, "what new affliction has happened to you?—what aggravated sorrow is it, that deprives you of the power of teaching me to sympathise in your grief?—Tell me, I beseech you! 'twere mitigation of the agony I now experience, to share with you the most complicated misery."

Alphonsus answered her not.

Sinking on her knees, she clasped his;—"Speak, I conjure you, if you love me: ease these cruel fears: what can I do to serve you?—Name what you wish, and you shall find me ready to obey you."

Springing from her side, "Hate me," he exclaimed with increasing wildness, "hate me! I know you will,—you must hate me."

"Never! witness heaven!—can you suppose so meanly of me, that accumulated misfortune shall win from me the regard of him I once have loved? The hard dealing of the world towards you, shall only strengthen my love for you; and if you still account it as worthy your possession as you once did, your loss shall be your gain."

"Oh that I were worthy of that treasure!" he cried: "but an angel's love like yours must draw down curses on a wretch, whose disobedience to a mother's last command has called her from the silent grave!—Yes, I have seen her!—seen her honoured shade, come to upbraid me for my want of confidence in her commands; to scorch my eyes, and swell with tides of grief my heart-strings till they crack, and end the torture of this maddened brain!"—Again he sunk into the chair.

Lauretta wept, and count Byroff supported her in his arms.— "Oh, my foreboding heart!" she cried, "this danger I foresaw."

" 'Tis here," cried Alphonsus, again starting up; "here, hot and rankling: a parent's curse for disobedience, shot from the glaring eyes of death!"—He turned to Lauretta: his eye regained its wonted calmness.—"Do not you curse me too: I never disobeyed you; say, you will not."

"Have I not this instant conjured you to listen to my vows of love, of truth, of constancy?"

"But you may turn cruel."—The tears stole down his cheek.— "My mother was once kind, as you are now; and for one, one act of disobedience, though my rent heart could no longer exist in uncertainty, she has—Oh, had you seen her!" a sigh, drawn from the bottom of his heart, followed:—falling on his knees, he clasped Lauretta's hand, and pulled her down by him;—"Pray with me; pray to my mother for her forgiveness."—He clasped his hands, and seemed to pray inwardly some moments, whilst his countenance underwent various changes of frantic sorrow and pain: at length he exclaimed, "Oh! revoke, revoke—" The remainder of the sentence died on his tongue, and he fell to the ground.

Count Byroff immediately called in the assistance of Jacques, and Alphonsus was conveyed between them to a bed; and it was, for nearly an hour, a doubt to the count whether he lived or not: at length, when he again raised his eyelids, his eyes which had before betrayed the wildest frenzy, bespoke the most painful sorrow: he looked anxiously round the apartment, and discovering Lauretta, he beckoned eagerly to her; she flew to his side: he grasped her hand in his,—"Do not leave me! promise you will not leave me."

"Indeed I will not," she answered.

"Why are you not in bed?" he rejoined: "I have had so horrid a dream!—Oh!"

Lauretta turned her face aside to conceal her tears.

Alphonsus looked stedfastly on count Byroff:—"You here, my friend? and you too?" observing Jacques—"Did you hear me call out in my dream?"—He then seemed suddenly to observe that he was not undrest, and lying only on the outside of the bed; he looked round in surprise, and tacit inquiry of the cause: then, seeming to recollect himself, he started, a degree of wildness flashed in his eyes, and he exclaimed, "It was reality; it was no dream; would to God it had been!"

The night passed on mournfully: Alphonsus answered rationally, but in slow and desponding accents, to every question that bordered not upon the subject which tingled on his heart. Once count

Byroff ventured to touch upon the tender chord; his words then became incoherent, and his gestures indicated a heated brain.

Lauretta became more affected, and count Byroff more alarmed. Jacques wept, prayed, consoled Lauretta, and advised the count by turns, not forgetting to whisper at intervals to the land-lord, "that he was sure the black devils had done all the mischief." The host on his part entreated the count, that a friar might be sent for, to pray by Alphonsus, from the monastery of the Holy Spirit, which he said was not above half a league distant.

Alphonsus continued in the same state; and towards noon Lau-retta entreated that the landlord's advice might be put in execution. Count Byroff had not much faith in the effect of prayer on a mind disordered by frenzy, but readily consented to the petition of his daughter; and the landlord offered himself to be their messenger to the monastery: some travellers, however, entering at the very mo-ment the host was about to set out, he was obliged to delay going; but Lauretta's anxiety making every lost moment of consequence to the salvation of her husband, a little boy from the neighbouring village, who happened by chance to be passing by, was prevailed on by the promise of a trifling reward to show Jacques the road to the holy mansion.

In little more than an hour Jacques returned, accompanied by a brother of the monastery, who, in addition to his holy office, was skilled in the art of physic.

Count Byroff met him at the door of Alphonsus's apartment, and leading him to the bed, solely informed him, that the senses of the youth, for whom he requested his assistance, had been de-ranged by some recent and aggravated calamities, which his state of mind had rendered it impossible for him to explain.

The friar requested him to name what he thought to be the cause of his malady; count Byroff declared himself ignorant of it.

The holy man took Alphonsus's hand in one of his, and placed the fingers of the other on his pulse: Alphonsus raised his eyes, and fixing them stedfastly on the countenance of the friar for some mo-ments, he exclaimed, "Who art thou!—Thy garb bespeaks thee a comforter:—dost thou bring me pardon?—Has she pronounced my forgiveness?"

"Compose thyself, my son: confide in heaven, and hope the best," was the answer.

"Shame, shame!" returned Alphonsus: "thou art a deceiver: thy outward garb speaks hope to wretchedness, and thy false tongue belies his expectations.—Away, away! in pity do not torture me."

Alphonsus placed his hand before his eyes, and sunk on his pillow. The friar turned to count Byroff and Lauretta;—"There is some concealed sense even in this seeming madness," he said; "has he been ever thus before?"

"Never," said Lauretta.

"The cause was sudden then?" said the holy man, addressing Lauretta.

"And unknown to us," she returned.

"I will lull awhile his imagination by a draught of a healing and composing nature, and trust its powers will add much to recall his wandering senses."

He then knelt, and prayed devoutly to the divine power to assist his earnest endeavours for the restitution of mental and bodily health to his patient.—Lauretta joined fervently in the prayer.

The friar then departed, and Jacques accompanied him to the monastery, to bring back the medicine he had recommended for Alphonsus.

CHAPTER XXIV.

Now o'er the one-half world
Nature seems dead, and wicked dreams abuse
The curtain'd sleep; now witchcraft celebrates
Pale Hecate's offerings, and wither'd murder,
Alarum'd by his sentinel, the wolf,
Whose howl's his watch, thus with his stealthy pace,
With Tarquin's ravishing strides, towards his design
Moves like a ghost.
                              MACBETH.

WHEN Jacques returned, count Byroff immediately saw by his countenance that he was brimful of some intelligence which he wished to communicate to him; and accordingly, a few minutes after he had left the chamber, he followed him out.

"Ah, *monsieur*," cried Jacques, on beholding him, "I am glad you are come down, I have got something so unaccountable to tell you, and I did not know whether I might mention it before *madame.*"

"To what does it relate?" asked the count anxiously.

"Why, *monsieur*, you shall hear. When I got to the monastery, the old friar desired me to wait in the *refectoire*, in one corner of which was a door a little way open, and behind it I could hear glasses jingling, and people talking and laughing; so, when the friar was gone, I crept a little nearer to the door to listen what they were after, for my curiosity was a good deal raised, I must confess: when I first overheard them, one was telling a story about the pope, I fancy; for it was a man that they said was a good deal like an old woman, and the cardinals wished him dead; so when it was done, says another, 'Come, father Francisco, give us a toast.' 'I will,' says he:—'Here's the ghost at the castle, and wishing it may ring as long as we all live.' Well, *monsieur*, they all laughed, and I could hear them pouring out the liquor, and then they repeated what father Francisco had said, and then I could hear them set down the empty glasses. 'I wonder where the young count is,' says another, after a minute or two's silence. 'Why, as to that,' said another—and just then I heard the old man coming back with the draught; so I stepped forward to meet him, and when I had got it he let me out, and so I heard no more."

Count Byroff having told Jacques to wait within Lauretta's call, walked out upon the green before the little inn, to indulge the reflections for which the conversation Jacques had overheard, had given him a subject.

It appeared to him evident beyond a doubt that the midnight bell at the castle was tolled by the friars belonging to the monastery of the Holy Spirit, as a confirmation of the castle's being haunted, which report they had probably been the first to circulate, to promote some private interest: thus he conceived also that the black figures which Jacques had seen issuing from the postern gate of the castle, were three of the fraternity, who had been to the castle for the purpose of raising the nightly alarm by sounding the bell, and were returning to the monastery when Jacques beheld them; that they had gone into the castle at first unseen by Alphonsus and

Jacques, and the open gate by which the former had entered the castle had doubtless been left so by them, whilst they were in the castle, unsuspicious of any one having ventured to approach so near a place of such general horror as that building was described to be by all that knew it. But how was he to account for Alphonsus's excessive alarm, which could not have been produced by the appearance of three friars, if even he had seen them, which circumstances seemed to contradict that he had, or they him?—for his getting out of the castle, as Jacques had said that the last figure had locked the gate?—and above all for Alphonsus's assertion that he had seen his mother's shade?—Might it not have been the work of priestcraft? he asked himself; but his knowledge of Alphonsus's manly courage, which, though his eyes might have been a moment deceived by any false appearance, would have led him to have investigated the truth, ere he gave himself up to those feelings which alone could have reduced his faculties to the state he was now in, instantly contradicted the idea. Lengthened conjecture tended but to perplex him, and he determined, if the potion administered by father Nicholas had not the desired effect, at all hazards to himself to attempt the solution of the mystery which clouded the castle equally with the real cause of Alphonsus's present state of mind, by personal investigation.

The draught given by the friar was of a somnific nature, and in a short time after its being swallowed by Alphonsus, produced the intended effect.

Towards midnight count Byroff with much difficulty prevailed on Lauretta, who had not tasted rest the preceding night, to retire to bed.

With the dawn Alphonsus awoke; he raised himself on the bed, and drawing back the curtain, seemed to listen,—"Hark!—was it not she that spoke?"

"Who, my friend?" said count Byroff, advancing to the bed.

"My mother."

A pause ensued.—Count Byroff wished to pursue the discourse, but knew not in what manner to continue it.

"Will you go with me to the castle?" said Alphonsus.

"Why do you wish it?—Is she there?"

"Not now, I fear," replied Alphonsus, raising his eyes to the casement, as indicating that day-light was beginning to appear. "It was in the dead of the night that I saw her; did I not tell you that she had a burning lamp in her hand?"

"No."

"But she was dead: her cheeks were pale and sunk; my disobedience called her from the grave: I would fain see her once more, and kneel for her forgiveness: and would she then but calm her angry looks, I should die happy."

"Did she speak angrily to you?"

"I know not whether she spoke at all, my eyes and heart ached so I could not bear her sight;—feel how my temples beat even now."

Count Byroff raised his hand in compliance with Alphonsus's request; he grasped it. "Do not ask me to go to the castle; indeed I will not, I shall double my crime; I must not go, I dare not see her again. If you should see her, tell her—; but you will not see her; you have not disobeyed her; she will not frown on you; think you no more of it; I must bear with it." He hid his face on the pillow, and the count forebore to interrogate him farther on a subject which he saw was beginning to overpower him.

This short conversation, which tended not to enlighten the subject discussed, strengthened however count Byroff's resolution of visiting the castle on the first opportunity offered to him, and endeavouring to gain some light on this strange mystery.

A few hours after sun-rise father Nicholas visited his patient; he pronounced him to have been much benefited by the composing draught, and gave the most encouraging hopes of a speedy amendment. Lauretta was not in the chamber when the holy man arrived, but being informed by Jacques that he was visiting her husband, she immediately entered the apartment, and eagerly inquired of him after the health of her Alphonsus.

The name seemed to produce a momentary surprise in the countenance of the friar, but immediately regaining his former composure, he answered to her inquiry: count Byroff alone perceived the effect which had been produced on father Nicholas, nor was he mistaken in imagining that the friar's a second time approaching the bed under pretence of feeling his patient's pulse, was an excuse for more closely investigating Alphonsus's features than he had yet done. Promising to visit his patient in the afternoon, and to bring with him such medicines as were necessary, the father left the chamber, and count Byroff accompanied him to the door of the inn, in order to prevent his holding any discourse with the landlord; and immediately on the old man's departure, he warned the host against acknowledging to any one that Alphonsus had visited the castle, being as yet uncertain whether benefit or harm to Alphonsus was to be expected from such an avowal.

Towards evening the friar returned. Alphonsus's mind was still in a state that baffled count Byroff's most ingenious attempt to draw from him the cause of his disorder. The friar seated himself by the side of the bed; he again inquired in a more exact manner than he had before done, whether they could form no remote conjecture of the cause of the malady under which his patient was labouring; he received the same answers from the count and Lauretta which had before been given him. He remained for some moments silent, his countenance by no means exhibiting a strong conviction of the veracity of their words. "Have you travelled far?" he then said.

"Many leagues," answered the count.

"And is the place whither you are going far from hence?"

"As soon as my friend is sufficiently recovered to proceed, he will determine our route."

"You are then on an excursion of pleasure!"

A slight inclination of the head on the part of count Byroff, was the answer to this demand.

Many other questions, answered with as little satisfaction to the friar's curiosity, were advanced by him, and he departed for the night.

Lauretta, who was not acquainted with the conversation which Jacques had overheard at the monastery, looked upon what the old man had said to have been dictated by a no more than common curiosity, excited by the situation of her husband; count Byroff, though he did not undeceive his daughter in this point, considered it in a very different light, and he even began to conceive that the solution of the mystery would prove count Frederic Cohenburg to have retired to the monastery of the Holy Spirit, to enjoy, unmolested, possessions criminally acquired. Still, however, as it was certain that if his conjecture was a true one, all the friars were privy to the plot, he saw no means of effecting the discovery but by ascertaining by whom the bell at the castle was nightly rung, and this he determined if possible to learn that very night.

The medicine last administered by the friar to Alphonsus, count Byroff perceived to possess the same quality, only in a less potent degree, as the former one he had taken, and this lessened his anxiety at the idea of leaving Lauretta for so long a space of time as was necessary to his purpose: he determined, however, not to inform her of the plan in agitation, and when she entreated him to retire in his turn for the night, which he well knew she would do, he pretended to comply with her request, on condition that Jacques might be her companion in watching over her husband. The landlord having provided him with a lantern, and implements for striking a light, reluctantly, as he trembled for the safety of the count, conducted him as far on his way as the intricacy of the road made it necessary for a stranger to have a guide; and then, with injunctions to secrecy on the part of the count, and prayers for the count's protection from evil spirits, on the part of the landlord, they parted,—the host returning home, and count Byroff proceeding along the road leading to the castle.

Count Byroff had advanced only a few yards when the distant sound of the bell fell on his ear; he regretted that necessity had obliged him to set out later than he had intended, but still resolving to pursue his enterprise, he proceeded forward with an increased speed.

Arrived at the castle, natural curiosity, which the shining moon favoured, induced him to eye it in every part as he walked round it, in search of the postern-gate: for an instant he thought he caught the glimmering of a light from a window in the second range of apartments; he stopped and looked, but it did not return, and he passed on, believing his imagination had deceived him.

At length he arrived at the postern-gate; it was shut; he pushed against it, and it yielded heavily to the pressure of his arm; he entered a few steps; he looked round; all was silence and darkness.

He stepped back without the gate, and having lighted the wick within his lantern, which he held in such a manner as to be able in an instant to conceal it in the skirts of a mantle which he wore over his shoulders, he again entered, and closed the gate after him as he had found it.

He proceeded along a vaulted passage, at the extremity of which a turn to the left conducted through a door into the great hall of the castle. He stepped forward a few paces, and raising his lantern, the better to view surrounding objects, nothing met his sight but cumbrous pillars of fluted marble, which were ranged on each side of the hall; and at the extremity, the dark iron-gates which seemed to form a blot in the azure-coloured wall. He turned himself round; facing the gates was a spacious flight of stairs, on each side of which was a high and narrow door; by one of them he had entered the hall.

He ascended the stairs; to the right and left lay an extensive gallery; he again held up his lantern, and directed his eyes first to the extremity of that on the right; he perceived doors on either side, and that it ended in a blank wall. He then turned to the left; the extent of the gallery was greater than that on the right, and as he viewed it, a figure seemed to flit quickly through the shade at the extremity.

He advanced swiftly along: at the end of the gallery was a turn to the right, which led, by the descent of a few steps, into another gallery, much resembling that he had just left: at the extremity of this a door, partly open, attracted his notice: hiding his lantern he looked in, and perceived that all was dark: he uncloaked his lantern, and entered a chamber richly furnished: there were no apparent signs of its having been lately inhabited, nor was there a second door in it: he returned to the gallery. The shutting of a door at some distance from him next attracted his attention; he could not determine exactly from what part of the castle the sound had proceeded, but he conjectured it to have issued from the gallery on the right of the flight of stairs which had conducted him from the hall: he followed the sound, and the gallery terminated, as the other had done, by a descent of a few steps into a passage of equal size.

After debating in his mind for some moments what plan to follow, he descended the steps: arrived at the end he found a door as on the other side: he used the same precaution with his lantern as he had before done, and was just grasping the handle of the door, with an intent to open it, when he heard a long groan, which seemed to be uttered by a person not far distant from him: he turned round his head; but nothing was to be seen: he was willing to imagine his

senses had been deceived, and was again applying his hand to the
door, when his action was arrested by what seemed a stifled shriek
in the apartment to which that door led. He listened, the same kind
of sound was twice more repeated; he was convinced that it had issued from behind the door, close by which he now stood. For a few
moments all was still, and he was a third time on the point of entering, when several voices seemed to break out together into tones
of supplication: his astonishment was now wound to a higher pitch
than before: suddenly the voices changed their tones into the notes
of a solemn chaunt; in this he immediately recognised the work of
priests, and determining at once to unravel the mystery, with his
lantern still concealed, he pushed open the door and entered.

Nearly opposite to where he had entered, was a small arched
door-way, from which issued a faint light; he proceeded a few steps
towards it, and on looking forward, immediately found that he was
now in a small vestry behind the altar of a chapel, into which the
arched door before him led. He ventured cautiously forward to a
spot where he could command a view of the greater part of the
chapel; at a short distance from the steps leading to the altar, knelt,
by the side of a coffin, a figure of a pale and emaciated countenance, in whose left hand was a cross, and in the right a knotted
cord.

On the other side of the coffin knelt three friars, who were singing the chaunt which count Byroff had heard begun, whilst standing by the outer door: the chaunt being finished, the friars crossed
themselves, and began a prayer, in which they supplicated mercy
for the guilty. Upon this the figure, whose sex the sable and loose
garments it wore, tended not to declare, rose, and began to lash its
shoulders with the cord, the pain occasioned by which caused it
to send forth sounds of lamentation, such as the count had before
heard: this done, the friars offered up another prayer, in which the
penitent figure joined, and they then together left the chapel by a
door opposite to the altar, taking with them a lamp which during
their devotions had been placed on the coffin round which they had
knelt.

All count Byroff's former plans of obstinate perseverance into
the mystery in which the castle was enveloped, were put to flight by
what he had seen: awe and reverence for the solemnity of the reli-

gious worship in which he had seen the friars and the suffering person engaged, whose salvation their prayers seemed meant to effect, had forbade him to interrupt their devotions; and when they were ended he felt an insurmountable objection to introducing himself to those who might have a right to dispute his unlicensed entrance into the castle, and refuse to attend to his excuse.

Some minutes were lost by him in reflection how to proceed, when he heard footsteps at a distance in the gallery; but they were no sooner heard, than they died away, and he doubted not, from what Jacques had told him he had seen on the night of his waiting without the castle for Alphonsus, that the friars were now departing; the shutting of a gate, with the sound of which the castle immediately after rang, confirmed him in his opinion.

He resolved to enter the chapel, and if possible, discover whither was gone the figure whom he had seen; for he strongly conceived, he knew not why, that it had not left the castle: as to who the figure was, his mind wavered between count Frederic, and the countess Anna; the former his own ideas taught him to believe it; but the words uttered by Alphonsus seemed to assign a degree of probability to its being the latter: arrived at the end of the chapel, he found that the door through which the persons he had just beheld had passed, was an iron grating; he pulled at it, but it resisted his efforts, being fastened by a spring, which he was not acquainted how to open. As he stood by it, a glimmering of light, at some distance, caught his eyes; he hid his lantern; the light advanced, and showed him that the iron gate led into a long and narrow passage; at the extremity of which, in a few seconds, appeared, bearing a lamp, the figure he had lately beheld in the chapel: it opened a door facing him, and having entered, immediately closed it, and all was again dark.

He again produced his lantern; but the door through which the figure had passed, was too far removed for him to distinguish it with the aid only of the light in his hand: he determined, however, if possible to find it; and, if he could, to address the person who had so strongly excited his attention and surprise.

After entering many chambers and passages in vain, a suite of rooms brought him to a chamber, from a door in which, a small closet, through which he passed, led him into the passage, at the extremity of which was the grated door from the chapel: he moved hastily to the other end, in search of the door by which the figure had vanished from his sight: the form of the wall was a semicircle, constituting, as he concluded, part of one of the turrets, of which there were four at the angles of the castle; but his most minute investigations could discover in it no door, or even crevice.

He placed his lantern on the ground, and for some time continued to pass his hands over every part of the wall, in the hope of discovering some clue to the object of his search; at length he imagined that he felt through the plaster a small elevation, which appeared to the touch like a flat hinge: he took up his lantern in order to examine the spot where he felt it, when, to his great disappointment, he perceived that his wick was dying out in the socket: he now found it necessary to return to the gallery as quickly as possible, whilst he had light to conduct him, lest from his being delayed a longer time than he wished, by searching his way in the dark, his absence should be learned by Lauretta, and add additional fears on his account, to her already too much afflicted mind: he accordingly precipitately retraced the path which had conducted him to this passage, and arrived in the gallery at the moment the last spark in his lantern became extinguished.

Day was fortunately for him beginning to dawn, and he easily descended into the hall, and gained, by recollecting his way, the postern gate, when, what had never occurred to him till he experienced it, the gate was locked, and thus all means of departing excluded from him.

He upbraided himself for not having forestalled the friars' departure, which, had he but considered the matter, Jacques's narrative of the occurrences of the night before the last had warned him to do; he returned to the hall, and attempted to open the great gates, but they baffled his endeavours; how had Alphonsus got out after the departure of the friars? was a question he next asked himself, but he found it not less a difficult matter to answer this demand, than at the present moment to effect his escape.

All he now felt was anxiety for what Lauretta would experience, should she discover his absence, and learn whither he was gone.

Nearly two hours were spent by him in vain attempts to leave the castle, and unavailing lamentations; on a sudden he imagined he heard a key turn in the lock of the postern gate; he stopped a few seconds to listen; no sound followed it; and he almost feared his expectations to have been falsely raised; he determined, however, to ascertain the truth, and accordingly proceeded to the postern gate; it was partly open, his heart leaped with joy, and eagerly crossing the threshold, he set forward without stopping to consider by whom, or from what cause, the gate had been opened.

Arrived at the inn panting for breath, count Byroff instantly inquired of the landlord whether Lauretta had asked for him, and with much satisfaction he learned that she had not. The host had, by the count's desire, sat up till his return, and count Byroff having, in recompence for his complacency, satisfied his curiosity in regard to the tolling of the wonderful bell, they both retired to their respective apartments.

Count Byroff threw himself on the bed, and immediately began to re-examine in his mind the occurrences of which he had been a witness in the castle; and severely did he task himself for not having, at all hazards, aimed at a development of the mystery which it seemed so necessary to the welfare of those with whom he was concerned to have explained; and yet he conceived that he had but acted consistently with the respect due to religious offices.

Unable long to bear this contest of opinions within his own breast, on a matter of so great importance, and of so tender a nature, he entered the chamber of Alphonsus, who was still lulled by the soothing influence of the draught he had taken; Lauretta refused to retire to bed that night; Jacques readily accepted the offer of leaving for a few hours his post of watching.

The count determined not to impart to Lauretta his visit to the castle, as he wished to make one more attempt at solving the enigma, now more perplexing to him than ever, and which he feared her entreaties and alarm for his safety, were she acquainted with his intention, or even surmised it, might induce him to abandon.

It was some hours ere Alphonsus spoke, though he had been long awake: he then called Lauretta to him and embraced her; the tears ran down his cheeks. "Is the holy friar here?" he asked.

Lauretta answered, that she every moment expected his arrival.

"Would he were come!" continued Alphonsus. "I would unburthen to him my heart: his counsel might relieve me, if his prayers and intercession cannot obtain my pardon."

"Am not I equally worthy the participation of your secret thoughts?" said Lauretta tenderly.

"Oh my Lauretta!" returned Alphonsus, "it is my love for you, that causes me to hide them from you."

"Do you then suppose that I am less moved to see you unhappy, than if you had acquainted me with all the particulars for your present anxiety?—Oh Alphonsus! can you believe my heart less feeling towards you, than yours has been to me?"

"You are too good, too kind," cried Alphonsus, "to one who, choked by melancholy and despair, has never given you a chearful smile, in gratitude for those endearments, which have been his only comfort."

"Indeed you wrong yourself. I have been happy, very happy— witness heaven, very happy," said Lauretta, stifling her tears.

"I fear I have said too much," replied Alphonsus, looking stedfastly in her face; "I have already told you what afflicts me; have I not?"

"Forget it, I entreat you," answered Lauretta.

"Never! never!" he exclaimed. "My senses have been lately so disordered, that I scarcely know what has passed; did I tell you that I had seen my mother's shade?"

Lauretta was at a loss how to answer for the best: she looked at count Byroff for advice; she saw he was perplexed not less than herself; the door of the chamber opened, and father Nicholas entered to their relief.

The father passed on to that side of the bed opposite to which Lauretta was standing; "A good and blessed day to thee, my son!" he said.

Alphonsus turned towards him, and said, "Wouldst thou indeed bless me?"

"Thou hast my most fervent prayers to heaven," returned the holy man.

"If thou hast my welfare at heart, thou wilt be secret, if I confess to thee my sorrows," said Alphonsus, with more composure than he had yet spoken.

"Secrecy is a bond of my office; speak freely my son and fear me not."

"Go to the castle of Cohenburg to-night; when the midnight bell has sounded, thou wilt find the postern gate open to thee: enter the chapel, and pray for me forgiveness for my disobedience, of my mother's shade: if thou seest her not, she will hear thee, for she inhabits there; tell her I repent my forbidden visit, though I have learned no secret by it; and if she refuse to pardon me, I will die to prove my penitence."

"Are you indeed the heir of Cohenburg castle?" said father Nicholas, surprise and pleasure mingling in his countenance.

"Oh no! no!" replied Alphonsus, "I am only the lost, abandoned, cursed Alphonsus."

"When did you visit the castle?" asked the friar.

"It was"—said Alphonsus:—he paused: "It was by night; but I cannot recollect whether last night, or not."

"It was two nights ago," said the count.

Lauretta had retired to the window; the friar went to her—"Are you the wife of this young man?"

"I am, father."

"Dry your tears, be comforted; happiness is yet in store for you."

"God grant your words be true."

"Trust to his mercy; through me he compassionates your afflictions."

He again approached the bed: "I will pray for you, my son; rest assured, and place faith in my endeavours;—I shall visit you again to-day; till then peace be with you: farewell."

He departed, and his words for some time occupied, in silent reflection, those he had left.

CHAPTER XXV.

There is but one, one only thing to think on,
My murder'd lord, and his dark gaping grave,
That waits unclos'd, impatient of my coming.

                                        ROWE.

TOWARDS evening father Nicholas returned; he found Alphonsus risen: his health was materially restored; but his spirits were still depressed, and a degree of wildness was at times visible in his countenance.

"Didst thou know my mother?" said Alphonsus, first reverting to the subject on which all were thinking, but none had yet touched.

"Full well," returned the holy man. "Is it possible you do not recollect me?" continued he with some hesitation.

"No," replied Alphonsus, "no; and yet methinks that scar above your eye claims place in my remembrance; pardon me, that my harassed brain excludes all thought but on one subject; I pray you tell me your name."

"Father Nicholas, many years your mother's confessor."

"I know you now." He took his hand, pressed it in his, then kissed it. "You saw my mother then before she died?"—The friar hesitated to answer; Alphonsus perceived it not, and continued—"Did she wish again to see her son?"—The friar was still silent; Alphonsus went on, "You doubtless know my sad story?"

"I do."

"Oh! why did she discard me from her affections? wretched forlorn Alphonsus! my mother cruel! my father murdered!—Oh God! grant me to know his assassin!—Father, I have a vow in heaven of vengeance against his murderer, and here again I swear——"

The friar interrupted him, "Calm thy agitation, my son: thou canst not recall him into life by shedding another's blood; why then stain thy hands in murder?"

"Thou say'st true: heaven will avenge the deed better than I can; my hate and curses must fall on him.—Oh, if he must have fallen, would he had fallen by any hand rather than that he did!"

Father Nicholas sighed deeply.

"Who that knew him, could have believed that count Frederic would have murdered his brother?"

"If you believe he did, you wrong his memory."

"Is he too dead?—none left to bear a load of grief but me!—I recollect my mother told me, when she sent me from her, he was innocent; but she had first taught me to believe him guilty:—'twas strange!"

A pause ensued.

Suddenly recollecting himself, Alphonsus exclaimed, "If you can exculpate the innocent, you can arraign the guilty:—confess to me, I conjure you, whom I ought to hate; and guide my vengeance by your own discretion."

"Lay aside all thoughts of revenge; we are enjoined to be charitable to all; and who more strongly claims our pity, than he who suffers from the pangs of a conscience, that reproves him with the commission of murder?"

"It is a sentiment too refined to bias the heart of a son, bleeding at the recollection of a father's untimely death."

"The more severe our trials, the greater will be the reward bestowed on us, if amidst their severity we still do not deviate from the exercise of christian duty."

"If my mother knew the murderer!" Alphonsus exclaimed wildly, without having seemed to attend to father Nicholas's last words; and suddenly he interrupted himself—"Did she know him?" he added.

The holy man was silent.

"Say rather that she killed him,—burst my swelling heart, and end at once my agonies in death, than torture me by this mysterious hesitation."

The old man was affected to tears, by the transports of Alphonsus's feelings.—"Wouldst thou not rather that thy father lived, though thou couldst never see him more, than know him dead?" he asked.

"If he were happy, witness heaven, I would."

"And if thy absence from him constituted but his negative comfort, and even caused thy sorrow, hast thou enough of filial piety in thee to obey him?"

"Oh yes! on any terms, 'twere happiness to know he lived. But to what end avail these questions? I know he lives not, and yet you dazzle my imagination with ideas of what cannot be?"

"You once thought a mother had an equal claim on your obedience."

"Forbear, forbear to rack my heart, by telling me I wanted fortitude to obey her commands."

"Rouse your strength of mind to execute them now."

"What mean you?—explain yourself, I conjure you."

"Know then she lives,—but you must never see her more."

Alphonsus had till this moment been comparatively calm:—"Lives!" he re-echoed, in the most piercing accents; then falling on his knees, and raising his hands to heaven—"Angels of mercy, I thank you!—It was then her living self I saw; my disobedience did not call her from the grave. The eyes she fixed upon me, were not those of death.—Oh God, I thank thee!"—A flood of tears relieved his full heart, swelled with a multiplicity of undescribable sensations.

A general silence prevailed for some moments, when Alphonsus could again articulate, "May I not once more see her,—only once, to implore her forgiveness?" he said.

"You have her pardon; rest satisfied in that assurance," returned the friar.

"Tell me, then," cried Alphonsus, "tell me why she refuses again to behold me?—And hard, very hard as I feel the struggle between duty and inclination, I will not press to see her."

"There is a just cause for her refusal. I have her permission to reveal it to you; and much I think, when you have learnt it, you will no longer press your late entreaty."

"Speak it, I beseech you."

"Have you fortitude to hear a tale of horror, which is nearly related to yourself?"

"Oh yes: my heart has felt too much substantial misery, to sink beneath recited ills."

"I need not warn a wife to secrecy, on a point of tender interest to her husband," said the friar, raising his eyes to Lauretta, and then passing them on to count Byroff.

"Nor her father," said the count, "to act for the welfare of both."

The friar gently inclined his head, in token of his satisfaction, and thus began:—"On the death of your aunt, count Frederic's wife, the kind attentions which the goodness of your mother's heart inclined her to use towards his children, raised in the breast of your deceased father a suspicion that her regards were bestowed on his offspring from the love which she bore their father.

"How this unhappy suspicion ever gained way into his thoughts, I can no otherwise account for, than that the single foible of his nature was an inclination towards distrust; and I am certain that your uncle and mother were both innocent of the false imputation which your father laid on them.

"The three first years after the loss of his wife were sorrowfully marked to count Frederic by the death of his children; and, unable to remain in the midst of scenes which gave him such ample scope for poignant reflection, he resolved to travel. He visited Venice; and here chance introduced him to a lady who seemed to promise a reparation of the loss he had sustained; but a mercenary father doomed her to the arms of a man she disliked, who carried her away from Venice; and his repeated journies and inquiries could never lead him to discover whither she had been conveyed."

The agitation here expressed by the count and Lauretta, induced the friar to break off his narrative, and inquire the cause of their emotions: count Byroff briefly explained it, to the great surprise of the friar, who in return informed them, that, after the count's departure from Venice, a report had been circulated by Arieno's servants, that count Byroff, having killed the son of a senator in a duel, had fled with his wife into Spain, to which kingdom count Frederic's researches after his Lauretta were then confined.

This, though a new instance of count Arieno's villany, was but a slight one, and count Byroff requested the friar to proceed.

"Every return of your uncle into Germany refreshed your father's fears, which his absence had lulled: he perceived his brother to be a prey to grief, and as he always refused to explain what afflicted him, your father's suspicion grew stronger on the repeated refusals of your uncle to divulge his cause of sorrow.

"The last time your uncle returned, was with a resolution no longer to pursue a fruitless search after her he loved; and he retired to his own mansion, where he determined to live a recluse from the world, visiting only his brother's castle.

"Every visit continued to increase your father's secret suspicion; and although he was always present when count Frederic saw his wife, he worked himself into a persuasion that a criminal intercourse was actually subsisting between them. At length, no longer able to bear the torture of suspicion, he resolved to clear his doubts, convinced that he could not be more miserable than he now was, be the result of his stratagem what it might.

"He accordingly gave out that an affair of consequence called him to Vienna. It was a probable circumstance, and gained belief; the day prior to his departure, he visited his brother: he told him that he had a matter of the greatest importance to confide to him, and in which he must entreat his assistance, which count Frederic readily promised. Your father then required of him to swear that he would be secret, before he communicated to him the matter in question: to this your uncle at first objected, but after many entreaties on the part of your father, he gave his faith not to reveal to any one what he should impart to him. Your father then told him that he suspected the fidelity of his wife.—Count Frederic, as it is easy to suppose, showed marks of no small surprise at this intelligence. Your father immediately misconstrued his astonishment with secret satisfaction at his own sagacity and penetration. Count Frederic proceeded to inquire whom his brother supposed to be the paramour of your mother? 'Suffice it that I know him,' returned your father; 'what I have to require of you is, that during my absence you will endeavour to win my wife to your love, and inform me of your success on my return.'—Count Frederic remonstrated warmly against measures, from which he could not possibly conceive that any discovery or advantage could be derived; but your father was so earnest in his entreaties, that count Frederic at length yielded to make the experiment.

"On the following day, a fatal day to him, your father left his castle, and taking with him old Robert his faithful servant, they proceeded to the cottage of my sister, about five leagues north of Cohenburg castle. I was in the secret of your father's plan, and had, at his request, there provided for him a reception.

"For nearly two months, your unhappy mother was constrained to bear the blandishments and caresses which count Frederic un-willingly tempted her with; she complained in private to me, and I could only give her such consolation as I taught her to derive from the innocence of her own heart.

"Repeated letters did your uncle write to his brother, assuring him of the fidelity of his wife; and as a proof of her nice sense of honour, added, that no male visitor, except himself and me, had been admitted at the castle since his departure.

"These letters your father read with very opposite sentiments to what they were meant to produce in him.

"The period now arrived which he had determined should stamp his happiness or misery. Robert, as it had been preconcerted, returned to the castle with information of your father's having been assassinated in the Wolf's Wood in his return from Vienna; and the late conduct of your uncle represented him to your mother as the murderer of her husband."

"Oh!" exclaimed Alphonsus, "I remember well the accusation which she then alleged against him; 'twas then I swore to—"

"No more of that now," interrupted the holy man. "Hear the conclusion of thy parent's fate:—when count Frederic arrived at the castle, and you left him with your mother, she accused him with the murder of his brother on the pretensions of his late conduct to her; he denied the charge, again urged his pretended love for her, and departed.

"On the next day, as you doubtless recollect, he returned to the castle; he re-iterated his love; she knelt to him, and implored him to cease adding pangs to the agony he had already inflicted on her. At this instant, as your mother has since told me, you entered the apartment:—this explains to you one mystery which you could not solve.

"Unknown to any one, I that night introduced your father into his own castle; for, as you may well suppose, he had not believed that his brother had written to him true accounts of his wife, and had only acted this farce the more deeply to entrap her, while the close of this hazardous experiment lay with himself.

"In the middle of that night a noise in your mother's chamber alarmed her,—she shrieked; a voice which she immediately concluded to be count Frederic's addressed her in accents of familiar love; she sprang from the bed, as the person advanced towards it; he held her arm; she stretched out her other hand to a table near the bed, and grasping a dagger which she had lately worn to defend herself from count Frederic, should he have attempted force upon her person, and which she now believed him to be doing, she pierced him who held her to the heart.

"Till the dawn arose, she thought herself the murderer of count Frederic; but alas! she beheld her bleeding husband, killed by her own hand! Immediately the vow she had exacted from you recurred to her, and constituted no small part of her agony; for the mad state of her brain taught her to believe you would fulfil it. What followed that morning, you know better than myself."

"Oh, God!" cried Alphonsus, in accents that seemed to proceed from a frame whose every nerve was racked by agony, "'till now I never knew what misery was! Oh, ye pitying angels, bless my unhappy mother!—Forgive my erring father!—Oh, father! thou said'st well that I should no longer press to disobey my mother, when I knew the cause of her commands:—'twere death to both to meet!—Oh, that vow!" Convulsed by pangs of sorrow he sunk upon count Byroff.

Recovering, he fixed his eyes on the friar:—"Oh, wretch! wretch! doomed to be cursed for parricide or perjury!" He inarticulately whispered, while sighs of agony partially choked his utterance.

"Comfort thee, my son: the church is able, and, I doubt not, will be willing to absolve thee from an oath of such a strange nature."

"Oh, her bloody hand!—methinks I see it now!—I would have embraced her, but she forbade me." He paused. "Oh, horrible! I swore to murder her who gave me being." He shuddered. "Fool that I was to say that misery had shot at me her keenest shafts, ere I had heard this tale of woe; she has but one other in her quiver that can pierce me. I will not part from thee!" he exclaimed, flying to

Lauretta, and clasping her to his bosom. He then turned to the friar:—"Go on, good father: I can hear any thing now; thou shouldst have blunted thus my senses long ago:—go on, I pray thee."

"I will briefly relate the sequel of my tale," returned the friar, with a look to count Byroff, which indicated that he feared to disobey the request of Alphonsus, and yet was apprehensive his senses were again perplexed. "At an early hour I was sent for by your mother; and frantic with grief she confessed to me her involuntary crime, and its consequences. Shortly after count Frederic arrived at the castle, the sad tidings were announced to him by me: never did I behold a man so agonised; he immediately declared to your mother the cause of his pretended love for her, and cursed himself for having been the blind instrument of his brother's jealousy and suspicion.

"The countess entreated me in the most supplicating terms to hide from the world the real means of her husband's death, and to circulate an immediate report of her death: to execute the latter, I was under the necessity of calling in the assistance of some of my brother friars, and we contrived by a pretended funeral to accomplish her wish; after this ceremony, as you was no where to be found, and that count Frederic declared himself determined to pass his future days in seclusion from the world, at the monastery of Saint Paul, the servants were discharged, and the gates of the castle locked.

"Your mother had during this interval been secreted in the apartment to which the secret door in the south turret leads. On the first night of the evacuation of the castle I visited your mother, whom I had constantly supplied with the little provision she had required, and she then told me, that she had formed a resolution of passing the sad remainder of her days in solitude in the castle. I reprobated this idea: but she was firm in her determination, and no arguments could divert her from her purpose.

"An empty coffin had been brought in pomp by means of Robert's adroitness from the Wolf's Wood; in this we contrived to deposit secretly your father's remains, and it was then placed in the vault beneath the chapel; but, by the earnest entreaties of the countess, again removed into the chapel: and by it she has every night since prayed, and inflicted on herself voluntary punishments."

"'Twas there I saw her,—methought she rose from the coffin when I beheld her!" cried Alphonsus.

"But the midnight bell—" said count Byroff.

"Was tolled by her," interrupted the friar, "for the double purpose of keeping idle visitants from the castle, under the idea of its being haunted, and to call to her two holy men of our monastery, who, by turns, together with myself, visited her every night to assist her prayers over the body of her husband."

"But you were not with her," said Alphonsus, "when I beheld her in the chapel."

"No: we had left the castle, but she remained praying by the coffin."

"How know you this?"

"She informed me, that on the night on which I now find you entered the castle, she had seen a man advance a few paces into the chapel, who on beholding her had fled away alarmed."

"Oh! the piercing recollection of that night!" cried Alphonsus. "Oh, what did I not then feel."

"How did you escape from the castle?" asked father Nicholas.

"Frenzy gave me strength to burst the window at the extremity of the hall, and through it I effected my flight."

"Count Frederic," continued the friar, "immediately retired to the monastery of Saint Paul, and did not long survive his brother. Ever since your father's death, the brethren of the Holy Spirit have, by your mother's permission, enjoyed the rents of the estate on which the castle stands, in recompense for their nightly visits, and the assistance of their prayers. I often entreated her to have you sought after, and restore you to your legal possessions: but a wild frenzy of alarm always forbade me to urge my petition, though she unremittingly grieved at the hard lot you were innocently suffering.

"Yesterday morning I visited her alone, for the purpose of informing her of my suspicions, drawn from the name I had heard you called by, and many words I had heard you let fall, of you, her son, being now in the vicinity of the castle."

"Was not your visit to the castle paid between the hours of three and four?" asked count Byroff.

The holy man answered that it was, and this explained to the count the means by which the postern gate had been opened to him.

Father Nicholas continued:—"In return for the information I brought her, she only entreated that you might not see her, scarcely, I believe, crediting what I told her I surmised relative to you; for her faculties have been impaired by her distress of mind. The words you this morning addressed to me confirmed my conjecture, and I again visited her this afternoon; she heard me, contrary to my expectation, with composure; wept when she learnt that you had beheld each other, still however thankful she had not known you; declared her intention of putting you in possession of your natural rights, by immediately departing from the castle; and above all entreated, that when I had related to you her unhappy story, you would confer on her the only proof of affection she could ever desire, or hope to receive from you, namely, your never attempting to see her more."

Alphonsus's spirits were exhausted even to infantine weakness; he seemed no longer to attend to the words of the friar; he urged no farther inquiry into this heart-rending business; but wept, and that without intermission.

The holy man advised that he should retire to rest, and endeavour to compose his spirits; he retired to bed, but without giving any signs that he knew what he did; he sunk on the pillow, and spoke no more that night.

Having addressed some words of comfort to Lauretta, who, except that she respired, existed not, or at least without a thought to bestow on any other object than her Alphonsus and his sorrows; and having told count Byroff that he was called away by an urgent concern, but would return in the morning as early as he was able, father Nicholas left the inn, bestowing a benediction on its inhabitants.

The night passed on in sorrowing silence, broken only by occasional comments on what they had heard from the friar, on the part of count Byroff and his daughter; and heart-drawn sighs on the part of Alphonsus.

The tenth hour of the morning had sounded ere the holy man arrived; he found Alphonsus fallen into a gentle slumber. Count Byroff and the friar had a copious topic for conversation; they indulged themselves in discussing it till Lauretta came to inform them that Alphonsus was awake, and had inquired for the father.

They ascended to his chamber.—"Father," said Alphonsus, on beholding the friar, "you did not tell me whither my unhappy mother was gone."

"When I left you last," replied the holy man, "she was still in Cohenburg castle; I have this night conveyed her to the convent of the Virgin Maria, seven leagues distant from hence, and whose votaries are not permitted, when they have once entered its walls, ever again to hold converse with the world."

"What said she at parting?—nothing which you were to repeat to me from her?"

"She bade me tell you, that her blessing would fall a curse upon you,—thus she forbore to speak it. She entreats your prayers, and that you will sometimes view with pity her resemblance."

The friar here put into Alphonsus's hand a small portrait of his mother.

Alphonsus gazed eagerly upon it, then kissed it. "Forgive her, heaven!" he exclaimed. A small ribband was fastened to the picture; he tied it round his neck, and turned the face inward to his bosom. "Lie there in peace," he cried: "and, oh! may the shades of my dear father and mother hereafter unite in scenes of bliss, with all the warmth and tenderness their images are now connected in my heart."

CHAPTER XXVI.

But happy they! the happiest of their kind!
Whom gentler stars unite, and in one fate
Their hearts, their fortunes, and their beings blend.
                                        THOMSON.

IN the course of a few days Alphonsus's health and spirits were sufficiently restored to permit him to visit Cohenburg castle; by the care of father Nicholas, the coffin which contained the remains of the late count had been replaced in the vault; but still it required more fortitude than Alphonsus could at that time command, to enter, unmoved, the chapel, and the chamber in which his mother had so mysteriously addressed him on the morning of her sending him away from the castle.

As the castle had required but little preparation to render it fit for the reception of Alphonsus and his Lauretta, count Byroff and the friar had given the necessary orders to that purpose, which had been performed by the daughter of the landlord, and her husband, who resided in the village.

As for Jacques, from the first moment of his receiving the intelligence of Alphonsus's restoration to his rank and possessions, he could find time for nothing but congratulations alternately bestowed on the count, Alphonsus, and Lauretta; and when they would no longer listen to them, he congratulated himself by singing and dancing, every step he moved.

The landlord, on the first arrival of the travellers at his house, had been an attentive and pleasing host; but no sooner did he learn that the heir of Cohenburg castle was an inmate with him, than his attentions became so over-strained, that they lost the very effect of pleasing, they had so strongly possessed, when nothing more than ordinary was meant to be conveyed by them: he was in a bustle all day long, whether he had employment to occasion his being so or not: and, communicative as he had before naturally been, he now seemed to make it a point of politeness, hardly to answer the questions which were asked of him.

Visiting frequently the neighbouring village in his twofold character of priest and physician, father Nicholas was well acquainted with its inhabitants, and readily engaged in it such servants as were immediately necessary to Alphonsus's new establishment; at the same time using his most sedulous endeavours to allay that surprise which would naturally be excited, on the sudden appearance of the heir of the castle.

On the day after Alphonsus became an inhabitant of the castle, he received the congratulations of the brothers of the Holy Spirit in person; how closely their lips and hearts were in unison, deprived as they now were of the rents they had been so long enjoying, it is not perhaps quite fair too accurately to investigate, considering in how handsome a manner they outwardly comported themselves. Jacques stood laughing unobserved in the hall as they went out. "Ah

mes amis," he cried, "you drank the ghost's health just in time; *plait
à Dieu*, you may never have the opportunity again."

Father Nicholas had immediately written to the bishop, stating
the peculiarity of Alphonsus's unfortunate situation with regard
to his oath, and entreating for him the utmost indulgence of the
church; and absolution was readily obtained for him, on the obliga-
tion of his bestowing a sum of money on a convent of poor nuns,
and undergoing a slight penance.

Alphonsus had resided nearly three months at Cohenburg castle, and the poignancy of reflection was beginning to be softened
by scenes of domestic happiness, when Jacques one day abruptly
entering the apartment, panting for breath, and hardly able to articulate, addressing himself to count Byroff, exclaimed, "Huzza,
monsieur! huzza! *graces à Dieu*, we have not an enemy in the world
now, but my uncle Perlet, and the Bastile."

Count Byroff eagerly inquired what occurrence had called
forth such extraordinary signs of joy; but it was some time before
Jacques could recover breath sufficient to answer: at length he said,
"I'll tell you, *monsieur:* Kroonzer and all the rest of them are sent to
the gallies."

"How have you heard this?" asked count Byroff. "Why, *monsieur*, I have just been as far as the little inn," (a very constant prac-
tice with Jacques, who had been in habits of great intimacy with
the landlord since the time of his residing at his house) "and whom
should I meet there, *monsieur*, but a man, a stranger; so the landlord
asked him what news; and so he told us, that a gang of robbers had
been discovered in an old castle, not a day's journey from Inspruck.
You may think I knew pretty well where he meant, *monsieur.* 'How
were they found out?' said I; so he told us, that a gentleman that
was travelling that way, had been attacked by them, and that his
servants had managed to take one of the banditti prisoner, who had
confessed all their tricks, and that the gentleman had had them all
taken up, and that they had been condemned by the emperor, to be
sold for galley slaves, and sent to the Turks. I wish, *de toute ma vie*,
they had been sent to the Bastile."

Count Byroff immediately took measures for inquiring into the
truth of this report; and to the excessive delight of Jacques, who,
since his escape from the banditti, had stood in great fear, though

he had endeavoured to hide it, of being fetched back by them and punished for his desertion,—and to the no small though suppressed satisfaction of count Byroff, who, from the threatened vengeance of Kroonzer, had thought himself in rather an unpleasant predicament,—the report proved to be a true one.

About this time Alphonsus employed a person recommended to his confidence by father Nicholas, to pass over into Italy, and ascertain whether count Arieno was still in existence; intending, if he was alive, to visit Venice himself, together with his Lauretta, whom he looked upon as entitled to become the heiress of count Arieno's property; and that it became him on this account to make her known to her grandfather; but the messenger returned with information, that count Arieno having been proved to be an accomplice with another senator who had embezzled some part of the public revenue, he had died on the scaffold, and his entire property been confiscated to the state.

Thus the wretch whose life had been a disgrace to humanity, was punished by a death equally shocking to the feelings of civilization.

The countess Anna lived but a few months in the seclusion in which she had chosen to end her days, and little doubtful of her forgiveness in a happier state, for the commission of an involuntary crime, Alphonsus could not lament, that her sorrows on earth were ended.

Some years after this, an accident introduced to each other's sight Alphonsus and the baron Smaldart; time had softened the resentment the baron had, immediately on the death of the chevalier D'Aignon, borne to Alphonsus; and Alphonsus had long wished a reconciliation to take place. Thus, though neither party proposed it, both visibly promoted it; and it was effected to their mutual satisfaction.

Shortly after the baron accepted an invitation given him by Alphonsus to visit Cohenburg castle, and beheld a scene that called forth in him the tenderest feelings; Alphonsus and his Lauretta, living in the splendor of rank, yet deriving their comforts from domestic happiness; count Byroff revered by his son and daughter; beloved and caressed by their offspring; that offspring growing up in the sanctioned felicity of innocence, sweetened by the indulgence of a fond grandfather, the endearments of a doating mother, and the instructions of a father, competent to give them. "Learn, above all, my children," Alphonsus would often repeat to them, "to avoid suspicion; for as it is the source of crimes, it is also the worst of crimes, attaching itself with equal mischief to the guilty and the innocent; it is an endless pang to him who harbours it; for it dies only when he dies, and then too often leaves a curse on those that follow him; it is the influence of evil that breeds suspicion, the noble spirit of charity that subdues it!"

THE END.

CPSIA information can be obtained
at www.ICGtesting.com
Printed in the USA
BVHW06s0807071018
529495BV00021B/708/P